TRAVELLER'S HISTORY OF BRITAIN AND IRELAND

Also by Richard Muir
MODERN POLITICAL GEOGRAPHY
THE ENGLISH VILLAGE
RIDDLES IN THE LANDSCAPE
GEOGRAPHY, POLITICS & BEHAVIOUR (with R. Paddison)
SHELL GUIDE TO READING THE LANDSCAPE
THE LOST VILLAGES OF BRITAIN
HISTORY FROM THE AIR
NATIONAL TRUST GUIDE TO PREHISTORIC AND ROMAN BRITAIN (with H. Welfare)
VISIONS OF THE PAST (with C. C. Taylor)
EAST ANGLIAN LANDSCAPES, PAST AND PRESENT (with Jack Ravensdale)
THE SHELL COUNTRYSIDE BOOK (with Eric Duffey)
SHELL GUIDE TO READING THE CELTIC LANDSCAPE
STONES OF BRITAIN
LANDSCAPE AND NATURE PHOTOGRAPHY
THE NATIONAL TRUST BOOK OF RIVERS (with Nina Muir)
NATIONAL TRUST GUIDE TO THE DARK AGES AND MEDIEVAL BRITAIN

Richard Muir

TRAVELLER'S HISTORY OF BRITAIN AND IRELAND

A Mermaid Book

First published in Great Britain by
Michael Joseph Ltd
27 Wrights Lane, London W8
1983
First published in Mermaid Books, 1987

British Library Cataloguing in Publication Data

Muir, Richard, *1943–*
  A traveller's history of Britain and
  Ireland
   1. Historic sites—Great Britain
  I. Title
  941   DA632

  ISBN 0-7181-2839-7

Printed and bound in Singapore

CONTENTS

Contents

ACKNOWLEDGEMENTS

The author and publisher wish to thank the sources listed below for their kind permission to reproduce the photographs which appear on the following pages:

The Controller of Her Majesty's Stationery Office (Crown Copyright): 48 right, 94 right, 132 top, 137 right and bottom, 195; Herbert Art Gallery and Museum for the Lunt Fort reconstruction by Alan Sorrell: 93; Christopher Dalton: 141; Dr Warwick Rodwell: 148 for both map and photograph; Walter Scott, Bradford: 173; Trevor Rowley: 177; Wales Tourist Board: 203.

All the section maps and the general map on page 296–7 have been drawn by Boris Weltman.

ABOUT THIS BOOK

There can be few nations as fascinated by the past as the British. Even so, one suspects that this widespread enthusiasm thrives in spite of rather than because of the examination- and syllabus-orientated history which holds sway in most classrooms. Learning about the Calico Act of 1721 or memorising the reigns of the Tudor monarchs may do us no harm, but one may undergo a great deal of formal teaching in history without realising that the subject is really concerned with *people*. The people who really matter—the mass of common folk—do not always emerge very clearly from the pages of the history books. They are often thinly sketched as legions of faceless extras who shuffle in the wings while the kings, generals and politicians perform great deeds in the centre of the stage.

It is also sad that while millions of British people devote large slices of their leisure time to visiting historical monuments, classroom history seldom devotes much time to explaining the reasons why prehistoric dwellings and medieval houses or castles were constructed in certain ways, what a medieval town or village really looked like, or how an Iron Age family might have organised their day-to-day affairs.

Here is offered a method of learning and re-learning history which is based on that most delightful pursuit of visiting historic buildings and antiquities. More than fifty main sites have been selected for special attention and each one is very evocative of a particular period and facet of the past. The choice of these monuments from the exceptional assemblage which comprises the British heritage has been difficult and, inevitably, controversial. The selection was made according to a number of rules: all the major regions of the British Isles should be represented, as should the different ages of history and prehistory. It was also felt that, wherever possible, lesser-known sites should be introduced to the exclusion of famous and sometimes over-crowded places. Thus, for example, Stonehenge is omitted while the great prehistoric complex of monuments at Avebury is included. In this case, it would be impossible to say anything original about Stonehenge while many would argue that the ethos of this truly unique and remarkable monument is submerged by the surging tide of visitors and the vast and incongruous car park. On the other hand, while the more extensive circle at Avebury is much visited, the other great monuments in its immediate vicinity tend to be overlooked.

By introducing a good number of lesser-known but exceptionally visit-worthy sites such as the Neolithic tombs at Cairnholy, the castles of Grosmont and Caister or the church at Llanddewi Brefi—it is hoped that the visitor will enjoy the hitherto unsuspected rewards of under-valued places. As tourists, the British do tend to single out a small number of famous places for special attention and then swamp them to the extent that concentration, enjoyment and the contemplation of the past become impossible amongst the jostle and throng. Yet while places like the Tower of London,

Stonehenge and Caernarfon Castle in the summer are clamorous and hopelessly overcrowded, scores of enthralling sites and monuments are virtually deserted. Much of the photography for this book was undertaken in July and the blazing August and September of 1981. Yet, while invaluable monuments like the Roman shore fort of Burgh Castle or the reconstructed Saxon village of West Stow heard only the patter of occasional feet, others, like the amazing 'stone circle' of Callanish, the deserted medieval villages of Houndtor and Wharram Percy, the battlefield of Sedgemoor and the prehistoric cave dwellings at Creswell Crags were found to be quite devoid of fellow visitors.

The selection of sites is of course a personal choice. While some of the places like West Stow, the Pimperne Iron Age house reconstruction or the venerable dwellings which have been rebuilt at Singleton are unique or so remarkable that they have, as it were, selected themselves, most imaginative readers will decry the omission of some particularly cherished site. In answer, I can only plead the constraints of space, the need for historical and regional balance and certain principles which governed the selection.

Although the places described amount to a very varied selection, I have sought to keep one major theme flowing through the book: that of 'the British at home'. The homes range from deserted settlements of the prehistoric era or the fortified stronghold of the medieval lord to the dwellings of medieval yeomen and mansions of nineteenth century industrialists. I can be certain that visitors to the many different types of home described will be impressed and fascinated by a remarkable variety of the visions of 'home' which were held by different classes of people at different times.

The choices have been made with the motorist very much in mind. For this reason, I have sought sites which are generally accessible to the motorist. Most are located in open countryside or in village or small town settings. Of course there are scores of important monuments which lie close to the hearts of large towns but it must be admitted that towns of a larger order than, say, Lichfield or Wells, tend to face the motoring stranger with frustrating searches for parking places, labyrinthine and unpredictable one-way road systems and other time-consuming problems of this kind. With a motor-borne tourist and day-visitor still in mind, I have accompanied each 'main entry' with a selection of interesting sites in the general vicinity. When route-planning, one is often tempted to accomplish too much, yet experience shows that it is generally difficult to visit and enjoy more than four or five quite closely-spaced sites in a single day. Several of the places described, like the open air museum at Singleton, offer the potential for a full day's entertainment and, in such cases, the suggestions for tours in the neighbourhood are accordingly shortened.

I have also catered for the amateur photographer. Today, the great majority of visitors to historic monuments arrive equipped with cameras, and the sophisticated 35 mm models outnumber the cheap and simple cameras. Even so, these outfits are not often used to the best effect and the really good shots tend to be missed when good vantage points go unnoticed and when inappropriate lenses and accessories are used. The photography of landscape and antiquities is a special craft with special rewards. A brief guide to the most useful sort of equipment and the basic techniques of this branch of photography follows in the next chapter, while in the case of each main site, particular 'Phototips' concerning viewpoints, lenses and effects are listed.

In the course of 1981 and 1982, every one of the main sites described was visited by me, a few for the first time and, in other cases, for the fourth or fifth time. The tours ranged from the Isle of Lewis to Land's End and from the west of Ireland to the Suffolk coast. Although the organisation of tourism in these islands is often criticised, the hospitality at the many small hotels was never less than good and, in the case of the

12

farmhouses of Ireland, quite unforgettable. The curators and officials in charge of the various monuments—with one cartoon-like and privately-employed exception—and the many people who assisted with directions and local knowledge also confirmed the impression that Britain is still a friendly and helpful place. Even so, those who travel in search of the heritage must expect some disappointments. The destruction of good old countryside by modern farming methods is a national scandal of gigantic proportions, while the closure of several important monuments as a consequence of short-sighted government spending cuts shakes one's faith in the state's custodianship of the national heritage.

There is just one thing that must be said: vandals do not tend to read books but in case one should, the use of metal detectors on archaeological sites is *illegal and may result in prosecution*. This apart, prehistoric and medieval villagers had no lasting possessions of any value so metal detecting at lost village sites is a waste of time apart from being anti-social and irresponsible. However, metal detectors can be exchanged for good secondhand cameras and thus a silly hobby can be substituted for one that is worthwhile and challenging.

Where a place name in the text is followed by an * that site is covered elsewhere in the book, either as a main or a secondary site. Refer to the index for further information, the **bold** entry indicating the chief reference. Ordnance Survey grid references have been given for out-of-the-way places. The small maps in each section give an approximate position for all the sites mentioned in that section.

If, at times, the narrative that follows seems to ring with superlatives, this is simply because it includes some of the most exciting and rewarding exhibits from our amazing legacy of historical monuments. I can only hope that in following some of the history trails that I have suggested, the reader will discover the same interest and, indeed, sheer enjoyment.

PORTRAITS OF THE PAST

Photographing monuments and their settings is a part of landscape photography which has its own particular techniques, challenges and demands. It can be very rewarding. It produces mementoes of excursions and events, gives full scope to the photographer's ingenuity and creativity, and encourages a better understanding of landscapes and buildings and the subtleties of light and shade.

Visitors to prehistoric monuments, medieval castles and stately homes who waste yards of film on bad or nondescript shots must surely agree that one really good photograph is worth much more than a packet of mediocre prints. The good pictures are there in the landscape waiting to be taken, but finding them demands extra thought and effort.

EQUIPMENT

In comparison to the costs of travel or holiday accommodation, photography is a relatively cheap hobby once the necessary equipment has been bought.

The 35 mm single lens reflex camera is the most popular with the amateur photographer. It is a versatile and convenient camera, being capable of producing monochrome negatives which can be enlarged to $10'' \times 8''$ without noticeable deterioration in quality, and good colour transparencies. Its lenses can be interchanged and for photographing buildings and landscapes well, the 'standard' 50 mm or 55 mm lenses with which it is usually sold need to be replaced by a lens with a wider field.

Taking photographs of buildings with a 50 mm lens is likely to cause 'parallex'—the effect of falling over backwards that results from tipping the camera axis away from the horizontal. Where tall buildings are concerned, you should either stand back or use a sufficiently wide-angle lens so that parallax is avoided completely. Alternatively, you can deliberately exploit the parallax effect: see page 263 where I have described the technique working well when photographing windmills.

The field of a lens is indicated by its focal length: a 300 mm lens is a powerful telephoto capable of bringing distant details closer, but it has a narrow field; the 150 mm is less powerful, with an effect comparable to small binoculars rather than a telescope. A moderate wide-angle lens—that is, one with a wide field—is a 35 mm, while the 24 mm has such a wide field that it will enable you to stand in one corner of a moderately sized room and photograph the other three corners. The lower the focal length of a lens, the wider its field.

My choice of lens is 35 mm for colour work and 25 mm for monochrome—the exceptionally wide field of the 25 mm enabling me to enlarge portions of the negative while still enjoying the panoramic effects.

When buying wide-angle lenses, it is important to remember that they are more

14

difficult to manufacture than telephoto lenses and are likely to be more expensive. If you wish to carry a second lens, I would suggest a zoom spanning 75–200 mm. This combines standard, portrait and telephoto and is reasonably priced. A zoom with a good wide-angle capability will cost a lot more.

Cost and convenience will decide the amount of equipment you carry. An item that is relatively cheap, often under-rated yet indispensable for interior work, is the tripod. While modern flash-units which can gauge the amount of flash needed for a perfect exposure are now available at competitive prices, there is really no comparison between an interior photographed in natural light and the harsh, brash divisions of light and shade which flash tends to produce. Inside prehistoric tombs or in murky medieval houses or churches, flash can be useful for lightening a dark corner in the course of a time exposure which uses the natural lighting.

A tripod can be unwieldy and should be used with discretion when there are other visitors around. Always seek the permission of the custodian of a site before using it because tripods are banned on some important sites. When buying a tripod, avoid light models which do not provide a steady base for the camera.

There are two forms of colour film: colour negative from which prints are made, and transparency film. It is generally accepted that transparencies offer the most subtle and life-like rendering of colour but they can only be viewed conveniently by being projected on to a screen or enlarged by a hand-viewer. Colour prints are very popular: they are comparatively cheap, easily shown to people and simple to keep in an album. However, mass processing by computer can produce some odd colour combinations and, at the moment, transparency film must be used for accurate work.

Professional photographers tend to favour Kodachrome 25 and Kodachrome 64 for transparencies, both being renowned for their fine grain and rich colour renderings. The 25 is a slow film and needs the use of a tripod in murky conditions when long exposures are required; the 64 is faster. Users of larger cameras can take advantage of Ektachrome 64, available in 35 mm but not very suitable for the smaller format.

Cheap colour prints have tended to reduce amateur interest in monochrome photography although it is arguably the most versatile, creative and telling medium. In poor weather conditions when the scenery shades from grey to khaki, it is particularly valuable. If you have a dark room, shots taken in dull conditions can be greatly enhanced by slightly over-developing the film, and by the use of 'hard' grade papers and high-contrast print developers. For monochrome work, I favour Ilford FP4, a film with a 'medium' speed ASA rating of 125.

Black and white film tends to bleach out the sky so that cloud patterns disappear. They can be retained by using a yellow filter which darkens blue sky and emphasises white clouds. The orange filter which I prefer to use produces an even more dramatic effect. Orange is also good for heightening the subtler tones of timbers, and yellow-green will bring out contrasts in vegetation. It makes prehistoric stone monuments look cold and slightly eerie.

There is a baffling array of filters for colour work. Starburst or multi-image filters are used for special effects which, although stunning to look at, might come to be regarded as gimmicky. Graduated colour filters should be taken more seriously: graduated blue will intensify blue sky and add interesting tones to cloud patterns on cloudy days—an effect also obtainable with graduated grey, tobacco or violet filters. Diffuser and fog filters create blurred and dreamy images while the clear centre spot diffuser produces a clear central subject in a halo of haze. For general colour work, many photographers fit

The effect of different graduated filters: (Above) *Fountains Abbey, magenta:* (Below) *Bodiam Castle, tobacco*

(Left) *Two photographs of Ludlow Castle showing the difference in the field of view between a medium telephoto and the standard lens*

a colourless skylight filter which helps to eliminate excessive blueness in a landscape and will penetrate haze to a limited extent. Polaroid filters can be used in monochrome and colour photography on those rare occasions when glare from water or windows is a problem.

TECHNIQUE

It is a mistake to become so obsessed with equipment and the more obscure technicalities of photography that you lose sight of the fact that they are simply means to an end. A memorable photograph comes from being at the right place at the right time and doing the right things. Although today's automatic or semi-automatic 35 mm camera with through-the-lens metering reduces the level of technical competence required to take a good photograph, it is very important that you remain master of the camera and override its decisions when you think it necessary.

Still photography is concerned with images set in rectangular frames and the good photographer, like a painter, sees the pictures existing in a landscape. Vantage points are very important. They may not be where most photographers are gathered, but perhaps on a nearby hillock or beneath a tree with branches which help to frame the subject. Luckily, subjects in landscape and architectural photography do not move around and it is normally safe to set the shutter at 1·125th of a second and forget about it unless you switch to a telephoto lens which needs a faster speed. The telephoto will pick out details in the main subject—part of a timber framing, a textured and weather-worn fragment of stonework, or the shapely silhouette of a weather-vane.

Capturing your subject in the right light is all important. Avebury on a cloudy day is barely the same place when seen in low sunlight, its details sharp and glowing. Beautiful results can be obtained in winter. Most people do their photography in the summer when the high sun at midday casts heavy shadows and an unsympathetic glare. Monuments and buildings look dramatically beautiful when side-lit by a sinking sun so they should be photographed late on a summer's day.

Our unpredictable weather can make excessive demands on your patience while waiting for the sun to appear between clouds in what you hope will be the right place for the best picture. People and cars can try your patience, too; I have a lady in a luminous red anorak who seems to constantly dog my footsteps! Should you wish to photograph people in landscapes or near buildings, you must decide which is to be the subject of the picture. Friends and relatives can make an attractive distant detail in a photograph of a castle; conversely, a distant or out-of-focus castle can provide an attractive background for a family group. It is usually a mistake to place equal emphasis on both.

A final technical point: do not neglect to make use of the camera's depth of focus guide. It shows precisely the area in which objects will be sharp according to the aperture setting. A small aperture (f16 for example) gives a great depth of focus, a wide aperture (f2) a shallow depth. Aperture affects shutter speed and there are occasions when using a small aperture for maximum depth of focus means such a slow shutter speed that a tripod is necessary—in a church for example. Here the wide-angle lens is invaluable, for the wider its angle, the greater its depth of focus. Used properly, it will make everything sharp, from close foreground to the horizon.

I have provided a section entitled 'Phototips' for each of the main sites described in the text and illustrated them with photographs especially taken for this book. Of course, they by no means exhaust the possibilities of the sites and I hope your search for the 'best' photograph will be as enjoyable as mine.

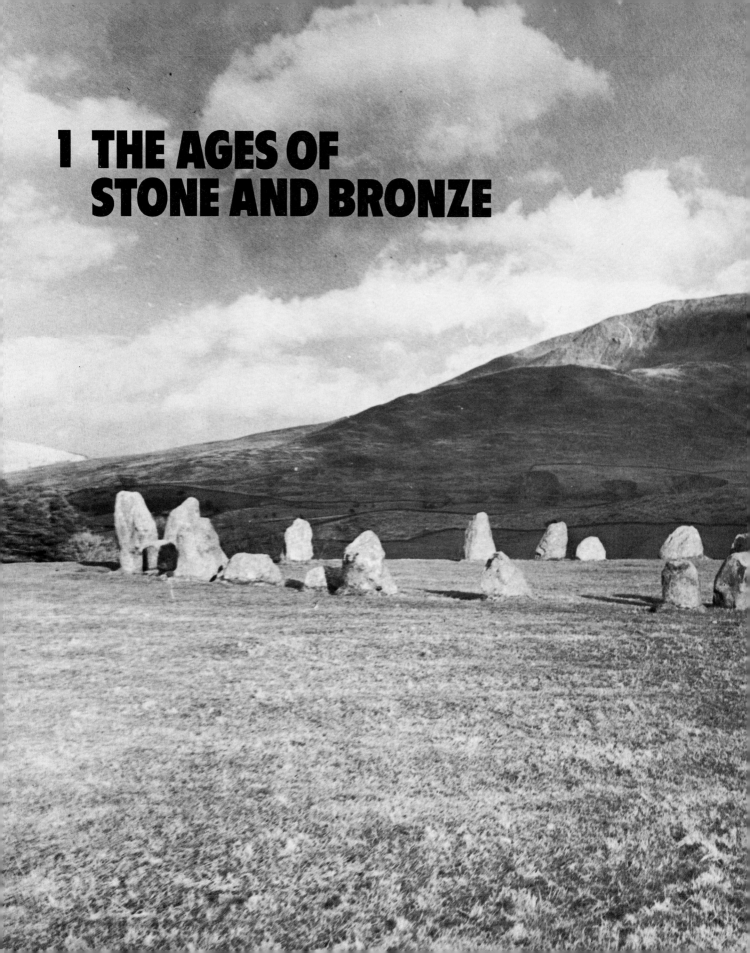

1 THE AGES OF STONE AND BRONZE

The story of man in Britain has no easily recognisable beginning. Instead, as we trace it back through the millennia, it becomes ever more misty until the human presence is only evidenced by discoveries of flint tools and fragmentary relics such as teeth and pieces of skull. The Old Stone Age or Palaeolithic period extends back for hundreds of thousands of years, beyond the last great Ice Age and into warmer 'interglacial' periods between ice ages. The modern human species, *Homo sapiens sapiens*, was probably not the original human tenant of these islands and there are suggestions that our close relative Neanderthal man and our older and more distant cousin *Homo erectus* may have wandered here. Our knowledge of Palaeolithic man focuses on the numerous discoveries of the finely wrought flint tools of this period, but most other questions remain unanswered. Bands of Palaeolithic hunters seem to have been quite active in the warmer, more southerly parts of Britain during the later stages of the last Ice Age and discoveries of their tools are not uncommon. Even so, we are unsure whether we should regard these hunting bands as permanent British residents, or whether they were continentals who came here to hunt in the warmer seasons and interludes, exploiting a land bridge spanning the present English Channel.

The deglaciation of Britain began around 14,000 years ago. For a few thousand years, there were warmer interludes and periods of glacial readvance, but then the warming trend became entrenched and tides of advancing woodland began to lap northwards. Hardy species like the pine and the birch formed the vanguard but they were to be displaced in the lower and more hospitable areas by deciduous trees like the elm, lime, ash and oak.

The Middle Stone Age or Mesolithic period spans the period when the old Palaeolithic hunting lifestyle was reshaped to exploit the resources of the forested environment and it ends with the introduction of farming to Britain in the fifth millennium BC. As is the case with the more ancient Stone Age folk, we tend to meet the Mesolithic people mainly through the survival of their tools of flint and horn. These tools, the flint-working sites and the fragmentary traces of Mesolithic dwellings suggest that hunting groups followed a semi-nomadic life within their hunting territories. There seem to have been permanent lowland winter base-camps and a variety of more ephemeral dwelling sites which were visited at different times of the year. So far as we know, the British communities of the Old and Middle Stone Ages created no durable monumental tombs or temples, while their dwelling sites tend to be recognisable and intelligible only to archaeologists. And so the only monuments to these formative periods which remain to excite the non-specialist are the natural caves which were, from time to time, occupied by ancient hunting groups. The caves at Creswell Crags in Derbyshire, therefore, will be our first visit.

Although the introduction of farming marks the break between the Mesolithic period and Neolithic era or the New Stone Age, it seems that the first steps in the removal of the natural forest blanket were taken by hunters rather than farmers. They may have been seeking to improve the browsing quality for the grazing animals upon which they preyed, or to create open hunting ranges. It is also possible that certain animals—the dog without doubt and possibly the red deer—were domesticated before the age of farming. The early stages of farming in the fifth millennium are shrouded in mystery, but the presence of Neolithic communities in the fourth millennium is visible in a most dramatic fashion through the construction of remarkable religious and ceremonial monuments in the forms of long barrows and chambered tombs, causewayed camps and, later, stone circles. Along with important flint and stone axe-making sites and the rediscovery of a number of important long-distance routeways, they tell us of a well-organised and capable series of societies which were strongly motivated by a religion demanding the construction of massive and imposing tombs and temples.

In many history books, the prehistoric period is dismissed in a few lines, but the contribution of prehistoric peoples to the shaping of the landscape and later patterns of development was profound. Many have visions of these people as being dwarfed by their forest environment, yet by the end of the Neolithic era, a large part of the natural woodland had been removed while extensive tracts of countryside seem already to have experienced the adverse effects of many centuries of continuous cultivation.

There is no doubt that farming will have supported much heavier densities of population than the old hunting and gathering lifestyle. The remarkable Neolithic monuments show that the peasant communities enjoyed leisure, for they could never have been built by people who were forever striving to achieve subsistence. The existence of these leisured farmers alone is not sufficient to explain the magnificent adventures in monument building, or the modern countryside would be packed with new creations. It seems that as society advanced and land became the subject of serious territorial contests, so the social hierarchy was stretched and new breeds of powerful chieftains and warlords emerged, men who could command and organise the building of prestigious tombs and temples. Also, it is worth remembering that the control of land was a matter of life or death to pre-Industrial peoples, while only in relatively recent times have we come to regard religion, politics, economics and law as being separate and distinct. Often, the Neolithic religious monuments seem also to have served as prominent symbols of territorial control. Recreation, entertainment and religion will have been similarly merged, and so the stone circles and earthen henge monuments will also have served as spectacular theatres for the staging of ritual ceremonies. Like medieval churches or the cinemas of the '20s and '30s, they doubtless offered a glamorous escape from the humdrum routines of daily life.

The New Stone Age does not end abruptly, but in a transition period from around 2700 and 2000 BC. This era is associated with the influence of groups known as the 'Beaker folk'. Formerly, we were certain that there was a considerable immigration to Britain by communities of powerfully built people whose burials were accompanied by the internment of a beaker-shaped and often highly-decorated pot. Now we are less sure whether there was a physical invasion and settlement rather than a spread of ideas. In any event, in the course of this transitional period, the rite of collective burial was generally superseded by that of individual burial beneath a round earthen barrow or in a stone-lined box or cist, while copper and then bronze technology was introduced from the continent.

The Bronze Age proper begins around 2000 BC and although the agricultural operations were further extended and population would have grown, the Bronze Age has not left such a rich and imposing legacy of great monuments. Doubtless, this partly reflects changes in religious outlooks but it also seems likely that the main population and ceremonial centres were relocated in river valleys where they may still lie entombed and masked by many feet of river silts. In the later stages of the Bronze Age, the pressure of an increasing population and the effects of a deteriorating climate which caused the desertion of many upland farms, contributed to the emergence of defenceworks and defined communal territories which were jealously guarded, establishing the political climate for the Iron Age which followed.

See Appendix II for other sites from the Bronze and Stone Ages.

Creswell Crags

(Derbyshire)

Many thousands of years before man appeared in Britain, a small river had been at work, gradually gouging out a narrow gorge through an outcrop of limestone. Such is the nature of limestone—a rock which tends to be fissured and soluble in stream water that penetrates these cracks—that it is vulnerable to underground as well as surface erosion. Subterranean streams create labyrinths of caverns in limestone beds, and a large number of such caves were exposed in the sides of the river gorge at Creswell. In due course, communities of prehistoric hunters made their homes in these natural shelters.

The tenancy of these caves was confined to no one human group, but it spans a period of more than 40,000 years during which different communities will have occupied the caverns for differing periods which will have been separated by phases of abandonment. The oldest excavated remains, some of which date back more than 70,000 years to the long warm interlude which preceded the last Ice Age, represent animals such as the red deer, hippopotamus and hyena and many of these bones may have been brought to the cave by carnivores. It was probably during the less frigid intervals in the last Ice Age that small hunting groups, seeking shelter from the biting winds and sleet storms, discovered the caves at Creswell Crags and there may have been fierce contests to evict sitting tenants in the forms of bears and hyenas.

The oldest traces of human occupation date back to around 45,000 years ago and are represented by quartzite fragments and rough stone handaxes, chipped from pebbles. Although this period of life at Creswell Crags has yielded the bones of many animals including lions, bears, mammoths, horses, woolly rhinoceroses, reindeer, wolves and hyenas, definitive human remains are lacking, but it is hypothesised that the cave dwellers who made the stone tools were not *Homo sapiens* but our close cousin *Homo neanderthalensis*. (Were we able to meet a Neanderthal Man, we might find his features slightly course, but his brain size was equal to our own, and sometimes even a little larger.) Apart from one recently discovered tooth, convincing remains of Neanderthalers have not been found in Britain but finds of characteristic stone tools testify to their presence here.

OPPOSITE *The Boat House Cave and* (left) *the peaceful lake at Creswell Crags. Photograph on pp 18–19: Castlerigg, Cumbria*

23

The most important age of cave life in Britain took place during the later phases of the last Ice Age, between about 30,000 and 10,000 BC. The greater part of Britain remained in the grip of ice sheets and glaciers and periodic colder spells will have occurred to drive the hunting communities southwards from northern and Midland England.

Nevertheless, the evidence of settlement at Creswell Crags during this 'Upper Palaeolithic' period is very rich. Most of the animals which Neanderthal groups had hunted were present and the reindeer seem to have been particularly abundant. The evidence from lost and discarded flints reveals a growing sophistication in the craft of tool-making; around 30,000 years ago, the tools which were shaped from flakes of flint included beautiful points shaped like laurel leaves. However, a severe drop in temperature followed and Britain was probably abandoned. By about 13,000 BC, the climate ameliorated and hunting communities returned and re-discovered the Creswell caves. By this time, the lion and woolly rhinoceros were extinct in Britain although horses, elk and reindeer ranged over the swamps and snowdrifts of the tundra landscape, feeding on stunted shrubs and lichens and perhaps browsing on the stands of woodland which had become established in the most sheltered places.

Creswell Crags has given its name to a culture—the Creswellian—which testifies not to the 'primitiveness' of cave life, but to the remarkable craftsmanship of the people and the birth of British art. The Creswellian toolkit was varied and versatile; it will have included flint blades of types with characteristically blunted backs, awls, burins and scrapers, and

The scene from the mouth of one of the caves at Creswell Crags

tools of bone and antler. There is no evidence of cave painting in Britain but a form of line drawing did exist here during the Old Stone Age and the Creswell caves have yielded a competent engraving of the head of a bushily-maned wild horse and a more puzzling sketch of what may be a dancer or a man-beast, both drawings being scratched on bone.

Finds such as these help us to see the ancient occupants of Creswell Crags as real people blessed with talents and sensibilities and, with a little imag-ination, we can visualise the hunting groups gathering in the mouths of caves to plan the chase, returning with the carcase of a horse or reindeer, dismem-bering it expertly with blades of flint, cooking and sharing the meat, cleaning the hide with flint scrapers, cutting it into garments which would be pierced

with an awl of flint or bone and sewn together with sinews. Nothing would be wasted, and while the families gossiped around their fire in the relative security of the cave mouth, the local artist might scratch out designs on bone or antler, perhaps recreating the figure of a shaman priest, a scene from a familiar ritual or a fluent animal outline in an attempt to charm the intended prey.

Although the relics which have been excavated from the Creswell caves help to colour our visions of life in the Old Stone Age, important questions remain unanswered. Archaeology has shown that the cave-dwellers seemed to prefer caves with relatively narrow openings and that they tended to occupy the portion of the cave closest to the mouth. But there are only a few parts of Britain which are well endowed with caves and we are left to wonder where the non-

cave-dwelling majority lived and whether the cave-dwellers occupied their caverns only seasonally? There is little evidence of 'open' camps in Britain, but various continental sites have sug-gested that ancient hunters also lived in skin tents. We know this from the discovery of arrangements of boulders or mammoth bones and tusks which were used to anchor and support the tents.

The occupation of the Creswell caves did not die with the Old Stone Age and excavations show that the caverns pro-vided shelter, if sometimes in-termittently, at all the main prehistoric and historical periods through to the nineteenth century. They were occupied in the Middle Stone Age when the climate warmed and forest began to blanket the landscape; later, prehistoric farmers and Roman shepherds used them, while relatively recent tenants are indicated by the discovery of clay tobacco pipes.

Although this is one of the most impor-tant places known to have supported Old Stone Age communities, many other sites have been located. However, Cres-well Crags is far more accessible than the majority and the site is less clamorous than a handful of other well-publicised and over-commercialised cave attrac-tions. Even so, the approaches hardly prepare one to contemplate ancient life for the site is tucked away within the gutsy and bustling heartland of the York-Derby-Notts coalfield. Although the tranquility is broken from time to time by traffic using the Crags Road to Creswell, the immediate setting of the caves is green and secluded.

Some twenty-three caverns and rock shelters lie along the northern and southern margins of a ribbon of artificial lake which was created when the stream

Jagged limestone rocks protruding from the roof of a Creswell Crag cave

at the foot of the gorge was dammed to form a fishpond in the nineteenth century. The most notable are Boat House Cave—which was used as a boat house until the lake level was lowered in the 1930s and which has surrendered the remains of bison and hyenas—and Mother Grundy's Parlour, Church Hole Cave, Pin Hole Cave and Robin Hood's Cave, all of which contained evidence of the earliest phase of settlement at Cres-well Crags. Pin Hole Cave produced evidence of a remarkable sequence of occupations representing not only the various Old Stone Age periods but also relics from all the major prehistoric periods which followed. Mother Grundy's Parlour brings the sequence through until recent times since it takes its name from a nineteenth-century occupant, reputedly a witch who is said to have lived in the cave.

I consider the caves at Creswell Crags to be the most fascinating of the Old Stone Age sites in Britain. The local authorities have provided a well-appointed information centre and picnic area a short distance from the caves, and a footpath runs around the lakeshore and beside the mouths of Boat House and Church Hole Caves. On the debit side, safety considerations prevent public access to the cave interiors while the approaches to caves like Pin Hole, Mother Grundy's Parlour and Robin Hood's which lie across the Crags Road could be improved.

Cresswell Crags is jointly run by Derbyshire and Nottinghamshire County Councils.

Phototips There are two basic possibil-ities: a general view of the setting of the caves and photographs of the individual cave interiors. The former is much the easier because fine views of the southern caves can be obtained from the opposite lake shore. In summer's late afternoon sunlight, the colours take on a wonder-ful intensity, with the pale yellow-grey limestone assuming an amber glow while the surrounding shrubs and lake-side vegetation display every shade of green. Although the lake is a modern creation, its blue waters add the final complement of colour and the scene is much more effectively captured in col-our than in black and white.

One needs rather more equipment and determination to do photographic justice to the cave interiors. The lens have to be poked through the bars of the cave-mouth grills and a steadying tripod is needed. The daylight scarcely penet-rates the gloom of the cave interiors and so photographs taken while using a long exposure alone will produce rather dark, flat results. On the other hand, flash produces harsh angular shadows and will dispel the mysterious subtleties of light and shade.

The best answer is to use the tripod for a long exposure while throwing in a flash to lighten the darker recesses. A wide-angle lens set at a small aperture such as f11 should capture a broad sweep of the cave interior while giving sufficient depth of focus from the cave mouth to the back wall. Depending upon the cave in question, the brilliance of the natural light and the speed of the film being used, an exposure of 1 to 8 secs will be needed and, during this time exposure, the flashgun can be fired and it should be directed towards the murkier recesses, avoiding the rock formations which are close to the cave mouth and are therefore quite well-illuminated by daylight.

Location Between Chesterfield and Worksop. From the A616, take the B6042 at Creswell village; from the A60, take the B6042 to Creswell. The picnic area is signposted from the B6042 Crags Road.

ROUND AND ABOUT

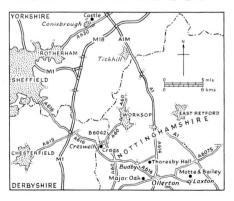

CONISBROUGH CASTLE
(South Yorkshire)

Several rewarding hours can be spent visiting the caves at Creswell Crags, but with the fast routeway lying less than 10 miles away, just to the east of Worksop, the drive to the magnificent Plantagenet stronghold at Conisbrough is easily accomplished.

Although Saxon fortifications prob-ably surrounded a nearby hill as the town's original name *Cyningesburh* or 'king's fort' implies, the earliest defensive work at Conisbrough Castle involved the building of the moated mound upon which the stone defences now stand. The earthworks were constructed after the territory around Conisbrough was granted to the Norman conqueror Wil-liam de Warenne who was created Earl of Surrey and held other great estates in Sussex and Norfolk. A timber palisade embracing wooden buildings originally crowned the mound and the erection of a stone castle was probably commanded by Hamelin Plantagenet, an illegitimate half-brother of Henry II. Hamelin married the de Warenne heiress Isabel in 1163 and the construction of his stone tower or keep began about 1180.

The keep is almost 100 ft in height, a cylindrical tower with a splayed stone base and clasped by six great turret-like buttresses and a formidable refuge. It is

at several later castles.

The modern visitor approaches the castle across a causeway which marks the position of the original drawbridge, while the last stage of the journey into the inner bailey via a formidable gatehouse was through the wall-flanked passageway of the barbican. A portion of the barbican and southern curtain wall have unfortunately slithered down towards the moat.

the then Earl of Surrey. This was all very much the stuff of medieval romance, but Conisbrough Castle owes much of its modern renown to a different romance—Sir Walter Scott's *Ivanhoe* which introduced a fictional Saxon castle and cast to Conisbrough.

The castle is in the care of the Department of the Environment.

Location From the A1(M), take the A630 towards Sheffield; the town of Conisbrough lies about 3 miles from the A1(M) and the castle is close to the town centre and clearly seen lying to the N of the A630 which runs through the town.

Conisbrough Castle: a superbly restored 12th-century fortress

so well restored as to seem almost newly built and only the conical roof and internal floors are lacking. Once built, the keep was surrounded by a curtain wall some 35 ft tall and 7 ft thick which embraced the inner bailey. The stern but gloomy keep probably served as a storage area, but was mainly a last resort should the castle be attacked. The south side of the fortress was more vulnerable than the north and the southern section of the curtain wall was studded with six great semi-circular projecting turrets—an innovation in design which was adopted

Despite the disappearance of the domestic buildings, servants' quarters and probably a chapel which huddled against the inner face of the curtain wall and the collapse of some sections of the curtain, Conisbrough Castle remains too much intact and imposing to be regarded merely as a ruin. Were it located in the southern countryside rather than near the heart of a northern industrial town, it would surely be a major tourist attraction. Even though it is overlooked by much of the town, the castle still manages to dominate its setting.

Formidable but not invincible, Conisbrough fell in 1317 to Thomas Earl of Lancaster, who retaliated following the abduction of his wife by John Warenne,

THORESBY HALL AND SHERWOOD FOREST
(Nottinghamshire)

The original hall was burned in 1745 and in the 1860s the present neo-Tudor hall was built to a design by Anthony Salvin. The Hall is now owned by the Countess Manvers and is open to the public. The surrounding estate was taken from Sherwood Forest in the late-17th century and the statue in the Hall's forecourt shows that the Robin Hood legend was also adopted. The actual existence of Robin Hood is uncertain and 12th-century records suggest a variety of Robin Hoods and various different locations to rival Sherwood Forest. The famous Major Oak is reputed to have been used by Robin as a cache for supplies. The tree has a diameter of $10\frac{1}{2}$ ft and is estimated to be 400 to 640 years old which makes it doubtful if it was even an acorn during the reigns of Richard I (1189–99) and John (1199–1216) in which the legends are set.

Location Reached via the minor road linking Budby village (on A616) and A614, 4 miles NW of Ollerton. The Major Oak is 2 miles from Thoresby Hall.

Note Laxton is also in the neighbourhood: *see* index for page reference.

27

The Cairnholy Tombs

(Dumfries & Galloway)

The contrast between the lifestyles of the Old Stone Age hunters who lived in the Creswell Caves* around 12,000 BC and those of the New Stone Age peasants who erected the Cairnholy tombs about 8000 years later was remarkable. The domestication of animals had probably been achieved well before 5000 BC and it was early in the course of the fifth millennium that grain cultivation was introduced from the continent. Gradually, the removal of forest to extend the agricultural stage will have transformed the landscape and, in the course of the fourth millennium, the peasant communities asserted their presence in new ways, constructing great tombs and then stone circles.

Two stone tombs were built at Cairnholy, on the hillslopes above the tidal marshes of Wigtown Bay, looking out to the Irish Sea beyond. Hundreds of chambered tombs were built in western Britain during the New Stone Age. Many were larger and more elaborate than those at Cairnholy; most have toppled, been robbed for building material or ploughed out of existence, but few compare with the visual dramas of the tomb which is known to archaeologists as Cairnholy I.

Excavations clearly show that, like the earthen long barrows of other parts of England, the chambered tombs accommodated skeletons from corpses which had been allowed first to decompose in mortuary houses or within stockades. The tombs were houses for the dead and doubtless built by peoples who were deeply concerned with their ancestors and the afterlife. The chambered tombs were probably much more than burial places; many probably featured in ritual ceremonies, the details of which we may never discover. Belief plainly demanded that a privileged minority of the people who died during the New Stone Age should have their remains installed in a house which was incomparably more durable and sophisticated than the homes of the living.

Chambered tombs of differing types are found throughout northern and western Britain and along the Atlantic margins of the continent but we do not know whether they represent a single great religious movement, nor the extents to which the various types are the products of local invention. However, there are close similarities between the tombs on either side of the North Channel which separates Ulster and southwest Scotland, and the sea seems to have been a uniting rather than a dividing force.

At Cairnholy I, where the tomb is 170 ft long by 50 ft broad, erosion has stripped away the elongated covering mound to expose the two burial chambers. The most stunning feature of the tomb, however, is not the internal stonework of slabs and partitions but the towering stones of the façade. These are arranged in the form of a shallow crescent and rise in height towards the centre of the crescent where the entrance to the burial chambers was located. The façade may have formed an eerie backdrop to rituals performed in the forecourt, its stones silhouetted like gigantic shark's teeth. The gaps between those stones were neatly sealed with drystone walling.

Whatever the changes in religious outlooks that may have accompanied the arrival in Britain of Beaker influence in the centuries following about 2700 BC, the tomb remained in use, at least for a while. Excavation revealed that the rear section of the burial chamber may have been modified to contain a chest-like burial cist, and fragments of Beaker pottery were found, along with a flint knife of a type sometimes associated with female burials of the early Bronze Age; shards of a type of early Bronze Age pot known as a 'food vessel', and a stone carved with the undeciphered 'cup-and-ring' marks which are commonly associated with prehistoric monuments were also found. Older relics included fragments of what was presumed to be a ceremonial axe in prestigious jadeite stone, a leaf-shaped stone arrowhead and pieces of New Stone Age pottery.

Clearly the tomb remained in use over many centuries, during the course of which it was adapted and received the relics of peoples belonging to different periods and cultures. Either the rear chamber was altered to accommodate the burial cist, or the outer chamber was a later addition, since one of the slabs in the rear chamber is so tall as to block access to the entrance. It is easy to assume that prehistoric monuments were created in single architectural outbursts, but modern archaeology is helping us to recognise the complexity of their evolution.

On higher ground just 150 yards away are the remains of a second tomb, Cairnholy II. Though less well preserved than Cairnholy I, this smaller tomb— 70 ft by 40 ft—has an equally outlandish silhouette. The essential design of the inner and outer compartments is similar to that of its neighbour though one chamber retains a stone slab roof and while there is no great façade, the entrance to the tomb is flanked by two great slabs, one of which rears and tapers, poised like the neck of some rudely awakened dinosaur. Again, the excavated pottery shows that interest in the tomb continued into the Beaker period.

Accessible though little known, the Cairnholy tombs lie in an attractive countryside of woodland and rough pasture where an outlying spur of the southern uplands slopes down to meet the sea. Like others of their kind, these tombs—which were excavated in 1949—offer tantalising glimpses of prehistoric life and belief, and the changes which affected them. However, the mysteries remain to the fore and in this case we do not know why the two tombs were built so closely together. Perhaps they stood at the margins of neighbouring clan territories, perhaps the local New Stone Age community was dominated by two distinct dynasties, or perhaps they simply chose to build anew rather than to enlarge an existing tomb?

The site is in the care of the Scottish Development Department, who also look after Torhousekie and Cardoness Castle.

Phototips Both tombs are easy subjects

and the possibilities offered by their outlandish silhouettes should be explored. By photographing from a low position, the height and drama of the stones can be increased.

Location (517538) The Cairnholy tombs lie about 4 miles to the SE of Creetown and

The tomb known as Cairnholy II is less well-preserved than its neighbour and its boulders create wierd silhouettes

are reached by a narrow but navigable track and are signposted from the A75. Parking space is available.

ROUND AND ABOUT

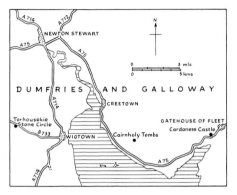

TORHOUSEKIE STONE CIRCLE

The façade stones at Cairnholy I are among the many examples which show that prehistoric peoples knew how to use large slabs and boulders to excellent dramatic effect. On the other hand, the stones at Torhousekie circle—well, they just seem to squat there like giant puffballs in a ring. There is little of the majesty of a Stonehenge or Callanish* although this circle is larger than the many scores of little circle temples which exist but fail to make the guidebooks.

Nineteen ice-smoothed granite boulders are arranged in a circle of about 60 ft diameter while three upright boulders are aligned across a diameter of the circle. This internal arrangement may be influenced by the 'recumbent stone circles' of north-east Scotland in which a part of the periphery is occupied by a large horizontal altar-like stone flanked by uprights. The construction of the circle began with the erection of a raised platform of earth and pebbles which supports the stones.

This part of Galloway offers better farmland than most other areas of Scotland and the presence of a numerous population in the early Bronze Age (when, presumably, the circle was built) is evidenced by the many smaller monuments which the area contains.

Location (383565) Immediately on the south side of the B733 and about 4 miles W of Wigtown.

The Torhousekie Stone Circle contains 19 boulders in its 60-ft diameter

CARDONESS CASTLE

The early military history of the area is uncertain although the remains of a Norman motte-and-bailey castle lie just to the west of this tower-house which appears to date from the middle of the 15th century, being built as the stronghold of the McCulloch family. The tower consists of four storeys and reaches a height of about 45 ft, which is not of dramatic proportions, but the approaches from the nearby sea cross broken, rocky ground and the tower controls the routeways across the sandflats. The walls of the tower are more than 8 ft in thickness.

Thus it is not surprising that in the reign of Elizabeth I, the English estimated that a force of 200 soldiers would be necessary to capture the stronghold by surprise attack. The McCullochs seem to have been possessed of a murderous and turbulent nature of a kind not uncommon on either flank of the Anglo-Scottish border and, during the 17th century, the ownership of Cardoness was violently disputed between the McCullochs and their Gordon neighbours. In 1668, the Gordon widow was dragged from her sickbed and left to die on a dung-hill while, at the end of the century, the last man to be executed on the Scottish guillotine was a McCulloch.

The tower has been uninhabited since

A stranded fireplace at Cardoness Castle

1697, and the internal floors have perished. Still, the external appearance of this starkly solid tower-house, the typical abode of the lesser Scottish noble in the 15th, 16th and 17th centuries, is well preserved. Inside, the bleak rubble walls and massive fireplaces testify to the draughty discomforts of baronial life. Children will love the 'murder-hole' or prison pit beneath the ground floor.

Location Beside the A75, 1 mile SW of Gatehouse of Fleet.

The Avebury Complex

(Wiltshire)

Around 800,000 people visit Stonehenge each year, and whilst many also visit Avebury, so often one meets people who have visited the remarkable circle there but remain unaware of the other components in this great prehistoric complex. They include the causewayed camp at Windmill Hill and the Sanctuary—which admittedly retain little of their former powers and glories—the West Kennet Avenue, the cavernous West Kennet chambered tomb and the enormous whatever-it-is of Silbury Hill which, in its way, is even more impressive than the stone circles.

This remarkable assemblage of monuments shows that during the Neolithic period, Avebury must have been a dominating cultural focus with an influence extending far across Wessex. It was clearly a great religious and ceremonial centre and probably a political core area too being the base of a dynasty of chieftains with the powers to command the construction of the gigantic monuments. Also, excavations have unearthed scores of stone axes which were brought to Avebury from many different regions, suggesting that this might also have been an important market and trading centre.

Causewayed camps are amongst the most puzzling of the British prehistoric monuments. They consist of a large area—often a hilltop—which has been surrounded by one or more erratic rings of banks and ditches. Evidence from a few of these camps suggests that battles may have occasionally taken place at these sites but the fact that the ditches and banks are breached at frequent intervals by level causeways argues against the camps as defenceworks. They may have been multi-purpose constructions which were used as assembly places for religious ceremonies, social gatherings and trading. They certainly represent major building schemes which will have required several gangs of organised workers and many man-hours of labour—in the case of Windmill Hill, sufficient to occupy fifty men for 300 days.

Windmill Hill was the first monument of this type to be excavated. It dates from the centuries before 3000 BC and the excavations produced evidence of people who grew primitive strains of wheat and barley, raised sheep, goats and pigs and, particularly, cattle; they kept fox terrier-sized dogs, hunted wild cattle and horses, cats and foxes and gathered crab apples and hazelnuts.

Despite their important but largely mysterious place in Neolithic society, neither Windmill Hill nor most other

---

OPPOSITE *Avebury: the remains of a great Neolithic religious and ceremonial centre*

(Below) *Some of the massive stones of the inner circle of the temple at Avebury*

causewayed camps survive as visually dramatic monuments but on the hill one can recognise sections of causewayed ditches as well as the bowl-shaped blisters which are much later Bronze Age burial mounds.

The West Kennet long barrow is one of the largest chambered tombs in Britain and the pottery which it contained shows that the construction of the tomb was roughly contemporary with that of Windmill Hill. Here, the skeletons of the territory's most important people would have been laid, probably after the flesh had decomposed in some sort of mortuary house.

The mound has the elongated wedge form which is characteristic of those in the Severn-Cotswold area but it is remarkable for the length of its partly collapsed covering mound—330 ft—and the magnificent façade of enormous sarsen slabs which stand in line across the entrance. The interior, which is more spacious than most other long barrows, can be entered. Two pairs of side chambers and a terminal chamber

run off from the entrance passage and several of the great constructional boulders are polished from their use in sharpening stone axes. As well as the remains of at least forty-six individuals, the tomb was found to contain pottery of types which spanned about 1000 years, predating the eventual sealing of the chambers by the erection of the façade and blocking sarsens (a local sandstone) around 2250 BC.

The Sanctuary is a more problematical monument, now represented by un-exciting concrete markers. Post holes which probably represent the supports for timber ceremonial buildings were excavated to reveal an original post ring and two stages of enlargement which produced a building with a diameter of 66 ft. It was probably in the con-struction of this third-phase building that stone circles inside and outside the

timber ring were erected. The initial building dated from about 2900 BC while the stone circles were probably con-temporary with the completion of the temple of Avebury around 2300 BC.

From the Sanctuary, a broad pro-cessional way, the West Kennet Avenue, curved its way towards the southern entrance of the great monument. It was flanked by sarsen slabs of apparently alternating long and lozenge shapes, perhaps symbolising the different sexes. Almost a mile in length, the avenue is now only a prominent feature for about the northern third of its length where most of the flanking sarsens still stand. A second and now largely obliterated processional way, the Beckhampton Avenue, looped off from the temple towards the west.

The temple at Avebury is a simply stupendous monument which covers

34

about twenty-nine acres and consists of an enormous roughly circular bank surrounding a ditch that was 30 ft deep. Ringing the inner sides of the ditch were the ninety-eight original stones of the outer circle. Inside, there were two more circles; the northern inner circle had three stones of which two survive, forming a cove-like feature at its centre. Apart from the two surviving northern stones, five remain to trace part of the perimeter of the southern inner circle, and the eastern end of the village of Avebury now obliterates portions of both circles.

Construction of the inner circles seems to have begun about 2600 BC; the surrounding earthworks and outer circle were completed around 2400 BC when the ditch, twice as deep as the silted trough of today, will have been a canyon-like gash in the glaring white chalk. When the ditch was complete, the diggers tossed in their antler picks, perhaps as offerings to the earth spirit. It was about this time that work probably began on the great avenues.

Avebury was famed far beyond Wessex before the great temple was begun: famed for the incredible man-made mountain of Silbury Hill where construction began around 2750 BC and continued for about a century. We know a good deal about Silbury Hill except what its function was, and so the most important question remains unanswered. If the hill took a century to build then this might represent the continuous employment of seventy men, but it may represent the seasonal efforts of much larger forces.

The hill stands 130 ft tall, it incorporates $8\frac{3}{4}$ million cubic ft of moved earth, rubble and chalk blocks and covers $5\frac{1}{2}$ acres, while its flat top alone has a diameter of 100 ft. Excavation has shown that the hill was built in steps like the stacked tiers of a wedding cake, with quarried chalk blocks being used to form the structures and the framework being filled with rubble. Then the ascending steps were infilled, leaving only the topmost step exposed. The bell-push-like summit which resulted is still evident and the hill remains well preserved although millennia of silting have partly filled the surrounding quarry ditches.

Although the villagers of Avebury systematically vandalised the surrounding circles in the medieval and more recent periods and some of the smaller monuments noted by seventeenth- and eighteenth-century antiquaries have been obliterated by farmers, Avebury remains a uniquely important complex of prehistoric monuments and it is unfortunate that so many visitors are aware of only one or two of the components.

Looking at Avebury more closely, one becomes aware of the enormous endeavours and resources of organisation and manpower involved. Even when one ignores the older tomb and causewayed camp, Avebury was a major ritual centre for around 1000 years before the complex began to decline in importance around 2100 BC. The Ave-

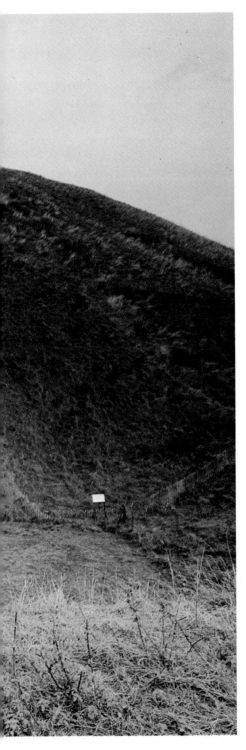

bury complex can hardly have been less revered or magnetic than the more compact monument at Stonehenge, a near contemporary whose completion dated from about the time of Avebury's initial decline.

The Department of the Environment looks after the Avebury complex; the National Trust owns part of Windmill Hill.

Phototips The potential is clearly enormous and the following notes suggest only a few of the possibilities.

When at the circle of the avenue, consider portraits of individual stones as well as groups. The knobbly, weather-worn sarsens are full of character and they change their appearances dramatically according to the weather, being brilliant in the sunlight and brooding darkly under cloud cover.

The outer circle is far too large and too much interrupted by the intruding vil-

The knobbly sarsen stones change their appearance dramatically according to the weather OPPOSITE *Silbury Hill, an incredible man-made mountain whose function is still a mystery*

lage to be encompassed in a single photograph but fine panoramas can be gained from the banks on either side of the southern entrance (which is used by the roads to the SE and Devizes), and from the northern entrance (used by the Swindon road) looking towards the village church. The cove stones just NE of the village centre and the biggest stones of all, the pair near the S entrance, are particularly photogenic.

Silbury Hill is impressive from all angles, but a fine view of the hill in its pleasant setting can be obtained from the track which leads up from the A4 towards the West Kennet chambered tomb.

The tomb, with its saw-toothed façade, offers many dramatic possibilities but one of my most cherished photographs was taken from the terminal chamber looking towards the entrance. A tripod and an exposure of 4–8 secs (if film of around 125 ASA is loaded) and a wide-angle lens set at around f8–f11 to give good depth of focus may be used. Inside the tomb, flash will produce glaring surfaces and black, featureless shadows, dispelling the eerie subtleties of the natural light, but a flicker of flash can be thrown in during the course of a time exposure to lighten some of the darker recesses.

The circle, avenue, hill and tomb all photograph well in colour and black-and-white, with colour perhaps having the edge in sunlit conditions and black-and-white giving more drama when the weather is brooding or gloomy. If conditions of sun and shade are alternating rapidly, as they so often do in England, it is worth waiting for a moment of clear sunlight to ignite a particularly appealing stone in a blaze of brilliant white.

Location Avebury lies just to the N of the A4, 6 miles W of Marlborough and the map shows the locations of the different monuments in the vicinity. The official Avebury guide contains a map.

Castlerigg Stone Circle

(Cumbria)

I find it impossible to visit the Lake District without having yet another look at the Castlerigg circle. The scene is never quite the same for the stones seem to mirror the elements: dark and brooding or light and lustrous according to the celestial state of play.

The stones are set on top of the spur of Chestnut Hill, a lofty platform which is surrounded by an amphitheatre of sterner mountains. The views in all directions are remarkable, but the star at the centre of this natural stage is a great circle of thirty-eight boulders which are arranged in a slightly pear-shaped ring about 110 ft in diameter.

Most of the stones are of fairly local origin and they will have begun their journey to Chestnut Hill as mountain debris which was trundled along in the slow-moving glaciers which gouged and smoothed the surrounding landscape. Only man could have assembled the boulders on the hilltop and so we must imagine teams of fifty to one-hundred members struggling with ropes and levers to haul each boulder upslope and into position. Tall stones were placed in the southern arc while an enigmatical arrangement of ten stones form a rectangle which touches the eastern arc and there is one outlying stone.

Any amount of space could be devoted to describing a circle such as this, but of course the important question is: 'What exactly is it?' This is a question that cannot be answered with any certainty. It is clear that the circles are a form of pagan temple since they perform no practical economic function, whilst the interpretations which cast them as astronomical observatories are not gaining in credibility. The cult of the dead and the after-life which is attested by the many chambered tombs like those at Cairnholy* was an important facet of a religion which was surely still alive when the circles were built. It should also be remembered that the circle builders will very largely have consisted of peasants whose survival depended upon the vagaries of the weather.

It therefore seems likely that the ceremonies which were performed at the circles were linked to the renewal of the fertility of the land and the placation of the deities which controlled the forces of Nature. In the course of such rituals, people may have danced around the ring until they became entranced. There is little evidence that they did, although an excavator reported that the ground around a Dorset barrow had been worn smooth by dancing feet.

During the historical period, right through until the nineteenth century, Cumberland was a thinly-populated and somewhat inaccessible backwater. In

OPPOSITE *Stones at Castlerigg in March, standing like black islands in a huge white sea of drifted snow*

(Below) *Stones silhouetted against the winter sunset at Castlerigg: the effect is enhanced by a pale violet filter*

the New Stone Age, and probably for much of the Bronze Age, the region was an important source of materials from which stone axes were made. No instrument, not even the modern bulldozer, has done so much to transform the British landscape, and Cumbrian axes, quarried from hard volcanic rocks such as tuff, rough-shaped on the mountain slopes and then ground and polished on the coastal sands, were exported throughout most of Britain.

Axe-makers and traders (both groups perhaps part-timers) will have been among the circle congregations and although no recent excavations have taken place at Castlerigg, the discoveries of concentrations of stone axes in association with other circles, including Avebury* and the Ring of Brodgar* have given rise to suggestions that they may have been linked to axe cults.

The questions concerning the meaning of the circles remain open but it should not be forgotten that, while serving primarily as religious centres, the circles could also have been places for trade gatherings and social events.

We do not know the age of the Castlerigg circle; the evidence for dating stone circles is limited although it is safe to generalise that the older circles belong to the second half of the New Stone Age and the younger to the first half of the Bronze Age. The archaeologist Aubrey Burl suggests that Castlerigg shows many of the features which he associated with the older circles, such as its large diameter and numerous large stones and the presence of an apparent entrance and an outlying stone. Thus one might guess that some 5000 years have elapsed since the circle was built.

Marked in some maps and guide books as Keswick Carles circle, Castlerigg is sufficiently tucked away from the beaten track and lakeshore hurly-burly as not to be completely overrun during the summer. However, to visit the circle in winter, especially when the surrounding peaks carry an icing of snow, is an unforgettable experience.

Castlerigg is in the care of the Department of the Environment.

Phototips Anyone failing to capture a satisfactory photograph of this exceptionally photogenic monument might be advised to consider a different hobby! There are two basic possibilities: photographs of the complete circle within its mountain setting and photographs of selected groups of stones. The less successful photographs are likely to be those which fall between the two stools.

Do not forget that in circle photography, as one moves back to include more of the circle within the frame, so the impact of individual stones or stone groupings will diminish, and when photographing stones in close-up, remember to check the depth of field guidelines to ensure that the background remains sharp.

The mountains form an attractive backdrop in every direction but one should decide whether the emphasis in the photograph is to be on the circle itself or the setting. Do not forget the sky: in full sunlight, the stones are brighter than their surroundings; otherwise they are darker and offer interesting possibilities as silhouettes against a dramatic skyscape. Crouch low until the selected stones are backed by sky and expose for the sky rather than the stones. The sky will then be shown with a wide range of tones to emphasise the cloud patterns while the stones will be portrayed as dark shapes rather than textures.

Location (292236) About 1½ miles to the E of Keswick; the walk is pleasant and not particularly steep. Signposted from the A591 Keswick–Ambleside and A66 Keswick–Penrith/M6 roads.

ROUND AND ABOUT

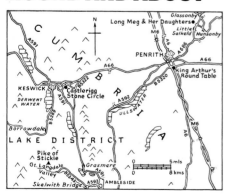

The Lake District is packed with interest and it would be impossible to visit more than a few of the fascinating monuments in the course of a day. Let us then save the intriguing sites such as the commanding Roman fort at Hard Knott Pass, the vertiginous Roman mountain road of High Street, the pack horse bridges, hamlets and quarrying relics for other days and explore a handful of the exciting prehistoric sites which are all close to Castlerigg.

GREAT LANGDALE AXE FACTORY

One by one, the sites of prehistoric axe-making are being discovered and the most celebrated of the known sites lies in the Langdales, on the flanks of Pike o' Stickle. The prehistoric peoples knew their geology well and the favoured rock was a fine hard volcanic tuff of a dull grey colour. The tuff juts up like the button on a bell-push to form the Pike's bulging summit: a mountain with gran-

The Pike o' Stickle

deur if not grace. The stone was quarried and shaped into the rough form of axes high up on the mountain flanks and it is still easy to discover waste flakes or, more occasionally, the rough axe-shapes upon the scree slopes. These slopes, however, are best left to experienced climbers and seasoned fell-walkers.

There are fine views of the Pike from the level valley floor below but the finest are seen from The Band, the steep spur which faces the Pike from across the valley. Going up The Band is more a steep walk than a real climb though there are places where the hands are needed.

The site is owned by the National Trust.

Location (292236) Leave the A593 2 miles W of Ambleside at Skelwith Bridge and follow the B5343 until it becomes a minor road near the head of the Great Langdale valley. Parking is available and the summit knob of Pike o' Stickle (272072) can be seen on the right (N) of the wonderful Mickleden valley panorama. Footpaths follow the Pike crestline, the spur of The Band and the stream.

KING ARTHUR'S ROUND TABLE

Nothing to do with King Arthur, this is (or was) a fine example of a henge monument. These have the surrounding bank and internal ditch which one often finds at stone circles, but lack the stone arrangements. This is an exception and the henge had two of its eight standing stones still erect outside the N entrance in the 17th century. Road alterations have vandalised much of the site and destroyed one of the two entrances although, 500 yds to the W, there is another and now better preserved henge known as Mayburgh.

The henges were roughly the contemporaries of the circles and they may have served similar functions; they are certainly no less mysterious. Excavation has shown that at the Round Table a stone structure covered a trench near the centre of the henge which had been used for a cremation. Originally, four stones formed a central rectangular setting and four more flanked the entrance.

The site is in the care of the Department of the Environment.

Location (523284) At the village of Eamont Bridge, 1¼ miles SE of Penrith. From the M6 (exit 40), go ½ mile E on the A66 and take the last roundabout exit to Eamont Bridge.

The ditch at King Arthur's Round Table

LONG MEG AND HER DAUGHTERS STONE CIRCLE

Being located off the main tourist trails on the eastern approaches to the Lake District, this circle, which probably dates from the earlier part of the Bronze Age, is not particularly well-known. Its relative lack of fame is surprising when one considers that the diameter is about three times that of Castlerigg while twenty-seven from an original membership of fifty-nine large stones still stand. In comparison with Castlerigg, the farmland plateau setting is merely pleasant rather than spellbinding though the circle has a distinct charisma of its own.

Long Meg probably dates from the earlier part of the Bronze Age, and is an angular, willowy slab of red sandstone

Long Meg, an angular, willowy slab of red sandstone forms a striking contrast to her ring of pudgy grey granite daughters. If you inspect her surface closely, you will see a display of mysterious concentric cup-and-ring engravings.

Location (571373) The circle lies 4 miles NE of Penrith. Turn N off the A686 towards Hunsonby; after Hunsonby carry straight across the Little Salkeld–Glassonby road and you will soon come to a passable track which leads to the circle with space for parking beside the track.

Meeting the New Stone Age on Orkney

There are two British locations in particular where one can see not just one magnificent prehistoric monument but a complex of exceptionally impressive creations. One, of course, is the Avebury* region in Wiltshire, the other, less well-known, is the northern portion of the Orkney mainland island. Orkney offers the visitor an almost perfectly preserved Neolithic village, two remarkably imposing stone circles and, in Maes Howe, a passage grave of such magnificence that it is only rivalled by the famous tombs of Ireland's Boyne valley, Newgrange, Knowth and Dowth.

These archaeological treasures lie within a few miles or less of each other in a sea-hemmed landscape of rolling pastures and meadows which is studded with lesser monuments in the forms of tombs, standing stones and settlement relics of many ages. Many people, I suspect, regard Orkney as a wind-lashed northern outpost, of interest mainly to sheep and oil men. To anyone with a feeling for the distant past it is—or should be—simply irresistible.

Many years will pass before we are in a position to be able to attempt a detailed reconstruction of life on Orkney during the Neolithic period, but as the evidence from excavation accumulates, it seems that people who practised mixed farming, cultivating grain and raising sheep and cattle arrived in the islands some time before 3500 BC. Before very much time had elapsed, they had begun the construction of the great clan or family tombs and circles. The evidence of excavated pottery, the Unstan ware and the flat-based 'grooved ware' suggests that the circles and tombs were roughly contemporary with settlements such as Skara Brae and less accessible stone hut dwellings such as Knap of Howar on Papa Westray island, and Rinyo on Rousay island.

While Avebury, Stonehenge, Newgrange and the other great circles and tombs have their undoubted attractions, on Orkney one can see not only the remarkable monuments to ritual and death, but also the dwellings of the unglamorous peasant farmers who might well have helped to build them.

Driving around Orkney, one sees many an abandoned post-medieval long-house type of farmstead and, as on Lewis, the suspicion arises that pre-

OPPOSITE *Ring of Brodgar: as impressive a prehistoric site as Avebury*
(Right) *The setting sun turns the great circle of stones into silhouettes*

43

historic communities were rather more adept at sustaining rural life than happens nowadays. Orkney, however, is much less of a rocky or peat-clad wasteland than most other parts of the Scottish Highlands and Islands.

The island platforms of pinkish Old Red Sandstone have weathered to produce gently rolling landscapes of plains and low plateaux, and soils which are more rewarding than most in the north. The nature of the Caithness flagstone of Orkney is such that it readily splits along the horizontal 'bedding planes' (which mark the divides between different sequences of deposition) to provide great 'planks' of stone which seemed purpose-made for the creation of homes and monuments. And so the prehistoric splendours of Orkney owe much to the natural endowments of attractive farming country and inviting geology.

The stone circle known as the Ring of Brodgar is a good place to commence the visit. Although only twenty-six of the sixty original sandstone slabs remain in place, the circle has the appearance of being more complete than many. The great ditch, with its opposed causeway entrances to the north-west and southeast, which encircles the stones is still impressive although originally it was cut into the bedrock to a depth of around 10 ft. Unlike most other henge monuments, there is no evidence of an outer bank surrounding the ditch.

With a diameter of more than 300 ft, the Ring of Brodgar is one of the largest stone circles in Britain and while some of the stones have surrendered to the elements and exist solely as shattered stumps, many still tower several feet above the heads of visitors. The Ring of Brodgar has a setting which is hardly less enchanting than that of Castlerigg* and an intrinsic beauty to compare with Callanish*.

The slabby stones are a light pinkish

buff in colour but they are also dappled with growths of lemon and blue-green tinted lichen. The circle stands near the tip of a peninsula which is interjected between the waters of the Loch of Harray and the Loch of Stenness. The summer visitor can look across the yellow and purple carpets of wild flowers and heather which garnish the circle, over the bright green hay meadows and mirrors of loch water which embrace it, to the muted greens and violets of the horizon plateaux. With the sunlit stones glowing like beacons, this is one of the most perfect vistas which Britain has to offer—even if the meaning of the circle remains mysterious.

One of the hut interiors at Skara Brae. Note how the slabby local sandstone was used to provide the furnishings

Facing the Ring of Brodgar across the fragile neck of the Ness of Brodgar is another circle: the Stones of Stenness. Far taller, far more compact, incomplete and interfered with by early efforts at reconstruction, this is much less in accord with the traditional perception of what a stone circle should look like.

There are three enormous pillar-like slabs, the tallest being some 17 ft in height, but impressive though they are, they can only give the mildest glimpse of the original grandeur of the monument.

A ditch with a single causeway entrance to the north surrounded the twelve or thirteen original members of what must have been a stunningly tall and compact ring of stones while, in the centre of the circle, four horizontal slabs outlined a square area which was found to contain fragments of pottery, charcoal and small stones and cremated bone suggesting that offerings had been made to the forces which governed the fertility and resources of the earth.

With its remarkably lofty and compact form, the Stenness circle will have contrasted with the vast circle of Brodgar which is clearly visible across the Ness. What was the relationship between the two great circles? Perhaps they were paired in great prehistoric rituals, with the Ness of Brodgar serving as a processional way to link the temples? Even if this were the case, the truth would probably have been more complicated because there were other great monuments in the vicinity.

The Watch Stone which stands less than 600 ft to the north-north-west is taller than the tallest of the Stenness stones and is the sole survivor of an original trio. Half a mile to the southeast is the Barnhouse Stone, while the great perforated stone known as the Stone of Odin stood to the east of the Watch Stone until it was wrecked by a farmer in 1814.

The positions of other great monoliths or stone groups are likely to be undiscovered, but even if we could reconstruct the original stone patterns in the Stenness-Brodgar area, we might not be able to decipher their meaning. Of course, it is possible that the two great circles were not paired in ritual, but rivals.

The Bays of Firth and Ireland and the lochs of Stenness, Harray and Wasdale form a watery waist across the centre of Orkney and a natural divide between the northern and southern sections of the

island. Had Neolithic Orkney been divided between northern and southern tribal communities, then the two circles could be seen as showpiece temples which proclaimed the powers of their respective builders across the territorial borders. We simply do not know.

The third site on this visit is absolutely supreme as an example of a prehistoric settlement site—Skara Brae. In the middle of the last century, storm winds shifted the sand dunes which fringe the Bay of Skaill to reveal a small village of stone-walled huts which had been buried and preserved for around four and a half millennia. So well had the

The Stenness Stones, a view looking westwards towards the sinking sun

sands cocooned the dwellings that not only were the walls intact, but so too were the hut furnishings.

Slabs of Caithness flagstone had been used almost as if they were planks of wood in the construction of dressers, cots, hearths and sunken tanks in which fishing bait might have been stored.

In the course of this century, a sequence of excavations have allowed the lifestyle of this Neolithic community to be pieced together. Skara Brae is thought to have been inhabited between about 3100 BC and 2450 BC—quite a long period because most prehistoric villages had a lifespan of between about twenty and two hundred years. In the course of this occupation, some of the sub-rectangular huts were rebuilt and the cycles of improvement complicate the archaeological picture, but it seems that six or eight of the huts were in use at any particular period.

With flagstone on hand to provide the perfect building material, the huts at Skara Brae were infinitely more durable than other more typical Neolithic dwellings. As yet, we know very little about the homes which were built in the remainder of Britain during this period, in areas where timber rather than flagstone would be the natural choice.

While Skara Brae might have been a Rolls-Royce amongst the other less durable settlements of Neolithic Britain, we might find aspects of the prehistoric village life rather unpleasant. The various families lived in intimate proximity, with the huts linked by tunnel-like stone-walled alleyways and, as the settlement gradually disappeared beneath enveloping piles of shellfish refuse, the stench must have been extreme. The excavated relics of village life seem to tell of a community which subsisted by fishing, raising livestock and growing a little grain.

At Skara Brae, there is evidence of members of the Orkney Stone Age community who raised the great stone circles and constructed the magnificent chambered tombs. They were just simple rugged peasants. They dug the local peat and burned it in their hearths, hunted the red deer, herded sheep and cattle, made coarse gritty pots, fished the surrounding seas and may sometimes have been so hungry that they turned to consuming the unpalatable limpets.

Their life will have been tough and demanding but it was not completely dominated by the struggle for economic survival. Such was the power of a religion which may have been deeply concerned with the after-life, ancestor worship and the propitiation of the gods controlling the fertility of the soil, the weather and the success of hunting or fishing that, from time to time, prosaic tasks were set aside as tens or hundreds of peasants gathered for a frenzy of building activity which culminated in the creation of a great circle or communal tomb.

Apart from a handful of Irish examples, the great 'passage grave' of Maes Howe is unequalled in its scale and sophistication by any other in these islands—or even in western Europe.

A rectangular central chamber is covered by a domed mound which is 24 ft in height and 115 ft in diameter and which is surrounded by a ditch ranging from 25 to 60 ft. The central chamber is reached by an entrance passage which is 36 ft in length. The chamber itself is 15 ft square and three of its walls contained rectangular burial recesses which were formerly sealed by massive stone blocks. The quality of the drystone masonry of the chamber and the stone corbelling of its inward-sloping roof is superb, while a number of the stones carry runic inscriptions made by Viking tomb robbers.

A stark description such as this does scant justice to the truly wonderful monument. Visit it by all means but be prepared to accept conditions which, by Orcadian standards at least, are clamorous. At most well-publicised monuments, crowds of visitors mean hasty conducted tours, queues, hurried glimpses of things which should be savoured and a quick departure to make way for the next coach party. Sadly, this is what I encountered at Maes Howe.

However, if the rushed and indigestible feast at Maes Howe stimulates in you an interest in the remarkable man-made landscapes of death in the Neolithic period, then next drive westwards along the A965. Within a couple of miles, you will see a small promontory reaching northwards into Loch of Stenness. Just before the junction with the A964, turn down the track towards the cottage which stands on the little headland. Here you can obtain the key to the Unstan or Onstan chambered tomb which is beautifully restored and where you can study the detail of Neolithic grave architecture in peace.

The burial chamber is covered by a bowl-shaped mound and it is reached by a cramped but neatly-built drystone-walled passage which is around 20 ft in length. The passage enters the tomb through one of the long side walls of the somewhat boat-shaped chamber. With the first glimpse of the interior, it is apparent that the chamber is divided by great slabs of sandstone into a number of side compartments.

A number of other Scottish tombs display the same type of arrangement—Midhowe on the Orkney island of Rousay is a more imposing example—and such tombs are known as 'stalled cairns'. In the case of the Onstan tomb, the wall which faces the entrance is breached by the opening of a small side cell.

The chambered tombs of the New Stone Age come in a variety of different forms: some of these forms are associated with particular localities while others, such as the portal dolmens like Chun Quoit or the passage graves like Maes Howe, can be found in widely separated areas. We still do not understand the implications of these differences in design. To what extent do they represent the migration of different cultures, the existence of different religious cults or the builders' responses to differences in the nature of local stone resources?

The Onstan tomb was opened by a local antiquary in 1884 and it was

The Onstan tomb: two crouched skeletons were discovered here in 1884

found to contain four finely-wrought flint arrowheads, human bones in the various stall compartments and two crouched skeletons in the side chamber. There was also an unusually profuse collection of pottery bowls of a low, round-based shape with rims decorated with geometrical motifs which became known to archaeologists as Unstan Ware—the name became entrenched before the map-makers chose to label the place as Onstan.

Although much smaller and less imposing than many other chambered tombs, the Onstan example is well restored. On the whole, people who suffer from claustrophobia should give these tombs a very wide berth, while others who fear the dark, ghosts and so on should do the same. In this case, however, a window has been set into the roof of the chamber and so the interior is quite brightly illuminated.

Phototips The Ring of Brodgar and the Stenness Stones are easy but very rewarding subjects, although a wide-angle lens is necessary to emphasise the height of the latter group. The tips given in relation to Castlerigg* apply here and, in the case of each shot, one should decide on the desired emphasis for the stones, their shapes or texture and their setting. Visitors are likely to be spending at least one night on the island and the stones lie within easy reach of all parts of Orkney. Therefore, if there are any hints of an exciting sunset, it is worth returning in the evening to photograph the stones as silhouettes against a blazing sky.

At Skara Brae, individual huts are much more photogenic than the panorama of the whole village. If the weather is dull, flash can be used to augment the natural light. Careful framing is needed to exclude the little official signposts and the legs of fellow visitors as details such as these seem much more intrusive in a photograph than they do in real life.

At Maes Howe, one can do no more than take a few hurried shots with flash and these are unlikely to excite. At Onstan, however, the opportunities are far greater and the natural light which pours through the ceiling is very favourable to photography. Here again, a wide-angle lens is needed to capture the broader dimensions of the chamber.

Location The Ring of Brodgar and the Stenness Stones lie beside the B9055 about 4 miles ENE of Stromness. Maes Howe lies just to the N of the A965 and is also about 4 miles ENE of Stromness. The Onstan tomb is also just N of the A965, around 2 miles ENE of Stromness and the turn-off is just to the E of the A964 T-junction. Skara Brae is around 8 miles N of Stromness and within easy walking distance of a car park beside the B9056.

ROUND AND ABOUT

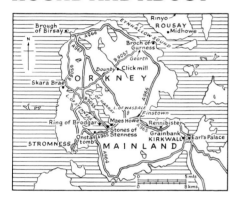

One could tour for a week on the small Orkney mainland island and still not see every monument and standing stone. A selection of some of the most interesting sites follows, but one would not be able to see them all and those which have already been described in the course of a single day.

The visitor should hire a car or bicycle; farmhouse accommodation is widely available while both Kirkwall and Stromness are attractive bases, with Kirkwall having the advantage in terms of historical interest.

BROCH OF GURNESS

This is one of the best-preserved examples of a broch, an Iron Age defensive tower of a type which is described in detail in the Dun Carloway* entry. Several circular Iron Age stone-walled huts surround the broch and there are fine views across Eynhallow Sound which separates Orkney and Rousay island.

Location (383267) The broch is about 13 miles NE of Stromness. A track runs down towards the broch from the A966 from just to the SE of Georth hamlet. Parking is available and the final walk to the broch is made across bracing sand dune country.

The interior of Gurness broch on Orkney

BROUGH OF BIRSAY

This is a fascinating religious and Viking settlement site covering many periods. Excavations suggest that the earliest

A jumble of excavated settlement remains at Brough of Birsay, with boat-shaped Viking long-houses just above the other relics

settlement was Pictish and a reproduction of the fine 'Pictish symbol stone' (page 141) which was found on the site is displayed. An early religious settlement of the Celtic church was then established, followed by the Vikings and the excavated foundations of boat-shaped Viking long-houses lie beside the religious buildings.

Following the conversion of the Norse community, more religious buildings were constructed and the 10th-century church was modified in the 12th and 13th centuries. One range of buildings remains controversial and it has been suggested that the ruins might be those of a 12th-century bishop's palace.

Location About 20 miles NW of Kirkwall. Follow a by-road from the junction of the A967 and A966 for a short distance to the car park. Brough of Birsay is a tidal island which can be reached at low tide via a concrete causeway.

THE EARL'S PALACE, KIRKWALL

Orkney has more than one Earl's Palace. The ruins of a palace which was built around 1574 can be seen on the mainland close to the Brough of Birsay. The

The Earl's Palace at Kirkwall, more like a mansion than a castle

Kirkwall palace was constructed early in the 17th century with a great hall and two smaller chambers on the first floor with cellars and store rooms below. The large windows are too vulnerable for this building to be considered a proper castle although there are corner turrets provided with gun loops. Just to the N of

the palace is the fine red sandstone cathedral.

Location In the centre of Kirkwall.

RENNIBISTER SOUTERRAIN

Rennibister Souterrain: the purpose of these mysterious earth houses remains obscure

Souterrains or 'earth houses' were common features of the Iron Age landscape in parts of Scotland and Ireland. The purpose of these stone-lined tunnels is almost entirely mysterious although they seem to have been closely associated with surface huts. It has been suggested that the souterrains were used as refuges, although families hiding in them would be trapped and incapable of escape; or refuges which might have been used to harbour cattle when raiders were abroad. Another explanation casts the souterrains as cool storage areas.

The Rennisbister example was discovered in 1926 when a section of farmyard collapsed with the introduction of a heavy threshing machine and subsequently the souterrain was restored and made accessible to the public.

It consists of an oval chamber about 10 ft in length which was reached not by the modern opening in its roof, but via a narrow passage which is about 12 ft in length. In this case, the passage was much too narrow to have admitted

cattle. Cupboard-like recesses can be seen in the walls of the chamber, suggesting a storage function although some sort of ritual use cannot be ruled out.

When first discovered, the passage was found to be packed with shellfish debris while the disarticulated bones of six adults and around twelve children were found within. This is most unusual and it seems likely that the chamber became a burial vault during only the last stage in its useful life.

Location About 4 miles W of Kirkwall, signposted and reached by a track which runs a short distance N from the A965. Another souterrain can be seen at Grainbank, a small suburb to the west of Kirkwall.

DOUNBY CLICK MILL

This is the last restored and surviving example of a type of small early 19th-century watermill which was once very common in the Highlands and islands and in which a stream was harnessed to power a little horizontally-mounted waterwheel.

Location Just beside the B9057 about 2 miles NE of Dounby village.

All these sites are in the care of the Scottish Development Department.

The last restored and surviving example of a type of early 19th-century watermill

Callanish Stone Circle

(Isle of Lewis, Western Isles)

Anyone who has been jostled around the perimeter fence at Stonehenge might envy me the days when I wandered around one of the very greatest of British prehistoric monuments and scarcely met a soul. Obviously this was not Stonehenge, nor Avebury* nor even the Ring of Brodgar*, but Callanish on the bare Outer Hebrides island of Lewis. Arriving on the margins of Callanish village with one eye on the suicidal flocklets of roadside sheep and half an eye on the map, the first glimpse of a stone circle at Callanish was disappointing and it seemed less majestic than the photographs that scores of archaeological books suggest. The disillusionment does not last long for the first-glimpsed roadside circle is just a modest satellite. As you raise your eyes to the horizon above the village, you see the magnificent silhouette of the main circle, with the lines of stones jutting from the skyline like the teeth in a crocodile's jaw.

Callanish fascinates not only because of its size and beauty but also because it is one of the few circles which have been the subject of a comprehensive modern excavation, accomplished in 1980–81. Now that a considerable amount is known about this monument, we are reminded that we should not regard the circles, tombs, causewayed camps, stone-flanked avenues and henges of

other digs as distinct and separate monuments since they tend to overlap and share several ritual features. Also, it should be remembered that most monuments are the result of several different phases, their final forms often differing greatly from the original vision.

Callanish has a complex form. A central megalith stands almost 16 ft tall and forms the western bastion of a chambered tomb. A ring of lofty stones stands around, two almost parallel lines of stones run out from the circle to form the north avenue while cross-like limbs are formed by other lines of stones running roughly to the east, south and west. The excavation reveals the complex history of the monument in so far as it can be understood. Grain seems to have been grown here until around 3500 BC, when some timber constructions were erected. Then the stone circle and central monolith were slipped into their sockets with clay and stones being packed around their roots. The chambered tomb does not seem to have featured in the original plan but perhaps some great local chieftain decided to have his mausoleum built at the heart of this remarkable ritual complex.

The site was levelled with a plastering of clay and then a trench cut through the ground to contain offerings of cremated bone and charcoal. Then the slabs which form the two chambers of the tomb were erected, a cairn put around it, with a surrounding kerb of coursed stones to mark its edge. The circle was

already an ancient monument by 2000 BC, when Beaker people ploughed the site and its surroundings. Later, in the Bronze Age, other occupants of the area dug pits at Callanish, erected vertical stones to form a new kerb around the north side of the cairn to show that this was still a revered religious centre. The avenue remains undated, but it probably belongs to one of the earlier phases in the life of the monument.

By around 1000 BC, Callanish seems to have been at least partly redundant since the spreading peat bog was allowed to extend across the site. Eventually, the peat accumulated to depths of almost 6 ft so all that could be seen were the tips of the fifty-three great slabs of Lewissian Gneiss—a pretty, striped stone. It was in 1857–58 that Sir James Matheson, the proprietor of Lewis, had the peat stripped away and the circle appeared with most of its former glory.

Archaeology has demonstrated the complex history of the wonderful monument, but for all its magical prescience, it is unable to tell us very much about the religion which had Callanish as one of its greatest cathedrals—whether the religion of the circle-builders was the same as that of the tomb-makers or similar to that of their Beaker and Bronze Age successors. Whatever colourful, frightening or solemn rituals may have been performed here, the ghostly towering stones provided an unsurpassed setting.

The New Stone Age peoples who

The great standing stone at Callanish

began the work at Callanish must have been skilful mariners with seaworthy ships or they would never have seen the shores of Lewis. Like the Bronze Age peoples who succeeded them, they were also competent farmers who could win a living from the soils of this wind-blasted island and still have time to spare to construct a monument which must have demanded the efforts of scores of labourers.

Phototips At Callanish, one should be able to concentrate on the art rather than the craft of stone circle photography since the crafty element—the ability to click at the instant that all the other visitors have disappeared behind different stones—should not be needed. Do not try to include the whole of the monument in a single shot. The north avenue alone is some 270 ft in length

and so it is inevitable that in such a picture, the most distant stones will appear as the merest dots. At a place such as Callanish, the photographic costs will be but a fraction of the travelling costs and so one may as well use plenty of film to commemorate the visit.

With its attractive loch-flanked setting and the streaky whites and greys of the banded gneiss stones, Callanish photographs well both in colour and black-and-white. In sunlight, the stones are quite dazzling but they turn leaden to match the clouds which roll in from the Atlantic. Black-and-white photographs are likely to be most successful as they capture and emphasise the atmosphere of the place. Here orange or yellow filters can be used to darken the blue sky to make the sunlit stones stand out, or to emphasise the rolling, lowering or op-

ABOVE and right: *Stones grained like weathered planks in the Callanish stone circle on Lewis*

pressive forms of clouds in heavier skies. There are innumerable good angles, some of the best are seen as one looks towards the central monolith from the eastern and western stone rows.

Location (213330) Near the W coast of Lewis about 13 miles W of Stornoway airport on the margins of Callanish village. There are various small car-hire outlets in Stornoway and a few bed-and-breakfast farmhouses in Callanish village. At the time of writing, it seems likely that Loganair with its lighter aircraft will replace the British Airways service from Glasgow.

ROUND AND ABOUT

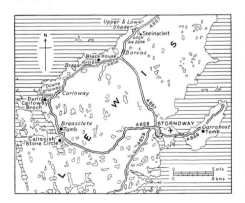

and black peat-blanketed interior, Lewis is attractive but in a barren manner which makes the Bronte country seem like Hyde Park. There are two other notable circles on the fringes of Callanish village to the SE.

BREASCLETE CHAMBERED TOMB

Most of the Neolithic cairn has been removed but four touching upright slabs form an arc and represent the remains of the burial chamber.

Location (211355) On the crest of the island's low hill surrounded by the A858 and Breasclete hamlet street.

GARRABOST CHAMBERED TOMB

Most of the material which formed the covering mound of this Neolithic cairn has been robbed but seven stones which were part of the surrounding kerb remain, along with internal settings which formed the stone burial chamber or lined the entrance passage.

Location On the Eye Peninsula, 6 miles E of Stornoway and $\frac{1}{2}$ mile SE of Garrabost hamlet, in the moorland at OS reference 523330.

Note Dun Carloway Broch (and subsidiary sites) are in the neighbourhood (*see* index for reference).

With its glaciated mountain country carved into the Lewissian gneiss to the south of Callanish, its rocky shorelines

Death in the Burren

(Co Clare)

Nobody can claim to have seen all the greatest landscape wonders which these islands have to offer until they have ventured into the Burren in the west of Ireland. The limestone geology is comparable to that of parts of the Pennines or the Mendips, but the bare and barren nature of the terrain is much more extreme and more reminiscent of the *karst* of Yugoslavia. 'I call it the Gobi Desert,' said a farmer from neighbouring Co Galway and, with the sunrays beating back from the blinding limestone pavements and scars one soon understands why. Although this is one of the wetter parts of Britain and the first stop for rainstorms driving in from the Atlantic, the rivulets of rainwater have hardly formed before they are engulfed in the criss-cross networks of deep fissures which pattern the limestone surface.

The Burren was not always as dry and denuded as it is today. In the Neolithic and Bronze Age periods, there was open woodland here with oak, elm, ash and hazel in abundance. Climatic change may have played a small part in the creation of the present scene, but forest clearance and the over-grazing of the cleared areas over many centuries resulted in the exposed soils being flushed away down the gaping 'grykes' which fissure the rock.

Even so, we should not imagine that in the prehistoric period, the Burren was regarded as prosperous. It was probably less thickly peopled than most areas with richer, deeper soils but the abundance of limestone building slabs and the retreat of population as the farmland deteriorated in the medieval and modern eras has ensured the survival of an exceptional legacy of prehistoric stone monuments. Small Stone Age and Bronze Age tombs are almost commonplace while there are more than 500 surviving examples of Iron Age ringforts—in places there seems to be one in every field.

Devoid of prominent landmarks, the Burren landscape may seem to be an interminable succession of bare pavements, grassy hollows or *turloughs* and rocky scars. Without a map and compass, one may easily become lost but two particularly fine little tombs lie within easy reach of roads.

The Stone Age tomb at Poulnabrone is of a type known as a 'portal dolmen' which is found in other parts of Ireland,

OPPOSITE *The Burren, a bare and barren terrain*   (Below) *The Stone Age tomb at Poulnabrone*

in Wales and in the west of England. This is one of the simplest forms of chambered tomb, consisting of a massive stone roofing slab or capstone perched upon great side-stones and a back-stone which formed the sides of the burial chamber. Quite how the Stone Age peasant tomb-builders managed to raise capstones weighing up to 100 tons into position is not known, though timber levers and cribs or earthen ramps may have been used.

In purely aesthetic terms, the savage grandeur and jagged geometry of the Poulnabrone tomb is surely at least the equal of any of the creations of modern sculptors intrigued by the possibilities of juxtaposing land, stone and sky. However, the living may have been denied this stunning vision once the stone burial chamber of the House of the Dead was complete, for it seems that some if not all portal dolmens were originally covered by an earthen mound.

Only about four portal dolmens are known in the Burren and the Poulnabrone example is the finest. Another type of stone tomb, the wedge-tomb, is very common in western Ireland, but only known in Britain from a single and uncertain Welsh example, Bedd-yr-Afanc in the Preselis. In profile and in plan, the wedge-tomb has the form of a somewhat wedge-shaped box which is neatly formed from stone slabs. The massive sheets of limestone which could so easily be prized from the pavements of the Burren were ideally suited to the task of tomb-making and these tidy car-sized burial boxes are abundant here.

The wedge-tombs seem to be a little younger than the portal dolmens; they may represent the introduction or development of a new religion in the early part of the Bronze Age or the gradual evolution of Stone Age beliefs. The entrance is at the higher of the narrow ends of the tomb box and these entrances almost invariably face towards the south-west, perhaps implying some connection with the sinking sun. One most peculiar feature of a number of the Burren wedge-tombs is the chipped-off corner of one of the end stones. Could this ritual practice have been undertaken to provide an exit hole for the escaping spirit? We really haven't a clue.

Some wedge-tombs have more than one burial chamber and some at least had a covering cairn of earth and stones; more than a hundred examples can be found in the Burren and in this part of Ireland they tend to be particularly simple, trim and box-like. No better example can be found than the one at Poulaphuca which overlooks a fine panorama of glistening and starkly beautiful limestone country.

These tombs pose many problems; they resemble types which are found in Brittany while many which have been opened were found to contain the beaker-shaped pots which are so often associated with Earlier Bronze Age burials in the north-west of Europe. Since the wedge-tombs with their beaker burials are much more common in the western uplands of Ireland than are the older portal dolmen tombs of the New Stone Age, it is tempting to think that they represent a concerted colonisation of the western woodlands by livestock farmers. Perhaps it was at this time that the landscape started to become impoverished as the forests began to be removed.

Phototips Monuments which seem quite massive and imposing when seen in the field may appear much less impressive in photographs. In order to capture or emphasise the visual powers and attractions of megalithic monuments like portal dolmens, it is often sensible to adopt a low and quite close viewpoint, whilst using a wide-angle lens to underline the perspective and provide the depth of focus which the close-up position demands. Too much emphasis on background landscape can prove distracting although attractive cloud patterns always seem to form an exciting but not diverting backdrop.

While specialist archaeological photography often requires a neutrally objective portrait, the creative photographer can treat monuments like portal dol-

The Poulaphuca wedge tomb perched high in the barren countryside of the Burren

mens as powerful, almost abstract collections of stone shapes—and studies which emphasise the power of the stone forms are likely to come closer to encapsulating the beliefs and emotions of the people who built the tombs.

Locations The Poulnabrone tomb (M24 20) is easily found as it lies just to the E of the country road which links Killinaboy and Ballyvaughan. It is clearly visible from the road and about midway between the two villages, about 7 miles NNW of Killinaboy. The Poulaphuca tomb (M26 02) is within walking distance of a turn-off to the W from the country road linking Turlough and Carran hamlets and midway between them. This turn-off forms a lane which is debatably drivable and emerges close to the Poulnabrone tomb. It is probably advisable to park at the end of this lane, especially since the ½-mile uphill walk along the track which passes immediately to the S of the tomb offers superb views of the Burren countryside.

ROUND AND ABOUT

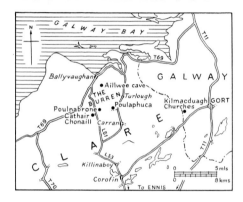

As with Dartmoor and western Cornwall, the choice of fascinating prehistoric sites is almost overwhelming. Visitors to the Burren can do no better than obtain a copy of T. D. Robinson's remarkable archaeological map which is sold in the area and identifies scores of tombs, forts and Christian sites.

CATHAIR CHONAILL STONE FORT

The multitudes of mainly circular stone forts which are so liberally sprinkled across the Burren landscape seem to have been the abodes and not very robust refuges of Iron Age farmers and their dependants. They clearly tell of a landscape which was once much more thickly peopled and some of them remained in use into the medieval period. Cathair Chonaill is one of the larger and more seriously defensive forts and the evidence of the dressed stone blocks by its gateway suggests that it was used during the Middle Ages.

Location (R24 00) Just to the W of the Killinaboy–Ballyvaughan road and less than 1 mile S of Poulnabrone. Open to the public and accessible via the roadside farm.

AILLWEE CAVE

Not strictly a prehistoric site since no human remains have been found here—however, visitors will see the remains of a long-extinct cave bear which was one of the Ice Age residents. Although the stalactite formations are unexceptional, the guided tour goes deep into the bowels of the limestone mountain along the unusually spacious channel of a former subterranean river. The landscaping and provision of shops and restaurant facilities are most impressive.

Location Signposted from the Killinaboy–Ballyvaughan road to the W, about 4 miles N of Poulnabrone.

KILMACDUAGH CHURCHES AND ROUND TOWER
(Co Galway)

An early monastic site in Co Galway on the eastern approaches to the Burren displaying a fine 'round tower' (page 152) an 11th- or 12th-century cathedral and two medieval churches.

Location 3 miles WSW of Gort, signposted from the T11, with a car park.

Note The other sites in Co Clare are Craggaunowen and Bunratty which are in the neighbourhood; and Clonmacnois is not too far away by car. *See* index for page references.

Cathair Chonaill stone fort: one of the larger stone forts of the Burren

Kilmacduagh churches and the fine round tower built on an early monastic site

Two Lost Villages on Dartmoor

(Devon)

Our lifespans are locked to an ever-steepening spiral of change. Most of us tend to regard prehistoric peoples as outlandish primitives, but it is worth reflecting that the peasant folk of the not-so-distant Middle Ages had much more in common with prehistoric farming communities than with ourselves.

OPPOSITE and below: *Grimspound, the most fascinating of the Bronze Age settlements*

The remains of prehistoric settlements abound on Dartmoor and the recent excavation of the lost medieval village beneath Hound Tor gives us the opportunity to compare the nature of the medieval settlement with that of Grimspound, the most fascinating of the deserted Bronze Age settlements.

Grimspound survives as a window on moorland life as it existed in the centuries before 1000 BC. The most obvious thing about the village is its height, for it is situated on a fairly steep hillside some

1500 ft above sea level. Faint ridges which can be discerned in the moorland and rough grazing pastures which blanket the neighbouring hillsides are the traces of prehistoric fields which must almost certainly have been used by the folk of Grimspound. Again, there is the uneasy realisation that prehistoric people were more adept at managing the upland margins than modern man.

Here, however, two points must be made. First, the Bronze Age climate was a little milder than that of today, giving more encouragement to moorland graziers and barley-growers like those of Grimspound. Second, the moorland—which was slowly beginning to advance as the climate gradually commenced its deterioration in Grimspound time and then spread rapidly as the curve of climatic decay steepened after 500 BC—is part of a shrinking heritage of wildscape. If the moorland with its wildlife refuges is allowed to continue being transformed into sterile pasture the nation will be the poorer.

The village covered an area of around four acres which was encircled by a low wall offering little in the way of defence but probably serving to pen the beasts which may have been driven into the enclosure at night. An entrance breaches the wall on the upslope side; it is flanked by large upright granite boulders and was cobbled to prevent the churning of the ground by passing hooves.

Inside the compound, there are the

remains of up to thirty circular stone-walled huts, some scarcely detectable, but some that are very well preserved as circular arrangements of boulders. These huts are more compact than the quite spacious examples seen at some other prehistoric village sites on the moor such as Kestor or Merrivale; their drystone walls will always have been low and their most obvious features will have been the conical roofs of straw or heather thatch. Some of the huts have low stone screens to protect their door-ways from the upland winds.

The drive from Grimspond to Houndtor via the narrow and deeply-engraved moorland tracks is an attractive one. The two deserted settlements are sep-arated by about four miles of moor but over two thousand years of time and so while there are similarities, there are also differences between them.

The first similarity—their apparent fate—has only been understood by research work in palaeoclimatology, the study of past climates, and by other archaeological techniques. Like the many other settlements whose hut deb-ris has sprinkled the moor with circlets of boulders, Grimspound surely fell victim to the changes in climate which caused the carpets of sour black peat to unroll across local areas of upland farming. By the Late Iron Age, there may have been no (or hardly any) settlements remaining on the moor above a height of 1000 ft and the uplands remained deserted until after about AD 800 when warmer, drier summers began to return. The Saxon colonists will have owed a debt of gratitude to the anonymous prehistoric farmers who had cleared boulders from the Bronze Age fields; these will have still been discernible with their walled or banked boundaries. Villages like Hound-

tor which were no less prosperous—or, at least, no more impoverished—than their lowland neighbours, developed on the moor.

However, in the late 13th and 14th centuries, the tide of climate turned again and peasant agriculture retreated when faced with unripened, water-logged or wind-flattened crops, sodden pastures and advancing moorland. Many of the lost settlements remain undiscovered but about 110 are known—mainly farmsteads, but also hamlets and villages—with about half of the settlement corpses lying at heights of 500 to 1000 ft and about half above 1000 ft.

Houndtor village was one of these casualties. The medieval village was established in an area which is littered with the remains of Bronze Age huts and compounds and patterned by the man-made scarps or 'lynchets' which mark the boundaries of Bronze Age fields. The villagers cultivated fields lying well above 1000 ft and excavations by the late Mrs E. M. Minter revealed the his-tory of the settlement.

The first evidence of the recol-onisation of the moor was found in the form of a trio of sunken-floored huts which were probably used as shelters by herdsmen who drove their stock up to graze the moor during the summer. The establishment of a permanent medi-eval settlement soon followed but, until the middle of the thirteenth century, the peasants lived in turf-walled huts. These were superseded by stone dwellings of the 'long-house' type in which the peasant family shared their roof with their livestock. By this time, signs of climatic decay may have been apparent and perhaps the cattle were wintered in the long-house to prevent the churning-up of waterlogged pastures.

The peasants of Houndtor were mixed farmers: the ridge and furrow patterns of their ploughlands corrugates the land leading up to Greator Rocks. The end of

The lost medieval village of Houndtor

The walls of the Houndtor long-houses

their village seems to have come slowly. The archaeologist Guy Beresford has described how the wet summers probably increased the incidence of stock disease, how the shortage of winter fodder caused cattle to be turned out too early in the spring which led to the pastures being over-grazed, while the drying of harvested grain became a problem. As individual families abandoned the struggle, the empty dwellings were converted into barns or corn-driers as one by one the houses were deserted in the course of the 14th century.

As the settlements of peasant communities which perished in the face of environmental adversity, Grimspound and Houndtor share much in common. The most obvious differences concern the remains of dwellings. At Houndtor, the walls of the rectangular stone long-houses stand about waist high. Three buildings in the north-western section of the village served as corn-driers while the eight remaining long-houses are of varying sizes, averaging about 50 ft by 20 ft. Evidence of garden plots are associated with the long-houses and though the houses are aligned on a north-east to south-west axis, the unplanned form of the village may suggest a Celtic tradition comparable to that of Chysauster*.

About 350 yards to the north-west of the village lie the remains of Houndtor farmstead, a 13th-century three-roomed long-house with a separate barn and corn-drier. This medieval farmstead is particularly interesting because it sits within a prehistoric pound and a hut circle was reconstructed to serve the farm as a stock pen. And so at this remote and plaintive little site, the successive struggles of Bronze Age and medieval peasants to harness the moor are encapsulated.

It was probably the exposure of the native peoples of Britain to Roman building styles which encouraged the transition from circular to rectangular buildings. Despite the differences in the shapes of their dwellings and the undoubted differences in language, the medieval peasants of Houndtor must surely have communicated about all the essentials of life and most details of farming with the people of Grimspound.

Phototips So far, I have said nothing about the scenic splendours of the two lost village sites. Grimspound lies in barren, rolling and perhaps rather oppressive country, while Houndtor has a magnificent situation, overlooking a green valley hollow with the great rockpiles of Hound Tor and Greator Rocks to dramatise the scene. Both sites offer many photographic possibilities: at Houndtor, it is possible to capture a panorama of deserted dwellings, flanking hillslopes and valley fields but at Grimspound one cannot do justice to the huts, the compound and the setting in a single portrait. Individual abandoned huts provide subjects for wonderfully evocative photographs, especially if the sky is dark and threatening, while good views of the compound can be obtained from the footpath which leads up to the jagged rocks of Hookney Tor.

Locations Grimspound lies about 4 miles SW of Moretonhampstead close to a minor road which is the first turn-off to the left after the B3344 junction as one heads SW on the B3212. The site is not signposted, so be guided by OS reference 701809; a short but stiff walk leads upwards from the roadside.

Houndtor (743790) lies about 2 miles SSW of Manaton. From the B3344, take the minor road running south via Southcott and Great Houndtor. At the junction of this road with three other roads, you will see Hound Tor Rocks. The rocks are signposted and visitors destined for the lost village site should use the Hound Tor parking place. The rocks are as impressive as they are likely to be crowded, but few of the visitors are aware of the lost village site. Continue up and past the rocks following the footpath leading SE towards Greator Rocks and the outlines of the long-houses will soon become apparent.

ROUND AND ABOUT

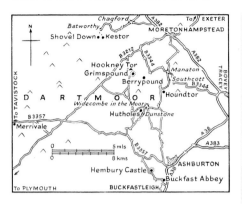

Dartmoor is an almost incomparable wonderland for the prehistory enthusiast, with small stone circles, stone rows and monoliths in abundance, but the following deserted settlements are especially exciting.

Any energetic visitor who would like to make the journey from Grimspound to Houndtor on foot will find the prehistoric compound of Berrypound (713803) on the direct route and about 1 mile ESE from Grimspound. More

The mysterious stone row at Merrivale, close to a prehistoric settlement

The deserted prehistoric settlement of Kestor

impressive deserted prehistoric settlements can be seen further afield, at Merrivale (554748) on the B3357 about 5 miles W of Tavistock (close to the parking place which is just E and uphill from Merrivale Quarry and S of the road) and Kestor, 3 miles SW of Chagford village and beside the lane which peters out at Batworthy, W of Teigncombe. Merrivale also offers a mysterious stone row, stone circle and standing stone and there are stone rows and hut circles on Shovel Down (660860) just W of Kestor.

Turning to the medieval period, the deserted village of Hutholes, which resembles Houndtor, slumbers at OS reference 702758 less than 4 miles SW of Houndtor, near crossroads about 1½ miles SW of Widecombe in the Moor.

BUCKFAST ABBEY

The Abbey was founded in the 10th century and existed as a small and generally impoverished foundation through the Middle Ages until its dissolution in 1539. In 1907, however, the Benedictine order began the construction of a new abbey, building it in a Norman–Gothic transitional style of architecture; it was finally completed in 1938. The monks have a fine line in honey and fortified wine.

About 1½ miles to the NW of the abbey and overlooking a rather precipitous minor road which ascends out of Buckfastleigh is the Iron Age hillfort site of Hembury Castle, its ramparts partly obscured by woodland.

Location The Abbey is about 2 miles N of Buckfastleigh on a minor road which leaves the old A38 Buckfastleigh–Ashburton road to the left.

2 THE AGE OF IRON

The Iron Age is thought to have begun in Britain around 750 BC. In most formulations, the last phase of the period is the Roman Iron Age which begins with the Claudian invasion of Britain and in this chapter we are concerned with the period between about 750 BC and the Roman Conquest in AD 43. The 'Three Age System' which divides prehistory into the Ages of Stone, Bronze and Iron has given good service but had the Iron tag not been invented, we might call this phase the Celtic Age, the Hillfort Age or even the Battle Age. It emerges as a period of new invasions and settlements, a time of turmoil when tribes and septs clashed over the control of territory and resources, and when defenceworks rather than temples or tombs were constructed to provide the most durable epitaphs to the Age.

If we could cruise above the Iron Age countryside in a time machine we might have some difficulty in knowing whether our timeship had been programmed towards the Iron Age or Bronze Age. The pasture ranges, the close networks of small bank-edged arable fields and paddocks would look much the same for each period, as would the circular thatch-roofed hut dwellings which are liberally scattered about as farmsteads, small hamlet clusters or the less frequent village-sized groupings. Before too long, however, we would see a hillfort with its formidable summit girdle of banks or ditches and recognise the brownish patches of spreading upland peat bog, and then we would know that we were visitors to the Iron Age. The forts and the advancing bog were not unrelated for both reflected the effects of a steadily deteriorating climate which caused families to retreat from many traditional farming areas and fight for stronger footholds.

Despite the decay of the climate and the endemic tribal warfare, the Iron Age was far from being a time of stagnation and decline. Before the Roman Conquest imposed a new stability and quickened the rate of material progress, the native peoples of Britain had advanced to the portals of civilisation. They had adopted different ranges of coinage, developed sophisticated and finely-wrought metalwork and jewellery and constructed the great agglomerations of rampart-guarded huts, workshops and royal estates of the tribal capitals or *oppida*. Sprawling and apparently little-planned, the typical *oppidum* will have contrasted greatly with the grandeur and functionalism of a Roman town. Even so, it is clear that recognisable towns would soon have developed in Britain without any Roman conquest.

The introduction of ironworking to Britain did not immediately transform the lives of the people. The date and the geographical origins of iron technology are uncertain and the discoveries may have been made in Central Europe or the Caucasus mountains. In any event, knowledge of the use of iron spread through Europe rapidly during the ninth and eighth centuries BC and by the seventh century BC iron had become widely accepted although it did not replace the much older and less demanding bronze technology. Although more difficult to smelt and forge, iron ores were more common than those of copper and tin and the resultant metal was in many respects tougher than bronze. As the smiths began to master the mysteries of the new craft, iron began to be used for items such as tools and harness fittings and prosaic products such as nails, wheel rims and cooking pots which could seldom have been afforded or would have served less well if made of bronze. At first, however, the new metal was reserved for prestigious items of military equipment such as longswords, battle-axes and spearheads.

We do not know what language was spoken by the Bronze Age settlers in Britain and therefore we cannot be certain that the Celtic languages were not spoken in these islands before the Iron Age. The Celts were never a unified people or race; they were as happy to fight with each other as with anyone else and it is most unlikely that they ever thought of themselves as forming any sort of nation. There was no one Celtic invasion but different Celtic-speaking peoples settled in Britain in the course of the centuries leading up to the Roman invasion. Very little is known about the origins of the Celts but they may be descended from peoples who spread westwards from Eastern Europe in the centuries following 1200 BC, built hillforts, had a well-armed warrior aristocracy and buried the remains of their dead in pots or urns in level cemeteries.

In the centuries after about 1000 BC, a Celtic culture which derived its wealth from iron-working and salt mining developed in Austria and the upper Rhine. It takes its modern name from an Austrian village called Hallstatt where a typical cemetery and salt mine have been explored. Hallstatt culture was probably introduced to Britain in the seventh century BC with the establishment of English and Welsh coastal trading settlements. We do not know whether there was any large-scale Celtic settlement and the rapid spread of Hallstatt iron technology may reflect native craftsmen in Britain who imitated the Hallstatt wares.

On the continent, Celtic peoples expanded, traded and fought with the Mediterranean civilisations of Greece and Rome. The La Tène phase—the great flowering of Celtic culture—takes its name from a Swiss site on Lake Neuchâtel where archaeologists have discovered the beautifully wrought votive offerings which people threw to appease their gods. Until the third century BC, Celtic armies and raiders threatened and sometimes defeated the Mediterranean civilisations but, following defeats in Greece and Turkey in 244 BC and pressure from German tribes in the north, the Celtic world was in retreat.

La Tène Celts became established in the east of Yorkshire in the fourth century BC and by the first century BC a La Tène culture, with all its military trappings and refined and elaborate artwork, was firmly established across Britain. The islands now lay on the fringes of written history and so Classical writers as well as archaeology reveal a new phase of Celtic settlement in Britain as the Belgae from the northern fringes of modern France took control of the Thames valley, Kent, Suffolk and the south-east Midlands. In their metal technology and art, the La Tèna and Belgic Celts were at least the equals of the Mediterranean civilisations although politically they remained barbarians. It was left for the Romans to impose visions of unity upon the English and Welsh lands.

The most enduring monuments to the Neolithic and Earlier Bronze Age worlds are the great ritual temples and tombs while the Roman legacy is dominated by the town and the road, but the hillfort, a symbol of fear and conflict, is the foremost Celtic relic in Britain. Celtic pagan beliefs gave rise to hardly any enduring monuments. Much less is known about the Celtic Druid caste than popular books and folklore would have us believe. The Celtic religion seems to have been associated with hordes of different gods and seasonal festivals used to promote the fertility of the land, but it also appears to have been fragmented amongst a multitude of local cults. Gruesome sacrifice rituals appear to have played a part, with a strong cult focusing upon the severed human head while in its less repugnant aspect, the religion seems to have involved the veneration of local wells, glades and trees. In the years preceding the Roman Conquest, Britain emerged as the focus of Celtic paganism, encouraging revolts and unrest in the Celtic territories of the Empire, thus providing further inducements for the Romans to invade.

Whilst we must admire the sophisticated metal goods of the Celts of Britain with their sweeping curvilinear decorations, the fearsome weapons and refined trinkets, we must remember that these were the trappings of an aristocratic minority in a predominantly peasant society. Dawning civilisation and unrepentant barbarism were wierdly intertwined in Celtic Britain, but this was not an age in which any but the least faint-hearted would choose to live.

See Appendix II for other sites from the Age of Iron.

Two Shropshire Hillforts

Change tended to occur more slowly in the prehistoric period, but it was always a part of the pattern of human life. Some of the changes were rooted in social evolution and new technologies— progress you might say. Others were made in response to changes in the climate which so closely affected the lives of the peasant farming communities. The many hillforts of Britain reflect the forces which caused them to be built: powerful forces, for even a modest and unspectacular example embodies an enormous investment of toil.

The hillforts are the most characteristic and majestic of our monuments to the Iron Age, a period which emerges as a time of turbulence and conflict. This was an age when there were few empty and unexploited areas left to beckon to the pioneer farmer or herdsman, when tribes competed to control existing farmlands and when a worsening climate caused peasant communities to retreat from the advancing upland peatbog or valley marshes. Over-population, soil exhaustion and wars for territory are things which we associate with the modern age rather than the prehistoric era, but perhaps we have simply failed to learn the lessons from the past.

Archaeology has shown that killing and perhaps even warfare took place even in the good times of the New Stone Age. The discovery of a burned and arrow-strewn hut in one place and the occasional finds of skeletons which are pierced by flint-tipped missiles in another reveal fragments of the story. Archaeology also shows that during the Bronze Age at the latest, aristocratic tribal dynasties had emerged, for the finely-wrought bronze daggers, the necklets, and bracelets of imported gold were not peasant baubles.

By the Iron Age, British society was divided between a number of tribes and governed by an array of powerful tribal chieftains. It was a class society, with chiefs, sub-chiefs, aristocratic warrior castes and probably a priestly class, all supported by the toiling peasants who will greatly have outnumbered all the others. Around 1000 BC, the climate became increasingly cool, blustery and moist. Farming began to withdraw from the uplands; families of refugees increased the pressures on the better farmlands: old territorial conflicts will have intensified, while spearheads and longswords flowered from the bronze-smiths' forges. It is not surprising that the first generation of hillforts was spawned in the years around 1000 BC.

New hillforts were constructed and older ones adapted and enlarged throughout the Iron Age. A few were destined to be stormed by advancing Roman legions while any which might have threatened the rule of Rome were evac-uated, though some of the ancient hilltop fortresses were refortified in the course of Dark Age turmoils. While the life span of the hillfort covers almost 2000 years and begins in the later part of the Bronze Age, the heyday of the hillfort covers about 800 years and the whole of the pre-Roman Iron Age.

These strongholds are common everywhere in Britain apart from the eastern lowlands of England. Some have ramparts which embrace dozens of acres, and others are small; some came to contain permanent settlements of town-like proportions, some housed villages, while others still seem only to have been occupied in times of war.

The Shropshire hillforts of Old Oswestry and Caer Caradoc are smaller than some more famous examples, but each has its special attraction and the contrasts between the two are quite striking.

Most of the more inviting hilltops in the west of Shropshire were crowned by hillforts. Old Oswestry is one of the most imposing of the strongholds, but the hill concerned is not in the same lofty league as the crests of the Long Mynd or Wenlock Edge, but rather a blister which swells to a height of just around 550 ft from the lowlands to the north of Oswestry. Although this hill will have commanded a number of old routeways converging at the strategic junction between the lower country to the east and the swelling ground of the Welsh Marches to the west, it cannot have

The view across the ramparts of Old Oswestry hillfort, an imposing Iron Age stronghold. Photograph on pp 64–5: Caer Caradoc hillfort

The ramparts of Caer Caradoc link up a number of craggy natural rock outcrops to bar the easier lines of attack

Fine panoramas of the Shropshire countryside are enjoyed from the ramparts of the summit hillfort on Caer Caradoc

seemed to offer particularly promising defensive material, in comparison to other Shropshire summits. However, a series of defenceworks, improvements and additional ramparts created girdles of banks and ditches and produced a formidable citadel.

As is so often the case, the hillfort of Old Oswestry is the product of several different building phases. Earlier in the first millennium BC, a defensive wooden palisade seems to have been erected on the hilltop. Around 250 BC, a sterner stronghold was created with the construction of two great rings of ditches and ramparts. Later, a third ring was

added, the western gateway defences were redesigned and finally the forty-acre enclosure and its ramparts were completely enclosed by a great double compound.

Whether the labouring peasants who toiled with picks, shovels and earth-filled baskets were unwilling conscripts or volunteers, we do not know, but one must walk up, down and around the pleated terrain of the ramparts to appreciate the scale of the achievement. In time, the Romans imposed their peace upon the unruly Celtic tribal territories, but some time after the collapse of Roman power in Britian, Dark Age

settlers made their homes behind the sheltering ramparts. Perhaps they were refugees from the uprisings and invasions which spluttered and flared in the aftermath of the Roman disintegration. Their settlement did not endure, while peace in the Dark Ages was always fragile and, in 641, the battle of Maserfelt (in which the Northumbrian king Oswald was killed by the forces of Penda, the Mercian king) was fought at Oswestry. Power passed to the Saxons and then to the Normans who built the new town of Oswestry at the foot of the old hillfort, naming it after St Oswald's Tree in memory of the slain and canonised Christian king. Celtic culture however did not die and the area was Welsh-speaking until the eighteenth century.

One can still sense a convergence of the Welsh and English worlds. As one walks the circuit of the ramparts, dif-

A view from the rampart bank at Old Oswestry; the inner rampart ditch can be seen lying to the left of the photograph

ferent pageants of fine scenery unfold: to the west, the rising hills of the Welsh Marches, good undulating countryside to the north and east, and wonderful panoramas of the town which has swelled from the Norman plantation to the south.

That which is pleasant and interesting at Old Oswestry is simply spectacular at Caer Caradoc. Let me be more precise, for there is more than one 'Caer Caradoc' hereabouts and we are concerned with the one which lies on the great ridge a couple of miles to the north-east of Church Stretton. The rugged peak is part of a line of hills composed of tough Pre-Cambrian volcanic lavas and ashes which are amongst the oldest of the British rocks. It rises above the trench-like Church Stretton gap to a height of over 1500 ft, providing an irresistible

site for the Iron Age hillfort builders. In the construction of a six-acre defended enclosure, the people displayed great effort and ingenuity, building a rubble rampart and rock-cut ditch which followed the natural contours of the summit, while incorporating outcropping vertical rock faces as links in the defensive chain.

Little that is certain is known about the history of Caer Caradoc. We know that the invading Roman legions established a Shropshire base at Viroconium near Wroxeter, but that a few years later, when Ostorius Scapula was seeking to strengthen the imperial grip on the area, he faced bitter resistance from British guerillas led by Caradoc (Caractacus to the Roman writers). Tacticus tells how Caradoc had a rampart of stones cast up around a steep hill which stood above a river which was difficult to

ford. Some historians have identified the hill where Caradoc's men made their last stand as Caer Caradoc although other possible candidates include the hill of the same name lying to the south of Clun, and Coxall Knoll which is south-east of Bucknell. Defeated and in flight, Caradoc was betrayed by the queen of the northern Brigantes tribe but he won the respect of Emperor Claudius and was returned to his family.

Whether approached from Church Stretton and the south, or from Willstone to the east, the walk to the summit hillfort is a sheer delight. No real climbing is involved and as the path steepens

towards the peak so the panoramas of the sweeping hill sculpture become ever more striking. From the top of Caer Caradoc, the gap below seems canyon-like with Church Stretton a sparkling red and white toy town. One sees the line of the Roman road running north-eastwards from the town as the A49 (T), forking near the hill's foot as the A49 heads north and the old Roman road continues on its course as a minor country road. One cannot help wondering whether British insurgents did not crouch above these ramparts to observe the Roman troop movements on the bright thread of new-built road? The fort itself must certainly pre-date the Roman invasion and it is best regarded as a local stronghold in an Iron Age landscape which was carved up between various competing and insecure communities.

From their lofty perches, the hillforts glared at one other, each threatening and each threatened from all directions. Caer Caradoc, Old Oswestry, Nordy-bank, The Ditches, Castle Ring, Bury Ditches and many other Shropshire hillforts bear witness to a long and

unsettled passage in the story of man in Britain.

Both sites are in the care of the Department of the Environment.

Phototips Hillforts offer many exciting opportunities and challenges to the photographer. Basic possibilities include views of the hillfort as a dominating feature of the landscape; portraits of sections of ramparts to highlight the man-made scarplands of banks and their fronting ditches, and landscape studies showing the fine passages of countryside which can be seen from the ramparts.

In photographing hillforts, the angle and direction of light are vital and you should look for a viewpoint which shows the banks casting strong shadows to accentuate the rampart profiles. Remember that the photograph is two-dimensional and so features which seem sharply defined to the human eye may appear much flatter in a photograph. Wide-angle lenses are needed to encompass the full sweep of ramparts or countryside but, if possible, take a telephoto lens; it will allow you to

Even without the historical interest of the summit hillfort, the ascent of Caer Caradoc would be worthwhile for the fine views of the Shropshire hill and plain landscape which unfold as one approaches the hilltop and the hedged pastures yield to bracken-clad slopes

extract interesting landscape cameos from the broad panorama. Some of my favourite photographs of field patterns were taken from distant hillforts.

Location Old Oswestry (296310) lies just ½ mile N of Oswestry in the sharp angle between the A483 (T) and the minor road from the town to Hengoed village. It can be approached from various directions and is clearly visible from the nearby A483.

Caer Caradoc (477953) is plain to see a couple of miles to the NE of Church Stretton. There are various approaches but perhaps the most convenient and attractive is from Cardington village to the E, via a minor road to Willstone and then by foot by the dipping track and rising footpath to the summit.

ROUND AND ABOUT

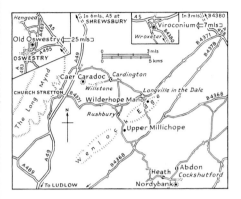

Transport me to Shropshire any time you wish; I think it may be my favourite county. How better to spend a day, week or lifetime than in following the tortuous little lanes from one fascinating site to another with little-spoilt countryside of hills and hedgerows all around? Dozens of possibilities beckon, but I am going to concentrate on the hill country to the east of Caer Caradoc. Although this landscape offers broad vistas across the plains to distant ridges of hard and ancient rocks it is also a very intimate countryside that is packed with fascinating details.

UPPER MILLICHOPE

This comes as something of a surprise. Norman churches and castles are quite common, but dwellings dating back to this period tend to be few and famous. Still, there beside the lane leading from Rushbury to the B4368 is a farmstead with an unmistakably Norman stone doorway. Enquire at the farm and you find that this little-known treasure has recently been opened to the public and you can enter a suite of unaltered medieval rooms.

Built as a forester's lodge around 1280, the dwelling has some of the features of a tower house. The walls are some 6 ft in thickness and the lodge

block has external measurements of 42 ft by 29 ft. The lower floor was an undercroft and the hall occupied the floor above and is dimly illuminated by two-light windows with window seats.

Location (522892) From Church Stretton, take the B4371 eastwards; turn off for Rushbury, follow the road through the village and up the steep face of Roman Bank; fork right near the crest of the ridge and the lodge is part of the first roadside farmstead on your left as you drive down the slope.

TWO LOST VILLAGES

Lost and shrunken villages abound in this area. Heath has its epitaph as the perfectly preserved example of a small Norman church, now isolated in the roadside pasture. Note how Roman blood red bricks, which were probably robbed from a decaying villa, have been incorporated amongst the yellow and white masonry. At Abdon, the medieval church nestles on the hillside and the grassy trenches or 'holloways' in the fields below trace out the streets and tracks of a village which has decayed, leaving only a manor and a couple of farmsteads to survive.

Locations Both are accessible by the network of narrow lanes in the hill

A simple stone church with a distinctive Norman doorway marks the site of the deserted Shropshire village of Heath

country about 10 miles SE of Church Stretton (557857 and 575865 respectively).

NORDYBANK HILLFORT

More fine views and breathtaking fieldscapes are seen from this well-preserved Iron Age hillfort.

A splendid panorama of hedged fields is seen from the ramparts of Nordybank hillfort

Location (576847) Follow the lane E from Heath for a mile or so towards the old quarrying hamlet of Cockshutford. It lies immediately to the S of the lane and ½ mile WSW of Cockshutford.

WILDERHOPE MANOR

A rather inaccessible 16th-century manor house with interesting 17th-century plaster ceilings. Owned by the National Trust and leased as a youth hostel, the manor is open to the public on Wednesday afternoons during the summer.

Location (545929) Can be reached by foot from Longville in the Dale village.

Note The other sites in Shropshire are Clun, Coalbrookdale and Stokesay; Offa's Dyke runs through the area as well. *See* the index for page references.

The Pimperne House, Butser Hill

(Hampshire)

The word 'prehistoric' has unfortunate 'primitive' connotations, particularly when applied to the later prehistoric periods. We cannot live in the past or replicate dead cultures, but if we could re-enter the Iron Age and view a typical English landscape from one of the many hillforts or 'hilltowns', the view would not strike us as particularly primitive. Instead of swelling seas of primaeval forest, we would see vast networks of fields, generously punctuated by the thatch-cones of farmsteads and small hut groupings. We would soon discover that this was a rather unsettled landscape and that the people were sometimes preoccupied with threats of war and raiding, but it would also be a well-managed and well-populated countryside. In comparison, the same landscape as it would appear centuries later in the Dark Ages might strike us as more thinly populated, untidy and more heavily wooded.

The time machine is a dream and, without it, times past are out of reach and beyond recreation, but at Butser Hill in Hampshire we can at least see a carefully authenticated reconstruction of the Iron Age concept of 'home'. As archaeology comes of age, some of the most far-sighted experts have realised the importance of combining specialist research with the essential task of capturing the public interest. Were there many more excellent reconstruction projects of the kind that can be seen at Butser Hill and West Stow*, then the insatiable popular interest in the past would be better served and greater public support would hopefully lead to more funds becoming available.

The Butser story began in 1972 with the formation of the Butser Ancient Farm Research Project and the reconstruction of a farm of 300 BC. The research ventures in experimental archaeology explored many aspects of farming practices, husbandry, cultivation and building construction and contributed enormously to the experts' understanding of the day-to-day lives of Iron Age countryfolk.

Soon the project had become a victim of its own success and the pressure from the visiting parties began to threaten research. In 1975, the Hampshire County Council made a 4-acre site available in a more accessible location, close to its new Queen Elizabeth Country Park where a demonstration area could be developed. It was realised that this area could serve as a useful adjunct to the work in experimental farming which was being practised on the Hill.

The centrepiece of the new experi-

The centrepiece of the Butser Ancient Farm Research Project is the reconstruction of an Iron Age enclosure and house. OPPOSITE *and right: the area which lies inside the encircling defensive bank and ditch*

ment was the reconstruction of an Iron Age enclosure and house, using precise data gleaned from an excavated site at Pimperne in Dorset. There it appeared that two successive dwellings on the same site had together spanned a period of about 400 years and so the reconstructed Pimperne House was not based upon one of the many ephemeral prehistoric buildings, but was built to endure. Small crop-growing paddocks surrounded the reconstructed hut, and a garden was planted with pre-Roman herbs.

The sense of a competent and durable construction permeates the Pimperne House and visitors will be impressed by the spaciousness of the circular interior. The diameter is over 40 ft; the wattled and daubed walls are low while inner

and outer rings of stakes and ring beams support the long poles of the rafters which carry the great covering cone of wheat straw. As with the less exacting reconstructions of huts at Craggaunowen*, the experiment underlined the enormous demands which home-making placed upon the resources of the local environment and of labour. Peter J. Reynolds, the director of the project, reports that the hut absorbed fifty straight coppice-grown oaks while the radiating rafters required straight elm and ash trunks which were around 30 ft in length. Prodigious quantities of coppiced hazel saplings were used in the wattle while the roof consumed the straw from more than three acres of cropland.

This and other evidence suggests that

The carefully reconstructed interior of the Pimperne House; the diameter is over 40 ft, giving an impression of spaciousness

the crafts of woodmanship must have been developed and well-established by the Iron Age if not before. With areas set aside for coppices, pollards and standards and the different trees felled according to various rotations, the Iron Age wood, rather than being primaeval and forbidding, was a much healthier and well-managed place than the neglected woods of today which tremble in the shadow of the subsidised bulldozer. Given the amount of effort and skill required in the construction of the house it was suggested that house-building and thatching were professional occupations during the Iron Age.

In keeping with its period, the house is surrounded by a bank and ditch. Again we encounter the apparent pre-occupation with defence. We can be sure that the Iron Age peasantry supported a formidable array of chieftains, sub-chiefs and warriors and we can guess that a sort of feudal system existed, with folk subscribing to some kind of aristocratic protection racket. Yet, if the chiefs had a responsibility for defence, why are most quite lowly dwellings provided with their own defences? We do not know. Being large and durable, the Pimperne House might have been an Iron Age equivalent of a medieval manor house.

Inside the house, an Iron Age interior with hearth, oven, firedogs and cauldron has been recreated, and one can

guarantee that a visit to the Pimperne House and demonstration area will be an unforgettable experience. The modest fee that the visitor pays is ploughed back into invaluable research work and, as with West Stow*, a Friends Society exists to assist the project and various events are organised for those enthusiasts who join. The scope and need for other reconstruction schemes is enormous, and personally I will not be content until some enterprising director gets a financial green-light to reconstruct a deserted medieval village!

Phototips From the outside, the house is a straightforward subject. As you proceed down the approach lane, the first sight of the house gives you the feeling of having stepped across a threshold of more than 2000 years and you should

try to capture this sentiment on film, taking care to exclude other visitors and intrusions from the modern world. The large interior may prove too much for most smaller flashguns and a time-exposure will produce much more authentic results. Tripods can be a pest to other visitors and you should not use one without getting permission from the curator on duty. It is also sensible to assure him that you are not on commercial business.

Location The Pimperne House is reached from the Queen Elizabeth Country Park which is beside the A3, 3 miles SW of Petersfield. The Iron Age farm area with two more houses is concerned with research and not accessible to the public, but these can be glimpsed on a spur as you approach from the N.

ROUND AND ABOUT

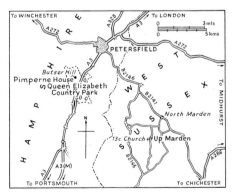

environments were extensive earlier in this century but they are rapidly disappearing as farmers plough up the ancient down or seed old pastures with rye grass, thus sterilising many of our most botanically diverse countrysides.

The Park is managed by Hampshire C.C. and the Forestry Commission.

Location As above. There is a large public car park.

UP MARDEN (West Sussex)

The site of this deserted medieval village is marked by a perfectly preserved and almost completely unaltered church of the 13th century.

Location From Petersfield, take the B2146, and B2141 to North Marden. Turn right onto minor roads, following

signs to Up Marden. The church lies 9 miles to the SE of Petersfield.

Note The Weald and Downland open air museum at Singleton in West Sussex is not far away: *see* the index for the page reference.

The simple, austere but little-changed church interior at Up Marden

THE QUEEN ELIZABETH COUNTRY PARK

Various outdoor pursuits are available and, the ancient farm demonstration area apart, the park is of historical interest because it contains an area of traditional chalk downland. Such

The Iron Age Brought to Life at Craggaunowen

(Co Clare)

How can we show that history is an exciting subject, bring the past alive in ways that will fascinate the layman and stimulate a nation to fight for the causes of conservation and archaeology? The answer can be found at places like Butser Hill*, The Lunt* and West Stow* in Britain and at Craggaunowen in southern Ireland. At Craggaunowen, you can see two distinct reconstructions of Iron Age settlements—with not only a genuine castle thrown in for good measure but also the boat used in the courageous and well-publicised if somewhat unprecedented Brendan Atlantic voyage. The reconstructions at Craggaunowen are of a crannóg and a stone fort and, as at most other major Irish historical tourist attractions, the presentation is superb.

Both these fortified settlements highlight the Iron Age obsession with defence. We know very well that the Middle Ages was a turbulent period which produced a bountiful crop of noble castles but, in the Iron Age, even the humble peasants seem to have been preoccupied by the need to defend their homesteads. The efforts involved in building defences often greatly outstripped those expended in building the home itself, and we do not know exactly why. Certainly, warfare and raiding were rife but, as I have said in the chapter's introduction, every area presumably had its controlling chieftain and one can only wonder why the needs for communal defence were not fully satisfied at levels higher than that of the peasant farmstead.

The crannóg is a homestead or small hut group which is built on an artificial island of stakes and brushwood and whose name derives from the Gaelic *crann*, a tree. Children of any period would, of course, love crannóg life with its wonderful opportunities for fishing, canoeing and getting wet but the construction of an island from stakes, rubble and prodigious amounts of brushwood was a large and time-consuming undertaking. Nevertheless, the crannóg was a remarkably persistent form of settlement; some were occupied in the medieval period, a few even defended in the seventeenth century, while currently Scottish underwater archaeological work is showing that crannóg building took place in the Bronze Age. Of course, to build a crannóg, you first need a lake and so crannóg life was always a minority pursuit.

The simulated crannóg at Craggaunowen has that feeling of purposeful solidity that one finds at all good reconstructions. The island is ringed by a palisade of posts and wattle and, while most original crannógs were only accessible by canoe, is reached by a modern timber causeway. A gatehouse overlooks the entrance and inside the palisade are a pair of huts, one circular and one sub-rectangular.

Not all the materials used in the simulation are exactly authentic or indigenous; this is not surprising for the reconstruction work has shown the enormous demands that prehistoric home-making imposed on the local environment. The surrounding palisade is about 100 yards in diameter and employs over one hundred 16-ft larch poles and 8000 pieces of wattling timber, while the circular hut alone has 3600 bales of rushes in its high conical thatch roof. About ten tons of mud were needed to provide the daub plaster on its wattle walls. (My wife, who was born in Kenya, was immediately struck by the similarity between the hut and those in the living villages of East Africa.)

The reconstructed entrance to the stone fort; the thick ramparts of drystone walling are crowned with a palisade of sturdy stakes

OPPOSITE *The simulated crannóg at Craggaunowen – a view from the footpath which leads to the reconstructed stone fort*

The Craggaunowen stone fort reconstruction showing the circular dwellings with their drystone walls, well-thatched conical roofs and *paved interiors. Note too the grass-covered rampart wall which encloses the dwellings, and the timber palisade which crowns the rampart*

There were no towns in Iron Age Ireland, relatively few villages and scarcely any that have been discovered, but there were many thousands of defended farmsteads. Known as 'raths' or ring forts, they consisted of a circular banked and ditched enclosure guarding one or more dwelling huts and a few storage buildings. The typical rath enclosure was around 40 or 50 yards in diameter and may perhaps have served as an animal compound in territories where cattle raiding was a national pastime. Larger raths, 100 or more yards in diameter and often with two or more rings of earthen ramparts, were presumably the homes of chieftains and of their principal retainers. In terrain which was strewn with stones, the rath had its counterpart in the stone-walled ring fort.

A fine reconstruction of one of the more substantial stone forts can be seen at Craggaunowen, with its thick ramparts of drystone walling crowned by an uninterrupted palisade of vertical logs. Inside, a group of huts has been built with conical thatch roofs similar to those of the crannóg dwellings, but with their circular walls made of neat drystone walling rather than wattle and daub. Again, there is a grand sense of authenticity which results from the skilful use of substantial materials.

Both raths and stone forts were often provided with underground passages or souterrains (presumably used for similar purposes as those at Chysauster* and Rennibister* and are similarly mysterious) and one of the stone fort huts has an underground chamber.

Many details of Iron Age life in Ireland remain mysterious. The national preoccupation with the Celtic aspects of its past may be at the expense of the pre-Celtic and later medieval heritage. In the Bronze Age and the early Christian period, Ireland occupied a special position on the European stage and the examples of Craggaunowen and of the Bunratty Castle Folk Park* nearby, suggest that Britain could learn much from the Irish about the presentation of the past—and do so in ways that would not only lighten lessons for schoolchildren but also encourage the tourist industry.

Phototips Both reconstructions present difficulties because they have an outside and an inside view so that a good photograph of the approaches to the ramparts will not do justice to the huts inside. Because film is relatively cheap, you should always take a number of photographs to portray the different aspects of a marvellous site such as this.

A good panorama of the crannóg can be obtained not from the causeway or lakeside so much as from the raised ground close to where the path leads off to the stone fort, the higher vantage point allowing a view over the palisade which reveals more of the interior. General views of the stone fort can be gained from the rampart walkway, and a shot of the huts within framed by the entrance through the ramparts is very worthwhile and can be dramatic.

Location Within easy reach of Shannon airport and signposted from the L31 road near the village of Quin. From Shannon, take the N19–N18 routes towards Ennis and then the minor road turn-off to the E which leads to Quin.

ROUND AND ABOUT

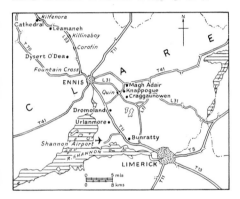

The surroundings are studded with castles: Craggaunowen itself, Urlanmore, Dromoland, Knappogue and Magh Adhair but the following places can be visited by visitors en route to the Burren* and the monuments described in Chapter 1.

DYSERT O'DEA

The church and round tower mark the site of an early Christian monastery founded by St Tola. The church fell into ruin and was rebuilt in the 17th century but the Norman-influenced doorway, with its chevron decoration surmounted by human masks and animal heads, was retained in the new building. Standing in a field to the NE of the church is a very fine High Cross of the 12th century which bears the figure of a bishop, possibly a representation of St Tola.

Location (R28 85) To the W of the Ennis-Corofin L53 road about 3 miles N of Fountain Cross village.

LEAMANEH CASTLE

This gaunt and roofless castle is in two parts. The tall narrow eastern portion with its slit-like window openings is a tower house built for the O'Brien family

Leamaneh Castle: the tower was built in 1840

in 1480. In the 17th century, domestic arrangements were made more spacious and comfortable by the addition of a large manor house of four storeys. Conor O'Brien, who held the castle, perished during the ghastly Cromwellian invasion of Ireland but his wife, Maire Ruadh, is said to have saved her estates by marrying a Cromwellian officer. With the ranks of mullioned windows gazing blindly like the eye sockets in a skull, the crows flapping from the tops of jagged walls and stairs ascending into darkness, this is a deliciously spooky castle.

Location At the T-junction where the L51 leading N to Poulnabrone leaves the L53 Killinaboy-Kilfenora road.

KILFENORA CATHEDRAL

The partly ruined church which is tucked away on a side road in an apparently inconsequential little town belies the fact that the Catholic diocese of Kilfenora has the Pope as its bishop. Inside the roofless chancel are effigies of bishops dating from the 13th and 14th centuries. Two High Crosses stand in the churchyard and a third and very lofty example bearing a crucifixion and interlace motif lies in the field to the W.

Note The Burren and the Bunratty Folk Park are both in the neighbourhood, and Clonmacnois is not far away. *See* the index for page references.

Chysauster Village

(Cornwall)

Occupied from the first or second centuries BC until the second and possibly the third century AD, Chysauster village spans the prehistoric and historical periods in Britain. There is no better site at which to explore the Late Iron Age concept of 'home'—or, at least, the idea of home as it applied to the stone-strewn landscapes of the south-west. The village or hamlet had no particular plan but consisted of four pairs of circular dwellings set on opposite sides of a street with a ninth house lying just beside the entrance to the site, and at least two more dwellings in outlying positions. The houses vary greatly in their states of preservation; some may still be undetected, several are scarcely recognisable but a few are roofless but otherwise remarkably intact.

The dwellings are of a type known as 'courtyard houses' of which a number of Iron Age examples are known in Cornwall while others have been found in Wales. The design of the courtyard house will strike most visitors as being rather odd. Each house consists of a rugged oval or circular outer wall while a series of separate rooms are constructed *in* the thickness of this wall,

each room facing on to an open central courtyard. The floors of these cells were paved and were originally roofed, some perhaps in thatch, others by the corbelling method using slabs of stone which were laid in courses which projected inwards until the roof space was spanned.

The evolutionary history of the courtyard house is not known, but these Cornish dwellings may represent attempts to translate the timber huts of Iron Age Wessex into stone in a part of the country which was rich in boulder scatters but perhaps already short of timber.

The Chysauster folk were doubtless peasant farmers; nearby, can be seen small garden plots in the form of stone-walled terraces while the faint outlines of what were presumably fields from the same period can be traced on the nearby slopes. Life in the village will have been somewhat spartan but not grossly uncomfortable. Indeed, these Iron Age folk may never have known the extremes of deprivation which were endured by the hovel-dwellers in many medieval villages. We may guess that each house was the home of a particular village family; individual cells within each house may have served as a workshop, a

Chysauster in Cornwall. OPPOSITE *The entrance to one of the courtyard houses, a threshold which may first have been crossed 2000 years ago. (Right) The living rooms and storage areas were built into the thickness of the great stone walls*

byre, a store and perhaps a corn-drying room while the largest of the circular cells was probably the living quarters. The house which is marked as '6' shows these features very well.

The open courtyard was perhaps a generally useful space which was sheltered from the strong Atlantic winds and in which craftwork and domestic tasks could be performed, livestock perhaps sheltered, and where children could play and food might be eaten. When the village was excavated, hearths were found in many of the rooms, along with fragments of pottery and the stone handmills which were used to grind the village grain. Stone-lined water channels ran across the floors of a number of rooms, some being used for drainage, others apparently to collect water for domestic use.

With a little ingenuity, we can imagine pots simmering above the hearths, the village women grinding bread grain while children tumbled about in the courtyards as leg-weary fathers returned from the fields carrying milk. Iron Age life at Chysauster will not entirely have conformed to such images of self-sufficient rural bliss, however. Doubtless, there was a local chieftain who was always ready to demand rent or tribute and although the village is somewhat unusual in having no defences, Castle-an-Dinas hillfort lay within running distance.

To the south-east of the village lies an example of the mysterious underground passages which are known in this part of the world as 'fogous', but whether they served as a refuge for people or livestock, as a cool storage chamber or some more mystical purpose, we do not know. A much more well-preserved fogou can be

Each house was probably the home of a particular village family: individual parts of each house may have served as a workshop or store

entered at Carn Euny village a few miles away where the surrounding huts belong mainly to the first century BC.

Although Chysauster occupies a special niche in Britain's incomparable archaeological inventory, its importance is mainly due to the fine preservation of many of the huts. We must not imagine that Chysauster was particularly special during its own lifespan. Rather we should imagine that the rugged sea-girt landscape of Penwith in western Cornwall was partitioned between many small communities and at least thirty separate settlements of courtyard houses are known to have existed in the wind-swept country which lies west of St Ives.

Phototips At sites such as Chysauster, it is often difficult to combine a general panorama of the whole settlement and good portraits of particular huts in a single portrait. At Chysauster, general views of the site are much more effectively accomplished by air photography but the individual huts make attractive subjects. On sunny summer days, the scene is very colourful with purple and yellow moorland plants flowering around the huts, the green pastures on the distant slopes merging with the heather moors above and billows of cloud cruising in from the Atlantic. On dull days, however, strong studies of the dwellings and background cloud forms in black-and-white will prove much more effective than drab and muted colour shots.

Location 2 miles N of Trevarrack and accessible via the minor road from the B3311 at Badger's Cross. Chysauster is quite easily found since the site is signposted from the A30 from about 2 miles E of Penzance. A small car park is available and a short but steep footpath leads to the village which has a DoE custodian.

ROUND AND ABOUT

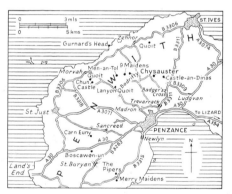

Oh dear! Where to begin and what to leave out? The Penwith area of Cornwall has a stupendous collection of prehistoric sites within this little area. Apart from the two subsidiary sites following, here is a selection of sites along with their OS map references: Chun Quoit (402340) Neolithic portal dolmen type of tomb; Chun Castle nearby (405339) Iron Age hillfort; Zennor Quoit

Chun Quoit, a Neolithic portal dolmen here photographed with a clear centre spot diffuser

The village of courtyard houses at Carn Euny. The fogou entrance is in the foreground, with one of the circular dwellings beyond

(469380) portal dolmen; Carn Euny (402289) Iron Age village and fogou; Men-an-tol (427349) mysterious holed stone with two flanking stones, perhaps remains of Neolithic tomb; Bodrifty (445354) Iron Age village site; The Pipers (434248) a pair of gigantic standing stones of uncertain date; Boscawen-un (412274) stone circle; Gurnard's Head (433385) Iron Age promontory fort, and Nine Maidens (434353) Bronze Age stone row.

MERRY MAIDENS STONE CIRCLE

The stone circle is more complete than most and all its nineteen stones still stand. The circle has a diameter of 79 ft. It is also known as Rosemodress and as the Dawns Men. Legends tell that the stones represent maidens who were petrified for dancing on a Sunday.

Location (433245) The circle can be seen from the B3315 Sennen-Newlyn road.

LANYON QUOIT

The original chambered tomb collapsed in 1815 and some of the original stones were erected to form the impressive but much-reduced monument. The enormous capstone, some 17 ft in length, rests head-high on three uprights. It is a National Trust property.

Merry Maidens: all nineteen stones of this circle still stand

The monument at Lanyon Quoit: the original chambered tomb collapsed in 1815

Location (430337) Just to the E of the Penzance-Madron-Morvah road.

Boscawen-un: the stone circle lies peacefully in autumn bracken

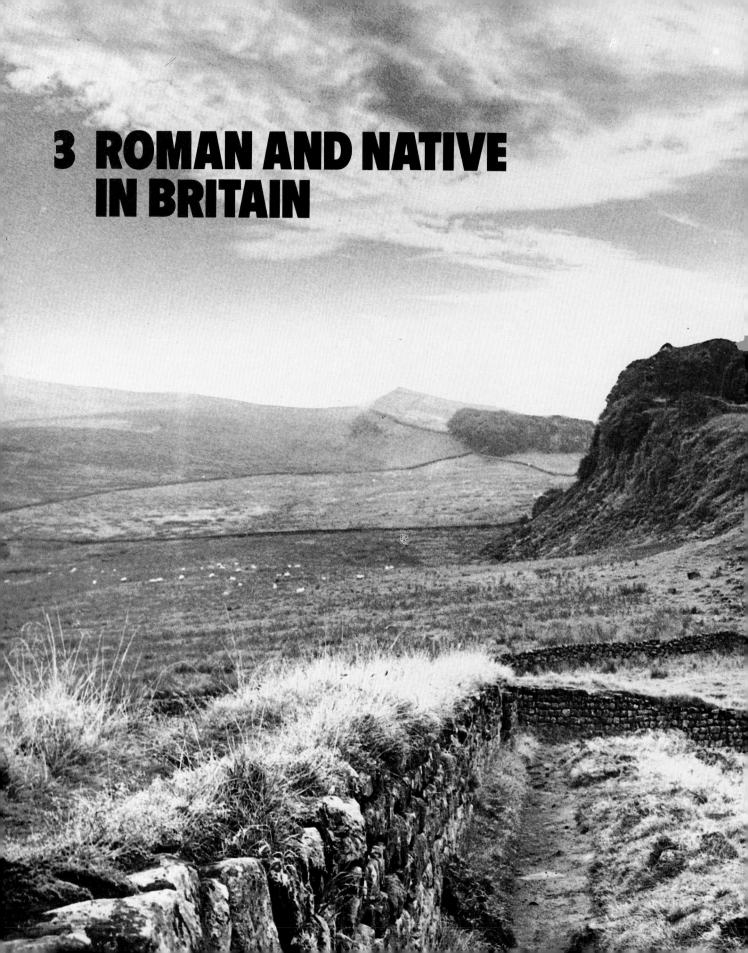

3 ROMAN AND NATIVE IN BRITAIN

The decades surrounding the lifetime of Christ witnessed in Britain the confrontation between two different worlds. There was the indigenous world of the Celtic societies which was rigidly partitioned between a series of tribal territories, and the civilised and highly-organised world of the Roman Empire which embraced much of continental Europe. We tend to regard the Roman Conquest and occupation of much of Britain as a triumph of civilisation over barbarism. In many respects, this was true, but this narrow view does not recognise the achievements of the native peoples. As we have already seen, the British territories were well-peopled and productive before the Conquest; metalwork in bronze, iron and gold was of an exceptional quality, while the loose and straggling native political capitals or '*oppida*' would surely have evolved to produce more populous and coherent towns without Roman interference.

Britain was therefore on the verge of civilisation, but the final steps had not been achieved. This was partly due to a lack of vision on the part of the native political leaders who continued to live in a world of tribal confrontation and rivalries, heroic displays and devious intrigues. Only after the Roman Conquest did visions of a united and integrated realm begin to flourish. Circumstances prevented the full fruition of such ideals, but the establishment of planned and prosperous towns, the basis for a national system of roads and a coherent pattern of defenceworks produced a remarkable transformation of the hitherto divided and fractious territories.

There were Roman contacts with Britain prior to the Conquest, while the southern territories seem to have enjoyed considerable prestige in the eyes of the continental, subjugated Celts. Britain appears to have been a major focus for Celtic religious instruction and to have been involved in the fermentation of unrest and resistance in Gaul. A Roman conquest of Britain would not only eliminate the outposts of Celtic unrest but also greatly enhance the prestige of the victorious commander. These motives inspired the reconnaisance in force mounted by Caesar in 55 BC; the practical results were insignificant although in Rome it was considered sufficiently important for a twenty-day public holiday to be declared. The following year, he mounted a more serious invasion with five legions and 2,000 cavalry, but the logistical factors were neglected and, having obtained the nominal submission of several tribes and established a native puppet king of the Trinovantes tribe, he was obliged to withdraw to the continent, where Gaulish resistance was again fermenting.

A new invasion may have been planned in the reign of Caligula (AD 37–41) but it did not materialise. In the reign of the emperor Claudius, a purposeful and successful invasion was staged in AD 43. The motives were quite complicated; some were similar to those which influenced Caesar, while the agricultural and mineral assets of Britain were obviously very attractive. Another important factor concerned Roman policy towards client rulers; Verica, the king of the Artebrates tribe, had been expelled in the culmination of a prolonged expansion of Catuvellauni territories. He fled to Rome and pleaded with Claudius to invade Britain. Had his appeal been rejected, the clients controlling the vulnerable eastern frontiers of the Empire would have had cause to doubt Roman support and might have transferred their allegiances to the Parthians.

The invasion fleets landed at Richborough in Kent and at two other unidentified sites. Before leaving Plautius to subdue the remaining territories, Claudius won a victory somewhere to the north of the Thames and captured the Catuvellauni capital of Camulodunum, near Colchester. Some tribes were defeated in battle but other chieftains readily submitted, realising that their choice was between Roman rule or eventual overlordship by the Catuvellauni federation. In AD 44, a substantial army, which was supplied by fleets working along the southern coast of England and led by Vespatian, achieved a rapid westward advance into Dorset, storming a number of hillforts in the course of the invasion. It seems that in the years which followed the fourteenth legion advanced through the Midlands while the ninth spearheaded the invasion of the eastern flank of England, establishing a base at Lincoln and then at York.

There were a number of insurrections and guerilla operations in the decades following the Conquest, the most serious being the briefly successful uprising of members of the East Anglian Iceni tribe led by their queen, Boudica, in AD 60 — the year in which Roman penetration reached Anglesey. Although the frontiers of Roman control fluctuated and the embers of native unrest flared from time to time, on the whole it is possible to imagine the British territory divided into a number of zones.

The lowlands, covering the greater part of England, were pacified, civilised and very agriculturally productive. The lowland landscape became punctuated by large and small towns and both Romanised and native villages, all bound together by an efficient and well-maintained road network. The countryside meanwhile was partitioned between the villa-centred estates of Romanised and immigrant landlords, and the farmsteads and hamlets of the indigenous peasants. To the west lay the upland zones of the Lake District, Pennines, Wales and Cornwall, where a more military climate endured and landscapes were exploited for useful metals, controlled by large and small fortresses and penetrated by military roads. Here, however, the old native lifestyles were less affected by conquest and defended hilltop villages continued to exist.

Meanwhile, Ireland to the west was completely unconquered while the bulk of Scotland lay for most of the time beyond the limits of Roman occupation, despite various invasions and forays. In the north, the Celtic lifestyle persisted but the southern Scottish tribes experienced Roman conquest and retreat, sometimes trading with or submitting to the alien legions and sometimes launching raids and invasions upon the imperial territories.

Perhaps I tend to see the heritage through the eyes of the photographer rather than the historian, but Roman relics sometimes seem a little uninspiring. Although archaeologists can deduce much from the evidence contained, one set of ankle-high Roman wall footings are inclined to look much like another, and it is seldom easy to appreciate the living villa, workshop or town house from such relics.

The Saxon Shore Forts are undoubtedly the most dramatic and stunning of the Roman remains, and fine examples can be visited at Porchester in Hampshire, Pevensey in Sussex, Richborough in Kent — where the weather-worn walls stand like gnarled battleships above the green sea of pasture — or Burgh Castle in Suffolk, the site I have chosen. Hadrian's Wall has its own unique ethos and a few sections of metalled Roman road endures to fire the imagination with visions of marching legions. Since the section of road on Blackstone Edge in Lancashire is currently the subject of fierce debate concerning its Roman credentials, I have written about the Wheeldale Moor road instead.

The indigenous people of Britain always vastly outnumbered their conquerors and several of their villages are preserved so well that it is much easier to visualise Romano-British country life than to picture the elegance and splendour of the major Roman towns.

See Appendix II for other sites from Roman Britain.

EASTERN GATEWAY

92

The Lunt Roman Fort at Baginton

(Warwickshire)

The first stage in the Roman overlordship of Britain almost ended in disaster in AD 60 with the uprising of the East Anglian Iceni tribe under the leadership of Boudica. The Roman population of Colonia Claudia Victrensis at Colchester was massacred and refugees fled from a wide surrounding area including London. A frenzied reappraisal of the military situation followed, and an important factor in the new strategy was the construction of a large and heavily-garrisoned fort at Barinton near Coventry and the decisive battle in which the insurgents were routed may have taken place nearby.

The Baginton fort occupied a central position on the military stage for about twenty years when, with England at peace following the annexation of the Brigantes lands in the north, Wales conquered and Scotland the target for further conquest, the troops moved on to new postings and the fort was eventually dismantled—although the site was briefly refortified during the third century.

The Baginton fort had a most unconventional shape for while the north and west sides were straight, the southern side curved and the western side was scalloped around a bulge in the ramparts. This bulge took in a large circular *gyrus* or paddock used for the training and exercising of cavalry horses inside the fort. Other structures which were set out inside the fortress in an orderly fashion include long timber barrack blocks, a centrally placed *principia* or headquarters building, fodder and harness stores, workshops, and others interpreted as a bath block and a very grand *praetorium*, the house of the commanding officer. Some experts have regarded the fort as an important training school for the Roman cavalry.

There can be few things that the modern traveller will less expect to see amidst the suburban scenery of a small Coventry suburb than the gateway defences of a Roman fort. The excavations at Baginton lasted eight years and were completed in 1973. The fort lay on land owned and scheduled for amenity use by Coventry Corporation and, in 1967, work on a partial reconstruction was begun by inmates from the local prison who constructed a

OPPOSITE *The timber parapet and gate house defences at the reconstructed fort.* (Right) *Alan Sorrell's reconstruction painting; note the representation of the circular* gyrus. *Photograph on pp 88–9:* Hadrian's Wall

93

section of rampart bank from turves. Then a detachment from the Royal Engineers moved in and the imposing replica gateway defences were erected in the course of one weekend and the rampart and ditch defences were extended.

Envigorated by their success with the gateway, the Engineers agreed to reconstruct an internal building. Timber, however, presented a problem until the site director, Brian Hobley, had the bright idea of appealing for diseased elms which were being removed by Coventry Parks Department. Work was able to begin on the reconstruction of the granary building which was 70 ft by 30 ft and presumed to be 30 ft in height. Those in charge preferred to call this a 'simulation' rather than a 'reconstruction' since the only firm archaeological evidence derived from the holes which had held the massive timber posts which raised the floor of the building about three feet above the damp ground. Elm weatherboarding and 5,500 wooden roof shingles completed the granary which then became a site museum.

The results of this simulation work will not fail to impress the visitor, but it must be remembered that only a small fraction of the perimeter defences could be rebuilt compared to the Roman palisade and ramparts which embraced an area of about four acres and which was crammed with military buildings. Even so, the cavalry fort was less extensive than the initial military complex which was hastily erected about the time of Boudica's revolt.

Phototips This is a fairly straightforward subject but try to frame photographs in such a way as to exclude fragments of the modern suburban setting. The more serious enthusiast can experiment with fog filters or clear centre spot diffuser filters to create the impressions of the formidable gateway defences looming out of the mist.

Location In Baginton suburb, 2 miles S of Coventry and signposted from the road leading to Coventry airport.

ROUND AND ABOUT

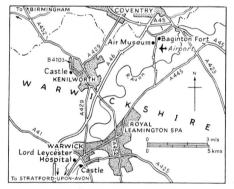

KENILWORTH CASTLE

The Norman keep was built on an older motte in the 1160s and 1170s. In the 13th century, a curtain wall was built to encircle the tower while an artificial lake

A magnificent view of Kenilworth castle; in the 1660s, Robert Dudley, the Earl of Leicester, converted the castle into a palace

strengthened the approaches. In this way, King John created a formidable royal stronghold and the surrender of Kenilworth was one of the conditions which the barons imposed upon the King under the terms of Magna Carta of 1215. In 1266 the strength of the fortress was underlined when the supporters of the rebel Simon de Montfort kept the army of Henry III at bay for 9 months until they were vanquished by starvation rather than assault.

MIDLAND AIR MUSEUM, BAGINTON

The museum is open on Sundays between April and October and a selection of aircraft are displayed. The American Super Sabre jet is one of the most popular exhibits but there are other less familiar designs including the Boulton Paul P 111A Delta research aircraft and a German WW2 helicopter.

Location Very close to the Lunt Roman fort, on the outskirts of Baginton by the airport road.

In the 1560s, the Earl of Leicester converted the castle into a palace which was intended to further enhance his standing with Elizabeth I who had restored the Dudley possessions forfeited in 1553 and created Robert Dudley an earl in 1560. Unlike some other suitors, Dudley maintained the Queen's favour; three times she was a guest at Kenilworth, one of these occasions being the subject for *Kenilworth* by Sir Walter Scott.

During the Civil War, parliamentary troops occupied and damaged Kenilworth and drained the surrounding lake. The castle is now in the care of the Department of the Environment.

Location 5 miles N of Warwick, signposted from the B4103.

LORD LEYCESTER HOSPITAL, WARWICK

Warwick is noted for its splendid medieval riverside castle but many tourists are unaware of the remarkably fine medieval timber-framed buildings

which constitute the Lord Leycester Hospital. The houses were built in the latter part of the 14th century as the headquarters for a guild. In 1571, Robert Dudley (*see* above) converted the guildhall and the adjoining chapel into a retirement home for servicemen—a role

which the hospital still fulfils.

Location At the top of Warwick High Street.

Note The Avoncroft Museum of Buildings is quite close; *see* the index for the page reference.

ABOVE *Warwick Castle, a splendid view obtained from the nearby road bridge. (Right) The Lord Leycester Hospital in Warwick, a fine medieval timber-framed building built in the latter part of the 14th century*

95

Hadrian's Wall, Housesteads

(Northumberland)

It has often been said of great empires that decline begins once the incentive for further expansion is lost and thoughts turn to the consolidation of the territories that have been gained. One can debate whether this is true of the Roman Empire in Britain, but Hadrian's Wall, which was built to secure the northern approaches of the valuable British outpost of Roman imperialism, performed its task well on the whole. Despite the serious but short-lived set-back of the Boudica revolt in the south and the rumblings in the Brigantes lands in the north, the easy conquest of the tribes of England was encouraging to the Romans.

The tribal leaders submitted with varying degrees of reluctance and sincerity, hillfort strongholds surrendered or fell to the sophisticated siege and storm techniques of the legions, and old tribal antagonisms made it easy for the new masters of England to practise divide and rule tactics. Before too long, the rich farmlands of the south and the mining areas of the north and west were pacified and productive.

For a while, it seemed that the Romans could bludgeon the Celtic tribes of the far north and west into submission and export the Empire across Scotland and perhaps Ireland too. From a fortress deep in the Highlands, beside the Spey at Inchtuthil, Agricola advanced to win a great victory over a tribal confederacy at 'Mons Graupius', somewhere in northeast Scotland, in AD 84. Scotland seemed to be Rome's for the taking but, on closer inspection, the price may have seemed too high.

The nature of the terrain favoured guerilla warfare. Four legions of the Roman army might have been needed to police the province and there must have been debate about whether the resources of Scotland were worth the effort? In the event, one of the legions in Scotland was withdrawn for use elsewhere in the Empire and another was shuttled south to cope with an uprising amongst the troublesome Brigantes.

There may have been earlier military schemes to stabilise and defend an imperial frontier between the Solway and the Tyne, but the final solution to the barbarian problem—the segregation of the warlike northern tribes by a fortified barrier wall—was imposed by Emperor Hadrian in AD 122 as part of a general policy to delimit and defend the frontiers of imperial expansion.

The construction of the wall took place between AD 122 and AD 130. Different lengths were the responsibility of different legions and the work was subdivided between the cohorts and centuries. When finished, it made the fifteen-year-old Stanegate system of forts, small forts and watchtowers far stronger and more watertight: a physical barrier 73½ miles long studded by mile-castles and buttressed by forts ran from Bowness-on-Solway across the narrow neck of northern Britain to Wallsend on the Tyne. The wall allowed movements across the frontier to be monitored and controlled and it insulated the bothersome Brigantes in the south from the unsettling influences of the Picts in the north and from their old allies the Selgovae of southern Scotland.

However, the wall was scarcely complete when the legions again marched northwards, taking control of southern Scotland and establishing a new frontier which was marked by a turf wall—the Antonine Wall—running between the Forth and the Clyde. This advance may have been inspired by politics and desire for attention directed at Rome rather than the Scottish situation. In about AD 163, Hadrian's Wall was again manned and the troops withdrew from Scotland leaving a few garrisons manning forts in the southern uplands.

Thenceforth, the military situation in the north fluctuated and the wall was battered and in parts overrun in the early 180s, in 197, 296 and in the particularly destructive invasion by an alliance of Picts, Scots and Saxons of 367. The badly damaged wall was rebuilt in AD 369 but abandoned within two decades. Thereafter, however, the worst threats and the ultimate death-blows to Roman rule in Britain came not from the old enemies in the north, but from the south.

A panoramic view of Hadrian's Wall, looking east from Housesteads

ABOVE *The ruins of one of the granaries at Housesteads, one of the seventeen forts which were sited behind the wall at 5-mile intervals*

RIGHT *The Wall near Cuddy's Crags. Even in summer the scene can seem damp and chilly as the mists leave droplets clinging to the turf*

OPPOSITE *Hadrian's Wall running eastwards from the ruins of Housesteads fort with the bleak landscape of Whin Sill behind*

There are many places at which one can view the wall but one of the most dramatic is near Housesteads where it bestrides the crumpled scarp of the tough basaltic rocks of the Whin Sill. Here one can see the four components of the defensive line: the northern ditch; the wall itself, punctuated by turrets, mile-castles and forts; the second ditch—the great *Vallum*, 20 ft wide, with its flanking earth banks—to the south of the wall, and the military road which runs behind the *Vallum*.

At Housestead too one sees the remains of one of the seventeen forts which were sited behind the wall at intervals of about five miles. Below the south gate of the fort, a civil settlement grew up, housing the families of soldiers, traders, craftsmen and the various hangers-on that one associates with large garrisons. After the great Pictish raid of AD 367, the destroyed settlement was not rebuilt and subsequently the civilians were accommodated inside the fort.

Legionary life on the wall was not all warfare and last-ditch-stands and for long periods of time the garrisons will have had little to do but keep look-out for rebellious tribes, check smuggling and prevent the natives from stealing each others' cattle. Even so, the climate in this part of the world is hardly perfect and although the forts were as solid and no more spartan than most—civilians were close by, plying their various wares and there were temples serving most persuasions— it is hard to imagine that a posting to the wall was greeted with anything but very mixed feelings. The legionaries came from all parts of the

Empire, and at various times there were cavalry regiments from Gaul, north-west Spain and Hungary and cohorts from Belgium, southern France, Yugoslavia and Syria. With the northern tribes in ferment, and freezing fog shrouding the approaches to the wall, how the patrols must have wished for transfers to the Rhineland, Spain, the eastern Mediterranean—or anywhere!

Phototips Probably the best photograph of Hadrian's Wall is that taken by the great Edwin Smith showing the wall undulating and then rising to ascend Cuddy's Crags just to the W of Housesteads fort in a landscape that is dappled by sunbursts and cloud shadows. For a splendid panorama of the wall, one can do no better than follow in his footsteps. Sunlight can be a mixed blessing, for

while it gives brightness, contrast and sparkle to the scene, more evocative and dramatic portraits are likely when menacing clouds are rolling by.

On a recent visit, I spent hours huddled beneath the wall waiting for fog and rain to clear and there is really no answer to these sorts of conditions except to try to capture the prevailing atmosphere.

Location Close to the B6318. Visitors from almost all directions should use the A69, following the signs for Hadrian's Wall and Housesteads in the Haltwhistle-Haydon Bridge section of

the A69. A car park and tourist facilities are available beside the B6318 and the last few hundred yards to Housesteads fort are made on foot. For the recommended section of the wall, walk to the top of the fort and turn W (left) and follow the wall footpath over Hotbank Crags.

ROUND AND ABOUT

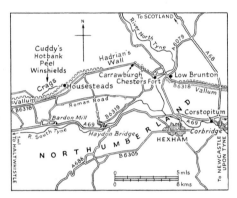

A series of fascinating Roman antiquities punctuate the stretch of Hadrian's Wall between Corbridge and Housesteads. There is a short stretch of wall which includes a well-preserved tower at Brunton (922698), while just across the North Tyne is the cavalry fort of Chesters where the riverside bath house is particularly evocative of the way in which the Roman lifestyle was transplanted into Britain. If you look across the river, you see the ruined abutments of the Roman bridge. About three miles further along the wall in the direction of Housesteads at Carrawbrough or Brocolitia are the ruined earthen ramparts of a fort and, just

outside the fort, the remains of a Mithras temple with a trio of altars. The one depicting Mithras has the halo pierced to allow a light to radiate from behind.

Several fine stretches of the wall can be explored to the W of Housesteads and (from a parking place around 754676) you can walk westwards over Winshields Crags or eastwards over the steep crest of Peel Crags and onwards via Hotbank Crags and Cuddy's Crags to Housesteads, a distance of about 5 miles.

Parts of the wall are owned by the National Trust while other parts are in the care of the Department of the Environment.

Corstopitum: the outlines of the Roman supply base are clearly visible

CORBRIDGE

The Roman supply base of Corstopitum lay $\frac{1}{2}$ mile to the W of the modern town of Corbridge and there is a small museum and the remains of granaries and military compounds: these are in the care of the DoE. One of the interesting sites in this border town is the Vicar's Pele of about 1300, a small defensive tower built to protect the vicar during Scottish raids and situated in the churchyard beside the market square. Two old bottle kilns from a 19th century pottery are preserved in Milkwell Lane.

Location Corbridge lies on the A68 and just to the S of the A69, 4 miles E of Hexham.

OPPOSITE *Hadrian's Wall running from Hotbank Crag over Cuddy's Crag – one of the most photographed vistas of the Roman Wall*

ABOVE *The Roman bath at Chesters fort, one of the least ruinous assemblages of Roman masonry in Britain*

The Roman Road on Wheeldale Moor

(North Yorkshire)

Roads probably comprised the most valuable legacy of Roman imperial rule, for while many of the Roman towns decayed or became deserted in the course of the Dark Ages, many Roman routes endured. Although they were seldom maintained in any really purposeful manner, the roads of Roman England provided a high proportion of the main arteries of the medieval realm. It was probably not until the Turnpike era of the eighteenth and nineteenth centuries that roads which were the equals or superiors of the Roman routeways were built in England.

Roman roads survive in many different guises. Some live on as modern trunk roads like the A4; others exist as they did in Roman times as difficult mountain trackways; High Street in the Lake District is an example. Many straight sections of country lanes and minor roads represent the disembodied fragments of an old Roman route, while in a few places one can see the original Roman surface or foundations of a stretch of road exposed. In this rather exclusive latter category, the two best examples in England are found in rough moorland settings, striding across Blackstone Edge in Lancashire near Little-

borough and over the swells of Wheeldale Moor in the North York Moors National Park.

Like all other roads, the Roman roads varied according to the local terrain and the amount of traffic which the planners anticipated. Some of them were insignificant winding country tracks which were quite indistinguishable from the native lanes and byways. Not all Roman roads were uncompromisingly straight, one could not ignore hills, marshes and inviting bridging points, and the road on Wheeldale Moor clearly sweeps and weaves a little to adopt the most practical line. On the whole, the higher grades of road were very well constructed, with legionaries providing the labour. Normally drains were cut on either side of the intended line leaving the space between as a central embankment or 'agger' upon which a foundation of stones was laid.

On Wheeldale Moor, one sees the Roman road foundations exposed by erosion. No cart could now travel very far upon this road without having its axles or wheel rims smashed as it rumbled over the jagged boulders. When the road was in use, however, this surface would almost certainly have been blanketed by a carpet of rammed sand or gravel. Centuries of exposure to frost and rain have resulted in the flushing-away of this surface, revealing the agger-making materials.

At the end of the first century AD, several military camps which could

have been used as training areas for the York-based legion were constructed upon the edge of the North York Moors quite close to the Wheeldale road but the routeway does not seem to date from this phase of imperial rule. For many years after the invasion, the Roman grip on the north was insecure and there were major northern rebellions in AD 117 and AD 119. Thereafter, Roman control was strengthened and for most of the second, third and fourth centuries the communities of the North York Moors experienced some prosperity.

Towns were established at Malton, Catterick and Northallerton and, in the latter part of the Roman period, even villas (which one normally associates with the most productive areas of lowland commercial farming) were introduced in situations which enjoyed good access to markets via a nearby waggon-worthy road. The indigenous peoples, members of the hitherto turbulent and unreliable Brigantes tribe, became subdued and settled farmers, but the far north remained unvanquished and threatening while, in due course, Saxons from the continental seaboard profited both by raiding the Roman territories and by serving the undermanned legions as mercenaries.

In the fourth century, the threats from the northern Picts, from the Scots of Ireland and the Saxon sea raiders increased. In the latter third of the century, a chain of fortified look-out posts was established along the Yorkshire

coast to provide warnings of sea-borne Pictish raids. These signalling stations may have used beacons or smoke to communicate their warnings but it is not certain whether they were used to pass messages down the coast, perhaps via great shore forts like Burgh Castle* to the fleet patrolling the Channel, or whether they were part of a more local communication system which was intended as an early warning system for the inland towns and villas.

In any event, life within the small garrisons at these stations will have been lonely and tedious except for the ever-present threat of ambush and extermination when an enemy fleet emerged from the coastal mists. Despite its leading position in terms of preservation, it is doubtful whether the Wheeldale Moor example was ever considered to be a leading routeway. It seems to have been built at a late stage in the Roman occupation to serve as a link between the town at Malton and the east coast signalling stations.

The road is in the care of the Department of the Environment.

Phototips Although the moorland setting is attractive, particularly in the late summer when the heather is in flower, the road is not an easy subject. Unless the photographer is able to inject an element of drama into the shot, there is a risk that the road will emerge as a rather nondescript cart track! In order to obtain a feeling of depth and recession, adopt a low viewpoint which will exaggerate the tapering perspective as the road narrows towards the skyline. A wide-angle lens will provide great depth of focus so that the horizon and the foreground pebbles, boulders and invading plants are all in focus. An orange or even a red filter can be used in black-and-white work to darken a blue sky and emphasise any cloud patterns.

Location On the southern fringes of the North York Moors about 8 miles N of Pickering. From Pickering, take the minor road running N through Newton-

Only sheep and ramblers now pass along the Roman road on Wheeldale Moor

---

on-Rawcliffe. After Newton, this road swings WNW and about 1 mile beyond the village, turn off right on the minor road which runs N through Stape hamlet. A little after Stape, this road deteriorates and one fears that it will come to a halt or disappear in a puff of dust. The track is definitely of sub-Roman quality, but one can drive along it. Within a couple of miles of Stape, one sees the Roman road marked by a white signpost on the right beside a rise in the track; one may park here.

The Roman road is seen intersecting the modern track at a sharp angle. The most clearly exposed section lies to the E of the modern track, but the road can be followed for some distance in either direction and it provides a good excuse for a ramble across the bleak and windswept moorland landscape.

ROUND AND ABOUT

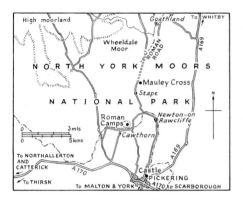

PICKERING CASTLE

A motte and bailey castle was built at Pickering following the Norman Conquest, quite possibly at the time of the evil butchery known as the 'Harrying of the North' of 1069–70, when vast tracts of northern England were depopulated. Between 1180 and 1236, the timber palisades which surrounded the motte and the bailey were replaced by walls of stone to create a castle of a type known as a 'shell keep'.

The later history of the castle was not particularly illustrious, for when the

Pickering Castle survived a demolition threat in 1652 and is now cared for by the DoE

invading Scottish army of Robert the Bruce advanced after burning Ripon to threaten Pickering in 1322, the townsfolk were reduced to bribing the Scots to spare the town and castle. The following year, Edward II stayed at Pickering and the castle defences were strengthened. The stockade guarding the outer ward was replaced by a stone wall with three rectangular towers; more towers may have been planned but never built since several stretches of the wall could not be reached by the bows and arrows fired from the three towers.

By the middle of the 17th century, the castle was in ruins and, in 1652, it was sold as a source of stone and scrap for just £200, but fortunately the demolition work never took place. It is now in the care of the DoE.

Location Close to the town centre of Pickering.

CAWTHORN ROMAN CAMPS

The four earthworks at Cawthorn seem to be the remains of camps which date from around AD 100. They are thought to have been dug as part of a military training exercise, probably by the legionaries based in York.

Location The camps lie about 4 miles N and NNW of Pickering, 1½ miles E of Cropton village within a sharp dog-leg on the minor road between Cropton and Newton.

The mysterious Mauley Cross

THE MAULEY CROSS

This tall stone roadside cross is somewhat mysterious; it could be a Christian replacement either for a pagan stone or for a Roman milestone as it stands beside a section of minor Roman road which may have been abandoned in the 2nd century.

Location About 3–4 miles NNE of Stape close to a track which forks off to the NE from the route leading to the Wheeldale Moor Roman road.

Note There are a number of other sites described in this book from North Yorkshire: Byland Abbey and the lost village excavations at Wharram Percy, together with their subsidiary sites. *See* the index for page references.

Dun Carloway Broch

(Isle of Lewis, Western Isles)

The hollow-walled cylindrical defensive towers known as 'brochs' are amongst the most distinctive of the Scottish monuments—and also among the most mysterious. Brochs seem to have been constructed in very large numbers in the years around 100 BC throughout the northern and western Highlands and Islands of Scotland and in ways which reveal a considerable standardisation of design and remarkable technical skill in the craft of drystone walling. At least five-hundred of these towers must have been built, yet within three or four centuries the broch seems to have become obsolete.

The causes which prompted this feverish fortification of mainly remote coastal localities have never been thoroughly explained, although recently Scottish archaeologists such as Euan MacKie have argued that the neatness and sophistication of broch construction suggests that they are the handiwork of professional masons rather than the products of local ingenuity.

The architectural expertise is particularly evident in the style of the wall structures and the adoption of hollow walls allowed towers to be built which were strong and lofty but not prone to collapse under the weight of the stone-work. The inner and outer walls were bonded together by horizontal stone slabs which sectioned the hollow space into a series of cells or chambers which were occupied or used for storage, while a stairway spiralled clockwise up through the walls, presumably reaching a parapet which surrounded some form of roof.

The topmost details of the broch are uncertain because none of the surviving brochs still stand to their original heights. The tallest example is the unusually large broch on the Shetland island of Mousa which is now about 42 ft high and may originally have been around 50 ft tall.

Mousa broch, however, is in a rather inaccessible location but the visitor to Lewis in the Outer Hebrides should not fail to visit the Dun Carloway Broch where the skilful construction of the hollow walls and wall cells is particularly well displayed. The broch lies about half a mile from the southern shore of Carloway sea loch overlooking Doune Carloway hamlet in a soulful but beautiful landscape of glaciated hills and small glacial lakes. Around 2,000 years ago, it must have been a local refuge for the peasant community which fished and farmed around Loch Carloway but it will not have served a large area for the ruins of another broch can be seen by the shores of Loch an Dùna which is only about six miles to the ENE.

We can still only guess at the nature of the threat which launched a frenzy of fort building amongst the communities of the Highlands. For whatever it may be worth, my own guess is that seaborne expeditions to capture victims for the insatiable Roman slave market may have been the spur. Work on the Orkney

OPPOSITE *The jagged ruins of Dun Carloway broch, jutting like a broken tooth from the bleak Lewis landscape*

(Right) *A section of the interior stone staircase at Dun Carloway broch, built within the hollow walls*

107

Dun Carloway broch in its lonely, but incredibly beautiful Lewis setting

brochs is also raising questions as to whether the broch should be seen as an isolated tower which served as a refuge for the surrounding peasant community or whether many brochs dominated surrounding villages, perhaps in the way that a Norman motte and bailey castle glowered over a subservient community? Riddles and questions such as these certainly add extra spice to a subject which is already packed with interest.

Phototips Jutting from a low spur like a hollow broken tooth, the broch is a fine subject in itself, but the most attractive photograph may be one which shows the ruined tower in its bleakly beautiful setting. The hillslope behind the broch provides good vantage points for photographs using a shortish telephoto lens (around 80–135 mm for 35 mm photography). Unfortunately, there is every chance that the weather will be unfriendly with rolling storm clouds or sheets of mist sweeping in from the Atlantic. In such conditions, try to underline rather than mask the atmospheric state of play, using an orange filter to emphasise clouds in black-and-white work.

Colour presents more problems but I have developed a trick to brighten and dramatise such scenes which serious amateur photographers might like to borrow. It involves using a graduated tobacco filter inverted to give an amber glow to dead grass and rock tones and a graduated violet filter to provide interesting sky tones.

Location (189412) Near the W coast of Lewis, 16 miles WNW of Stornoway. Just off the A858 Callandish–Doune Carloway road, 1 mile SW of Doune Carloway, signposted with a car parking space and the rare luxury of toilets. The site is in the care of the Scottish Development Department.

ROUND AND ABOUT

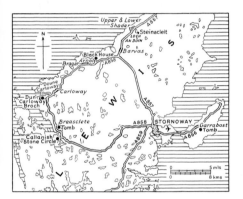

STEINACLEIT CHAMBERED TOMB

Not very much remains of the Steinacleit chambered tomb. Three stone slabs of the burial chamber protrude through the rubble of the ruined cairn.

Location (396540) The tomb lies at a short distance from a track which leaves the A857 between Upper Shader and Lower Shader hamlets.

THE ARNOL BLACKHOUSE

Until very recently, the farming and crofting population of these islands lived in blackhouses which had some prehistoric features and other features shared with the long-houses of medieval English peasants. Many can be seen in ruins, or superseded by the rendered and whitewashed modern 'white houses'. The walls had an inner and outer skin of stones and a central core of peat. The low and rounded roof of thatch did not overlap the walls but shed its water into the core, helping to improve insulation by moistening the peat. The interior was partitioned in long-house fashion to provide living quarters on one side and a byre on the other. A barn resembling a miniature blackhouse was often built against one of the long sides of the main house.

At Arnol, a blackhouse which dates from about 1875 has been lovingly restored to recreate its nearly original form (a land mine explosion in 1940 damaged part of the building and the barn was then shortened); it is in the care of the SDD. Although the design is surely archaic, many a ruined *tigh dubh* or blackhouse is a relative youngster and the *tigh geal* or whitehouse only began its advance in the 1850s. The Arnol blackhouse was still a home in the 1960s.

Location Beside a short lane leading N from Arnol village which is the next village E of Bragar along the A858.

Note Callanish Stone Circle is not far away; *see* the index for page reference.

Part of the interior of the Arnol Blackhouse on Lewis, showing the drystone walling in the peat-filled walls

Two Native Settlements in North Wales

(Gwynedd)

The imposition of Roman rule did not immediately transform the lives of most indigenous communities in Britain. With the passage of time and the consolidation of control, however, the side effects of the new imperialism were considerable.

Despite the occasional uprising and the peripheral skirmishes, life for many peasant farming communities became more secure and the control of the province, the improving trade and transport conditions and the expanding urban and garrison markets for food encouraged the growth of a more productive and commercial agricultural industry. Native aristocrats joined with privileged outsiders in establishing large commercial farms or villas in many of the more favourable farming locations. In the upland margins, the changes may have been less forceful, with the survival of traditional practices and institutions. In Wales, the Pennines and the south west, however, the old order was still affected by the Roman policing patrols, the mushrooming mining industries and the growth of commerce.

In the north-west of Wales, the two rather contrasting native settlements of Tre'r Ceiri and Din Lligwy are very well preserved and they help to illuminate life on the Welsh margins of the Roman Empire. The Roman Conquest of Wales was part of a second phase of campaigning in Britain in the years AD 74 and 78. Wales was divided between two military commands based on the great fortresses of Chester and Caerleon; subsidiary forts were established and roads were built to link them.

Despite the Roman presence in the area, however, it is clear that many communities were allowed to keep their defences and Tre'r Ceiri is uncompromisingly fortified. The settlement pre-dated the Roman Conquest but whether it should be termed a hillfort, a hill town or a defended village is debatable. Round huts were clustered in considerable numbers within a stone rampart which followed the hilltop contours.

The effect of the changes which were made during the Roman occupation is interesting. A new rampart was built to enclose an additional area of the hilltop to the north-west, new stone dwellings were erected to swell the number of huts

Tre'r Ceiri hillfort. OPPOSITE *A scatter of stones marks the site of a group of dwellings, with circular patterns of debris marking the position of individual houses.* (Right) *Looking down on the hillfort from a nearby summit*

to about one-hundred-and-fifty while many of the old ones were modified and rebuilt to roughly rectangular plans. It seems plain that the British peasants were copying the Roman preference for rectangular buildings.

The settlement is about 1800 ft above sea level and sections of stone rampart walling still stand over 12 ft tall. One can only conclude that whatever the effects of Roman influences and policing policies on the area, the peasants were still prepared to accept the hardships of hilltop life and considered their defences to be valuable. At the same time, the tribesmen of Tre'r Ceiri can not have constituted any threat to the Romans or we can be sure that the troops would have stormed their ramparts and evacuated the hillfort.

Din Lligwy on Anglesey was a much smaller settlement. The architectural uncertainties which Roman rule had created are reflected in the designs of the boulder-walled buildings, for there are two great round huts which seem to have served as dwellings and other rectangular stone buildings of which two at least were used as iron smelting workshops. Perhaps Din Lligwy represents an exercise in native entrepreneurship, with the iron produced being sold to Roman military blacksmiths or merchants?

During the occupation, the settlement was protected by the fortress of Segontium which guarded the Menai Strait. The fort was evacuated around AD 385 and it seems to have been about this time that the local chieftain was forced to consider his own defence and the huts were surrounded by a pentagonal stone wall which contrasts with the irregular

ABOVE and below: *Some of the boulder-walled buildings at the Din Lligwy settlement on Anglesey may have served as dwellings or even as iron-smelting workshops*

curves of traditional native ramparts. The threat came from Ireland but we do not know the fate of the Din Lligwy folk.

Although they contrast in terms of size, setting and in the ways that their people earned a livelihood, Tre'r Ceiri and Din Lligwy are amongst the best-preserved of the native settlements of Roman Britain and both can be visited in the course of a day: the former is owned by the National Trust and the latter is in the care of the Department of the Environment. The walk to Tre'r Ceiri is a long and ultimately rather steep walk but one is rewarded with wonderful views of the Lleyn peninsula. Din Lligwy is much more accessible and the walk from the roadside parking place across

The remains of 30 people were found in the Din Lligwy burial chamber in 1908

pasture, past a ruined church and then through trees imparts a flavour of mystery which reminds me of passages from *The Lord of the Rings*.

Directly by the roadside close to the ancient village is a low burial chamber of the Late Neolithic and Earlier Bronze Age periods. When the tomb was opened in 1908, the remains of thirty people were found beneath the gigantic cap.

Phototips The shattered peaks in the Tre'r Ceiri area might have been made for the photographer. Here, as with other prehistoric settlements, one must not fall between two stools by trying to combine panoramas and shots of individual huts. The best general view of the settlement can be obtained with a telephoto lens, looking down from the *next* mountain top (the one which is closest to the car park) but it is a very stiff

climb and the boulders which litter the summit are separated by deep gaps which are often masked by vegetation.

Din Lligwy offers some attractive studies including close-up views of the tortured, lichen-blotched ancient boulders which were used to build the huts and gateposts. A good shot of the largest round hut can be gained from opposite its entrance or from the rampart behind.

Locations For Tre'r Ceiri (373446), leave the A499 for the B4417 between Pwllheli and Clynnog-fawr. In Llithfaen village centre, take the track which leads N towards the cliff-top car park; the final 1 mile is walked. Do not climb the mountain which looms closest to the car park; Tre'r Ceiri lies on the one further back and to its right as you face it.

Din Lligwy (496862) lies between the A5025 and Moelfre village on Anglesey.

ROUND AND ABOUT

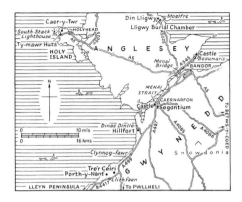

The great medieval castle of Caernarfon stands beside the Menai Strait about midway between the two villages already described, but let me introduce some less familiar relics.

PORTH-Y-NANT

A quarrying village which was deserted in the years following the Second World War. The terraced quarryworkers' cottages, the houses of the foreman and manager and the chapel still stand in the cliff-foot landscape of granite quarrying. This is one of the most magical places that I know of and currently attempts by

Some of the ruined houses at Porth-y-Nant which are currently undergoing restoration by the Nant Gwythryn Trust

The chapel at Porth-y-Nant – the scene of a local controversy in former times because services were given in English rather than in Welsh

the Nant Gwythryn Trust are being made to renovate the village as a centre dedicated to the revitalisation of the Welsh language.

Location From the same car park as used for Tre'r Ceiri, follow the track which winds down the cliff face. The path is quite safe but the return journey is exhausting.

DINAS DINLLE

A coastal hillfort of the Late and Roman Iron Age. The double ramparts were dug in a mound of glacial debris and the sea has eaten into one side of the fort so that the truncated ramparts overhang the edge of the cliff. There are fine views of Snowdonia in the other direction.

Location (437563) About 6 miles SSW

A view over the ramparts of the Late and Roman Iron Age coastal hillfort of Dinas Dinlle, looking towards the distant peaks of Snowdonia

of Caernarfon and signposted from the A499. The hillfort is very close to the rather unexciting little resort of Dinas Dinlle where there is a car park.

TY-MAWR HUT GROUP

Marked on some maps as Cytiau'r Gwyddelod, some fifty round and sub-rectangular huts straggled up the slopes of Holyhead Mountain and around twenty can still be seen amongst the bracken. This was thought to be a Romano-British village and, indeed, a Roman hoard was found in one of the dwellings. Excavations currently in hand, however, provisionally suggest a much more exciting prospect, for one of the excavated huts has yielded a Late Neolithic–Early Bronze Age date and if future work supports this date, then this is a remarkably well-preserved village site dating from a period which had previously offered very little in the way of settlement remains. Overlooking the huts from the nearby summit are the Iron Age stone ramparts which linked up a series of jagged natural outcrops to form the defenses of Caer-y-Twr hillfort. The site is owned by the National Trust.

Location (212820) On Holy Island, 2 miles W of Holyhead and a short distance ESE of South Stack lighthouse. The huts are just above the roadside and a car park is available.

One of the ruined farmsteads on Holyhead Mountain, where the settlement is now thought to belong to the Early Bronze Age

BEAUMARIS CASTLE

Regarded by many as the most perfect of the British medieval castles, Beaumaris is also the best-preserved example of a 'concentric castle'. The level site demanded few concessions to terrain and so Master James of St George, the military architect employed by Edward I, was able to produce a geometrical design based on a rectangular and heavily fortified enclosing ward, with a tide-filled moat providing the outer line of defence.

The work was begun in 1295 and in the course of the first five years of work, the equivalent of about £6 million was

spent. The ultimate cost of the castle was close to about £10 million in modern values, although the work was never finished and the towers never raised to their intended height. While, like Caernarfon Castle, Beaumaris helped to guard the Menai Strait, it was never put to the test of siege.

Location On Holy Island, about 4 miles NE of the Menai Bridge on A545.

A less familiar view of Beaumaris Castle: the scene from the rear of the castle was photographed in June with the yellow water flags in bloom

Note If you are driving down to south-west or south Wales, you will pass Harlech having left the sites described above; *see* the index for the page reference.

Burgh Castle: A Saxon Shore Fort

(Norfolk)

The collapse of Roman power in Britain is swathed in mysteries and we do not know whether the legions withdrew from the province in the years around 410, or whether they stayed and were dissolved in the tides of mercenary warfare, Saxon settlement and factional fighting which heralded the Dark Ages. In a sense, the beginning of the end for Roman Britain came in the latter part of the third century, with the escalation of 'barbarian' coastal raiding. The seriousness of this problem was recognised in the years 287–96 with the creation of a system of great shore forts which was designed to protect the coast of south-eastern England against the Saxon threat. In due course, the shore forts formed a separate command under the Count of the Saxon Shore.

The forts studded the coast from the Wash to the Solent; four defended the shores of East Anglia and one of the East Anglian forts, Burgh Castle near the modern town of Great Yarmouth, ranks with the other well-preserved survivors at Richborough in Kent and Portchester near Portsmouth. In most cases, the forts were sited to guard the mouth of a natural estuary in which an attached naval unit could anchor. In this way, Burgh Castle, known to the Romans as Gariannonum, guarded the Waveney estuary which will then have been more extensive than the present river.

The fort is very impressive. It is built to a rectangular plan with its eastern and western walls some 640 ft in length, and those on the north and south 300 ft long. Only the west wall, which overlooked the river, has disappeared while excavations have shown that there was a quay at the foot of the riverside bluff on which the fort stood. The remaining walls stand around 15 ft high and almost preserve their original appearance. They are built in a manner which was commonly adopted in the southern and eastern chalklands, with courses of flints embedded in mortar alternating with narrow courses of red tile-like Roman bricks. The gathering together of the enormous quantities of flints necessary to build the walls must have been a massive undertaking in its own right.

By inspecting the construction of the walls, we can learn a little about the building operation. In certain places, one can see that there are irregular joins between sections of the brick-bonding courses and so it is clear that different

OPPOSITE and right: *The Roman walls and a corner turret at Burgh Castle, a Saxon shore fort. Such turrets were often added to existing walls to accommodate the artillery weapons of the day*

A view of the Broads from Burgh Castle which is easily reached from the water

lengths of wall were built by different gangs. The solid semicircular bastions which stand at the corners and at intervals along the walls and which served as platforms for artillery pieces like the boulder-hurling *ballista* were apparently not a feature of the original plan. The walls were about half their intended height when the bastions were introduced for they are only bonded into the masonry above heights of about 8 ft.

Not a great deal is known about the subsequent history of the great fort but it seems that around the time of imperial collapse in Britain, the fort housed a force of Yugoslavian cavalry. It is hard to imagine what these Mediterraneans thought of their posting to a coast which was blasted by north-eastern winds and which formed one of the most perilous frontiers of a strife-torn province. In the course of the Dark Ages, the fort must have been abandoned while its setting surrendered to advancing woodland.

In due course, however, around 630, the interior of the dead fortress was chosen by the Irish missionary St Fursey as the site for a monastery. In his history of the English church and people, the Saxon chronicler Bede relates that 'This monastery was pleasantly situated in some woods close to the sea, within the area of a fortification that the English call Cnobheresburg, meaning

Cnobhere's Town. Subsequently, Anna, king of the province, and his nobles endowed the house with finer buildings and gifts.' Whether there was already a settlement here may be questioned, because a more exact translation of *burg* is 'fortification'. St Fursey's foundation endured into the ninth century and the final stage in the fortification of Burgh Castle is represented by an earthen motte and bailey castle which was constructed in the south-west corner after the Norman Conquest and which was finally obliterated in 1839.

The castle is in the care of the Department of the Environment.

Phototips The castle is a good subject for black-and-white photography but, with the contrasts between the grey and white flint work and the red Roman bricks, the big East Anglian skies and the blues and greens of the Broads below, it is an excellent colour subject as well. Direct frontal views of the walls are unlikely to succeed and when one has retreated far enough to allow the entire length of a stretch of wall to fit within the viewfinder frame, the walls will only appear as a narrow ribbon of masonry juxtaposed between the sky and the farmland. Some of the best shots are obtained by shooting at an angle to one

of the corner bastions—the south-eastern bastion in particular, although one may have to wait a short while for a gap in the intermittent pedestrian tourist traffic. The contrasting textures of the courses of flint and brick can make interesting close-up studies.

Location About 4 miles SW of Great Yarmouth and signposted from minor roads running from the A12 or A143 Beccles road. Car parking is available near Burgh Castle church and the final $\frac{1}{4}$-mile of the trip is made by foot. The fort can also be reached by boat from the R. Waveney.

ROUND AND ABOUT

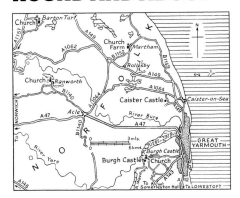

Edward the Confessor (1042–66).

At some stage, the upper part of the tower must have blown down for there are differences in the flint work above 16 ft while a brick top was added about 1663 to house a tenor bell. The nave and chancel, whose walls are interspersed with Roman bricks robbed from the nearby castle, reveal several phases of medieval rebuilding and the north aisle

is Victorian. It was in the middle of the last century that the thatch roof was replaced by one of Horsham stone tiles from Sussex—an unusual innovation in this part of the world but doubtless encouraged by the river access to the coastal shipping lanes. The fine Lion Font is more typically East Anglian, octagonal in form with shield-bearing lions and angels on alternate faces. It dates from the 14th century.

Location The church is passed by all pedestrians *en route* to the castle.

BURGH CASTLE CHURCH

The parish church of St. Peter and St. Paul at Burgh Castle hamlet is a gem. The round tower is of a type which is hardly ever seen outside East Anglia and which seems to be a response to the problems of building corners in flint and so flint towers are either round or have imported stones forming the quoins. Some of these towers are Saxon, others Norman; in this case, it is not easy to tell, but Domesday Book of 1086 shows that a church stood here in the reign of

Burgh Castle church has one of the distinctive flint round towers which are common in the region but rarely seen outside East Anglia

CHURCH FARM, MARTHAM

This working agricultural museum re-creates country life in the second half of the 19th century, before farm mechanisation obliterated the East Anglian countryside.

Location 9 miles N of Great Yarmouth, leaving the A149 at Rollesby.

Note Both Caister Castle (Norfolk) and Somerleyton House (Suffolk) are in the neighbourhood; *see* the index for page references.

119

4 THE ROAD TO CHRISTIANITY

In the early years of the fifth century, Roman power in Britain collapsed. The former province of the Empire was precipitated into a period which is aptly known as the Dark Ages, and the history of these centuries is almost as shadowy and difficult to recreate as that of the Iron Age. In Ireland and Wales, Christianity survived the traumas, while the re-establishment of civilisation in the English lands owed much to the conversion of the pagan Saxon overlords.

We do not know whether all the Roman legions were withdrawn from Britain in the years around 410, or whether they were absorbed into the ranks of indigenous warlords, but we now realise that more features of Roman life endured in the fifth century than was previously thought. The later decades of Roman rule had been punctuated by barbarian raids and invasions by Scots, Picts, Angles and Saxons. As we shall see, the authorities sought to buttress the over-stretched legionary armies by recruiting mercenary forces of various kinds which included significant numbers of Saxon warriors. Before the Roman collapse, retired Saxon mercenaries are known to have established themselves both in towns and in rural communities. The policy of recruiting Saxons to defend the former Roman province against raids by their kinsmen continued during the fifth century when other Saxon immigrants began to arrive as agricultural settlers.

There was no single or concerted Saxon invasion of England but, in the course of time, some form of Saxon ascendancy was established. There will have been various bloody confrontations between the forces of Saxon and native overlords, but it is hard to accept the traditional view that the native British were either massacred or driven into the rocky confines of Wales and Cornwall. The new settlers could not have arrived in sufficient numbers to overwhelm the population of what had been a highly productive, organised and well-peopled province. In places where the Saxon intrusion was large and forceful, native British communities may have been segregated and enslaved, but in many others Saxons may only have formed a tiny élite.

Contrary to popular belief, the Saxon settlers did not achieve a transformation of the British landscape, carpeting the countryside with their open strip fields and sprinkling the landscape with their villages where no villages had previously existed. This happened later and, during the early centuries of the Saxon ascendancy, the immigrants seem to have used the same fields and patterns of farmstead, hamlet and village settlement as were already established. Neither do the Saxons seem to have accomplished the great feats of woodland clearance which have been credited to them. Instead, it seems that they inherited a countryside that was scarcely more wooded than that of today but which became, in places, neglected and overgrown. It appears that even by the Norman Conquest, England supported less people than it had in Iron Age and Roman times. One must wonder whether this lapse into partial decay can be wholly explained by reference to the political disruptions and skirmishes which followed the Roman collapse? There were probably episodes of climatic deterioration and certainly the possibility of severe if scarcely documented outbreaks of plague cannot be ruled out.

Christianity probably gained a precarious toe-hold in the Roman province during the third century and by very early in the fourth century, St. Alban became the first British martyr. During the fourth century, Christianity gained official acceptance within the Roman Empire and the first overt Christian churches will have been built in Britain, partly superseding the chambers in private dwellings which had been used for less open forms of worship. The periodic changes in imperial religious policies, persecutions of Christians and the survival of pagan Celtic and Roman cults make it seem unlikely that Christianity was strongly entrenched in the Roman province. When power passed to pagan Saxon overlords, Christianity in England will have receded, but it is doubtful that it was completely extinguished.

In Ireland, a form of Celtic and monastic Catholicism created the basis for a remarkable early Christian civilisation which provided much of the inspiration for European monasticism, while in Wales, communities of Christian monks preserved the vitality of their religion when England subsided into pagan rule. The reconversion of England was not pursued with any vigour by its Christian Celtic neighbours but was achieved from Rome. In 597, Augustine and a small band of monks landed in Kent where Aethelberht the King was soon converted and the remaining pagan kingdoms adopted the Christian faith in the course of the seventh century.

In the centuries following the conversion a new indigenous civilisation arose. Whatever the mysteries concerning the true nature of the Saxon conquest, the Saxon language emerged as the language of England, albeit with several distinctive regional dialects. Around the ninth century, husbandry seems to have become more efficient with the establishment of open field strip farming probably providing an important stimulus to the creation of permanent village settlements. A series of provincial kingdoms had emerged from the chaos of civil strife and Saxon settlement and, by processes of conquest, intrigue and diplomacy, they gradually became welded together into a single realm which was generally dominated by the rulers of the powerful Wessex dynasty.

The progress towards Christian civilisation and English unity was severely afflicted in the final centuries of Saxon rule, however, by the debilitating effects of Danish invasion and raiding. The question of the Danish presence in strength in England raises similar problems to those which we associate with the Saxon rule. For while Danes and Norsemen donated many dialect words and place-names to the areas of eastern and northern England where they settled, they have left few distinctive archaeological monuments and many of the materials excavated from their settlement sites have a markedly Saxon appearance.

Of the surviving monuments to the Dark Ages, the overwhelming majority—including crosses, inscribed stones, churches and church fragments—are associated with Christianity. Most of the older churches appear to have been provided by nobles and some of the early minster churches seem to have been sited in royal estates, while a substantial number of churches appear to be associated with older pagan sites.

Sadly, the inclusion of the selected early Christian monuments which follow has meant that other delightful and intriguing monuments have had to be left out—like the wonderful assemblage of crosses and inscribed stones at Nevern near Fishguard, or the group of Saxon crosses erected in the market place at Sandbach in Cheshire.

Note: See Appendix II for other sites from the Age of Christianity.

The Pagan Saxon Village

(Suffolk)

Saxon settlers appeared in Britain before the collapse of Roman power. Many were welcomed as mercenary troops recruited to defend the province against pirate raids by their kinsfolk and others. Some settled in towns like Cambridge where they intermarried with the Brit-

West Stow: this reconstructed Saxon village is built on the original site. Photograph on pp 120–1: Offa's Dyke

ish. The recruiting of Saxon mercenaries seems to have continued after the Roman collapse, when other Angles, Saxons and Jutes left their homes on the north-western fringes of the continent to settle in England. In places, there may have been bloody struggles to wrest territory from the native British while, in others, the colonisation was peaceful.

The details are blurred, but out of the chaos, internecine power struggles and intrigues which heralded the Dark Ages, kingdoms ruled by men with Saxon names emerged, and gradually a simplified form of the Anglo-Saxon Germanic language supplanted Celtic and Latin tongues. The amount of contemporary literature is small and was written in the main by Christian monks whose monasteries and churches endured in the west. The Saxon settlers were pagan outsiders and so the violence of their rise to supremacy was probably exaggerated.

At West Stow, a very early example of a Saxon village was discovered and it differed from the already described Celtic or British settlements in many ways. The huts were rectangular rather than round and their floors seemed to be hollows scooped into the ground. The most obvious difference was the absence of any defences. British communities are known to have been living near to West Stow but there is no evidence of conflict, but rather, of friendly contacts. This was a settlement of mixed farmers and 'cottage industries' rather than a military encampment.

It is one of the most fascinating archaeological and reconstruction sites to visit—although its initial prospects were less glamorous for the site was earmarked as a rubbish dump. Local government amalgamation provided a superior dump and the local authorities conceived the area as an excellent setting for a country park—a reconstruction of a number of huts from the excavated Saxon village forms its crowning glory.

Two types of dwellings referred to as

125

'huts' and 'halls' have been reconstructed while there is also a reconstruction of the traditional perception of a tent-shaped Saxon hut of the form known as *grubenhauser* (some experts refer to these as 'grub-huts' to the annoyance of other, more formal archaeologists!). All the huts have floor pits in the characteristic early-Saxon manner. The purpose of these sunken floors is rather puzzling, but the West Stow reconstructors believe that these floors must have been boarded over and, certainly, sunken floors would have surely become swampy and extremely uncomfortable were this not so.

Each hut is faithfully based upon the excavated evidence of the original dwelling upon which it stands. In contrast to the Iron Age huts like those reconstructed at Butser*, the walls are not made of earthfast posts with wattle and daub panels, but are built of split oak logs which are jointed together and stand upright. Six internal poles serve as supports for roofs of straw thatch carried on ash rafters and hazel wattle, and the excavations supported this interpretation.

In earlier years, the Saxon village had been regarded as a particularly squalid and uninviting place. However, the reconstructed dwellings are clearly perfectly serviceable and quite homely.

As I have already said regarding Butser*, reconstructions of this type not only provide a wealth of experimental archaeological information but they are also the most effective means of stimulating public interest in the heritage. No visitor to East Anglia who has the remotest interest in history should miss West Stow but I am often surprised by the numbers of East Anglians who are unaware of this spendid recreation which is run by the West Stow Saxon Village Trust. Since the project began in 1972, the number of huts has gradually grown and the director, Stanley West, and the site warden have had much voluntary help: as at Butser, there is a Friends society which organises special events and is open to all subscribers.

West Stow had a relatively long life for an early Saxon village; it had begun by at least AD 400 and endured until about 650—but none of its inhabitants could ever have imagined that after more than 1300 years of abandonment the settlement would be brought back to life.

Visitors to the Saxon village reconstruction should spare time to look at the attractive church which serves the modern village. It is built of flint in the Perpendicular style of the later medieval period and its size and peripheral pos-

BELOW One of the reconstructed dwellings at West Stow early-Saxon village showing the vertical plank walls and thatched roof. (Right) A reconstructed lathe inside a hut

ition suggest that, in the Middle Ages, the village was larger and more extensive.

Phototips The site offers many attractive angles; individual huts are quite simple subjects but, if you have a telephoto lens, it is worthwhile bringing as there are good views of the entire reconstruction from the approach footpath and from the edge of the trees which fringe the valley of the river Lark. The Scots pines nearby form an attractive backdrop of spiky silhouettes even though they are not 'authentic'.

Location About 5 miles NW of Bury St Edmunds; from the A45, take the A134 Thetford road which runs N from Bury and, shortly, left onto A1101 Mildenhall road through Hengrave. Then follow signposts to the right to West Stow. At modern West Stow village, take the minor road which runs westwards. A short terrace of cottages will soon be seen and the entrance to the Country Park is opposite. There is a large car park.

The size of West Stow church suggests the medieval village was larger than the modern one

ROUND AND ABOUT

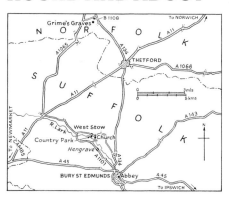

BURY ST EDMUNDS

The bustling market town has many important historical associations. When the East Anglian King Edmund was murdered by Danish raiders in 870, his remains were interred at the Saxon monastery which preceded the medieval Abbey. The destruction of the medieval foundation caused by the Dissolution and then the use of the ruins as a quarry for building materials by the townsfolk is comprehensive and so it is not easy to imagine the former grandeur of this important and affluent foundation.

The two great gateways, one Norman and the other of the 14th century, are the best preserved relics of the abbey. The Abbot's Bridge which spans the River Lark at the NE corner of the abbey park is a fine example of its kind and dates from the 13th and 14th centuries.

The town of Bury St Edmunds is notable for its remarkable grid-iron layout and the planning of the town took place in different stages. When the Abbey was founded in the 10th century, the main highway was diverted around its precincts and a long triangular market place was created by broadening the diverted road as it passed the abbey at Angel Hill. In due course, the Normans enlarged the town by building on some of the furlong blocks of Bury's West Field—and the shapes of the furlongs are still evident in the layout of the town. The French market was also created at this time; it is now known as Buttermarket and has been reduced in size by the encroachment of buildings.

The rather unsympathetically restored Norman building which stands beside the market is sometimes described as being the oldest domestic building in East Anglia, but it is probably neither and experts believe that it was a Jewish bank. It is now a museum.

The ruinous abbey: the loss of the east-facing stones reveals how rubble was used to form the inner core of the walls

This building which is now a museum was probably once a bank

Location Bury St Edmunds is close to the A45, between the towns of Ipswich and Newmarket.

GRIME'S GRAVES

The most important instrument in the making of the British countryside was the prehistoric stone axe. Axe-making was a specialised industry and a number of axe factory sites have been discovered. Various types of stone were used, including the tough volcanic rocks of the Langdale Pikes* in Cumbria. Because of a hardness which was combined with a readiness to flake and fracture when worked by an expert, flint was the most popular material.

Several Neolithic flint-mining sites are known and the most impressive is at Grime's Graves in Norfolk where major excavation has taken place since 1914. Here the miners rejected the uppermost bands of flint nodules in favour of the layer known as the 'floorstone'. Vertical shafts reached down as far as 40 ft to reach the floorstone, and radial horizontal galleries extended in all directions from the bases of the shafts. The quarried flints were then roughly shaped at the surface and exported over great distances. At Grime's Graves, the landscape is pock-marked by the remains of scores of shafts and littered with mounds of discarded flint flakes. The site is in the care of the Department of the Environment; there is an information centre and access is provided—via a steel ladder—to one of the excavated shafts. Protective head-gear is provided.

Location (817898) About 7 miles NW of Thetford, and the minor road and access track are signposted from the A134 and the B1108. Car parking is available.

Note Lavenham in Suffolk and Castle Hedingham in Essex are both quite close to the sites just described; *see* the index for page references.

One of the flint-mining galleries at Grime's Graves, the scene of great activity in Neolithic times

The Pictish Stones of North-East Scotland

In the years when Ireland and England were developing their own Christian traditions, the Picts of northern Scotland were regarded as a strange people, and were the subject of several outlandish legends. We still know remarkably little about these descendants of the tribesmen who had poured south to raid the Roman province, and the enigma of the Picts is coloured and intensified by their most obvious epitaphs: carved stones which are decorated by mysterious but elaborate symbols.

Around 250 of these stones survive and they seem to belong to three periods which chart the conversion of the Pictish kingdoms to Christianity. First, and presumably the oldest, there are the boulders and rough slabs which contain only pagan carvings; second, there are slabs which display both pagan symbols and the cross which appear to portray an intermediate stage in the conversion of the Pictish lands while, third, there are the slabs which contain the cross alone and reflect the ultimate success of the Christian missions.

The pagan symbols come in a variety of forms. There are fluent representations of real animals like the eagle, wolf, boar, bull or salmon; mythical animals like the so-called 'Pictish beast', which seems half-elephant and half-dolphin; portraits of domestic items, the

mirror and comb. Finally, there are the numerous wierd, undeciphered symbols; commonly-used motifs include the 'spectacle and Z-rod' or the 'double disc and Z-rod', the 'crescent and V-rod' and the 'serpent and Z-rod'. These are not simple decorative geometrical devices, but intricate and sophisticated designs which surely conveyed a message.

We neither know the function of the Pictish stones, nor the code of the symbols. If the stones are tombstones, it is surprising that they are hardly ever associated with burials and it could be that they are territorial markers. Some stones have a single animal symbol and it has been suggested that these are tribal emblems. More normally, the stones have an array of several symbols, and one may wonder if these groups contain a message like the stacked symbols on Red Indian totem poles. In fact, we are scarcely any closer to cracking the Pictish code than we were when attempts began almost a century ago.

The Pictish heartland lay in the north-east of Scotland. Many of the stones there have been gathered for protection in museums, but a number of good examples survive *in situ* in the former county of Aberdeenshire. One of the most beautiful of these is the Maiden Stone. It belongs to the second period and the pink granite slab has a cross and shaft and a man between two fish monsters on one side, while the reverse carries the strange Pictish beast, the mirror and

comb, a centaur-like creature and a 'rectangle and Z-rod' symbol.

A few miles away is the Picardy Stone, a more angular slab similar to the first period with good representations of the 'double disc and Z-rod', 'serpent and Z-rod' and mirror devices. Thirdly, there is the Brandsbutt stone on the outskirts of Inverurie, another stone of the first period which carries the 'crescent and V-rod' and 'serpent and Z-rod' symbols and, in addition, a line of undeciphered Ogam script, a non-Roman alphabet which appears in various forms in Dark Age inscriptions in 'Celtic' areas.

Finally, visitors arriving by air will find it easy to compare stones of the first and second periods, for virtually within walking distance of the airport at Dyce is the church of St Fergus, with two stones incorporated in the outside walls. One has the 'double disc and Z-rod symbol' and Pictish beast, the other has a cross and shaft, 'crescent and V-rod', mirror, 'double disc and Z-rod' and triple disc symbols.

The adoption of the cross motif and known historical events have enabled loose dates to be put on the Pictish stones. In the sixth century, St Columba penetrated Pictland and in those which followed, the Picts adopted the Christian faith. In 843, beset by Vikings to the north, Saxons to the south and the advance of Scots from Ireland the Pictish realm finally succumbed to a Scottish take-over under Kenneth McAlpin. Much of what we know about the

The Maiden Stone in its original setting

131

TOP *The Brandsbutt Stone and stone at St Fergus, Dyce;* below *The Picardy Stone*

Picts—and this is not very much—comes from contemporary Irish annals, but no interpretation of the Pictish symbols is provided. In the years following the Scottish annexation of Pictland, the 'Q' or Irish form of Celtic replaced the Pictish language or languages and, gradually, the memory of the Pictish code faded forever.

The stones are in the care of the Scottish Development Department.

Phototips It is possible that the symbols were originally picked out in bright paint, but no traces remain and some of the stones are weather-worn. The symbols still stand out quite sharply when they are side-lit by the sun which then casts shadows in the engravings and highlights relief. In this part of the world, the sun is not always co-operative. The detachable flashgun which can be attached to a lead offers a solution in cloudy conditions and it should be held in a position to side-light the engraving—most easily, by an assistant. Exposure in such cases may be a matter of guesswork but if the flash is adjustable, it should be set on 'manual' to deliver a good burst and the daylight metre on the camera should be over-ridden, stopping the lens down a setting or two to compensate for the flashburst.

Locations The Maiden Stone (703247) is right by the roadside on a minor road about 1 mile WNW of Chapel of Garioch hamlet which is about 5 miles NW of Inverurie via the A96. The Picardy Stone (609302) is also beside a minor road, between Netherton and Myreton farmhouses, about 2 miles NW of the village of Insch which is between Inverurie and Huntly on the B9002. The Brandsbutt Stone (760225) is on the NW outskirts of Inverurie and signposted.

St Fergus church is about 2 miles NNW of Dyce overlooking the River Don on a track which leads N from the road between Dyce and Pitmedden House.

ROUND AND ABOUT

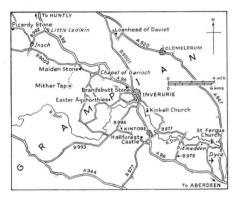

The area is particularly rich in antiquities and, apart from the two described below, the following lie close to the route which links the Pictish stones already described: Kinkell Church (786191), Mither Tap hillfort (682223) and Hallforest Castle (777153).

LOANHEAD OF DAVIOT RECUMBENT STONE CIRCLE

Recumbent stone circles are numerous in the north-east of Scotland and may have evolved from the famous Clava cairns of the Inverness region. Although the Clava cairns are tombs, they are surrounded by kerbs and stone circles in which the stones rise in height to the SW. The recumbent stone circles often enclose tomb cairns and their stones also rise to the SW, where a large horizontal or recumbent stone lies between two upright flankers. They seem to date from the years around 2500 BC.

The Loanhead of Daviot circle surrounds the rubble of a ruined cairn and has 10 upright stones and a massive recumbent.

The circle is in the care of the SDD.

Location (NJ 747288) The circle is about 4 miles NW of Old Meldrum and is reached via a by-road from the B9001.

The Loanhead of Daviot circle surrounds the rubble of a ruined cairn

Part of the Easter Aquhorthies stone circle

EASTER AQUHORTHIES RECUMBENT STONE CIRCLE

This equally impressive stone circle also lies close to the crown of a gentle summit. It has 11 vertical stones and an enormous granite recumbent. The circle is in the care of the SDD.

Location (NJ 732208) The circle is about 2½ miles W of Inverurie; it is reached via a 1-mile journey along a farm access road which leaves the A96 to the left, and lies about 1½ miles W of Inverurie.

Offa's Dyke near Chirk

(Clwyd)

The period which some historians refer to as the 'Dark Ages' is well-named. Even important facts about this period remain shadowy and much remains to be discovered. Whether or not Angles, Saxons or Jutes ever amounted to more than a minority of the population living in England, in the course of the fifth and sixth centuries the reins of power came to be held in Saxon hands. Pagan kingdoms emerged, some of them resembling the pre-Roman tribal territories, while fierce rivalries governed the relationships between the neighbouring realms.

One of the most important of these was the great Midlands kingdom of Mercia. Mercian power reached its peak under the eighth-century kings Aethelbald and Offa. Aethelbald had been described by Bede as king not only of the Mercians, but also of the South English. Offa, his successor was much more than a provincial potentate who ruled most of the territory between the Thames and the Humber. Offa reigned from his capitals at Tamworth and Lichfield from AD 757–96 over a kingdom which had been Christian for little more than a century; he felt sufficiently powerful to quarrel with Charlemagne, had enough influence with the Pope to have the Bishop of Lichfield elevated to the rank of

Long stretches of bank and fronting ditch are well preserved on Offa's Dyke

Archbishop and styled himself 'Emperor' and 'King of the English'.

He is, of course, best remembered as the man who caused Offa's Dyke to be constructed as a barrier between Mercia and the Welsh principalities. In this case, we do not seem to be dealing with myth and folklore and there is every reason to believe that Offa actually did initiate the work. Given that the great ditch and bank run with few interruptions from the northern to the southern coasts of Wales, it cannot be imagined that it was ever intended that the defencework should be manned along its whole length. The archaeologist Sir Cyril Fox found grounds for thinking that the line might have been negotiated between the Mercians and the Welsh, and that the Dyke might best be regarded as a massive and unambiguous boundary marker. No Welsh force could cross the Dyke unaware that they were trespassers on foreign territory and, although sections of bank might have been enhanced with palisades or manned during raids, the Dyke was probably more a great statement of ownership than a defencework.

It still exerts a powerful presence in the Welsh Marches. Long stretches of bank and fronting ditch are well preserved while the old field patterns clearly honour the line which has separated parishes and properties for more than a thousand years. There are many places where one can meet the Dyke and follow it for miles across expanses of some of the best countryside which the British Isles

can offer. Parts of the Dyke are owned by the National Trust.

Probably the most popular section is at Knighton in Powys, on the banks of the River Teme which forms the boundary with Shropshire. A less well-known stretch near Chirk in Clwyd rewards the walker with splendid views across the verdant, pitching border landscape. The Dyke intersects the River Ceiriog where a small bridge carries a minor road across the river to link with the B4500 just south of Chirk Castle. Walking SSW along the public footpath, you soon join the bank of the Dyke and there are fine vistas back across the valley where the Dyke can be seen dipping down to meet the river and then ascending the hillslope just to the west of the silhouetted castle.

Phototips The landscape, with its magnificent patterning of old curving field shapes and woodland offers many possibilities. As for the Dyke itself, it is worth remembering that earthworks are difficult subjects; with our two eyes, we have three-dimensional vision but a photograph is two-dimensional. Consequently, features which seem prominent and impressive may appear flat and unexciting when photographed. Lighting plays an important part in photographing earthworks such as Offa's Dyke and sunlight is obviously helpful to highlight the bank and shadow the ditch. Features like trees, branches or fence posts can be included

The view into Wales from Offa's Dyke

to provide reference-points which reveal the size of the earthworks.

Location Between Wrexham and Oswestry. Visitors coming from most directions should leave the A5 at Chirk townlet for the B4500 running W along the N side of the Ceiriog valley.

Turn left about two miles after joining the B-road to cross over the bridge; you can park here, and take the public footpath which joins and follows the Dyke.

ROUND AND ABOUT

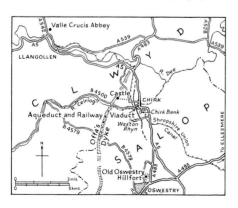

CHIRK AQUEDUCT AND RAILWAY VIADUCT

The impressive stone aqueduct which carries the Shropshire Union Canal across the Ceiriog valley was designed by William Jessop and built in 1801. It is 750 ft long and has 10 arches. Paralleling it, just to the W, is the railway viaduct of about 1850.

Location Just to the SW of Chirk and accessible via the B4500 or the minor road which leaves the A5 for Chirk Bank and Weston Rhyn.

CHIRK CASTLE

This medieval fortress of the Mortimers was begun in the late 13th century. It was twice besieged during the Civil War and fell on the second occasion through the failure of its water supply. In the 18th century, it was converted into a more comfortable country mansion.

Chirk Castle, begun in the late 13th century

but shortly after the establishment of the Abbey, the community received a reprimand from the headquarters of the Order at Cîteaux on account of the laxity of their observations. Thereafter, the history of the Abbey was rather uneventful until its dissolution in 1538. The ruins of the small foundation are dominated by the buildings of the east range and the early 13th century church.

Location Signposted from the A542 about 1½ miles NNW of Llangollen.

Note Other sites in this area which are described in this book are the hillforts of Caer Caradoc and Old Oswestry, the planned town of Clun and the fascinating industrial complex at Coalbrookdale near Shrewsbury, all in Shropshire.

Valle Crucis Abbey. ABOVE RIGHT *The west doorway of the early 13th-century church and* (below) *the east range across the cloister*

It is now in the care of the Department of the Environment.

Location About 1½ miles W of Chirk and signposted.

VALLE CRUCIS ABBEY

The Cistercian Abbey was founded at the beginning of the 13th century by Madoc ap Gruffydd Maelor, Prince of Powys. The valley in which it lies takes its name from the Pillar of Eilseg, a 9th-century cross which symbolised the importance of the Powys dynasty and which now exists as a broken cross-shaft ¼ mile N of the Abbey.

Valle Crucis was colonised by a small community of monks and lay-brothers from Strata Marcella near Welshpool,

Greensted Saxon Church

(Essex)

Each surviving Saxon church has its own strong personality. There is one, however, which has special claims to be both typical and unique. This is the timber church of St. Andrew at Greensted-juxta-Ongar. It is typical because it is probable that many, if not most, of the smaller churches which the Saxons erected in lowland areas which were devoid of good building stone will have been constructed of logs. It is unique because it is the only surviving English church of this kind and, in fact, it is thought to be the oldest timber building in Europe.

The antiquity of the church is uncertain, and although tests have suggested a date of AD 850, dating by the Carbon-14 process is complicated by the problems which result from the past use of a wood preservative on the logs. We are all familiar with the timber building techniques based on timber-framing with wattle and daub infill panels or weatherboarding, both of which were used in the Roman periods: here, however, there is a different technique which employs vertical split oak logs and is rather reminiscent of the Saxon hut reconstructions at West Stow*.

This may not have been the first log-walled church to stand upon this site, while later generations of church-

Greensted church (OPPOSITE and right) *thought to be the oldest timber building in Europe*

The simple church interior will be of great interest to photographers but good results need more effort than might be expected

builders masked the simple outlines of the surviving Saxon architecture. The Normans added a flint chancel which was reconstructed in brick in the 16th century, during which dormer windows were added; a weatherboarded spire was added at an uncertain date in the church's history. The church was restored in 1846 when the rotted stumps of the perhaps 1000-year-old logs were removed and the timber walls were mounted on a plinth of brick. It is therefore not easy to imagine the orig-

inal building, though it will almost certainly have been thatched and very dark inside, with slender shafts of light filtering through the auger holes which were drilled through the logs to provide ventilation. In the north wall there is a small aperture which is sometimes described as a 'leper-squint' but is, in fact, a 13th-century niche for holy water.

The church lies outside Chipping Ongar, with a farmstead and the Elizabethan-and-Victorian Greensted Hall for company. I have to wonder whether this is not a lost village site?

The Greensted area has one much more recent historical association, for after their pardoning and return from exile in Australia, some of the Tolpuddle martyrs (who had been persecuted for

forming an agricultural trade union) were resettled near Ongar. The parish register records that one of them, James Brine, was married at Greensted in 1839.

Phototips Although this seems to be a perfectly charming subject, the church poses problems to the camera which are not at first apparent to the eye. First, the prettiest face of the church turns away from the sun for the greater part of the day and second, its most interesting feature—the log walls—are stained pitch black. Therefore if one sets an exposure for the general scene, then the walls will appear as little more than a dark blotch; on the other hand, if one exposes for the logs then the remainder of the scene will appear over-exposed and washed out. Short of hiring a generator and battery of photographic lamps, the only solution is to direct a flashgun towards the logs while exposing for the general scene. It is probably wisest for those without a flashgun not to attempt interior shots.

The simple church interior with its warm wood tones is dark but inviting and the best results will be gained using a wide-angle lens for breadth of view and depth of focus, natural light from the opened door and dormer windows, a time exposure and a burst of flash to brighten the darker recesses. Good pictures can be taken at Greensted, but with more effort than one might expect.

Location The church is on the outskirts of Chipping Ongar, 12½ miles W of Chelmsford. Approaching from London on the A113, turn left at the small roundabout on the edge of the town where the church is signposted and proceed along the lane for about ¾ mile; the church is just to the right of the lane and parking space is available.

ROUND AND ABOUT

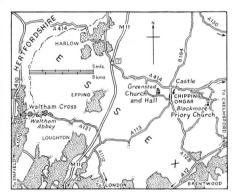

ONGAR CASTLE

The substantial motte and ditch are the remains of the Norman defences built at Ongar by the Count of Boulogne in the 11th century.

Location At Chipping Ongar, 12½ miles W of Chelmsford.

THE PRIORY CHURCH OF ST LAURENCE, BLACKMORE

The 12th-century nave represents the remains of a priory but the church is most noted for its remarkable wooden belfry tower of the 15th century which rises in a series of steps to culminate in a shingled broach spire.

Location Close to the A414 about 8 miles WSW of Chelmsford and about 4 miles E of Greensted.

WALTHAM CROSS (Hertfordshire)

Queen Eleanor died at Harby in Northamptonshire in 1290 and Edward I erected a series of lavishly decorated crosses at every place at which the funeral cortège had halted overnight on its journey to London. He may have been influenced by a similar practice enacted in France in 1271 after the death of Louis IX.

The crosses survive at only three of the eleven stopping places: Geddington and Hardingstone in Northamptonshire, and Waltham in Hertfordshire. Waltham Cross was begun in 1291; it is 50 ft in height and has experienced various restorations. It is hexagonal and has three figures standing in niches under the canopy; it is heavily decorated.

Location Waltham Cross is a mainly suburban area not far from London. It is on the A10, 3 miles NE of Enfield.

Note Castle Hedingham is not far away, and the air museum at Duxford in Cambridgeshire is a quick journey up the M11. *See* the index for the page references.

The wooden belfry tower of Blackmore church rises in a series of steps to culminate in a shingled broach spire

Early Christian Relics at Llanddewi Brefi

(Dyfed)

At first the scene seems medieval, with a great church tower dating from around 1200 soaring above a small market square. As you explore the church more closely, however, you begin to recognise the ancient relics of Dark Age Christianity. Fragments of carved stone which tell of a much older Christian tradition can be found in a number of English medieval churches, but they are more common in the Celtic west where Christian communities survived the pagan settlements.

One soon realises that the church seems to be built upon a massive artificial mound. Some churches, like Edlesborough in Buckinghamshire and Maxey in Cambridgeshire, are similarly situated and it is often suggested that such churches have taken over ancient pagan sacred sites. The origin of the mound at Llanddewi Brefi remains mysterious although a legend tells that around 519 St. David came here to address a Synod which had been convened to refute the Pelagian heresy. (The Pelagian heresy is named after a Briton, Pelagius, and was at its height in the early 5th century, and was condemned by St. Augustine. The points of heresy were largely concerned with technicalities of observance and the relative

Llanddewi Brefi. OPPOSITE *The church stands on a mysterious mound and* (right) *the view from the church tower*

143

Inscribed stones of the early Christian period, now grouped outside St David's church

status of man.) The earth is said to have risen up to form a platform from which the saint could address the great gathering, while the Holy Spirit in the form of a dove settled upon his shoulder.

The next puzzling relic is a fragment of stone built into the outside wall of the north-west corner of the nave. It is about two-fifths of a stone carrying an inscription in Latin which was copied in 1698: 'Here lies (Bishop) Idnert son of Jacobus who was slain because of the plunder of the Sanctuary of David.' The stone was probably smashed during 19th-century rebuilding operations and the remainder must be buried somewhere in the walls. Probably dating from the early seventh century, this is the oldest surviving reference to the saint.

Inside the church, large inscribed stones have been placed at the base of the tower. One of them reflects the close links between Dark Age Welsh and Irish Christianity; it has a mutilated inscription in the Irish 'Ogham' script on the face which is turned to the wall, a later cross carved on the other face and it could be the tombstone of a Pelagian Christian dating from before the Synod which David attended. Alongside it is a tall burial stone known as St. David's staff, and the other burial stones in the collection surely indicate the existence of an important Christian centre at Llanddewi Brefi six or more centuries before the great church was built around 1200. Even older is the fragment of a Roman soldier's tombstone which is at ground level just to the east of the door in the walled-up south transept.

It is clear that the medieval church at Llanddewi Brefi was both massive and important. The former positions of two great transepts are easily recognised on either side of the tower; the north transept collapsed at the end of the eighteenth century and the south transept at the start of the nineteenth century. The reconstruction of the ailing fabric was hampered by the poverty of the parish and the conversion of the majority of the people in the neighbourhood to Methodism. The nave was hastily rebuilt in 1833–4, but a more competent rebuilding was undertaken in the 1870s and 1880s.

Its historical associations apart, the church exerts a beautiful and commanding presence over the attractive village, but its definite though still mysterious association with the early centuries of Christian life in Wales gives it a very special importance. The village lies beside a Roman road and the Roman camp of Loventium stood nearby, providing other tantalising clues to the antiquity of Christianity in the locality.

Phototips The church is a straightforward subject providing that one has a 28 mm or wider wide-angle lens which is necessary to capture the full height of the tower without tipping the camera upwards and getting a parallax or falling-over-backwards effect. A tripod will be needed for photography inside the church. Enquiries in the village should produce the key to the church tower. The ascent of the tower is safe providing that you are not afraid of the dark and are careful of the worn stone steps. From the parapet, the views of the village and hills are ample reward.

Location In the heart of the village which is on the B4343, about 8 miles NE of Lampeter.

A Roman fragment, set upside down and built into the walls of Llanddewi Brefi church

ROUND AND ABOUT

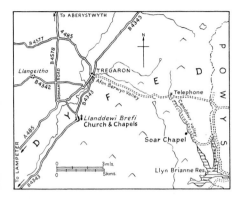

BETHESDA CHAPEL, LLANDDEWI BREFI

Many Welsh chapels appear austere and even barn-like from outside, but inside they often display beautiful proportions and woodwork of remarkable quality. The Welsh Calvinistic Methodist cause began in Llanddewi Brefi in the 1770s and one of the greatest of the Welsh Methodist preachers, Daniel Rowland (1713–90), ministered at nearby Llangeitho. At first, the Calvinistic Methodists held services in their homes, then two houses were bought and converted into a chapel which now lies ruined near the village centre. The present chapel stands on the site of two predecessors and dates from 1873. It has one of the finest interiors in Wales and combines elegant restraint and a wealth of masterly carpentry.

BETHLEHEM WELSH CONGREGATIONALIST CHAPEL, LLANDDEWI BREFI

The Nonconformist tradition in the area dates back to the 17th century. This chapel was built on the eve of the great Welsh religious revival of 1904–5 and included the Marxist and poet the Rev T. E. Nicholas (1879–1971) as one of its

The interior of Soar chapel

ministers. The building is more compact than the Bethesda Chapel, but again the quality of the woodwork is exceptional. It may be necessary to enquire in the village for the keys to these chapels which, together with the medieval church, form a remarkable collection of Christian buildings.

I remember Llanddwei Brefi with a particular fondness having been involved as photographer on a most unusual village co-operative project to produce a comprehensive guide to the parish which should appear and be available in Llanddewi Brefi in English and Welsh shortly after the publication of this book.

SOAR CHAPEL

Yet another important religious monument can be found in the vicinity of Llanddewi Brefi. The Soar chapel is the most remote chapel in Wales. Built in the 19th century to serve a number of isolated farming families who would come to services on horseback, the chapel lies stranded in depopulated hill country which is now surrendering to the advance of ugly coniferous plantations. Although most of the congregation of tough hill farmers has disappeared, the cottage-sized Soar Chapel receives a steady stream of modern visitors.

Location From Llanddewi Brefi, take the B4343 to Tregaron, then the minor road running east along the Afon Berwyn valley for 5 miles. Take the S (right) fork at the telephone box where the chapel is signposted, and continue along the Camddwr valley for 3 miles. A small car park is available and the chapel lies amongst the trees on the opposite side of the stream.

146

Barton on Humber Saxon Church

(Humberside)

Most churches are the products of many different phases of building, rebuilding and modification. Often we can detect some of these phases from the evidence of door and window openings, carving and woodwork which clearly date from different centuries. In the small number of cases where churches have undergone archaeological excavation, it emerges that the building history was often much more complicated than could ever be deduced from the visible architecture. In 1978, work began on the excavation of the church of St Peter at Barton on Humber—and nobody could be sure what might emerge as the old floor levels were stripped away.

St Peter's was no run-of-the-mill parish church but, along with its East Midlands cousins at Barnack in Cambridgeshire and Earls Barton in Northamptonshire, it is one of the most celebrated of the surviving Saxon churches. The Saxon origin is clear from the fine examples of 'flatband' or 'stripwork' decoration on the tower, and the semicircular and triangular heads of doors and windows. However, the church was much enlarged during the twelfth to fifteenth centuries.

What then was the appearance of the original church and does the surviving

OPPOSITE and right: *The church of St Peter with its outstanding Saxon tower*

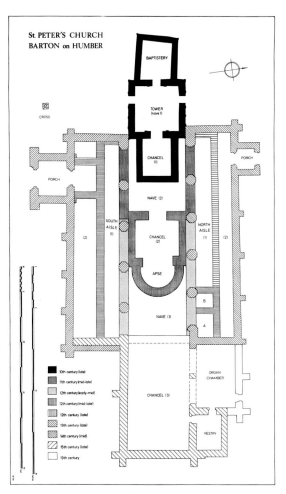

Successive building stages at Barton are revealed by the recent excavations

Saxon architecture represent this first church or a newer building on an older church site? Only excavation could provide the answers. Early in the 1970s, St Peter's was declared redundant, worship was transferred to the small town's other church and, because of its exceptional architectural importance, St Peter's was taken into the Department of the Environment's guardianship. A research and rescue programme under Dr Harold Taylor, and Warwick and Kirsty Rodwell commenced and gradually the story of the church was uncovered.

Contrary to many opinions, it was shown that the tenth-century church which survives as a tower and the adjoining 'porticus', which form the western extremity of the present church, had no older Saxon predecessor. This original church was only a fraction of the size of the medieval church which grew in stages to the north, east and south. It consisted of the tower which was its dominating feature, a tiny chancel to the east of the tower, and the porticus which was interpreted as a

baptistry. The base of the tower served as a small nave, about 18 ft square, while the gritstone used in the decorative strips and mouldings seemed to have been salvaged from important Roman buildings. A gallery ran above the nave at first-floor level while the second floor of the tower was the belfry. The chancel was even smaller than the tower/nave and the altar stood in its centre. In the baptistry, the base of the original font was discovered and it was found to have been converted from a Roman doorstep.

Excavation of the surrounding area shows that the first church was built in an area that was already used for burials and that the church builders exhumed the bodies from the space which the church would cover. About the end of the Saxon period of rule, the little chancel was demolished and replaced by a much larger nave, chancel and an 'apsidal' or round-ended sanctuary. The new church had the lofty slender proportions which make some Saxon buildings so attractive and the tower was given an upper belfry to harmonise with

the new arrangement. This church, however, disappeared amongst the later medieval extensions and so it is the tower and baptistry of the original church which survive to give St Peter's its very special appeal. The excavation work, research and restoration were still in progress at the time of writing and, when they are complete, Barton on Humber will boast one of the most attractive and thoroughly understood monuments to Saxon Christianity.

Phototips St Peter's is an attractive subject and it will not present many problems providing a wide-angle lens is available. This allows the choice of a close viewpoint uncluttered by the surrounding distractions. There are good views from the path which enters the churchyard from the SE and through the framing trunks and branches of trees in the yard to the S of the church.

Location In the little town of Barton on Humber which lies just to the S of the Humber bridge.

ROUND AND ABOUT

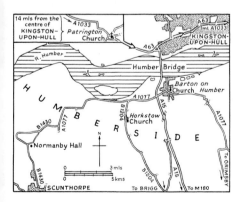

CHURCH OF ST MAURICE, HORKSTOW

The church of St Maurice is an unusual

Knights Templar church with a raised chancel and a number of memorials to the Shirley family who held estates in the area.

The Knights Templar was a religious and military order suppressed with great brutality by Pope Clement in 1312. Horkstow Church is dedicated to St Maurice who was supposedly martyred for being a Christian.

Location In Horkstow, 4½ miles SW of Barton on Humber by the B1204.

NORMANBY HALL

The famous architect, Sir Robert Smirke,

designed Normanby Hall which was built in 1830 for Sir Robert Sheffield. A late Victorian sitting-room, a 19th-century nursery and an Edwardian bathroom offer fascinating glimpses of past aristocratic lifestyles.

The house, with 40 acres of lawns and gardens, is open to the public.

Location Signposted from the B1430, 4 miles N of Scunthorpe.

Note There are a number of major sites close to Barton on Humber—firstly, the Humber Bridge itself and then, on the north bank of the Humber river, Patrington. *See* the index for page references.

Clonmacnois Monastic Town

(Co Offaly)

While pagan and Christian beliefs confronted each other across an English landscape which was racked by warfare and provincial dynastic rivalries, Ireland developed a Christian civilisation which influenced the whole of Europe. Scores of monastic sites, culminating in the splendours of places such as Kilmacduagh*, Glendalough, or Monasterboice ensure that the landscape of the country still resounds to the tune of these former glories. But of all the early Christian sites, the most celebrated is beside the broad Shannon at Clonmacnois. Here, there is a remarkable collection of different types of monastic masonry combined in a great pageant of Christian creativity which, once seen, will never be forgotten.

The vigour of the monastic movement is even more impressive when we remember that in the preceding centuries Ireland had been an obscure Celtic backwater, adrift in the Atlantic beyond the frontiers of the Roman Empire and fragmented into a multitude of kingdoms and minor principalities.

Palladius was despatched from Rome as Bishop of the island around AD 431 and St Patrick followed about two decades later. As in England, the Christian missionaries assumed control of the sites

RIGHT *A finely-carved cross at Clonmacnois; note the round tower* (also seen opposite) *to the left and medieval church behind*

151

One of the early Christian tombstones, recently set into a wall at Clonmacnois, showing a well-covered cross motif

Colmcille or Columba who founded several Irish monasteries before proceeding to establish the monastic school on Iona.

The subsequent history of Clonmacnois was punctuated by a truly remarkable sequence of destructions and recoveries. Between its foundation in 545 and its final reduction by the English garrison of Athlone in 1552, the monastic settlement and town is said to have faced about forty separate assaults by Viking raiders, medieval English armies and, on twenty-seven occasions, by jealous Irish neighbours.

One of the most striking features of the site is the avenue which is flanked by an astonishing collection of grave slabs which traces the evolution of cross forms from the eighth to the twelfth centuries. The modern presentation has often been criticised but I thought it impressive. The gallery culminates in a Round Tower which was completed in 1134 when it stood to twice the height of the 60-ft stump which remains. A second and shorter but more complete example stands nearby. These towers are thought to have served, at least in part, as refuges and strongrooms for the monastic treasures in times of raiding, although the risks of being burned alive inside such towers must have been considerable.

If one monument is supreme amongst this wonderful collection, it is the beautiful high cross known as the 'Cross of the Scriptures' which may date from the tenth century. Panels represent hunting scenes, soldiers, saints and angels and one may show the local chief, Diarmuid, helping St Ciaran to erect the corner post of the original wooden church. The older South Cross with scenes of the Crucifixion stands to the south.

The original timber monastic buildings have perished, of course, but the ruins of the medieval cathedral and two other stone churches remain. From the graveyard, a path runs eastwards to the site of the Nun's Church which has a fine

which were held as holy by the native pagan religions, but Celtic Ireland differed from England in its lack of larger settlements which could become the ecclesiastical and administrative centres of dioceses. Therefore, Christianity developed upon a monastic rather than a diocesan model. In the Roman Empire, Christianity had been the religion of the enslaved and oppressed classes and had won its conversions gradually, from the bottom of society upwards, while in Ireland the missionaries converted the mass of the population through the process of first winning the support of their leaders.

In the course of the missionary activity, scores of self-governing monasteries were established; many were small and situated in barren and impoverished surroundings but others grew to embrace wonderful collections of religious monuments. The influence of Irish monks was not confined to the island and their impact on continental Christianity was so great that, in 870, Heiric of Auxerre complained that 'Almost all Ireland, disregarding the sea, is migrating to our shores with a flock of philosophers.' Clonmacnois made major contributions to this flock in the ninth century, including Alcuin the most influential scholar at Charlemagne's court and Scotus Eriugena who was Europe's leading philosopher.

Clearly Clonmacnois was maintaining the standards set by its distinguished founder St Ciaran, a sixth-century pupil of St Finnian and a fellow student of St

Romanesque doorway and a chancel arch which is decorated with heads and masks and dates from the 1160s. In the pasture which runs down to the Shannon, you can see the faint earthworks of the settlement which accompanied the monastery and the most impressive approach to the site is by boat from across the Shannon.

Phototips The scope is so enormous that one should be prepared to photograph a variety of subjects, and no single portrait can do justice to the complex. One of the most attractive general views is from where the boat lands beside the Shannon; here the silhouettes of the round towers and ruins are seen to crown a slight rise.

When photographing the carvings, angled sunlight is needed for the best results and if the weather is variable, wait, if possible, for the clouds to clear the face of the sun. All stonework changes its appearance dramatically when sunlit. A less conventional study of the intact round tower can be taken using the window of the ruined cathedral as a frame.

Location On the S bank of the River Shannon 7 miles S of Athlone and signposted from all directions.

ROUND AND ABOUT

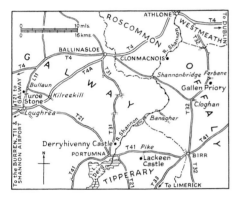

One should allow several hours for any visit to Clonmacnois, while in the vicinity, as in most parts of Ireland, there is far more to see than time can ever allow.

About 15 miles to the SSW and S are, respectively, the remains of Derryhivenny and Lackeen castles, the former close to the T31, 3 miles N of Portumna, and the latter S of the T41 between Portumna and Birr. About 8 miles SE of Clonmacnois are the ruins of Gallen Priory (N12 23) where early Christian grave slabs of the Clonmacnois type have been inserted into the gables of the medieval church.

Visitors heading for Shannon airport or the wonders of the Burren* along the T4A should divert at Kilreekill village to see the celebrated Turoe Stone

(M63 22). Isolated in a lovely meadow and reminding one of a huge decorated Easter egg, this smoothed 4-ft high granite boulder is carved with curving decorative patterns associated with the Celtic La Tène culture (page 67) and

The Turoe Stone showing curvilinear decoration in the La Tène style. It probably dates from about the 1st century BC

dates from the 1st or 2nd centuries BC. Its function is unknown. The Turoe Stone is signposted from Kilreekill village.

Note Distances in Ireland never quite seem to be so important as in Britain; therefore, the sites in Co Clare (the Burren, Craggaunowen and Bunratty Folk Park—*see* the index for page references) are almost considered to be 'in the neighbourhood'.

5 THE NORMANS

History is full of Ifs. The disaster of Hastings should never really have happened. Without the cruelly-timed havoc caused to Saxon preparations in resisting what seemed at the time to be a more frightening invasion by Hardrada's Norsemen in September 1066, the Normans should never have secured an English foothold or a victory at Hastings in October. We do not know what manner of history would have unfolded in England had the fates been less unkind to Harold. He was a respected and capable king even if his claim to the throne and the reputation of his House were somewhat dubious. Perhaps the cruel injustices of a fully-developed feudalism and the mindless destruction caused by aristocratic and dynastic rivalries would still have occurred under Saxon kings. However, the romantic can cling to the belief that, with all its faults, Saxon England contained the germs of a higher, more refined and more sensitive civilisation than anything which evolved under the Normans.

History is also full of myths. The old perceptions of the Saxons as stodgy, dull-witted backwoodsmen are slow to die. The Normans, on the other hand, have been described as progressive people whose invasion exposed the English backwater to the stimulating currents of continental civilisation. In fact, in almost every field of learning and art, Saxon England was a medieval Athens to the Dark Age Sparta of Normandy.

In chapter after chapter, the Norman story is one of great enterprises and ultimate failure. A recurrent theme is the almost incredible single-minded vigour and enterprise of the hero and his band. But another theme concerns the failure of the grand design which founders on the reefs of avarice and intrigue. So often the Normans seem to have been possessed of a boundless dynamism but rarely could they harness their energies to the lasting common good. It is not easy to like the Normans and the attitudes enshrined in many of their actions, but we cannot fail to be impressed by the explosive energy of this remarkable young nation.

The Normans were a sizzling ethnic and cultural brew of Viking and Gallic strains. In 911, the traditional founder of the Norman realm, the Viking, Rollo the Ganger, sailed up the Seine, passing lands which his forbears and compatriots had ravaged for the past century. This time, however, he had not come to pillage but to stay. He captured the Seine valley and his immediate successors rolled the Viking frontier westwards towards Brittany. In Normandy, the Vikings adopted Christianity and a French dialect, intermarried with the indigenous peoples and soon regarded this province rather than Norway as their spiritual motherland. Within little more than a century of Rollo's landing, a coherent nation of ruthless adventurers, pirates and visionaries had developed a small nation which soon provided the rulers and aristocracies of Italian and Mediterranean states and the steel core of Crusading armies; they utterly conquered England, advanced into Wales and ultimately into Ireland, and humiliated the Kings of Scotland.

Not all the noble adventurers and fortune-hunters who followed a Norman banner were themselves Normans and when William had won at Hastings and secured his grasp upon the new kingdom, he was careful to pay off and be rid of the mercenaries in his host. Many Normans came to England after the fighting was over, but it is doubtful whether Norman settlers amounted to much more than one per cent of the English population. With this in mind, their achievements in building and their success in subjugating the unwelcoming population are quite surprising.

Henry I perhaps excepted, the Norman kings of England were a thoroughly unpleasant collection of men. Neither William nor his heirs had any great liking for the English, but England gave its conqueror the one thing which was probably most dear to him: a king's crown and status. It provided his wolfish and often impecunious followers with vast new estates and wealth, for very few of the old Saxon landowners retained their possessions. At the same time, the Norman kings and greater nobles tended to value their homeland territories more than their English conquests. At first, the English lands were often treated as sources for revenue which could be invested and enjoyed in the homelands beyond the Channel. Meanwhile, ecclesiastical foundations in Normandy were endowed with grants from lucrative English estates. Only at the end of their tenancy of England did the Normans begin to appreciate the true worth of their victory at Hastings.

If the effectiveness of kingship is to be gauged in terms of will-power and might, then William I was an effective king. He was forceful, brave, worldly-wise—and ruthless far beyond the point of brutality. These qualities helped him to curb if not to eliminate the ravenous instincts of his barons; he imposed strict oaths of fealty, and fragmented the rebellious earldoms of Saxon England. Most of the new baronial holdings were wisely scattered in several blocks amongst different counties. In 1087, while pursuing his passion for war in France, William fell from his horse, ruptured his stomach and died the painful death that most of the English population will have considered he deserved. The Norman empire was then divided: the motherland was the inheritance of the Conqueror's eldest son, Robert and England passed to William Rufus, who added some unpleasant perversions of his own to the ruthlessness and greed which he inherited from his father.

Following the death of Rufus in a mysterious hunting accident in the New Forest, the kingdom was taken by William's third son, Henry, who was able to combine some instincts for good government with the martial traditions of his dynasty. Henry had been born in England and he had married into a Saxon royal line. In the course of his reign, England began to recover some of its natural identity. It became rather more than an exploited colony of Normandy, the desire to learn began to revive, trade and town life recovered and monastic establishments—particularly those of the newly-introduced Cistercian order—expanded rapidly. Henry also reversed the achievement of his father by capturing Normandy with an essentially English army. In a small way this may have restored the self-respect of the oppressed and exploited peoples of England. However, whether the kingship lay in good hands or bad, life remained more harsh than we can easily imagine for the peasant folk who formed the overwhelming majority of the population.

The rapacious ambitions of the Norman kings were shared in full measure by their barons. Henry's failure to provide a male heir and his unprecedented attempt to establish his daughter Matilda as the future Queen of England provided the fuse to ignite the powder keg. The barons preferred Stephen, the son of the Conqueror's daughter, Adela. Neither Stephen nor Matilda displayed the qualities of judgement, fortitude and conciliation which were needed to forge a coherent kingdom. The England of the Normans disintegrated in a conflagration of looting, intrigue and terror.

It fell to Matilda's son, Henry II, to provide the gifts of political astuteness and will-power combined with a genuine interest in justice and government which were needed to restore respectability and some calm. Through inheritance and marriage, Henry controlled enormous estates in France and his abilities were spread far beyond the bounds of England. He should be included amongst the most gifted of the Kings of England—had he been less capable, he would never have survived the diplomatic and domestic intrigues which regularly punctuated his reign. Although a great-grandson of the Conqueror, Henry belonged to the House of Anjou on his father's side and he was therefore associated with a new dynasty, the Angevin line, usually referred to as Plantagenet (a term derived from the plant which was the family emblem).

If the success of a nation or a dynasty is to be measured according to its ability to survive and maintain its identity, then for all their boundless energy and far-flung conquests, the Normans failed. Their French-based language was obsolete in England long before the close of the Middle Ages. Wherever they conquered and settled, the Norman élites were eventually absorbed and assimilated by the vanquished. Even the cherished homeland failed to retain its political identity for long and was annexed to the French crown in 1204.

There are several dates which one might adopt as marking the end of the Norman tenancy of England. In narrowly historical terms, the era ended when Henry II succeeded to the throne in 1154. The year 1204 marked the point after which the Norman nobles in Britain were obliged to accept England as their homeland. Perhaps more significantly, it was in the final quarter of the twelfth century that the massive Romanesque architecture of the Norman period of building began to yield to the more elegant refinements of the Early English style—a manner of building which has strong links with continental architecture but which still symbolises the reawakening of English sensibilities and the advancing obsolesence of the heavier Norman style.

Despite their ultimate failure to preserve their cultural identity, the Normans left a quite remarkable visible legacy of monuments. First, there are the thousands of English churches which are largely or partly built in the massive—and sometimes oppressive—masonry of the Norman period. It is hard to believe that older Saxon churches in timber or stone were much less numerous in England. One suspects that many a useful Saxon church was dismantled, giving way to a Norman replacement which helped to stamp the new realities of ownership upon a hostile countryside. However, here, as in other fields, English influences were assimilated for while the earliest of the Norman churches, such as survive at Blyth or Winchester, closely resemble their austere contemporaries in Normandy, the later Norman churches seem increasingly to show the influence of the Saxon enthusiasm for surface decoration. Before the Norman style became redundant, its original austerity had given way to almost florid decorative enrichments.

In the area of castle-building, the Norman contribution was quite phenomenal. In the aftermath of the Conquest, scores of simple motte and bailey earthen castles were built, mainly to intimidate the surrounding populations. As festering jealousies swiftly developed between the ruling families, then sterner, stronger citadels appeared. Half a century after the Conquest, England probably contained around 6000 castles of one type or another, and thousands more were built in the course of the civil wars of Stephen's reign.

Less obvious but of more lasting importance was the Norman contribution to the making of village England. Though plenty of villages existed before the Norman Conquest, there are scores of others which, from the evidence of surviving street and property lines, can still be seen to preserve the geometry of early medieval planning. In many places, the new Norman overlords seem to have herded peasants together in purpose-built settlements. The planning is most plainly evident in the villages of north-eastern England, where William launched a vile campaign of genocide, the Harrying of the North of 1069–71. Unlike the villages which were exterminated by the Conqueror's enlargement of the New Forest, the villages which were razed and depopulated in the north seem later to have been superseded by new ones which served as barracks to accommodate the peasant labourers who were the creators of Norman wealth.

In 1072, with his fleet and army in support, William met King Malcolm of Scotland at Abernethy and enforced recognition of Norman overlordship. In Scotland, the Normans of England were regarded as powerful enemies. Few opportunities to capitalise on misfortunes in England were missed, and few Scottish invasions escaped the consequences of massive reprisals. Even so, the Norman influence upon Scotland was considerable. The example of the well-organised and full-blooded feudal system which the Normans had refined (but probably not created) in England did not pass unnoticed by the Scottish kings. It was seized upon as a vehicle for pacifying and controlling all but the least penetrable of the Celtic Highland fastnesses.

Though partly protected by its difficult military terrain and agricultural poverty, Wales did not entirely escape the attentions of the Normans of England. The protection of the frontier region was entrusted to the freebooting Norman lords of the marchlands some of whom then established strongholds deep within Welsh territory, and the forays by rampaging Norman hotbloods were frequent. However, it was not until the 1280s that a large-scale, costly and concerted English campaign of invasion and castle-building consolidated claims to overlordship which extended back to the tenth-century reign of the Saxon king Edgar.

Ireland had escaped both the Roman and the Saxon conquests of England. Ravaged by Norse raiding and internal strife, the island which had given birth to monastic Christianity was weak and divided in 1170 when Richard Clare, Earl of Pembroke, responded to an appeal from Dermot, King of Leinster. Clare won back the kingdom for Dermot, married his daughter and succeeded to the throne. When Henry II visited Ireland in 1171, many of his chieftains received him as an overlord. Here the Norman settlers attempted to recreate the feudalism of village England and the clearest legacy of this period consists of the overgrown remains of lost villages: artificial settlements as short-lived as the interludes of peace in which they were created. In Ireland, as elsewhere, the Normans lost contact with their homelands—some claim that they became more Irish than the real Irish.

Note: *See* Appendix II for other sites from the Norman period.

The Motte at Laxton

(Nottinghamshire)

No tour of Norman England would be complete without a visit to one of the earthen mote or motte and bailey castles which mushroomed as local or regional strongholds in the years following the Conquest. Originally, these mottes were crowned by timber palisades although some later gained stone towers or 'keeps' or curtain wall defences. Mottes which lack the drama of ruined keeps and walls may not greatly excite the imagination, but Laxton castle is included as a good example of such a castle which is situated in a parish which is exceptionally interesting for its other medieval survivals. The motte is in the care of Newark District Council together with Nottinghamshire County Council.

At the start of the twelfth century, the marriage of Robert de Caux to one of the heiresses of the Alselin family of Laxton brought the hereditary stewardship of Sherwood Forest to Laxton. The castle became the seat of the de Caux barony and the administrative centre for the Forest. The Forest Courts were held here and the medieval kings stayed at Laxton in the course of royal progresses through Nottinghamshire. With these important administrative responsibilities, it is not surprising that the motte and bailey castle was one of the largest in the East Midlands, while the nearby village grew to town-like proportions.

The castle site is reached by a lane which runs north from the village street near the church. First, you pass through the earthbank of the outer bailey; the pasture in this enclosure is like a rippling sea of bumps and hollows which mark the outlines of buildings which once stood here. Then you pass through the more imposing bank and ditch defences of the inner bailey; the en- closure is empty now, but a map of 1635 shows that a large house and its gardens stood here, and this may explain some of the earthworks which can be seen. The earthen blister of the motte itself is now crowned by a clump of trees, but is still quite a prominent feature although far less formidable than the mounds at places such as Clun* or Clare*.

The settlement at Laxton did not fulfil its early promise, but shrank as the boundaries and importance of Sherwood Forest retreated. The village, which is now mainly composed of red brick

The Norman motte or castle mound at Laxton (right) is quite a small example and appears here as a blister beneath the trees. The handsome church (opposite) is built of one of the poorer building stones, a soft local marl. Photograph on pp 150–1: Byland Abbey

One of the medieval open field strips, seen here as a broad band of green pasture; note the typical slightly curving form

houses of the eighteenth century, is quite attractive and it will fascinate those who are interested in the history of village plans and forms. It is clearly a 'polyfocal' village, consisting of at least two components, each of which forms a limb of the 'L'-shaped plan, and the gaps between the still surviving dwellings show where others have now disappeared.

However, it is not the castle earthworks or the plan of the village that have made Laxton famous throughout the world, but the survival of an essentially medieval field system. Originally, villagers' strips were scattered through four great open fields. East or Town Field has gone, but West, Mill and South Fields remain and although the strips have been amalgamated to form broader ribbons of land than was originally the case, many features of open field farming survive. The office of bailiff has been preserved and the many and complicated decisions about the organisation of farming and the fining of offenders who flout the common code still take place at the Court Leet held in the village pub. There is still a brick pinfold where straying cattle can be penned, although the original stone-walled pinfold lay on the opposite side of the road.

The medieval church at Laxton was once considerably larger and it was not improved by rebuilding in 1861. The interior, however, is full of interest; a stone 'terrier' or inventory set in the north wall of the tower specifies the land which composed the glebe of the parson in the eighteenth century. There are several monuments to the medieval land-owning nobility of the area. One is quite remarkable and concerns Adam de Everingham, who died in 1341, and his two wives. The figures of Adam and his first wife are in expensive white lime-stone brought from Aubigny in France and lie side by side beneath a canopy. Margery, Adam's second wife, however, has a later effigy, not of costly stone, but carved from wood and the ravages of time have given it a strangely witch-like appearance.

The attraction of this unique village is enhanced by the creation of a Village Trail which the visitor can follow from church to castle and back, along the main street to the holloway of Hollowgate Lane, an old access to West Field, and down to the fish ponds which will have provided carp for fast days and important guests at the castle and which lie to the south of the church. A copy of the Laxton Trail leaflet is normally available in the church.

Phototips Mottes do not generally provide particularly inviting subjects, but Laxton is an exception. The tree forms on the mound are interesting; look for a viewpoint where the branches form attractive silhouettes or where boughs reach out towards the camera.

Location On a minor road about 4 miles S of Tuxford which is just to the W of the A1, north of Newark on Trent.

ROUND AND ABOUT

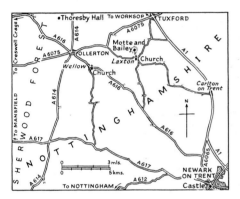

NEWARK ON TRENT

The 12th-century castle was built by the bishops of Lincoln and it was here that King John died in 1216. Most of the castle was destroyed during the Civil War, but the W wall and gatehouse survive.

The Church of St. Mary Magdalene in Newark has a fine 250 ft high spire, and the chancel, dating from the late 15th century, has a vast E window.

Location Newark, which is now bypassed by the A1, lies about 15 miles NW of Grantham.

WELLOW

The village is noted for its ducking-stool and stocks, and for the 300-year-old case clock in the 12th- and 13th-century church: the face of the clock was made locally and added in 1953 to commemorate the coronation of Elizabeth II.

Location Off the A616, 12 miles NW of Newark on Trent.

Note Creswell Crags are in the neighbourhood; *see* the index for the page reference.

Newark on Trent (right and above): *Fine buildings of many different periods from the 13th century onwards flank the vast market square*

163

164

Hedingham Castle

(Essex)

Gaunt, cliff-faced, with no later frills or comforts to mellow the spartan image, Hedingham Castle is just as a battle-worn stronghold should be. This castle is not in the same crowd-pulling league as Caernarfon or Windsor. Even so, from the outside and within, it preserves the stern, overbearing ethos of a major Norman baronial citadel. In some ways, it is more compelling than many of the large castles which spread and sprawled in the course of the Middle Ages: the defences are compact and largely of a single period so that the visitor can easily follow the military thinking behind the design. Inside the castle, overlooking the cold, bare masonry of the armoury, one seems to be breathing the very air of Norman England. Only at the most exciting of the British monuments can this feeling of a genuine communion with the past be sensed.

Hedingham Castle was very much a product of its age. It was the main stronghold of one of the mightiest of the Norman families of England and it was largely built during the strife-torn reign of King Stephen when strongholds large and small mushroomed and when many were put to the test of war. Constructed between 1130 and 1152, Hedingham played a role in many of the civil conflicts which afflicted the realm between the time of Stephen and the conclusion of the Wars of the Roses more than three centuries later.

The castle was built as the family stronghold of the Earls of Oxford, the de Veres. Aubrey de Vere was a leading member of the Conqueror's invading army. He was rewarded with grants of estates in five south-eastern counties, and these he held directly from the king. His son caused the castle to be built. No less powerful than his father, this Aubrey served Henry I as Lord Great Chamberlain of England—a title inherited by his heirs throughout the Middle Ages.

The de Vere citadel faced its sternest test in the reign of King John: Robert de Vere was among the twenty-five barons who imposed Magna Carta upon the king in 1215. Shortly afterwards, John temporarily forestalled an alliance between the barons and the Dauphin of France by taking Colchester castle and laying siege to Hedingham. The castle received a fearful battering by the king's artillery, and then surrendered. John's triumph was brief for, in 1216, the garrisons that he had installed at Norwich, Colchester and Hedingham surrendered to invading French forces and the de Veres were reinstated. In the same year, John died.

The de Vere insignia was the five-pointed white star or 'molette'—it can be seen in many church carvings in the de Vere territories. It is said to have been adopted after the Crusades battle of

---

OPPOSITE *The impressive Norman keep at Hedingham Castle. Note the deliberate use of the parallax effect.* (Right) *The great arch in the Great Hall is believed to be the largest surviving Norman arch in Britain*

The attractive Queen Anne house in mellowed red brick is a contrast to the massive austerity of the masonry in the nearby castle

Antioch, during which a divine star had been seen to alight upon the standard of Aubrey, the castle builder. Legend tells that, thereafter, the molette brought the family mixed fortunes. At the Battle of Barnet in 1471, confusion broke out in the Lancastrian ranks when the troops of the Earl of Warwick mistook the star for the 'streamers of the sun' emblem of the forces of Edward IV. They fired upon their allies and the Lancastrians were then defeated.

In due course, the de Veres aided the seizure of the throne by Henry Tudor. Anxious to assert his will over the haughty and turbulent provincial dynasties, Henry forbade the wearing of family liveries. Later, dining with his old

supporters at Hedingham, the king noticed that the servants were still wearing the molette star. Unable to condone such a flagrant flaunting of his edict, Henry imposed a hefty fine upon his host. The castle still remains in private hands.

Aubrey de Vere's castle is a wonderful introduction to the Norman concept of a stronghold. The essence of many important later Norman defenceworks—the successors of the palisaded earthen motte and bailey castles which are often the creations of the earlier Norman period—was the Great Tower, *donjon* or keep of stone. Aubrey clearly wanted a castle to match his needs and status and he was ready to pay a high price.

East Anglia is almost devoid of good building stone and the silvery dressed or 'ashlar' blocks which comprise the tower were brought all the way from the celebrated Barnack quarries which lie in the northern tip of the present county of

Cambridgeshire. The expense of transporting the stones via the narrow fenland 'lodes' or canals and then by carts to the building site, over distances of at least 40 miles, must have been stupendous. (I always find these building problems far more exciting than the perennial questions of whether Queen Elizabeth I slept in such-and-such a house or castle. Just for the record, she did stay at Hedingham, for four nights in August 1561.) We do not know the name of the man who designed the castle, but there are some similarities with Rochester castle and so perhaps they are the products of the same mind?

Norman masonry tends to be massive, but often the great thicknesses of stonework mask mediocre or poor technique. Notice how some of the Barnack ashlar blocks in the 'quoins' or corners of the tower have come away to expose the packing of flints and rubble which comprises the greater part of the 10 to

The planned medieval village of Castle Heding-ham contains a number of attractive houses in the local timber-framing style

12 ft-thickness of walling. See too how the lowest courses of the walls splay outwards to resist ground-level assaults. The entrance to the castle is set defensively at first floor level and the doorway is typically round-arched with decorative zig-zag carving in the surrounds. The small, rounded Norman window openings have also been retained.

Moving inside the castle, you can see the stark walls lined in a pink or blackish stone. Do not be deceived—this is still the fine product of Barnack but it has been scorched and seared by fire. Move directly into a vast chamber which served as a storeroom and which will have held the main garrison in times of siege. A stone stairway—which spirals to the right to force the intruder to use his weaker left limb as a swordarm—leads up to the armoury and Great Hall. With its cold stone walls and round or 'Romanesque' arches and their zig-zag

decorations, all is splendidly Norman. The great arch which spans the entire chamber is believed to be the largest surviving Norman arch in Britain. High above the four walls of the armoury runs a minstrel gallery and from here you have a superb view of the stark chamber and its solemn masonry.

The chamber above served as domestic accommodation and a last resort when the castle was besieged when the several alcoves may have served as bedrooms. In these troubled interludes, wooden walkways and hoardings will have been extended outwards from the battlements to be patrolled by bowmen, while oil and lime were kept heated, ready to be dumped through gaps in the walkway when attackers gathered to assault the wall base below. Decked-out for war, a castle such as this must have been a daunting and breathtaking sight.

What really appeals about the interior of Hedingham Castle is the absence of

the wood panelling, furniture, *objets d'art* and bric-à-brac accumulations of later centuries. Thus we see what is really important—the austere stony setting of embattled castle life during the troubled times of the later Norman kings.

Hedingham is arguably the most complete surviving tower keep in England. Even so, much has changed since the reigns of Stephen and John. The enormous weight of the great stone keeps was usually too great to be borne by an artificial earthen motte. Hedingham takes advantage of a natural ridge top and stands within the remains of its walled inner bailey which is embraced by a dry moat. The de Veres

The church at Castle Hedingham shows good examples of the late Norman transitional style of architecture. Note the circular wheel window in the centre of the picture

will have used the armoury for ceremonial banquets but in peacetime they lived outside the keep in a stone hall which formerly stood to the south-west of the tower. Their chapel stood nearby. Originally the keep had four great corner towers, though only two still jut above the battlements. The forebuildings which guarded the entrance and which may have contained a prison are now in ruins.

The tall trees which fringe the inner bailey are attractive but they are in discord with the Norman ethos, for woodland was removed from the environments of medieval castles to guard against a sneak assault and to clear a flightpath for bolts and arrows. A walled outer bailey lay beyond the moat and contained stables and storerooms while a stone building which may have been the guest house stood upon the site of the pleasant brick house in the Queen Anne style of the early eighteenth century. Linking this house to the inner bailey across the moat is a splendid red bridge in medieval brick which dates from about 1500

Down below the castle is the attractive village of Castle Hedingham with several fine houses in old brick and red pantiles or built of timber-framing. So many of the castle villages of England seem to have been planned by the Norman lord of the nearby castle. This village has a distinctly triangular lay-out. We know that in the reign of Henry VII, John de Vere was given many high offices of state and also the right to hold a Monday market at Castle Hedingham. Even so, the planning of the village may be much older.

The church of St Nicholas in the heart of the village is a lovely and an important building. The mellow brick tower is in the late-Perpendicular style of 1616 but the body of the church is much older. It was built in the Transitional manner at the behest of another Aubrey de Vere, the son of the castle-builder. It displays some very early examples of pointed Gothic arches and they are still surrounded by the decorative carving of the Norman style. Some experts have argued that it was here that the new Early English church style was pioneered—though many more would disagree. Such important questions apart, it is an enchanting building which is graced by a rare and beautiful example of a circular Norman wheel window.

Castle Hedingham: an outstandingly evocative Norman tower keep; a remarkable church, and one of the prettier of the East Anglian villages. One thing puzzles me. All this lies within the 'outer bailey' if not on the doorstep of London, so why is Castle Hedingham not a more popular venue for visitors? For the moment at least, the setting is peaceful, so visit it soon.

Phototips Wide-angle lenses help when photographing tall buildings. Such lenses increase the 'parallax' or 'falling backwards' effect when the camera is tipped upwards, but here you can use this 'bad' technique to good effect. Stand quite close to the tower base and really tip the camera towards the battlements to emphasise the feeling of a towering stronghold. Inside, the large chambers will defeat all but the most powerful of flashguns. Use the natural light, it is much more subtle but a time exposure of about 2–4 secs at f8 for 64–125 ASA film will be needed—it is darker than you may think! If you do not have a tripod, you will need to find a very steady support.

A good shot of the distant tower as it thrusts through the ridge top woodland can be taken from the lane on the other side of the A604, but you will need a very powerful telephoto lens. A most attractive colour shot can be taken from the drive in front of the Queen Anne house, showing the red bridge, the dark cluster of trees and the tower silhouette behind.

Location 9 miles NNE of Braintree in Essex and 16 miles NW of Colchester. Parking is available in the inner bailey. Take the road into the village from the A604. The castle lies above the village, at the end of a signposted drive.

ROUND AND ABOUT

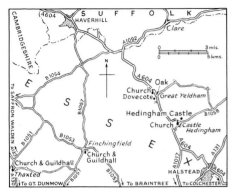

GREAT YELDHAM

This enticing village is notable for at least three reasons. First, there is the charming late-medieval church of St Andrew, built of local flints and rubble, with imported limestone for the dressings. Most of the church is in an early version of the Perpendicular style and of the mid-14th century. For reasons that seem odd, a tower was begun on the south side of the nave but not completed and the stump was topped with a stepped gable in brick. A more normal west tower was added in the

The weatherboarded dovecot at Great Yeldham manor farm

15th century. Inside, there is an Elizabethan pulpit.

Second, the manor farm has a square dovecot in the typical weatherboarded and pyramid-roofed style of the south-eastern counties. This well-maintained example is occupied by a flock of white fantails, not the traditional rock doves which were bred for the young squabs, then considered a delicacy. The dovecot stands on private land opposite the village and just across the A604 and it can be seen perfectly well from the roadside.

Third, there is the 'Great Yeldham oak', which lies inside an iron corset in the island at the junction of the village street and the A604. Now just a large gnarled stump, the oak is said to have been a massive old tree in the 18th century. If this is so, then it just might have been a sapling before the Middle Ages had run their course.

Location Beside the A604 between Halstead and Haverhill.

FINCHINGFIELD

The former medieval spinning town of Finchingfield is now a much-photographed 'showpiece' village and its genuine charms tend to be submerged by visitors, so that it is best seen 'out of season'. The partly Norman church stands in a churchyard that is entered through a late-medieval timber-framed guildhall.

Location On the B1053, about 8 miles NW of Braintree.

THAXTED

The little town of Thaxted is as attractive as any of the former industrial towns and villages in the E of England. In

addition to its textile industry, Thaxted had an important cutlery industry, although why such an industry should have been attracted to a spot which lies far from any sources of raw materials is unexplained.

Relics of Thaxted's medieval prosperity include the magnificent timber-framed guildhall of the late-15th century which overlooks the broad main street, and the Church of St John the Baptist with its 180-ft high spire and superb late-15th century font cover.

Thaxted: the magnificent timber-framed guildhall in the main street

Well restored almshouses stand beside the churchyard, and beyond the churchyard extension is an equally well-restored tower mill.

Location On the A130 about 6 miles SE of Saffron Walden.

Note There are a number of main and subsidiary sites in the neighbourhood, all within fairly easy distance by car: Greensted church in Essex, Lavenham village and the West Stow reconstructed Saxon village both in Suffolk, and Duxford air museum in Cambridgeshire. *See the index for page references.*

Kilpeck Norman Church

(Hereford & Worcester)

Much of the early Norman church architecture in England was rather bleak and oppressive. The technical competence and quality of masonry was often quite poor and the builders tended to compensate for their uncertainties by building walls that were massive and sometimes excessively heavy. Decorative masonry was largely confined to the heads of the round-arched or 'Romanesque' door and window openings, and motifs based on the chevron or V-shape were very common. At its worst, this architecture could be gloomy and repetitive—and also rather prone to collapse when the bonding of the beds of rubble forming the cores of walls and pillars failed.

Before the Norman Romanesque style yielded to the greater opportunities which the first of the Gothic manners offered, however, it had become freer and more adventurous in decorative terms and some examples which survive are positively florid and exuberant. Some experts see this tendency as a reassertion of the Saxon expertise in fluent and flowing decoration—an enthusiasm which is much more obvious in their drawings and manuscripts than in Saxon buildings.

Norman decorative work at its very

In a pasture behind Kilpeck church are the remains of a medieval village still recognisable from the mounds which mark the old property boundaries

best is displayed in the parish church of Hugh de Kilpeck, the grandson of the first of a group of gifted stone carvers that has not particularly Christian in their behaviour) and so the frequent inlcusion of St Pedic', suggesting an early missionary foundation, and a church is recorded here from about AD 650. The Norman church had at least one Saxon predecessor where the quoin in the north-east of the chancel was composed of Saxon 'long and short work' of alternating large vertical and horizontal stones. The greater part of the building is unmistakably Norman and we know that it was built in the middle of the twelfth century under the instructions of Hugh de Kilpeck, the grandson of the first Norman landlord.

It is also regarded as the finest product a group of gifted stone carvers that has come to be known as the Herefordshire School. The carving in the portal above the south doorway at Kilpeck, now restored to a pristine appearance, is as vigorous and skilful as can be. It is certainly not particularly Norman in its inspiration: Viking, Celtic, North Italian and Burgundian influences have all been detected. It has been suggested that a steward employed by a kinsman of Hugh de Kilpeck and who designed the now ruined church at Shobdon (6 miles WNW of Leominster and which was dismantled and re-erected as a hilltop folly) may have employed masons during a pilgrimage to Santiago de Compostello, and these masons may have

formed the nucleus of the Herefordshire School.

While they are certainly eclectic, the images on the portal are not particularly religious. Along with the mythical creatures, there are beasts of the chase surmounting a Tree of Life and while the artist may be representing the Creation, the pagan fertility symbol of the Green Man which crowns the right-hand column of the doorway is unmistakable. A much more explicit fertility symbol, the mother figure or 'sheila-na-gig' can be seen on the corbel above the apse. The appeal of witchcraft and the survival of some sort of Old Religion in medieval times has been grossly exaggerated. The lords who built the churches of Norman England were sincere in their beliefs (if not particularly Christian in their behaviour) and so the frequent inclusion of pagan symbols is puzzling. They are probably more than purely decorative additions; perhaps the essentially Christian designers were prepared to enlist the help of all conceivable deities in order to meet the onerous responsibility of the church to gain the favour of the forces of Nature which governed the productivity of the village lands.

Fine carving can also be seen in the interior of the church where the great chancel arch is decorated with moulded orders which show typically Norman chevron, lozenge and pellet motifs while the figures of three apostles appear on each shaft. Although Kilpeck is not a particularly large church, the interior

171

has an atmosphere of dignity and tranquility and the view from the small gallery, through the nave and the chancel arches to the round apse, reveals Norman parish church architecture at its very best.

The historical appeal of Kilpeck does not end with the remarkable church. Immediately to the west of the building are the earthworks of the substantial motte and bailey castle which the Conquerer's kinsman William Fitz-Norman built when he was granted these estates. Fragments of masonry survive from the shell keep which was later erected upon the motte, probably in the twelfth century.

Medieval parish churches and castles were not normally paired in isolation

The carefully restored carving in the doorway of Kilpeck church – as fluent and vigorous as any Norman decoration in Britain

LEFT *The church interior at Kilpeck, looking towards the great Norman chancel arch*

and this is not the case at Kilpeck. The church receives a steady trickle of visitors, but few are aware that behind and to the east of the church there are the remains of a deserted medieval village which are still recognisable from the mounds which mark the old property boundaries. The original village may have been a Saxon intrusion into Welsh-speaking territory though the causes for the failure of the medieval village are not known. Although now reduced from their original extent of over six acres, the earthworks suggest that the village dwellings flanked the lane which approaches the church from the north-east.

Phototips The restored carving around the south doorway is so deeply incised that fine details will emerge in photographs taken in dull conditions but the clarity and contrast are greatest under sunlit conditions in the afternoon, just before the sun slips behind the SW corner of the church. Beautiful pictures of the interior can be taken from the gallery, using a tripod—or, failing this, the gallery rail—for support, or from beneath the gallery, looking towards the apse. A telephoto lens can be used to pull in details of the fine carvings on the corbels.

Location About 9 miles SW of Hereford, beside a minor road and signposted from the A465.

ROUND AND ABOUT

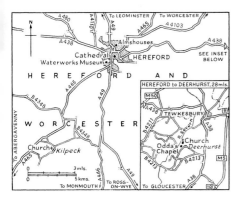

HEREFORD

The Saxon cathedral was rebuilt and almost immediately plundered by Welsh and Irish raiders in the years preceding the Norman Conquest. Norman reconstruction work was completed about 1200 and additions included the Lady Chapel in the Early English style and central and western towers of the 14th century. In 1786, however, the western tower, west front and part of the nave collapsed and the restoration by James Wyatt is widely criticised.

Other monuments worth visiting in the town include the almshouses in Widemarsh Street of 1614 which in-corporate the chapel and hall of the Knights of St John of Jerusalem and now contain a museum of the Order, and the Waterworks Museum on Broomy Hill where a working Victorian pumping engine is preserved.

DEERHURST (Gloucestershire)

Excavation at the church between 1971 and 1976 showed that the building passed through at least six building phases during the Saxon period alone. A high-pitched chancel roof shown in a drawing of 1794 may well have been a late-Saxon survival, but perished in the course of Victorian restorations. Although the exterior is a rather bland and unharmonious jumble of building styles, much of interest still survives and the lower part of the tower, the front and the triangular-headed windows in the nave are all of the Saxon period.

Location 4 miles S of Tewkesbury, on a minor road off the B4213.

Note 'The Three Castles' of Grosmont, Skenfrith and the White Castle are all in the district, as is Ewyas Harold village; *see* the index for page references.

The window with hood, fluted jambs and central pillar is one of the finest Saxon examples

Clun, A Planted Town

(Shropshire)

Old ideas die hard and just as the English village is often wrongly perceived as a timeless and unchanging place, so the town is often seen as being the product of slow and haphazard growth. Many towns, however, were deliberate and artificial creations of the medieval period. Some, like Oswestry and Caernarfon, prospered but others, like Caus in Shropshire, failed completely, shrank rather than grew as did New Winchelsea in Sussex, or failed to fulfil the creator's expectations like the delightful if demoted village at Clun.

The clues that Clun was a planned creation are not at first obvious and it seems like any other attractive and undisciplined Shropshire village. To the extent that it has a shape, it is that of a gingerbread man, with the castle mound as a head and the church at the end of an outstretched right arm. The town was not set out in an unpopulated area; Domesday Book of 1086 records a substantial manor and there was probably a Saxon village around the church. After the Norman Conquest, a particularly impressive set of motte and bailey earthworks were constructed at Clun, doubtless with the threat of Welsh raiding in mind. The threat materialised

When the massive stone keep was added to the earth motte mound at Clun, there were doubts that the earthwork would support it and the castle was built on the edge of the mound

in an irresistible form about 1195 when Prince Rees laid siege to the castle and burned the timber buildings and palisade.

The decision was taken to rebuild the castle in stone and in a big way. The resultant keep, now ruined, stood about 80 ft tall with walls 11 ft thick. It was so heavy that there may have been doubts that the motte would bear its weight without spreading, and the castle was set half on and half off the Norman mound. It was probably at this time that the decision was taken to create a castle-guarded town. It was built according to a rectangular design across the river from the older church and settlement site, on land which seems to have been partly wooded for a few of the later plots or 'burgages' were cleared from woodland. In 1204, the brave new town was granted a three-day fair and the archaeologist Trevor Rowley notes that 1272 saw the establishment of some 183 burgages—house plots each owned by one of the families of acredited townsfolk. However, there was disappointment when, in about 1300, some sixty burgages were untaken or empty.

Why one hopeful town should prosper and another fail is sometimes a mystery, but trade, competition from neighbours, individual entrepreneurship or genius, or plain and simple luck are often involved. Clun is a pretty place and may not bemoan its failure, but there is some irony in Housman's poem 'A Shropshire Lad':

Clunton and Clunbury, Clungunford and Clun,
Are the quietest places under the sun,

On walking round the planned part of the village which lies to the north of the river, the plantation origin becomes apparent. The High Street may have been the first part to be set out and it can be seen that streets lead off in a northerly direction to join at right angles with Newport Street which runs parallel with the High Street. The market square lies at the western end of High Street, but a larger trading area may have filled the triangular space between the market place and the river bridge which leads to Church Street. I find planned villages especially interesting and there are many fine examples—as at Castle Hedingham* and Appleton-le-Moors on the south side of the North York Moors. One does not have to be a history buff to enjoy Clun; there is a lovely Norman church, a charming river bridge, a pleasant walk through the pastures which cover the castle earthworks and several pretty village cameos as well.

Phototips There are no great challenges here, just a pageant of inviting scenes. The castle earthworks may be most effectively portrayed if you include a fragment of the ruined walls to provide scale, while the church is at its loveliest in the late afternoon sunlight.

Location Clun is about 8 miles W of Craven Arms at the junction of the A488 and B4368.

ROUND AND ABOUT

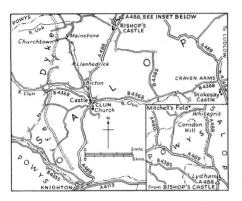

BISHOP'S CASTLE

This is another plantation town of the Welsh Borders with an obviously rectangular lay-out. The castle dated from the 1120s and the town was established in the second half of that century. It failed to grow and, as the photograph shows, the present village traces the confines of the planned medieval town nucleus.

Location Beside the A488 about 5 miles N of Clun.

OFFA'S DYKE*

The Dyke runs about 3 miles to the W of Clun; a popular section can be joined at Knighton a few miles S on the A488 from Clun, but there is another fine but less well-known section which can be reached from Mainstone and Church-town hamlets which are about 5 miles NNW of Clun and reached by the minor road from the A488 via Bicton and Llanhedrick. The National Trust owns part of the Dyke.

The lovely Norman church at Clun with its impressive square tower

Bishop's Castle: the planned rectangular layout

MITCHELL'S FOLD STONE CIRCLE

The circle has a diameter of 75 ft and there are 14 stones surviving, some as stumps and others 6 ft tall. The stone circle is in the care of the Department of the Environment. A lesser hill to the S of Corndon Hill which rises to the S of the circle provided volcanic rock which was quarried in the Neolithic period as a source of stone axe-making material. The exact quarry sites are not known, but probably lay on the NE side of the hill.

The view into Wales is spectacular from this area.

Location (305984) Mitchell's Fold is approached by foot, and lies about ½ mile NW of Whitegrit hamlet which is reached via a minor road from the A488 about 5 miles N of Lydham, above Bishop's Castle.

Note Other Shropshire sites in the neighbourhood include the hillforts of Caer Caradoc and Old Oswestry, Stokesay Castle near Ludlow and the industrial complex at Coalbrookdale near Shrewsbury. *See* the index for the page references.

Byland Abbey

(North Yorkshire)

In 1069, following a series of assassinations, revolts and a Danish-backed uprising in the North, William the Conqueror launched a grotesque campaign of genocide against the northern population. One chronicler reported that 100,000 people perished in the slaughter of people and livestock, the burning of crops and dwellings and the inevitable famine which followed. Vast tracts of countryside must have silently surrendered to encroaching weeds and woodland which followed. The killings, however, had created the wildernesses in which isolated monastic communities could thrive and the depopulated northern environments particularly appealed to members of the Cistercian order whose rule forbade unnecessary contacts with the outside world.

The founders of Byland Abbey were not originally Cistercians, but belonged to the Order of Savigny. In 1134, the monks of Furness Abbey attempted to establish a daughter colony at Calder in Coupland but four years later they returned, the new foundation having been razed by the Scots. Abbot Gerold was not prepared to accept defeat and renounce his rank and he set off with a party of followers to seek help from the Archbishop of York. On the way to York,

the party was helped by the de Mowbray family and a small base was offered at Hood near Thirsk. The community flourished and soon outgrew the resources of Hood, and Roger de Mowbray provided a new abbey site in Ryedale. The monks' wanderings were not yet over, however, for the new foundation was deemed to be too close to the great Cistercian Abbey at Rievaulx; the clanging of two sets of abbey bells caused confusion and annoyance and the newcomers were obliged to leave.

In 1147 they moved to another site which Roger de Mowbray provided in wasteland in a territory called Cukwald. A small church was built, but in 1177 the community drifted eastward and finally came to rest on a site reclaimed from marches near the foot of the hill of Cambe. In 1147, the Order of Savigny had been absorbed into the Cistercian order and in the years which followed, a network of prosperous estates was acquired and the abbey of Byland endured until it was suppressed in 1538.

The ruins of Byland Abbey are less celebrated than those of Fountains* or Rievaulx*, but no less fascinating to visit. The church is severely ruined, but enough survives to suggest its former magnificence. The west front is particularly fine, with three slender lancets in the Early English style surmounted by the great semi-circle of masonry which traces part of the outline of a gigantic wheel window some 26 ft in diameter. As the fragments of masonry in the site

museum show, the interior of the church was painted white with details picked out in red. At Byland, it is literally possible to stand where the monks once stood for, most surprisingly, large expanses of the original floors survive with the surface decorated in geometrical patterns of green and yellow glazed tiles.

The monastic buildings form a compact rectangular cluster and most of the masonry dates from the period 1170–1225. The square cloister forms the heart of the complex and it is bounded by the church to the north, the lay brothers' range to the west, the kitchen, cellar and warming-house to the south and the chapter house to the east. From the jagged ruins which remain, it is not easy to imagine the days when these austere but splendid buildings provided self-sufficient accommodation for a large community of monks and lay brothers. As the monastic orders became rich and influential, power often tended to corrupt, while the Cistercians were particularly severe in their eviction of peasant communities from the abbey estates. Even so, one cannot fail to admire the tenacity and courage which carried the founders from the smouldering ruins of Calder in Coupland to the marshes under the hill of Cambe, where they began to build their majestic abbey.

Phototips At the time of writing, the west front of the church is undergoing restoration inside a spiky forest of scaffolding, but there are many other fine

Ruins at Byland Abbey framed in one of the doorways. The setting sun illuminates the stone with a warm, golden light

179

views to beckon the photographer, particularly in the areas of the transepts and east end. In photography, the main subject—whether a building or a view—often seems most appealing if it is framed by foreground details such as an overhanging bough or the sides of a doorway. At Byland, there are several door and window arches which can be used to frame more distant views, but remember to use the depth of field indicators or the stop-down setting on automatic cameras to ensure that both the foreground and main subject are in focus—unless one deliberately chooses a 'soft' frame.

Location About 9 miles SE of Thirsk, beside the minor road which runs south from the A170 through Wass to Cox-

The ruins of Byland Abbey showing the round-headed Norman windows. Note the medieval glazed floor tiles which have survived the ravages of time

wold. There is a small car park, and the site is now in the care of the Department of the Environment.

ROUND AND ABOUT

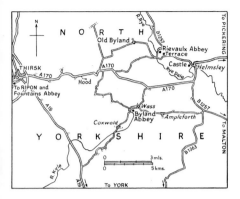

RIEVAULX ABBEY

The ruins of this magnificent Cistercian foundation of 1131 are more complete than those of Byland. While the most important of the monastic buildings were completed by the end of the 12th century, substantial additions were made in the 13th century. The abbey was one of the most important in England and controlled far-flung estates.

At the height of Rievaulx's importance, during the High Middle Ages, a population of more than 600 monks and lay-brothers may have been supported, yet by the time of the abbey's Dissolution in 1538, the lay brothers had long since disappeared and there were only 22 monks.

Some of the best views of the abbey are gained from the famous terraces in Duncombe Park which were begun by Thomas Duncombe I in 1712.

The Abbey is in the care of the DoE while the National Trust owns the terrace and temples.

Location From Byland, drive through Wass to the A170 and thence to Helmsley. Then take the B1257 and the signposted minor road which leads to the Abbey.

OLD BYLAND

When Abbot Gerold and his followers arrived in Ryedale in their third attempt to establish a monastery, a village occupied the chosen site. On several

Old Byland church was provided by the monks in the alternative village they built

occasions, villagers were evicted from newly chosen abbey sites and given no alternative home, but in this case a replacement village was built, about a mile from the original dwellings. The lay-out of this village, with the dwellings set back from the road beside a rectangular green, is still preserved, along with much of the fabric of the church which the monks provided.

Location About 3 miles WNW of Rievaulx via signposted minor roads.

HELMSLEY CASTLE

The jagged ruins of the castle which dates from the years around 1200 dominate the small pretty town. The castle was slighted after the Royalist garrison surrendered following a three-month long siege by Parliamentary forces. It is now in the care of the DoE.

Location Helmsley is on the A170, 13 miles W of Pickering.

Note The Roman road on Wheeldale Moor and the excavations at Wharram Percy are both nearby; *see* the index for page references.

Rievaulx Abbey supported 600 monks and lay brothers at the zenith of its power

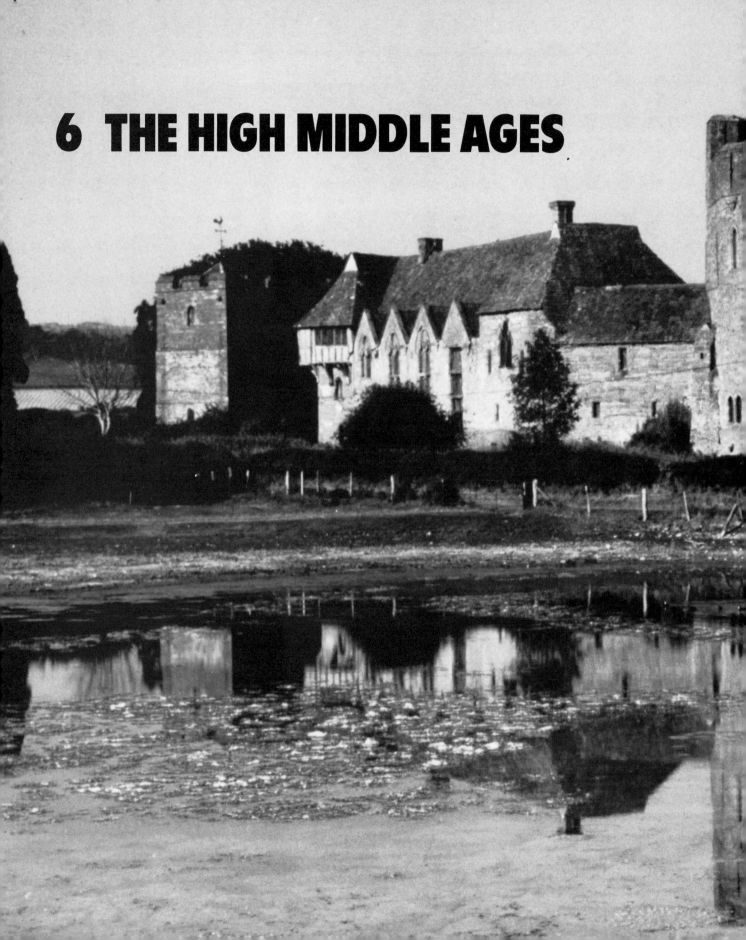

6 THE HIGH MIDDLE AGES

Perhaps it is our existence in a world of hurtling, disorientating change which often leads us to regard the Middle Ages as a period of stagnation? The arrival in Britain of the Pestilence or Black Death in 1348 marks a major watershed in the medieval period, but the British realms which faced the onslaughts of Pestilence in the middle of the fourteenth century had experienced many important changes since the last Saxon monarch had perished at Hastings. Saxon England had few truly imposing fortresses, and scarcely any built of stone; its cathedrals were mainly simple buildings of parish-church proportions while the monastic movement did not become a really powerful and numerous force until after the Norman Conquest.

In the centuries which followed the Norman Conquest, the population of England grew steadily, several of the older Saxon towns expanded while scores of new towns were deliberately established, some decaying into villages but others flourishing. At the same time, before the Black Death, medieval society tended to be conservative, autocratic and rigidly divided by almost insurmountable class barriers. There can be little doubt that systems of bondage which condemned most of the peasant classes to be scarcely more than the chattels of their landlords and masters had existed widely before the Norman Conquest, and bondage was probably at least as old as the Iron Age. The details of servitude were catalogued and enforced in the years following the Conquest and the grinding burden of feudal obligations persisted virtually intact until the watershed of 1348.

To the extent that the rates of progress and development were slow during the medieval period, a large portion of the blame is due to the rigidities of the feudal order which did not encourage the emergence of innovators or entrepreneurs. Blame can also be attributed to the disruption caused by recurring civil wars and the economic burden of the Crusades. For much of the period, the stability of the realm was directly proportional to the strength of the monarch. From the beginning of his reign in 1154, Henry II began to impose strong and, by the standards of his time, just government on an English realm which was emerging from the anarchy and civil strife which had been the hallmarks of Stephen's tenure (1135–1154). However, neither Henry nor his successors regarded themselves as exclusively nor always primarily Kings of England and their periodic attempts to retain or regain possessions in France drained the resources of both countries. Meanwhile, in England, the periodic dynastic wars and breakdowns in central control encouraged the provincial aristocrats to look to their own defences and thus the twelfth, thirteenth and fourteenth centuries were the hey-day of the private fortress.

Despite its internal setbacks, England was emerging as a considerable European power and the Celtic kingdoms and principalities of northern and western Britain were made forcefully aware of the ambitions of their powerful neighbour. Freebooting Norman barons had carved castle-guarded empires in the Welsh lands, but the conquest of Wales began in earnest in 1277 under Edward I. In Scotland, the situation was more volatile than clearcut; various early medieval Scottish monarchs had been forced to pay homage to English kings, but vows made under duress were seldom heeded once the immediate threat of English invasion receded. At the same time, the border barons on either side of the political divide pursued their own private feuds and raids. In 1291, when there were no less than thirteen claimants to the disputed Scottish throne, Edward invaded and overran the country. A Scottish uprising under William Wallace was defeated in 1298, but in 1314 Robert Bruce defeated the English forces of Edward II at Bannockburn and the 'auld alliance' with France which threatened England with wars on two fronts helped to preserve Scottish independence. Ireland, meanwhile, had not escaped invasion by Norman warlords and the Pope had granted overlordship of Ireland to Henry II but, although foreign feudalism was imposed on many parts of Ireland, the country was able to absorb and reorientate its conquerors and the medieval English grip on the island remained uncertain.

While kings and magnates pursued their dynastic and territorial disputes, the church enjoyed a far greater measure of stability, rivalling the monarchy in wealth, and, sometimes, in power. The church occupied an enviable position in the political establishment and was the major source of learning and education. Disputes between the church and the monarchy were relatively rare in the earlier medieval centuries, both being concerned to maintain the *status quo*. Fortunately, the two great forces were equally balanced, for while the king could choose bishops, the Pope could veto them. Taking advantage of this relative stability, the dynamic church-building process which was launched in the Norman era was pursued almost without interruption until it met the effects of the Pestilence. The church was not only a powerful political and intellectual influence, but also the recipient of remarkable riches obtaining bequests, endowments and all manner of soul-saving bribes from the wealthier classes as well as the proceeds of pilgrimage and tithes, and fines and dues of many kinds extracted from the peasant masses. Our great cathedral and abbey buildings provide epitaphs to the splendour of the medieval church.

However, an attempt to understand medieval Britain on the sole basis of the legacy of the surviving monuments would lead to an unbalanced view. Nobles, churchmen and townsfolk together only formed a small fraction in the population of what were essentially peasant realms. Although the scenes of village worship may be partially encountered in our thousands of medieval village churches, the hovel homestead of the typical medieval peasant family has perished everywhere. It is important to remember that the kings and bishops, abbots and knights who populate the history books were just the glossy froth, buoyed up by the deep tides of peasant toil and sacrifice.

In recent years, the excavation of deserted villages like those described at Wharram Percy* and Houndtor* has begun to illuminate our understanding of the home life of the peasants who were victims of the feudal system. Lost villages and their archaeological features apart, there is nowhere that we can go to see the world of the village peasant. England contains thousands of villages, some of them pretty, most of them fascinating and a number which contain many medieval or almost-medieval buildings. But because none of the peasant homes endures, the timber-framed dwellings of yeomen, merchants and craftsmen which survive leave a very unbalanced picture of the old village landscape. Even more frustrating is the fact that by the time that maps appeared at the end of the Middle Ages, most villages had already undergone the changes which determined their general lay-out. Therefore, the shifts, twists, mergers, drifts and shrinkages which have given the surviving villages their shapes and street patterns usually remain unknown.

Note : *See* Appendix II for other sites in the High Middle Ages.

Wells Cathedral

(Somerset)

Wells Cathedral is regarded by some authorities as the loveliest of the British cathedrals. It certainly exemplifies many of the best features of medieval Gothic architecture in the Early English and Decorated styles. However, the history of Christian worship here goes back much further than the commencement of work on the present cathedral building in the 1180s; there was an earlier Saxon cathedral which was itself preceded by a minster church dating from the start of the eighth century.

In 1978, the need to extend the Masons' Yard gave the opportunity for excavations which could explore the misty beginnings of the church. Numerous Roman finds suggested a hitherto unknown Roman settlement at Wells and part of the Saxon cathedral complex were discovered. The Saxon remains explained the peculiar misalignment between the medieval cathedral and the Market Place for it emerged that the Saxon cathedral was orientated along a line which linked the ancient holy well of St. Andrew to the east with the axis of the market square to the west. The new cathedral adopted a more conventional east-west alignment.

Wells was the first cathedral to be built entirely in the Gothic style and

Wells Cathedral exemplifies many of the best features of medieval Gothic architecture. Photograph on pp 182–3: Stokesay Castle

187

although the building spanned the period from about 1180 to the building of the south-west tower in the fifteenth century, the transitions between the different building phases do not jar and the cathedral is a coherent entity. The remarkable west façade, which is currently undergoing extensive restoration inside a thicket of scaffolding, was completed in 1282 as a stunning pageant of statuary with niches containing the effigies of almost 400 biblical figures, saints, bishops and kings. To imagine the original impact of this display, visualise the stone figures as being brightly painted in reds, blues and gold, so that from a distance, the façade will have seemed like a brilliantly spangled mosaic. The twin towers which crown the façade were not completed until the fifteenth century but they are perfectly integrated into the design.

The great central tower was raised to its present height by 1322 but by the 1330s, cracks in the walls beneath showed that it was too heavy to be supported. The massive inverted arches in the crossing were an ingenious answer to the problem, transferring the weight of the westward-tilting tower to the east.

The cathedral at Wells was one of several which were served by secular canons and the chapter house of about 1306 was the place where the business of the cathedral was discussed. Each member of the chapter had a place in one of the stalls which were arranged around the walls of this great octagonal building, facing inwards towards the massive central pillar. Thirty-two ribs radiate outwards from the top of the shaft and then converge in the clusters of vaulting shafts between the windows. The combination of Decorated window

Weathered sculptures awaiting restoration of the façade at Wells Cathedral

tracery and the 'tierceron' vaulting of the roof is splendidly effective while the central pillar and its sprouting ribwork have been compared to a great spreading palm tree.

Wells is also famous for the quality of its masonry and carving. The cathedral was fortunate in having access to the wonderful golden stones of Doulting quarry, only eight miles away. Many of the masons who worked upon the cathedral left their individual marks on

The busy market square at Wells with the cathedral towering behind

the stonework and these masons' marks are most easily spotted amongst the chapter house stalls. The quality of the foliate decoration on capitals in the nave is comparable to that seen at Patrington*—and do not miss the carvings of the fruit stealers in the south transept, where the capitals tell the story of a farmer's discovery, capture and punishment of the two orchard robbers.

There is also a magnificent collection of tomb effigies of former bishops. Seven of these represent the Saxon bishops of Wells, and although five of the effigies date from around 1200 and the two others a little later, the remains of the Saxon bishops were gathered from their

original resting places and placed in the tombs beneath their recumbent statues. All seem to have died in late middle age and to have suffered from arthritis, while one had suffered a severe blow to the skull, perhaps from a sword.

Among the other fascinating relics at Wells are the fourteenth-century astronomical clock in the north transept of the cathedral with its models of mounted

The beautiful stone steps that lead to the chapter house at Wells Cathedral

knights which emerge when the clock strikes, the moated Bishop's Palace which lies beside the cathedral and Vicar's Close, a well-preserved medieval street.

Phototips The best photographic exterior views of the cathedral will be denied to the photographer while the extensive restoration work to the façade is completed; then easy shots will be available. The interior offers a pageant of attractive subjects—all of which require the use of a tripod. Official attitudes to tripods vary from place to place but I

have found that permission is granted at Wells on request, and a donation to the fabric fund is a small price to pay for the privilege. A wide-angle lens is essential if one is to capture panoramas of the wonderful interior—the wider, the better. A telephoto lens is also an asset as it helps one to capture the wonderful carved details on the capitals. One of the best subjects is the winding Prior's Staircase which leads upwards to the chapter house.

Location On the A39 between Midsomer Norton and Glastonbury.

ROUND AND ABOUT

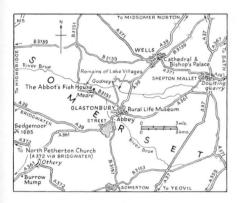

GLASTONBURY

Although there may have been a pre-10th-century monastic community, the original abbey at Glastonbury dated from 940, when St Dunstan established a very important monastery there. The medieval abbey was dissolved in 1539 and the extensive ruins date from the 12th and 13th centuries. These are now under the care of the Bath and Wells Diocesan Trustees. Subsequently, Glastonbury became associated with the Arthurian cult. The George and Pilgrim Hotel in the main street was built a little before the Dissolution as a hostel for pilgrims.

No visitor should miss the Somerset Rural Life Museum which lies on the high ground to the SE of the town centre and includes the 14th-century abbey tithe barn as one of its exhibits.

A series of small mounds lying to the E

The extensive ruins of Glastonbury monastery date from the 12th and 13th centuries

of the Glastonbury to Godney road are the remains of a Late Iron Age and Romano-British lake village and the results of its excavations (together with those from the Meare lake village) are housed in the 15th-century Tribunal building in Glastonbury which was formerly the Abbot's courtroom.

Location Glastonbury is on the A39, 6 miles SW of Wells.

THE ABBOT'S FISH HOUSE, MEARE

Situated close to the summer palace of the abbots of Glastonbury, the 14th-century fish house was used for the preservation and storage of fish which were netted in the lake nearby. The Fish House is in the care of the Department of the Environment.

Location On the B3151 about 3 miles NW of Glastonbury.

Note The site of the Sedgemoor battlefield, with its accompanying subsidiary sites, is very close to Glastonbury; *see* the index for the page reference.

Bayham Abbey

(East Sussex)

The most popular gems in the British treasury of abbey ruins are without doubt the great northern Cistercian foundations like Fountains and Rievaulx, but there are other ruined foundations which are much less publicised but hardly less appealing. Bayham Abbey is a good example, although it never experienced the wealth and power of its northern cousins. It was a house of the Premonstratensian canons regular, an order which derived its name from Prémontré in France, where Norbert, the founder, established a community of followers early in the twelfth century. The Premonstratensian canons sought to inject more rigour and zeal into what they considered to be the somewhat relaxed Augustinian rule, rather in the way that the Cistercians stiffened Benedictine practices.

Like the Cistercians, the Premonstratensian canons sought at first to establish their houses in isolated places which were insulated from the evils of secular life. However, they arrived later than the Cistercians on the British scene, when empty but potentially rich places were in short supply and so many of their foundations struggled from a lack of revenue. Two poverty-stricken monasteries at Otham in Sussex and Brock-

Bayham Abbey was built of pale yellow stone from Tunbridge Wells. The great tree (right) makes a marvellous photographic frame

193

The ruins of Bayham Abbey are rich in fine shafts and arches

ley in Kent, both founded in 1182, united to form Bayham and endowments were provided by the de Thurnham family. Canons from Otham and Brockley arrived at Bayham about 1210. The new Abbey enjoyed special prestige within the order as a daughter of Prémontré.

In the centuries which followed, the history of the foundation was similar to that of most other monasteries, with periods of laxity and squabbling over monastic politics, revenues and endowments alternating with phases of spiritual renewal under reforming abbots.

The masons who built the Abbey had easy access to better stones than are generally available in the south-east. These are the pale mellow yellow pro-

ducts of the Tunbridge Wells Beds which are soft and easy to work when quarried, but which form a tough protective skin after exposure to the weather. On the whole, the building followed the norms of Premonstratensian architecture, being austere with a very lofty, narrow aisleless nave. About the 1260s, however, the abbey church was lengthened with the provision of a late-Early English east end which is remarkable for the quality of the shafts and arches and the lavishness of the 'stiff-leaf' decoration.

Bayham perished in 1525 in a prelude to the general Dissolution of 1536–7. In due course, the Abbey and its lands were granted to favourites of Henry VIII and the estate came into the hands of the Pratt family in 1714, at which time the transept was still roofed. The building which contains the present ticket office and the Department of the Environment's custodian's house consists of a villa of the first half of the eighteenth

century with additions of about 1800. It was sited to provide romantic vistas of the Abbey ruins.

In 1799 and 1814, the then Pratt owner, the 2nd Lord and 1st Marquess Camden, invited advice from the celebrated landscape gardener and architect Humphry Repton. Repton suggested that the villa or 'Dower House' should be removed and a mansion built on the overlooking hillslope. The advice was not accepted although, in 1870, a neo-Gothic mansion house was built near the site which Repton had favoured. Other of Repton's ideas were accepted with rather unfortunate consequences for the archaeological integrity of the Abbey ruins; some sections were buried while others were made more 'picturesque'. One of Repton's famous Red Books with its 'before and after' drawings of the site survives.

Despite these changes, the ruins of the Abbey which the monks erected in what was then a clearing in an isolated Wealden valley remain enticing—and surprisingly undiscovered by the touring public, even though it is almost on the doorstep of London. No less an authority than Professor W. G. Hoskins has described Bayham as 'the Fountains Abbey of the South'.

Phototips There are several quite splendid views. The best is probably when one stands to the E of the 3-sided apse which terminates the E end extension. The jagged ruins of the nave, quire and transept are seen beneath the cascading summer foliage of the great tree whose roots twist and twine to gain a foothold in the ruined apse.

However, there is a problem of choosing the correct exposure, and the owners of automatic cameras should resort to manual override. Does one expose for the deep shade beneath the tree, or for the (perhaps sunlit) abbey ruins behind? It depends. If you choose to have the ruins exposed correctly, the tree will appear as a dark silhouette and the attractive contortions of its roots will be largely lost in shadow. In this case, step out of the shade and take a meter reading on the well-lit buildings. Alternatively, you can expose for the shaded area when the ruins behind will be pale and under-exposed. Photographers who have dark-rooms can enjoy the best of both worlds by 'burning-in' the background ruins during the printing stage.

Location About 5 miles E of Tunbridge Wells and signposted from the B2169. There is a small car park.

ROUND AND ABOUT

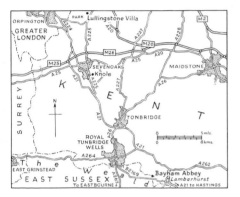

LULLINGSTONE VILLA (Kent)

This is one of the most important and well-presented of the Roman villa remains in England: it is in the care of the DoE. In the 2nd century, a wealthy Roman landowner extended and enriched the flint-built dwelling of a native farmer, adding baths, kitchens and a cult room dedicated to three water nymphs. For most of the 3rd century, however, the villa lay abandoned and decaying. Towards the end of that century, a prosperous Romanised family took over the site and reconstructed the villa as an orderly complex of flint-walled and red tile-roofed buildings, and fine mosaic floors were laid in the dining and reception room. A temple-cum-mausoleum dedicated to pagan Roman deities was added nearby. In the final decades of Roman rule, however, the family was converted to Christianity and

Excavation at Lullingstone began in 1949

one of the rooms was remodelled for Christian worship, thus making it one of the oldest surviving Christian monuments in Britain.

Early in the 5th century, Lullingstone became one of the many villas to perish in flames in the turmoils which marked the beginning of the Dark Ages.

The site was discovered in 1788 and proper excavation began in 1949.

Location About 6 miles N of Sevenoaks and signposted from the A225. There is a large car park within Lullingstone Park and the villa ruins are enclosed by a fine modern building with excellent display areas.

KNOLE (Kent)

A palace was constructed from a nucleus of older medieval buildings by the Archbishop of Canterbury, Thomas Bourchier, who purchased the site in 1456 for £266.13.4d! The palace was taken over by Henry VIII and expensive improvements were carried out; in the reign of Elizabeth I, it was granted first to Robert Dudley, Earl of Leicester, and then to her Lord Treasurer, Thomas Sackville who carried out further improvements. The house preserves the attractive details and rambling character of late-Gothic domestic architecture and looks over some fine gardens.

Knole belonged to the Sackville family until 1946 when it was bought by the National Trust.

Location Knole lies to the SE of Sevenoaks and is reached from the S of the town's High Street.

Note Bodiam Castle is also in the neighbourhood; *see* the index for the page reference.

Patrington Church

(Humberside)

The story of the development of church architecture has been told many times, how the Romanesque style which was used by the Saxons and Normans yielded to the exciting new possibilities of the pointed arch of the Gothic forms, and how the solemn restraint of the first Gothic style, the Early English, was superseded by the exuberant embellishments of the Decorated form, which was in turn replaced by the soaring vertical lines of the Perpendicular. The delicious details of the deeply-cut carving associated with the finest of the church building from the Decorated period of about 1275–1350 are displayed in a number of celebrated cathedrals such as Exeter, the Lady Chapel of Ely and Wells*.

One of the finest examples of the style can be seen in the parish church at Patrington to the east of Hull. One does not expect to find a splendidly large and ornate church here; the windswept peninsula of Holderness seems about to come to a point and disappear into the sea, but the low and level horizon increases the impact of the great spire which stabs through the distant skyline like a stiletto. As Sir John Betjeman writes in his preface to the guide to St Patrick's, 'It sails like a galleon of

---

stone over the wide, flat expanse of Holderness.'

The church is unusually consistent in style. There are traces of Norman and earlier thirteenth-century work in the fabric, and of Perpendicular tracery in the east window, but the building is essentially an essay in the Decorated style. Most of the work was completed between 1310 and 1349. The Great Pestilence, the Black Death outbreak of 1348–9, caused awful disruption and mortality with the result that building work was suspended and the final stages which were completed in 1410 adopted the new Perpendicular manner.

The question of why we should find an exceptional building in such an isolated and peripheral position can not be answered with total certainty, but two factors can be taken into account. First, although modern Patrington seems to be little more than a large and rather sleepy village, as a medieval market town it had two weekly markets and two or three annual fairs. The town served most of Holderness and before the fearsome storms of the fourteenth century inundated the Humber ports of Ravenser and Ravenserodd and a clutch of villages on nearby Sunk Island, considerable traffic must have passed through Patrington. Second, the manor was held by the Archbishops of York who may have encouraged or initiated the ambitious building programme.

St Patrick's is impressive in many ways. The first feature to strike the visitor is the spire which makes its impact not only from its great height of 189 feet, but also from the perfection of its proportions; the lantern storey—an octagonal corona—forms an elegant bridge between the spire itself and the square tower which supports it. Then there is the effect of the sheer size of the building, 150 ft long by 90 ft broad, with twenty massive piers supporting the roof. In the pierless chancel, bounded to the west by a late fourteenth-century screen and illuminated by the great Perpendicular east window, the feeling is one of space and light. The nave and transepts are more dimly lit so that the piers rise through the gloom like the trunks of trees in a stately forest.

Then there is the wonderfully fluent and vital carving which blossoms from the capitals and corbels and embellishes the font, piscina and sedilia, the Easter Sepulchre and the Lady Chapel. On the capitals, the clusters of foliage are an elaboration of the 'stiff-leaf' motifs so popular in Early English carving, while elsewhere there are around 200 representations of human faces, animals and grotesque creatures.

We know a good deal about the aristocrats and great churchmen of the Middle Ages, but very little about the men whose sweat and skills actually created the cathedrals and churches—the masons and master masons. Occasionally their names are preserved in building accounts and contracts, but otherwise they are very shadowy fig-

ures. Often they began their careers working in quarries and many have names which derive from quarrying localities like Corfe in Dorset or Barnack in Cambridgeshire. It is known that Yorkshire spawned a great dynasty of masons who took their surname from Patrington and members of the family are known to have worked at Westmin-

OPPOSITE and right: *Patrington 'sails like a galleon of stone'*

ster and York Minster, and there are close similarities between the carving of the capitals at Patrington and those in the choir at York Minster.

Phototips Churches with lofty spires present a real problem and a suitable wide-angle lens may be indispensable. Without one, you may not be able to get far enough from the church (because of the presence of surrounding buildings) to get the whole of the spire in frame — and chopped-off spires seldom appear acceptable. Fortunately here there is

quite a large expanse of churchyard to the S of the church and so a modestly wide-angle lens will suffice. Anyone who has a tripod will find an enormous range of possibilities in the interior and the view from the font, through the nave and crossing to the chancel beyond, is exceptional. The wide-angle lens can also be used for interior panoramas, but the tele-photo (if available) should also be used to pull in details from the carving on the capitals, roof bosses and gargoyles.

When photographing in church interiors, do not direct the exposure meter directly at a window, but towards the more dimly illuminated recesses, otherwise the reading will be artificially high. Small stops such as f11 should be used to get a good depth of focus even though this may demand the use of exposure times as long as 8 secs. The eye is a remarkably adaptable instrument and it is usually much darker inside a church than you think it is.

Location Beside the A1033, about 15 miles E of Hull. Getting lost in Hull is too easily accomplished and the A1033 is not well signposted, so when you *do* get lost, aim for the dockside road and follow it eastwards until you are taken out of the city.

ROUND AND ABOUT

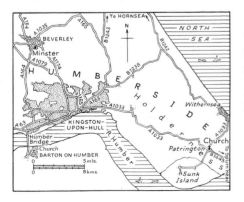

BEVERLEY

The town offers a feast of attractive buildings in brick with the fine stone minster church of St John the Evangelist as the crowning glory. This is the largest parish church in England, incorporating work in the three great Gothic styles and many fine carvings in both wood and stone.

The Percy Shrine is particularly notable. The canopy is regarded by many as the finest 14th-century work in the

country. There are sixty-eight misericords, which is the biggest collection in England.

Location About 8 miles N of Hull near the convergence of the A164, A1079 and A1035.

Note Just across the Humber Bridge, which is also a main site, is the Saxon church at Barton on Humber; *see* the index for page references.

199

Harlech Castle

(Gwynedd)

Between the construction of Offa's Dyke* and the killing of the first and last native prince of all Wales, Llywelyn, near Builth in 1282, Welsh history was a story of internal rivalries and attempts to resist English overlordship. Saxon settlers had penetrated the Marchlands, then Norman motte and bailey castles advanced deeply towards the heartlands of Wales while military strategy was stiffened by the constructions of greater fortresses like the Three Castles*. The later stages in the subjugation of the principality came in the years 1277–89 when Edward I launched a quite staggering programme of castle building, completion and reconstruction which produced no less than fourteen massive and formidable citadels, throttling the refuges of Welsh resistance like a mailed fist.

Although the rock of Harlech is mentioned in Welsh mythology, there does not seem to have been a fortification here until work on Edward I's castle began in 1283. The amounts of effort and resources which were devoted to the programme were quite stupendous and at Harlech alone there was employment for some 546 unskilled labourers, 227 masons, 115 quarrymen, 30 smiths, and 22 carpenters by

1286. The scale of the operations at some other castles like Caernarfon and Beaumaris was even greater and, at one stage, the latter castle provided work for no less than 1000 labourers, 400 masons and 200 carters. We do not know very much about the labourers and craftsmen involved, but the identity of the man who masterminded the design of the Welsh castles is known: Master James of St George was summoned by the king from Savoy in 1278, and in 1290 he came to live in Harlech where he served as Constable.

At Harlech, a relatively straightforward concentric plan was adopted. The Inner Ward which contained the great hall, kitchen, chapel and stores was surrounded by a roughly rectangular wall of massive proportions with round towers set at each corner. About 25 ft outside the fortifications of the Inner Ward ran the less imposing battlements of the outer wall which enclosed the Outer Ward. The toughest of all the defensive components was the mighty gatehouse which commanded the entrance to the Inner Ward, three storeys tall with walls up to 12 ft in thickness. Any attack which sought to breach the gate defences faced a barred wooden door, a portcullis, a barrage of arrows from the slits which guard the passage, another portcullis, another door, a third portcullis and a third door. The natural rocky knoll supporting the castle provided an ideal platform, while the proximity to the sea—which formerly lap-

ped the base of the castle rock—gave a possibility of relief in times of siege.

Like many other Welsh citadels, Harlech had a fairly active life. In the uprising of Madoc ap Llywelyn of 1294–5, Harlech was isolated from the Welsh interior but sustained by sea with supplies from Ireland until the siege was lifted. In the aftermath of the siege, the approaches to the shore and landings were strengthened by a loop of walls. At the start of the fifteenth century, however, the castle fell after a long siege during the uprisings led by Owain Glyndwr who himself lived at Harlech between the capture of the castle in 1404 and 1409, when it fell to an English siege. By this time, it had become established that Harlech could be taken—but only after a serious and sustained siege campaign.

The pattern was repeated in 1468 when the Yorkists, under the Earl of Pembroke, took the surrender of the Lancastrian constable. By the middle of the sixteenth century, the defences were decaying and the interior buildings ruinous but a 'small garrison of 42 gentlemen and soldiers' was installed during the Civil War. In 1647, Harlech surrendered after siege for the fourth time in its history and the taking of the castle by the Parliamentarians under Colonel Mytton was an historic event which marked the end of the Civil War. The old stronghold was then partly dismantled but not demolished and so restoration work carried out in the

course of the present century has allowed the castle to be preserved in a state that resembles its original appearance. It is now in the care of the Department of the Environment.

Phototips The view of the Harlech Castle as seen from the neighbouring knoll which lies to the SW has long been one of the most popular British landscape subjects. However, the artist has the freedom to mudge and fudge the intrusive details from the modern world and present the thrusting castle profile as a silhouette against the mountains of Snowdonia which lie to the north. In reality, the view is marred by ill-sited caravan parks, telegraph poles and a jumble of undistinguished nineteenth-century buildings.

Photographic mudging and fudging can take on a creative dimension if one uses what is known as a 'clear centre-spot diffuser filter'—a grand name for a bit of optical plastic which has a clear centre and stippled surround. As one might expect when this is used, the object in the centre of the composition is clear while the surrounding details are blurred. Photographs taken with such filters have a rather dreamy quality which can be quite attractive, and at Harlech there is the extra advantage that the distracting modern details around the castle are fuzzed. Fog filters and graduated fog filters which lack a clear centre spot can also be used to create a misty effect. Like the diffusers, they can be used with colour or monochrome.

Inside the castle, a fine view of the gatehouse is gained from the top of the ramparts in the E section. As ever, patience must be used as you wait for a break in the seemingly endless tide of visitors to the Inner Ward. The wait may be long but, in the summer especially, holidaymakers and the stark ethos of a medieval citadel are, photographically incompatible.

Location Close to the A496 in the rather uninspiring resort of Harlech.

A view from the ramparts

ROUND AND ABOUT

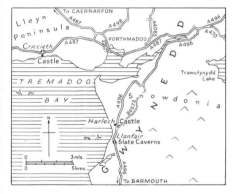

LLANFAIR SLATE CAVERNS

During the 19th century, enormous quantities of Welsh slate were exported and the roofs of most English towns display an abundance of the blue-grey rock. Although in private hands, a labyrinth of slate-mining caverns and passageways can be explored at the disused Llanfair workings, where guided tours are organised.

Location About 1 mile S of Harlech, just to the E of the A496 and signposted.

CRICCIETH CASTLE

This castle, which lies on the south side of the Lleyn Peninsula and faces Harlech across Tremadog Bay, was begun by Llywelyn the Great in the 1230s but was captured during Edward I's campaign in 1283. The concentric plan was gained in two stages for Edward's castle was built inside the circling wall of its predecessor. Like Harlech, Criccieth survived the siege of 1294–5, but was burned and destroyed by Owain Glyndwr in 1404. The National Trust now owns the land around the castle.

Location Signposted from the A497 about 5 miles W of Porthmadog.

Note Further north on Anglesey is the Din Lligwy site and its subsidiary sites; *see* the index for page reference.

Criccieth Castle, begun in the 1230s

Grosmont Castle

(Gwent)

Grosmont is one member of a knot of Marcher defenceworks known as 'the Three Castles', the others being Skenfrith and White Castle; they are all in the care of the Department of the Environment. Together they defended the approaches to Herefordshire, Worcestershire and Gloucestershire against invaders from the south of Wales. Grosmont developed from an older Norman motte and bailey castle although it has been suggested that the site was previously occupied by a Celtic hillfort. The Norman earthworks might date from around 1100 but in the reign of Henry II the castle and the two neighbouring fortresses were seized by the king, the two Fitz-Count heirs to the castles and estates both being lepers. King John granted the castles to Hubert de Burgh; they were confiscated in 1232 and granted by Henry III to his son, Edmund of Lancaster.

Rising from the ranks of the lower gentry, de Burgh rose to positions of enormous power, becoming Justiciar following Magna Carta. During the minority of Henry III, most of the effective government of the realm was accomplished by de Burgh and the Archbishop of Canterbury, Stephen Langton. Though always loyal, when de Burgh was accused of a variety of crimes—including poison-ing—in 1232, Henry III, whose judgement was often bad, chose to regard him as a traitor. The de Burgh empire and fortunes withered and when he died in 1243, his Earldom of Kent lapsed.

The construction of a stone castle at Grosmont was begun by Edmund after he gained the site in 1267. A very formidable ditch surrounded the square mound upon which the polygonal castle was built from the blood-red local sandstone. Semi-circular turrets studded the encircling curtain wall and a strong rectangular keep was incorporated into the western part of the curtain. The gate, in the position where the present walkway stands in place of the original drawbridge, was less elaborate than most and was protected by projections from the curtain wall. A remarkable feature of the castle is the survival of a chimney which probably originally served a fire in the lord's 'solar' or sitting-room. Chimneys were considerable status symbols in this period and the lofty octagonal structure is capped with a pierced lantern which served in the manner of a pot and cowl.

The castle stands upon a plateau edge which drops away sharply towards the modern village. Today, Grosmont is just a shrunken remnant of the medieval castle-guarded town which was said to have been the third largest settlement in the south of Wales, after Carmarthen and Abergavenny. The bulk of the town seems to have stood upon the plateau beside the castle.

With its situation in an unsettled marchland, it is not surprising that Grosmont did not always enjoy a quiet life. The decision to build a stone castle may have been inspired by events in 1233. Henry III was encamped with his army below the castle earthworks and was surprised by the combined armies of the rebel Earl of Pembroke and the Welsh prince, Llywelyn, and obliged to make a hasty retreat. In 1405, the army of Owain Glyndwr was defeated by the forces of Henry of Monmouth in the fields outside Grosmont.

Phototips I last visited Grosmont late on a summer's afternoon when the slanted sunlight ignited a splendid blaze of colours, pale ambers where the stones were sunlit and deep reds where they were shaded, all shades of green from the rolling networks of hedged pastures around the blue-black shadows amongst the trees which fringe part of the moat. In short, if the time of day and weather are right, this is a marvellous subject for colour work. It is hard to choose a 'best' angle, for you can walk all around the sturdily compact fortress and see a succession of fine views, either shooting through gaps in the tree fringe or at an angle to the walls towards the field-patterned hillsides to the E.

Location About 14 miles SW of Hereford, accessible from the A465 via the B4347. There is a limited amount of parking in the short lane leading up to the castle from the village's main street

Good photographs can be taken at an angle to the walls with the lovely countryside beyond

ROUND AND ABOUT

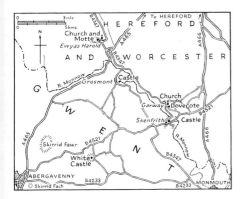

SKENFRITH CASTLE AND WHITE CASTLE

Skenfrith Castle began as a Norman fortress dating back at least to the reign of Henry I and the motte and bailey defences were enhanced with the addition of a stone keep in the reign of Henry II, while the drum towers were added when the Three Castles were held by Hubert de Burgh. This is the smallest of the trio and, as the first to become obsolete, the least affected by later alterations.

White Castle is said to be so-named because its walls were once covered in white plaster. It occupies a lofty position guarding a pass over the Skirrid Fawr mountains and it may have been held by a small garrison which was reinforced in times of trouble. It was begun in the 12th century and remodelled in the 13th century in the reigns of Henry III or Edward I. It has the form of an asymmetrical hexagon with drum towers at each angle, two of them set close together to guard the entrance. Outworks guard the gatehouse and the rear of the castle.

Grosmont: the great Marcher castle built by Edmund of Lancaster

Locations Skenfrith Castle is about 7 miles NW of Monmouth and reached via the A466 and B4521; from Grosmont, follow the B4347 SE and turn left on to the B4521 for the village. White Castle (380168) is about 7 miles NE of Abergavenny and reached by a minor road which leaves the B4521; from Grosmont, take the B4347, turning right on to the B4521.

GARWAY (Hereford & Worcester)

The Church of St Michael and All Angels dates from the late 12th century and was founded as one of the round churches of the Knights Templar. The surviving nave is of the 13th century, but a part of the original round nave survives, as does the Norman chancel arch, while the early 13th-century tower was originally detached from the body of the church.

The lovely medieval church at Ewyas Harold

To the S of the church is a fine dovecote of the early 14th century; although privately owned, it can be visited at specific times.

Location On a minor road leading NW off the B4251 between Skenfrith and the A466.

EWYAS HAROLD (Hereford & Worcester)

The village boasts a particularly lovely medieval church with a square stone stair turret adjoining the tower which has a low pyramidical cap, while the porch is timber-framed. The great motte mound which lies in private grounds is interesting because it is thought that it may be one of very few pre-Conquest mottes; it can be seen from the village.

Location About 12 miles SW of Hereford and reached from the A465 via the B4347.

Note Kilpeck church and Hereford are not far away; *see* the index for page references.

Stokesay Castle

(Shropshire)

The name is misleading, for this is not a castle but a fortified manor house. The Saxon manor passed to the de Lacy family after the Norman Conquest, and the name seems to be a combination of the Saxon 'Stoke'—which can mean a holy place or meeting place, cleared land with three stumps or a dairy farm—and the family name of the de Say family who gained the manor at the start of the twelfth century. The manor house buildings were probably already quite imposing when the then owner, Lawrence of Ludlow who was an extremely wealthy wool merchant, gained a licence to 'crenellate' or fortify his home in 1291, the house and manor having been bought by his father ten years previously.

Hundreds of such licences were granted by the medieval English kings to up-and-coming local notables. Sometimes the need for home defences was a genuine reflection of the insecure times, but often the boastful battlements served as status symbols built to underline the self-importance of the occupant. Since the fortified manors were seldom of such size as to cause real problems of national security, the kings will seldom have cared about the motives for crenellation—but will have been delighted to pocket the licence fees.

The oldest large component of Stokesay is the North Tower, dating to 1240, and Lawrence crowned this with a jettied, timber-framed top storey. The original hall was demolished and replaced by the magnificent 52-foot long open hall which survives as perhaps our finest example of its kind. The hall may date to about 1285, but elements of older work of around 1200 survive in the solar cellar and undercroft, which were used for storage. With the granting of the licence to crenellate, the stone tower was added to the south end of the west front and a surrounding moat and stone curtain wall completed the works.

In his book *English Castles*, R. Allen Brown remarks that 'It would be easy enough to joke that Lawrence of Ludlow, being a merchant, was not quite a gentleman, and therefore his house was likewise not quite a castle, but one would be more justified in supposing that this *mercator notissimus* of the reign of Edward I could have done better than this in terms of fortification had he chosen.'

There have been many changes since the completion of the defence works. The moat has been drained and various timber-framed additions were gained and some of them subsequently lost. It seems that an original stone gatehouse which guarded the bridge across an eastern section of the moat was replaced by the surviving fine timber-framed gatehouse in the years around 1620.

Although the manor has the trappings of a fortified building, it is doubtful whether Stokesay could have resisted an attack by any force other than a small raiding party. On the one occasion when real danger threatened, the then occupant, the 1st Lord Craven who was a fervent Royalist, lost little time in surrendering to a Parliamentary force in 1645 and so the house was spared. Whatever its military virtues, Stokesay was just the sort of country seat which appealed to *nouveau riche* merchant families like the Ludlows and Cravens.

The church which stands beside the manor house contains some Norman work and may have been rebuilt during Lawrence of Ludlow's reconstruction of Stokesay, although the village of South Stoke or Stokesay which it once served is lost.

Phototips There are many good views at Stokesay, especially the timber-framed top of the N Tower as seen from the entrance pathway which crosses the former moat. However, the castle is owned privately and anyone hoping to photograph the great hall may be disappointed since visitors seen approaching with tripods may not be made welcome. The best view of Stokesay is from across the glassy expanse of the former mill-pond which lies to the W of the manor. The area concerned is privately owned and visitors are not encouraged, although you may be able to negotiate permission at the nearby farmhouse.

Location About 7 miles NW of Ludlow and signposted from the A49.

An unusual combination of timber-framing and masonry at Stokesay

ROUND AND ABOUT

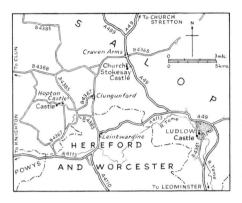

LUDLOW

This extremely attractive town was founded in the years following the Norman Conquest and is a superb example of a planned Norman town. The castle which still dominates the site was built around 1085 on a natural cliff bastion overlooking the River Teme. The town was probably set out by the de Lacy family after the completion of the castle. In the following century, the town plan seems to have been reorganised and the lay-out of the developing medieval town is clearly preserved in the surviving street plan.

Though hemmed in by later development, St Laurence's church is an impressive building when seen from a distance and it embodies some of the wealth created by the town's buoyant medieval wool trade; look out for the misericords. There are several fine post-medieval timber-framed buildings in the town, notably the Feathers Hotel of 1603 and the 17th-century extension to the stone Reader's House which was built in the 13th century and occupied by the local schoolmaster. These lie on

Stokesay: the South Tower, with the 16th-century timber-framed gatehouse to the left

either side of Corve Street, just to the E of the church.

HOPTON CASTLE

The picturesque ruins of a square Norman keep which incorporates some 14th-century additions lie on a valley slope amongst wooded hills. Like many other venerable castles, it was pressed into service during the Civil War. In 1643, its tiny Parliamentary garrison resisted a 500-strong Royalist force for three weeks. When the defenders surrendered, they were first mutilated and then stoned to death in a muddy pit.

Location About 5 miles SW of Stokesay, beside the B4385 Clungunford-Clun road.

Note Other main sites in Shropshire include the hillforts of Caer Caradoc and Old Oswestry, the planned village of Clun and the industrial complex at Coalbrookdale near Shrewsbury. *See* the index for page references.

At Ludlow, the planned Norman town is dominated by the great castle (above). *There are many fine buildings* (below) *in the town*

211

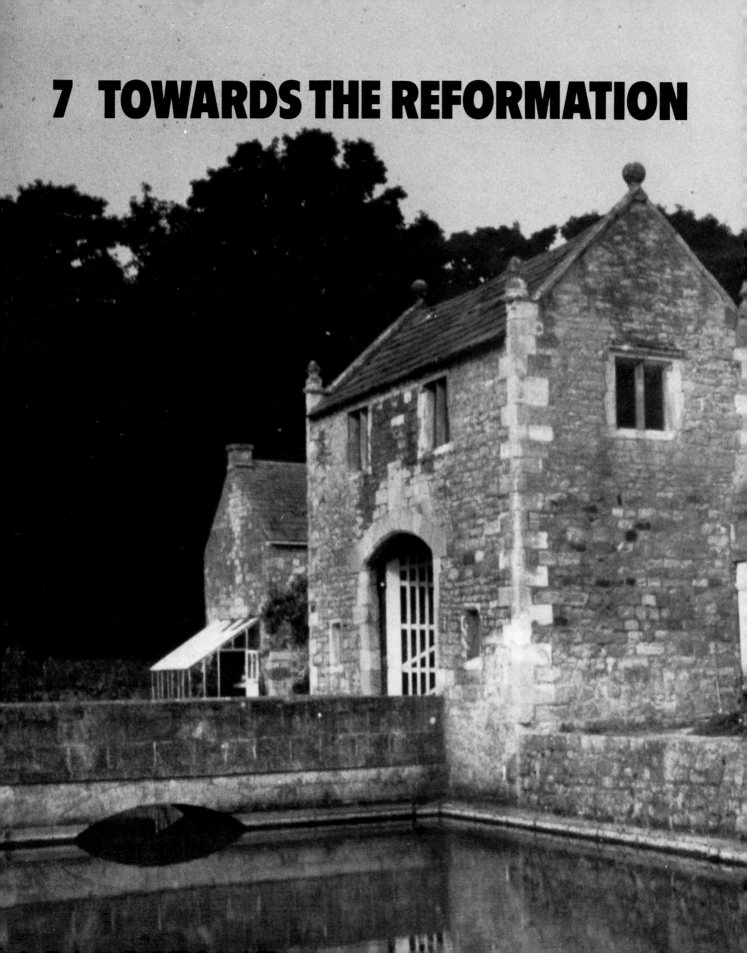

7 TOWARDS THE REFORMATION

The Middle Ages did not end suddenly but, rather, the features which were most characteristic of the period were gradually overtaken by change. The Reformation, climaxing in the first waves of the Dissolution of Monasteries in 1536, is often taken as a convenient landmark signifying the end of the period. The beginning of the end, however, occurred much earlier, with the arrival of the Pestilence in 1348. In the course of the two centuries which followed, there were important social and political changes and disruptions marking the steps in the establishment of a new order.

On the eve of the Great Pestilence, a buoyant spirit may have prevailed in England for a great victory over the French had been won at Crécy in 1346 and Calais was captured in the following year. Nevertheless, the kingdom was afflicted by more deeply seated ills. Not only was it over-populated in relation to the existing levels of rural and industrial production, but the effects of a gradually worsening climate were beginning to be felt. Already land hunger had enticed peasant colonies into many marginal and unrewarding environments while the demands of the swollen population exhausted the poorer soils. Labour was cheap and abundant and in consequence the peasants experienced ruthless exploitation by their masters.

Between 1348 and 1351, it is thought that the Pestilence wiped out between one third and one half of the English population, while in Scotland, Wales and Ireland its impact may have been almost equally severe. Almost overnight, labour became a scarce and valuable commodity. The English establishment attempted to peg wages and preserve the *status quo* under the provisions of the Statute of Labourers of 1351. The legislation was largely ineffective, and although the more radical peasant ambitions perished in the aftermath of the Peasants' Revolt of 1381, gradually and inexorably the feudal village, which was peopled in the main by peasants who were racked by feudal dues and obligations and required to devote a portion of the working week to labouring on their lord's demesne, was superseded by that of the wage-earning labourer and the rent-paying copyholder—the latter having a copy of the entry of his holding in the manor roll.

Conditions for the peasant masses still remained severe. The typical village homestead was still a squalid and poky hovel and, while a number of yeoman farmsteads and artisan or merchant dwellings have survived from this period (*see* Singleton*), many of the details of the peasant home still remain mysterious.

Throughout most of the medieval period, by far the most important English product was wool. Not everyone benefitted from the wool trade and many powerful landlords chose to drive villagers from their lands to create vast, depopulated sheep runs after the Pestilence and its consequences had created fractious and demanding rural labour forces.

Although the Great Rebuilding, which was to create new generations of more substantial dwellings for the less deprived sections of the rural population, still lay in the future, the later medieval period witnessed considerable changes in the concept of the aristocratic home. Throughout most of the period, the provincial magnates had good cause to seek the relative security of castle life. This need was underlined by the events which took place during the main campaigns of the Wars of the Roses, contested between the supporters of the rival York and Lancaster dynasties between 1459–61 and 1469–71. Many aristocratic families were related to the descendants of Edward III and his successors; the blood royal flowed through too many arteries nourishing the ambitions of potential kings and king-makers.

Following the Battle of Bosworth Field in 1485, the throne passed to a new Tudor monarchy and firm, centralised government was gradually imposed upon subjects great and small. Faced by monarchs of the formidable mould of Henry VII and Henry

VIII, the nobles were dissuaded from provocative ventures in private castle-building, while the more stable political climate encouraged them to explore the comforts of domestic life. There was some uncertainty concerning the form and appearance of a home designed for pleasure rather than security, while turrets, moats and battlements had long been the symbols of noble status. At first, there were attempts to build mansions which had the outward trimmings of castles, Oxburgh in Norfolk for example, but eventually the remaining pretensions were abandoned and the age of the stately home arrived, with the readoption of brick providing an equally prestigious alternative to stone as a building material.

The period between the Great Pestilence and the Reformation was the heyday of the final great development of Gothic architecture, the Perpendicular. We cannot be sure how far the introduction of the Perpendicular manner was a natural evolutionary process, or to what extent the rise in wages and inflation and the loss of many gifted masons caused by the Pestilence encouraged the master masons and their sponsors to place the emphasis on soaring lines and brightly-lit interiors rather than detailed and expensive embellishments which were the hall-mark of the preceding, Decorated, style.

The various changes in social and economic life had considerable effects upon religious outlooks. In the later medieval period, parish church projects and extensions tended to attract endowments which might earlier have been granted to monastic communities, while the main energies and ideals which had fuelled monastic expansion were already spent.

Finally, this was the period when the bud of English nationalism, which had been severely nipped by the Norman frost, began to open. It would be quite wrong to attribute nationalist motives to the coerced peasant masses or to mercenaries and aristocratic freebooters who followed the banners of most medieval monarchs. Some form of national sentiment may have motivated the Welsh supporters of Llywelyn who died in 1282, or the fourteenth-century Scottish supporters of Wallace and Bruce while, in England, a precarious sense of national identity began to emerge in the fourteenth century.

Norman French had been the language of the kings and Latin the language of religion and learning. After centuries of official neglect and disparagement, the creation of prose and poems in the native language by writers such as Chaucer, Langland and Gower announced the new respectability and acceptability of English.

Note: *See* Appendix II for other sites in the period preceding the Industrial Revolution.

Markenfield Hall

(North Yorkshire)

The private fortified house or castle of the medieval period came in many shapes and sizes, as the examples of Stokesay*, Bodiam* and Caister* show. Markenfield Hall is a remarkably well-preserved example of an early fourteenth century fortified home that belongs to the small end of the scale. The owner clearly did not have money to lavish on great towers and battlements though the hall may have been more seriously defensive than many of the fortified residences in the south. In the course of the medieval period, many northern timber-framed manor houses were burnt in the course of Scottish invasions and raids, and the nobles of the North had very good reason to expect that their defences might one day be put to the test.

John de Markingfield gained a licence to crenellate a house in 1310. Eight years later, in the aftermath of their victory at Bannockburn in 1314, the Scots poured into Yorkshire, burning the town of Knaresborough just a few miles away and many local villages—but Markenfield luckily escaped.

The house and outbuildings at Markenfield enclose a square courtyard and the whole is still surrounded by a well-filled moat. There was a drawbridge in

OPPOSITE, right *and photograph on pp 210–11: Markenfield Hall, a very well-preserved early 14th-century fortified home*

place of the present stone bridge and the entrance via the drawbridge was guarded by the surviving gatehouse. The house itself is 'L'-shaped and, as was often the case with stone-built medieval houses, the main rooms are at first-floor level. The great hall, which served as a general reception room, the banqueting and court room occupied the shorter limb of the 'L' and a chapel and another room formed the longer, while the kitchen and storage rooms occupied the lower levels. Access to the hall was by an external staircase.

The hall, chapel and gatehouse buildings endure, but over the years the other buildings which enclose the courtyard have been rebuilt more than once and

the remains of fifteenth- and sixteenth-century buildings are included amongst the later stonework. On the whole, though, the atmosphere and appearance of a compact fortified manor house and farmstead is maintained and although the interior could be improved by a small amount of restoration, it is uncluttered by later embellishments. It is not hard to imagine the lord, his family and retainers gathered around the logs which blazed in the great fireplace while the winter gales blasted around the draughty hall.

Phototips When buildings are clustered closely around a courtyard, there is an 'inside' and an 'outside' view and so it is

not possible to capture the whole story in a single shot. At Markenfield, there are fine views from the outside, looking across the moat towards the gatehouse, and also from inside the courtyard, looking towards the hall building.

Location The hall is much less well-known than it deserves to be and, being privately owned, is only officially open to the public on Mondays between May and September. Some care is needed in finding the hall which lies at the end of a poorly-marked but easily accessible field track which runs westwards from the Ripley–Ripon section of the A61 about $1\frac{1}{2}$ miles N of the hamlet of Wormald Green.

ROUND AND ABOUT

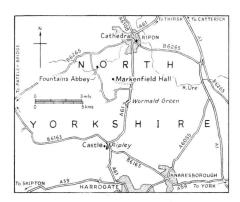

RIPLEY

The village, with its authentic cobbled market square, cross and stocks and 'Gothic' stone cottages has an 'olde worlde' charm, though in fact the dwellings were provided when the Ingilby family had the village rebuilt and pret-

The medieval cross and stocks in the cobbled market square at Ripley

tified around 1826. The Ingilbys have held Ripley Castle for 700 years and legend tells that the estates were granted after Thomas Ingilby saved his king from a charging boar while hunting in Knaresborough Forest—hence the stone statue to a boar beside the square. The castle was rebuilt in 1780 but an original tower remains and in 1963 a 'priest hole' was discovered in the Knights Chamber of 1555.

The family was Catholic and refuges such as this were essential during the religious purges of the 16th and 17th centuries: in 1557, Francis Ingilby, the family priest was hanged, drawn and quartered at York. The Ingilbys supported the Royalist cause during the Civil War and both Sir William and his sister 'Trooper Jane' fought for the king. While they were thus engaged, Cromwell stayed a night in the castle but his reception by the lady of the house is said

to have been chilly in the extreme. Bullet holes in the east wall of the medieval church at Ripley are believed to be grim relics of the execution of some Royalist prisoners.

Location Just by-passed by the A61, about 3 miles N of Harrogate.

ABOVE *Ripley church in winter*
Ripon Minster, one of the views not ruined by careless modern building and tree-planting

RIPON

The church, which gained cathedral status in 1836, is rather hemmed in by the bustling little market town and is a patchwork of 19th-century restoration, Perpendicular and Late-Norman architecture. It was severely vandalised by Puritans during the Civil War and in 1660 a spire collapsed causing extensive damage. The cathedral is, however, unique as the only one to include a 7th-century crypt, part of a church which was attached to a Benedictine monastery which was destroyed by Danish raiders in 950.

Location At the junction of the roads A61 and A6108 and B6265

Note The spectacular Fountains Abbey is close by, and the Aire Valley industrial complex lies to the south-west; *see* the index for the page references.

Bodiam Castle

(East Sussex)

Some history enthusiasts—myself included—like castles which are tough, craggy and uncompromising such as Hedingham* or Grosmont*. Others prefer the fairytale ethos of moats and turrets at castles such as Beaumaris*, Caerphilly and Bodiam. This last-named castle might almost have been constructed on a Hollywood set, and although it was never particularly important, its aesthetic charms are unsurpassed. It is also interesting because it occupies a transitional zone in the story of castle development.

In the earlier medieval centuries, an abundance of private strongholds were built by nobles who often had good reasons to fear their neighbours, to choose sides in the recurrent dynastic struggles or to proclaim their aristocratic status in a flourish of towers and battlements. However, during the course of the Wars of the Roses, many great lords perished and many strongholds were ransacked, while in the aftermath of the Wars the Tudor monarchs succeeded in bringing the haughty provincial aristocrats to heel. Few could consider resisting the newly found might of central government, the large mercenary armies which the kings could recruit or the destructive power of the improving cannon. Most of the later medieval castles were not private fortresses, but royal bastions, built in the main as components in a policy of national defence against foreign invasion and coastal raiding.

Bodiam bridged the gap between the two types of castle in a way that was almost unique. The medieval kings of England derived an important part of their revenue from the sale of licences, including licences to crenellate or fortify manor houses through the addition of towers or battlements (*see* Stokesay*). In the case of Bodiam, the licence which Richard II issued to Sir Edward Dalyngrigge in 1385 involved a private stronghold in a policy of national defence.

The logic behind this peculiar arrangement is not hard to fathom since French coastal raiding and the threats of more serious invasions caused much alarm. The nearby channel port of Rye had been ransacked and put to the torch in 1377 and New Winchelsea, which lay downstream from Bodiam by the mouth of the River Rother, was raided three years later. Bodiam was obviously well placed to stem any French invasion which sought to penetrate to the interior via the Rother valley.

Despite its incidental prettiness, Bodiam was built as a tough defence. Appearances can be misleading for as medieval castles go, this is quite a small example. The plan is quite simple, a square interior being guarded by massive and lofty curtain walls with rugged drum towers guarding the corners and rectangular towers set in the middles of the east and west walls.

By this time, the keep had been superseded as a last-ditch stronghold by the installation of the formidable gatehouse tower which was a castle in its own right and also concentrated defences around the vulnerable entrance. The Postern Gate in the south curtain at Bodiam is defended by a strong tower, but invaders who cracked this nugget of defensive masonry would still have to contend with the linked rectangular towers which overlooked the barbican and comprised the great or northern gatehouse. As a sign of the times, the towers were fitted with gun loops for cannon. Gatehouses such as this, or the fine example which towers above the ruined remainder of Donnington Castle in Berkshire, were as much defences against internal mutiny or treachery as against external attack.

In the event, Bodiam was not put to the acid test of French invasion for by the time of its completion, England had gained supremacy in the Channel. In 1483, Lancastrian rebels who were sheltering at Bodiam swiftly surrendered to a sieging force led by the Earl of Surrey and the castle was scarcely harmed. During the Civil War, the now obsolescent castle capitulated to a Parliamentary force which was strengthened by a powerful complement of artillery and the interior structures were severely 'slighted' or reduced.

Bodiam Castle, one of the brightest gems in the National Trust crown; the water lilies provide the finishing touch

In 1916, the site was bought by Lord Curzon who launched a series of excavations and discovered the piles which had supported various timber bridges which crossed the moat. He carried out a programme of restoration and, on his death in 1925, Bodiam was bequeathed to the National Trust. The castle is one of the most beautiful and popular monuments in the Trust's treasury, but it is also an unusually revealing example of military thinking from the declining years of the private stronghold.

Phototips The photographer who fails at Bodiam is unlikely to succeed elsewhere! When photographing castles, the most impressive pictures are often taken from an angled rather than a 'full frontal' position. In this case, there are

Looking across the wide encircling moat to Bodiam Castle

spectacular views from all four corners, particularly the SW, with the Well Tower in the foreground, and the WNW.

Location About 12 miles N of Hastings, taking the minor road through Bodiam village from the A229 or A268.

ROUND AND ABOUT

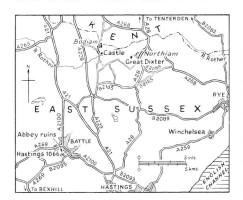

GREAT DIXTER

The wonderful house is a most unusual combination of an original 15th-century timber-framed house and a second house of a Tudor vintage which

was rescued from Benenden where it was languishing in bad repair and reassembled here. The great architect Sir Edwin Lutyens supervised the marriage of the two dwellings in 1909 and, with the help of Gertrude Jekyll, designed the gorgeous gardens.

Privately owned, it is open to the public at specific times.

Location At Northiam, a short distance to the SE of Bodiam and reached via a short lane from the A28.

The glorious gardens at Great Dixter, designed by Edwin Lutyens with Gertrude Jekyll, show a beautifully organised but relaxed effect with splashes of midsummer colour

BATTLE

The ridge of Senlac Hill, the scene of the Battle of Hastings in 1066, lies on the outskirts of this small town and is one of a relatively small proportion of British battlefields which still retain an aura of destiny. Some ruins survive from the Benedictine Abbey (now in private trusteeship) which is said to have been built as an expression of the Conqueror's gratitude, with its High Altar marking the spot where Harold fell. Perhaps most impressive is the gatehouse at the head of Battle High Street which was a late addition, and erected after Abbot Alan had gained a licence to crenellate in 1338.

Location By the B2095, ½ mile SW of Battle. There is a limited amount of parking in front of the gatehouse and the entrance to the area of countryside which includes the site of the Battle of Hastings is nearby.

The peaceful fields where the Battle of Hastings was fought in 1066

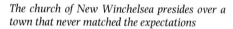

The church of New Winchelsea presides over a town that never matched the expectations

NEW WINCHELSEA

The town was the creation of Edward I, a planned replacement for the original Winchelsea which received many batterings from the sea before it perished finally in a storm in 1287. The new site was divided into a gridwork of plots, but they were probably not all filled and, after a very short life as a port, New Winchelsea declined when its harbour became silted and Rye took over the port trade. Visitors to the much-shrunken town may still be able to trace the outlines of the planned urban blocks in the surrounding fields.

Location On the A259 between Hastings and Rye.

Note Bayham Abbey is in the neighbourhood; *see* the index for the page reference.

The Church of St Peter and St Paul, Lavenham

(Suffolk)

Development, of course, did not come to a standstill during the Middle Ages and the Britain of the fifteenth century differed in many important ways from that of the eleventh. Many vital social and economic changes were mirrored in the pattern of church buildings. They often reflect the growth of towns and industries, and the rise of *nouveau riche* families who owed their wealth to manufacturing and trading ventures rather than land inheritances and changes in attitudes to personal salvation. All these changes can be recognised in the palatial church of St Peter and St Paul at the failed medieval textile town of Lavenham.

Lavenham rose from the ranks of the surrounding humble villages as a collection centre for the export of wool and it developed its own textile manufacturing industry in the fourteenth century when a colony of Flemish clothworkers was established. The industry expanded during the fifteenth century when the town was renowned for its blue cloth, but decline became apparent at the start of the sixteenth century.

The reasons were various; there was competition from the worsted cloths of Norfolk, periodic losses of continental markets as a result of wars and blockades, restrictive practices operated by the guilds and, perhaps most severely, a shortage of water power to drive the new fulling hammers which replaced the old foot-stamping process in the production of felted broadcloths. The industry gradually drifted to water-powered sites further to the west of England and the development of steam-powered textile manufacturing at northern coalfield sites in the eighteenth and nineteenth centuries sounded the final death knell.

Dating from the period 1444–1525, the church of St Peter and St Paul symbolises the years of Lavenham's greatness and embodies some of the wealth which the blue cloth earned. It also reflects changes in the pattern of endowment. Earlier in the Middle Ages, the wealthy feudal landowners had tended to purchase the salvation of their souls with endowments to monasteries. In time, however, the monastic reputations became tarnished and monks the subjects of ridicule. Meanwhile, the rich often sought more personalised monuments to their generosity and chose to endow palatial church buildings, resplendent with the family coat of arms, ornate family chapels or other extensions to existing buildings. Perpendicular architecture, the style of the later medieval period, is apparent in a few monastic buildings and in some of the cathedral rebuilding operations, particularly in the west of England — Gloucester and Worcester, for example. More than any other Gothic style, however, it is associated with a magnificent array of majestic parish churches — none more imposing than the example at Lavenham.

The church mirrors the evolving pattern of wealth for it combined the old wealth of the de Vere family, the Earls of Oxford, with the new wealth of the rising local clothier families of Branch and Spring. The de Veres held the manor from the Norman Conquest until the sixteenth century and their boar and star emblems are displayed throughout the interior. Two generations of the Spring family, however, were responsible for financing the tower, which is encrusted with their newly-awarded arms.

Whereas the preceding Decorated style of architecture which we have met at Wells* and Patrington* derived much of its impact from the elaborate and fluent details of the stone carving, the Perpendicular style placed the emphasis on the soaring vertical line which is carried through the window tracery and accented in lofty towers. The tower at Lavenham is remarkably tall even by Perpendicular standards; it rises to a height of 141 ft and, even so, it has an unfinished appearance and legends suggest that a taller tower was planned.

In spite of the riches which flowed from the textile industry, the endowments could not cover the enormous costs of making an entirely stone-built church in this stone-poor countryside. Stone was imported from Barnack near Peterborough to provide the structural de-

The church of St Peter and St Paul, a symbol of Lavenham's one-time vast wealth

The church porch at Lavenham

framed town beneath from the top: an affluent settlement of clothiers, merchants and weavers fossilised by the industrial decline.

There is a pageant of fine buildings and monuments in the town: there is the Corpus Christi guildhall of 1529 which overlooks the market place and the cross of 1502, the Woolstaplers and De Vere House of the fifteenth century, the Elizabethan Swan Hotel and many other fine buildings.

Phototips The church is a splendid sight at any time of the year, but in the autumn when the tourists have departed and the nearby trees are red and gold, the scene is unforgettable—as it is also in snow and sunlight. The great height of the tower makes the use of a wide-angle lens almost essential. The best pictures are probably those taken from vantage points in the churchyard near to the entrance from the main road. The entrance has attractive details which can be used for framing the church if you stand—with all necessary wariness—in the road and photograph through the gateway. From this position, the whole building can be covered with a standard lens. Visitors to the church tower should take a telephoto

Lavenham is a picturesque town

lens, if available, which can be used to 'pull in' house details from the little town down below.

Location On the A1141 between Bury St Edmunds and Ipswich.

tails, but in the walls and towers it is combined with the local flint in attractive 'flushwork' panels. The tower is normally open to the public and although the ascent is arduous, one gains a wonderful panorama of the timber-

ROUND AND ABOUT

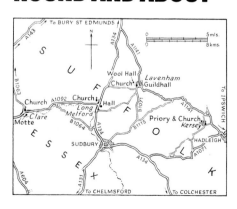

The impact of the medieval wool industry was by no means confined to Lavenham and there are several other villages in the locality with palatial churches and substantial timber-framed houses which testify to former glories. Here is a selection:

LONG MELFORD

This village has a 15th-century church

to rival that of Lavenham although the tower is mainly 20th-century. Note also Melford Green, the vast triangular village green that slopes down towards the village and the 16th-century Trinity Hospital buildings below the church and Melford Hall of 1560 beside the green, owned by the National Trust and periodically open to the public.

Location On the A134 about 3 miles N of Sudbury.

Long Melford's superb 15th-century church

CLARE

The church is of the 13th, 14th and 15th centuries. Also note the particularly fine and early 'pargetting' or plasterwork on the 15th-century priest's house by the churchyard and the gigantic motte mound which survives after the decay of the 13th-century keep which crowned it.

Location On the A1092 about 8 miles NW of Sudbury.

KERSEY

This village gave its name to a very popular type of cloth and the stream which bisects the main street was used in the fulling of cloth. Poor Kersey has far more visitors than it can really cope with and is therefore best visited out-of-season.

Location Between Sudbury and Ipswich and about 2 miles NW of Hadleigh and reached by a minor road from the A1141.

Note Castle Hedingham in Essex is nearby, and a little further north is the reconstruction of the Saxon village of West Stow; *see* the index for page references.

Fine plasterwork on the priest's house in Clare

Kersey: (Top) *The stream was once used for the fulling of cloth.* (Above) *The attractive village street leads up to the parish church of St Mary* (below)

227

Caister Castle

(Norfolk)

Although not particularly formidable as a defencework, Caister Castle is of special interest both to literary enthusiasts and to those who are fascinated by the study of architectural history. First, the literary associations: the castle was built by Sir John Fastolfe (1378–1459), at a time when the austere private stronghold was becoming redundant, homes more comfortable, and when battlements and moats symbolised status rather than impregnability. Sir John provided Shakespeare with a model for Falstaff, although the real Sir John was a sterner warrior than the Shakespearean character and gained a considerable reputation in the French wars.

He built his castle in the 1430s, and his use of brick rather than stone was a remarkable innovation. Useful technologies are hardly ever abandoned and so the disappearance of the craft of brickmaking in the centuries following the collapse of Roman rule in Britain is most puzzling. Saxon masons incorporated slender Roman bricks in several of their churches and the great Norman cathedral of St Albans displays prodigious quantities of red bricks salvaged from the ruins of Roman Verulamium. Although the manufacture of clay floor tiles seems to have been started by the end of the Saxon period and roof tiles were being made in the twelfth century, the first post-Roman brick-built construction of any size seems to have been Little Coggeshall Abbey, erected towards the end of the twelfth century.

It was only in the Tudor period that brick came to be adopted in the creation of fashionable and prestigious mansions and palaces. Compton Wynyates in Warwickshire, which was begun in the 1480s and enlarged in the 1520s, pioneered the use of brick. The material was used on an even grander scale in the building of Cardinal Wolsey's palace at Hampton Court, which was begun in 1514 and employed 2,500 men for five years in its construction.

It has been said that the bricks which were used in England in the later stages of the Middle Ages were brought as

OPPOSITE and right: *Caister Castle, built by Sir John Fastolfe in the 1430s*

ballast in wool trading vessels returning from the Low Countries. This does not seem to have been the case at Caister, however, for the bricks were baked in kilns on the castle site and Sir John may have introduced techniques which he had seen in practice in the course of his soldiering on the continent.

Not all of the castle has survived, but the 90-ft round tower with its hexagonal side-turret remains intact up to its parapet and a well-filled moat still laps around its base. The original moat and castle were more extensive, for the remaining great tower guarded the western corner of a rectangular complex of buildings including a great hall and state apartments which surrounded an inner courtyard. These were linked by a drawbridge to another collection of buildings which flanked three sides of an outer courtyard, while both groups were surrounded on all sides by a great moat.

The gardens in Caister Castle's inner court

The moat was filled by a channel which ran to the River Bure and was navigable by Sir John's barge of state..The remains of the barge house lie to the south-west of the castle complex.

The castle was built on the site of a flint-walled manor house destroyed in the Peasants' Revolt of 1381. However, it was probably not the possibility of a repetition of these events which persuaded Sir John to construct such a well-fortified home. It was more likely that he was preoccupied by the threat of Flemish invasion or coastal raiding. Both gun loops and arrow slits were provided and the garrison of thirty to forty armoured men would have offered stiff resistance to raiding parties, although the castle was much less formidable than many of its great stone predecessors. When Sir John died, Caister Castle was bequeathed to John Paston but in 1469, when he was away in France, the Duke of Norfolk's forces besieged the castle which, after five weeks, surrendered through a shortage of food and gunpowder.

Preservation work at Caister has been carried out by the present owner, Alderman P. R. Hill who is also a veteran car enthusiast. A large collection of vehicles is housed in a modern display area nearby, well-sited so as not to intrude upon the remains of this unique building which marks a late stage in the history of the private stronghold, but an important pioneering stage in the reintroduction of brick.

Phototips There are fine views of Sir John's tower either from the bridge which crosses the moat or from the remains of the inner court. In the former case, the moat provides an excellent foreground, while in the latter, the flowerbeds give colourful details. The best results will be achieved in slanting morning or late afternoon sunlight, at instants when other visitors have momentarily passed out of view.

Location Signposted on a minor road from the A1064 and just $1\frac{1}{2}$ miles W of the resort of Caister-on-Sea, N of Great Yarmouth.

ROUND AND ABOUT

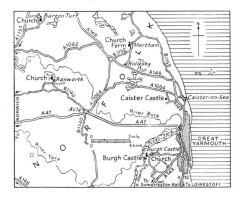

RANWORTH

The Church of St Helen is unusual in having retained its rood screen and rood loft intact, as such highly decorated features of the medieval church were commonly destroyed in the troubled years which followed the Reformation. The rood screen, which is decorated with paintings of the twelve Apostles, St George and St Michael and other saints, has recently been very beautifully restored. It has been described as 'probably the finest coloured screen in the country'.

Location Ranworth lies between two broads, about 8 miles ENE of Norwich, on a minor road off the B1140. From Caister Castle, take the A1064 to Acle, then the B1140.

BARTON TURF

Another fine painted screen can be seen in the Church of St Michael and All Angels at Barton Turf. The building dates mainly from the 14th and 15th centuries and has a fine, battlemented tower. The beautiful screens are 15th-century.

Location Barton Turf is about 11 miles NE of Norwich, on a minor road off the A1151.

Note Burgh Castle lies just to the south, and further south still is Somerleyton; *see* the index for page references.

The Story of the House at Singleton

(West Sussex)

The Weald and Downland open air museum at Singleton is one of the most lustrous gems in the crown of conservation. It is not only a magnificent collection of carefully restored and preserved dwellings, but is also guaranteed to lift the spirits of those brought to despair by acts of official and unofficial vandalism. Like a splendid beacon, the Singleton project signals what can and could be done in the field of conservation. Nobody who has followed a group of suddenly absorbed and enthusiastic schoolkids around this vast museum as they discover what history is *really* about would ever again accept the worthless platitudes about the heritage which drop like dead old leaves from the lips of officials entrusted to protect it.

The vocation of the museum is that of rescuing not the stately homes—of which we have an abundance—but the best examples of 'vernacular' buildings: the homes and work-places of commoner folk. The museum was the brainchild of J. R Armstrong MBE and it occupies a site provided at a peppercorn rent by the Edward James Foundation; it is spacious and allows the buildings to be grouped or dispersed as seems most fitting within the country park (where picnics are allowed). Much of the nec-

essary work is accomplished by volunteers although a small team of professional craftsmen is employed. The museum is non-profit-making, responsible for raising its own funds and receives no regular grants or subsidies.

The collection of reassembled and reconstructed dwellings and farm buildings is large and varied. The oldest dwelling reconstructed is a Saxon 'grubhut', rather less substantial than the West Stow* version. The dwelling which interested me most was the Hangleton cottage. No medieval peasant dwellings have survived but excavations have

shown that they were almost always flimsy and squalid, unlikely to endure for even half a century. In areas where stone was available for house or hut building, as at Houndtor*, then more substantial dwellings might have been built. The Hangleton house is based on two fairly similar examples excavated at the lost village site of Hangleton near Hove, which was abandoned in the fourteenth century when the Pestilence or Black Death, climatic decay and economic ills seemed to form a deadly conspiracy against village England.

The original of the cottage probably

The conservation project at Singleton. (Opposite) *The Boarhunt Hall and* (right) *a reconstructed Saxon 'grub hut'*

The Hangleton house: this semi-partitioned room would have housed an entire peasant family

dated from the thirteenth century and has low walls of flint rubble gleaned from the chalky ploughlands. A thatched roof has been provided, but roof materials are perishable and the roof of the original might almost equally as well have been of turf, broom or wooden shingles. A simple partition sections off a small area which contains an oven. There is no chimney, and smoke from the hearth filters away through a smokehole in the gable. The entire peasant family would have shared this single semi-partitioned room.

The most imposing dwelling at Singleton is the Bayleaf farmhouse which is a type of home known as a 'Wealden house'. It dates from around the middle of the fifteenth century and consists of three components, those at either end of the unjettied central bay having 'jetties' or overhanging upper storeys, the central section extending right from the ground floor to the rafters as an open hall. The reasons for the construction of jetties are uncertain; in a cramped town, the jetty offered a little more space on the first floor, but this was no great advantage in country areas. The jetty may have been a status symbol adopted in the homes of more affluent farmers. The inclusion of a privy during an early stage of improvement is another sign of the rising status of the occupants!

The Bayleaf farmhouse, one of three Bough Beech Reservoir houses donated by the East Surrey Water Co., underwent several alterations before it was reconstructed at Singleton when the experts faced problems concerning the choice of authentic roofing materials and the nature of the original infill between the great timbers of the frame. It was decided that the house had probably been roofed in tiles from the outset and the infill panels were formed of a mud daub on a framework of hazel woven between oak staves.

Other particularly notable exhibits include the Boarhunt Hall (Hampshire) of around 1500, built according to the cruck—rather than the more common box—method of timber framing, with each bay defined by a pair of massive curving blades joined to form an 'A'-shaped support for the roof.

Then there is the delightful Pendean farmhouse, a small yeoman farmstead of the late sixteenth century brought from near Midhurst in W. Sussex. Built near the close of the Middle Ages, it has the unglazed windows and ceilingless upper storey rooms of the medieval homestead combined with the efficient internal chimneystack which was adopted in later dwellings.

In addition, there are several fascinating non-residential and industrial buildings including a granary which is perched above the reach of rodents on staddle stones, cattle sheds, a fine watermill and a beautifully restored market hall from Titchfield in Hampshire.

Having walked around a number of these remarkable buildings, one is left in no doubt that medieval domestic life was much different from that of today. Although the farmsteads tended to be quite small, the generally open nature of the interior provides a feeling of spaciousness. The lack of ceilings or continuous partitioning walls, the unglazed windows and the open smokeholes suggest that most homes were draughty places. They probably were, but fires smoulder in open hearths in some of the rooms at Singleton and it is surprising how much warmth they create.

The Wealden House at Singleton and (bottom) *a reconstructed fireside scene*

Another feature of the homes, further evidenced by the survival of early inventories, is the sparse nature of the furniture—a wheelbarrow could have served as a removal van for most peasants and small farmers. The designation of rooms was also different from that of today. Outside pits generally served as inadequate substitutes for the modern loo, beds were scattered about the home and specialised bedrooms were unusual, while much living space was sacrificed for the storage of produce and the kitchen as such often did not exist; home-brewing was generally the main activity practised in the small chamber known as a 'buttery'.

The museum at Singleton offers much more than the available space will allow me to describe. But nobody with the remotest interest in the history of English home life and architectural history should miss the chance to visit this very special museum.

Phototips From the outside, the buildings are all easy and attractive subjects. The key to success is patience; one must choose the best viewpoint and then wait as long as may be necessary for other visitors to move out of frame, for their presence in photographs is much more intrusive than in real life. After experiencing a few of these delays, one learns the advantage of having the lens, focus and shutter settings ready and the ability to draw and shoot quickly is not confined to cowboys!

Interior work will test everyone's ability to the full. Flash alone will destroy all the beautiful effects of the natural light which trickles through doors and windows and dances along the venerable beams. In the course of a time exposure, however, it is often desirable to throw a little flash into a dark and gloomy corner. There is no substitute for the tripod although it may be a pest to carry around, and a pest to other visitors if used selfishly in inconvenient places. When using a tripod on private land, it is always courteous to ask permission, but the patient and well-equipped photographer can obtain some beautifully evocative results in the interiors at Singleton. In such houses, it is very important to check the depth of focus settings to ensure that nearby and distant parts are as sharp as possible. Even so, one should not stop-down more than is necessary as most lenses will perform better at f11 than at f16 or f22.

Location About 6 miles N of Chichester, just off the A286, SW of Singleton village.

ROUND AND ABOUT

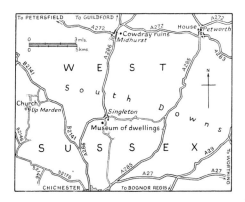

A whole day can be spent at the museum and fascinating things may still be left unseen.

Visitors approaching from the N could pause at the Cowdray ruins on the outskirts of Midhurst. The great house was burned in 1793 but the ruins are starkly romantic and a fine granary is preserved on the neighbouring green.

Petworth House, with its 13th-century chapel and 17th-century mansion is about 8 miles E of Midhurst, just off the A272 at Petworth village. Owned by the National Trust, Petworth House deserves a full-length visit, however, and it would probably be a mistake to try to combine in one day this magnificent house with Singleton which has so much to offer.

Note Not far away in Hampshire is the Iron Age house reconstruction at Butser Hill; *see* the index for the page reference.

The Cowdray ruins, with the gatehouse in the centre of the range

The Lost Village at Wharram Percy

(North Yorkshire)

In the course of the Middle Ages, thousands of villages were deserted. The causes were varied. For more than a century after the Norman Conquest, the climate seems to have been a little warmer and drier than today and this, combined with the pressure of a growing population, enticed settlers to colonise some of the less rewarding uplands and claylands. After 1200, the climate began to deteriorate and the poorer villages on the marginal farmlands bore the brunt of the adverse conditions. A few medieval villages were destroyed in the course of warfare and rather more by Cistercian monks in the clearance of farmlands around monastic farms or 'granges'. The year 1348 witnessed the arrival in Britain of the ghastly Pestilence or Black Death and a number of villages—but not as many as folk legends suggest—were depopulated by the plague.

The greatest onslaught upon the ranks of village England came in the fourteenth, fifteenth and sixteenth centuries when hundreds, perhaps thousands of communities were evicted from their homelands, to be replaced by flocks of sheep. Many landlords considered that it was more profitable to raise livestock than to collect rents from peasant farmers, and the uncertainty of

---

the fates which awaited the evicted villagers was seldom considered.

There are several thousand lost village sites in Britain. In many places, the relics of village life have been completely obliterated by modern farming practices, a large proportion are inaccessible to the public, but there are two sites in particular which are especially rewarding: Houndtor* on Dartmoor and Wharram Percy in Yorkshire. Wharram was deserted around 1500 and, although the details are not clear, it seems that it was destroyed by the Hilton family, to clear the way for sheep—and sheep can still often be seen grazing the pasture which cloaks the footings of the lost homesteads.

Wharram Percy would be just another name on the ever-lengthening list of re-discovered deserted villages were it not for the fact that in 1952 the newly formed Deserted Medieval Village Research Group (now named the Medieval Village Research Group) undertook the onerous task of excavating the site. Volunteer diggers under the direction of John Hurst have been continuing the excavation ever since, although only a fraction of the village area has yet been explored in great detail. The evidence which has emerged from Wharram has done much to transform our understanding of the medieval village and its life. There are ample traces of prehistoric and Roman activity, although a village as such did not develop here until late in the Saxon period but, when it did, its lay-

out was influenced by old field boundaries dating from the Romano-British period. The original settlement had two focuses and it was only in the middle of the thirteenth century that a unified village resulted from the merging of the two village manors.

The excavations also revealed the insubstantial and ephemeral nature of the typical peasant dwelling of the Middle Ages, and the exploration of house sites showed the partly overlapping remains of many dwellings. It was calculated that, once built, a peasant hut or house might only endure for around twenty-five or thirty years before a complete rebuilding was necessary.

Although still the subject of active excavations, visitors are welcomed at Wharram; one must, however, respect the delicacy of the areas which are currently being explored and not interfere in any way.

There is only one entrance to the site; as one approaches down a deep cleft in the side of the chalk valley of Deep Dale, the ridges or earthworks which define the old village streets and property boundaries can be seen on the opposite slope. Crossing the small stream which runs in the bottom of Deep Dale, one then joins the grass-covered trough or 'holloway' which marks the main village street. It can be followed up and along the slope and the ridges and trenches on either side represent the turf-clad outlines of former dwellings and the boundary banks separating the

long plots or 'tofts' which were attached to each homestead.

Following the holloway southwards, the remains of the village church come into view, lying on low ground in the valley bottom. The first church at Wharram was built about the tenth century, though it was probably preceded by a cemetery and a preaching cross which was used for outdoor services before a field church was provided. In the course of the Middle Ages, the church at Wharram Percy grew and then shrank, being at its largest in the thirteenth and fourteenth centuries. A decline in the numbers or wealth of the congregation before the final desertion is shown by the reduction in the size of the church. The excavators have marked the outlines of the larger church on the surrounding turf. The church survived after Wharram was deserted, providing services for the people of Thixendale, who obtained their own church in 1870. Occasional services were held at Wharram until the late 1940s, but thereafter the fabric swiftly decayed when thieves stole the lead from the roof, while a part of the tower collapsed in 1960.

Just to the south of the church lies the village millpond which is interesting because analysis of materials from the dam show that the mill site dates from around AD 700 and is therefore older than the village.

As a result of the remarkable information about the medieval village in England which accrues from each season of excavation at Wharram, this Yorkshire village is far more notable today than it ever was in its lifetime. Its historical importance apart, however, Wharram is one of the loveliest of our many lost village sites and Deep Dale has a special quality of tranquil beauty.

The church at Wharram Percy remained in use until the late 1940s

The research achievement at Wharram impresses even more when one realises that it is the accomplishment of volunteer diggers and supervisors operating on a shoestring budget with very little official funding.

Phototips The ruined church is an evocative and soulful subject from all angles, but the best views are to be taken from the slopes which overlook the building, either from the NW, where bushes provide foreground detail, or from the SW, where it is seen nestling deeply in the valley. Earthworks are the most difficult of subjects to photograph, for while they may seem quite clearly defined in real life, in photographs their impact tends to be much less. The best results are often obtained when shooting into a low sun which casts long shadows towards the camera. If possible, therefore, wait for late afternoon when the earthworks will be clearly defined by the sinking sun, and you should expect to take good shots with the aid of a telephoto lens from approaches across the valley.

Location (858642) About 7 miles SE of Malton; take the B1248 to Wharram le Street village and then travel in a SW direction for a short distance on a minor road. A small car park is provided close to the roadside and the final stage of about $\frac{1}{4}$ mile is made on foot.

ROUND AND ABOUT

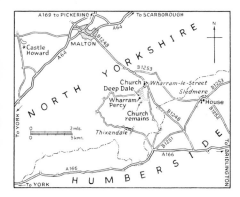

Not far from Wharram Percy is the lavish and palatial Castle Howard, built by Sir John Vanbrugh and his assistant, Nicholas Hawksmoor. However, to visit both places in one day would prove most exhausting.

WHARRAM-LE-STREET

The partly Saxon church at Wharram-le-Street is an especially attractive example, dating from about 1050. It stands in a slightly isolated position on the uphill side of the village.

The rather isolated Saxon church at Wharram-le-Street

Location See directions for Wharram Percy

SLEDMERE HOUSE (Humberside)

Generations of manor houses had stood on the site of the present house; the estate was inherited by the Sykes family in 1748 and has remained in that family ever since. The surviving Georgian mansion, which contains Chippendale and Sheraton furnishings, was completed in 1787, a decade after the landscaping of the surrounding park by 'Capability' Brown. An important racehorse stud farm has operated here since 1803.

Location 7 miles N of Great Driffield, close to the B1252.

Note The Roman road at Wheeldale Moor and the Cistercian foundation of Byland Abbey are both in the neighbourhood; *see* the index for page references.

239

8 INTO THE MODERN AGE

If we liken the course of history to a staircase, with each important change and development represented by a step, then our imaginary structure will have a peculiar form. The first steps, representing stages in the perfection of flint-working technology, the introduction of farming or the discovery of bronze- and iron-using techniques, would be widely spaced. In the course of the Middle Ages, the staircase would steepen, but the middle of the eighteenth century onwards the steps come ever closer together until they are stacked almost vertically like the strata in a rock face. Until the modern period, the landscape and its settlements tended to evolve at a more leisurely pace, so that a man would not be lost and disorientated in his grandfather's world. During the Industrial Revolution, which began around 1760, the rate of change was quickened, becoming hectic, then frantic, creating vast and impersonal urban societies helplessly addicted to new technologies but deprived of the deep roots in community and place which buttressed the older lifestyles.

Before the nineteenth century, an interest in the past and its monuments was largely monopolised by a small number of upper and upper-middle class antiquaries who were generally regarded as eccentrics. Today, perhaps because of a subconscious disenchantment with the materialistic world which we have created and a deep-seated need for roots and identity, an interest in the past is a major national passion.

Not that this need is being served by government, for the rate of the destruction of worthy vernacular buildings and the good old countrysides in which they lie is both appalling and accelerating while those conservationists who look for help are offered platitudes. In the course of this book, several most praiseworthy reconstructions have been introduced—most of them the fruits of sparsely-funded private initiatives rather than of official creativity and innovation. Poland is a sad, bankrupt and insecure country. For years, it has been the economic failure within an East European empire of faltering economies. Yet, on an archaeological site which the Nazi invaders tried to destroy, the Poles have reconstructed the Iron Age village of Biskupin. It utterly dwarfs any and all of the reconstructions which this book has described. It attracts some 140,000 visitors each year and, despite the ravaged state of the Polish economy, the Poles have never regretted the recreation of this facet of their heritage. In Britain, meanwhile, farming subsidies underwrite the bulldozing of old hedgerows, and important monuments are closed down to save the wages of their curators.

The sites which are included in this chapter are selected as typifying stages and facets of the advance from the medieval to the modern world. Fountains Abbey, where the ruined monastic buildings lie in a landscaped wonderland created by hard-headed men of affairs, typifies the Revolution and its aftermath; this is followed by Lichfield Cathedral which bears witness to the destructive bitterness of post-medieval dynastic and religious conflict, the neglect of great religious buildings in the early stages of the Protestant supremacy and the zeal of later generations of church restorers. The importance of the garden and recreational landscape in the setting of the great houses can be explored at Lyveden and Kirkby Hall in Northamptonshire, where much of interest has survived. Sedgemoor in Somerset is the scene of the last great civil battle in England where the records show that medieval forms of brutality were inflicted upon the defeated.

The Industrial Revolution was parallelled and partly preceded by a revolution in the countryside which had less drastic influences upon modern life but which reshaped most countrysides and, largely through the effects of Parliamentary Enclosure, extinguished the last traces of the old peasant existence. Fragments of the old rural landscape with its handsome and homely buildings, locally wrought in local materials, are found at the Avoncroft museum, while the traditional dwellings of the Irish countryside which are preserved in replica at Bunratty are described. Two landscapes which were forged in social and economic furnaces of the Industrial Revolution are included; that of the Ironbridge Gorge in Shropshire will have been visited by many readers, but the fascination of the industrial relics of the Aire valley in Yorkshire are probably new to most. At Cliffe Castle near Keighley, Wimpole Hall in Cambridgeshire and Somerleyton House in Suffolk we are introduced to the homes of nineteenth-century magnates, no less men of their times than the knights and barons of the Middle Ages.

The twentieth century poses the most daunting problems in the selection of sites for it offers so much—and yet so little that seems outstanding. History begins yesterday and our own period is as worthy of study as any other. I have chosen to represent it by a Battle of Britain airfield—a relic of perhaps the most crucial summer in our history—and by the Humber Road Bridge, which may be the most elegant monument to the age of the internal combustion engine.

Each of the many sites described in this book has its own distinctive beauty and romance but, in exploring the appealing qualities of lost ages and lifestyles, we should not lose sight of the genuine advantages of the present world. Most prehistoric and medieval peasants lived out their lives in conditions of abject servitude and the small minority of people who lived into middle age and beyond often had bodies contorted by arthritis, worn and pitted teeth and the legacies of malnutrition and vitamin deficiencies. They had no pensions, no health service, no education and no insurance. Their masters were not immune to the horrors of life either; epidemics of any of a wide range of ghastly diseases could afflict them all at any time and, in the absence of antibiotics and skilled dentists, even toothache could cause weeks of suffering and maybe death.

The future lies beyond the scope of this book except in just one respect. In the middle years of this century, we confidently anticipated a world in which new technologies and social policies would raise all standards of living while the working week was steadily shortened. Now we are less hopeful; but if this Golden Age should ever arrive, it is unlikely that our successors will be content to pass their leisure in suburbs, urban parks, museums and galleries, no matter how well planned and provided they may be. They will want to visit the heritage of monuments from bygone ages—but while the grander gems in this heritage may not be at risk, many others are. The past does not belong to us; we are just custodians and we are not performing our duties very well. It is one thing to drive to monuments like Caer Caradoc* or Castlerigg* past a pageant of glorious countryside, but quite another to visit showpiece sites which are set like islands in a monotonous ocean of featureless and defiled prairie fields. Conservation is not a luxury but an obligation—and the time is running out.

Note: *see* Appendix II for other sites in the period between the Industrial Revolution and the modern age.

Fountains: An Abbey Dissolved

(North Yorkshire)

Founded in the 1130s by a community of Benedictine dissident monks who craved the greater austerity of the Cistercian rule, Fountains Abbey rose from a scene of pioneering hardship to become one of the most wealthy and powerful forces in the medieval realm. As the fortunes of the community established beside the River Skell rose, and endowments flooded in, whole villages were swept away to clear the way for new monastic farms or 'granges'; the empire of Abbey estates extended across the Pennines and into the Lake District.

In this chapter, however, the Abbey is described in a different light, as a symbol of the Reformation and the redistribution of monastic assets which occurred in its aftermath.

On the eve of the Reformation, the realm of Henry VIII included some 10,000 male and female members of monastic orders, thousands more of their lay associates and servants and more than 800 religious houses. The causes of the Reformation were complex and involved more than just the political intrigues and wrangles concerning papal opposition to Henry's divorce and remarriage to Anne Boleyn. In 1534, an Act required every man to swear an oath in support of the validity of the marriage,

but although some Franciscans and Carthusians had refused, this could not justify the indiscriminate assault on all monastic foundations.

For perhaps two centuries, there had been a mounting popular disenchantment with various features of organised religion and particularly with the wealth, callousness and clearly evident corruption of many monastic communities. Meanwhile, the religious fervour which maintained the great church and monastery building programmes of the High Middle Ages had abated; the Great Pestilence of 1348–51 and the numerous outbreaks of plague which followed had removed monks and laymen alike and in the fifteenth and early sixteenth centuries many of the monasteries had less than half their full complements of monks. Probably more important than the internal corruption and decay of many foundations was the simple cause of greed on the part of the King and his supporters.

The monasteries, their lands, rents and treasures represented a vast empire of real estate and a treasure house of goods and profits. The problems of Henry's first marriage and its failure to provide the male heir—which he correctly regarded as crucial to the stability of the Kingdom—and the ensuing unsuccessful wrangle with the Pope created a political climate in which the Dissolution of the monasteries could be considered.

The first round of dissolutions took

place in 1536 and suppressed only about a third of the monastic houses, mostly quite small foundations. This, however, was the year of the great northern-based rebellion of the Pilgrimage of Grace, perhaps more concerned with popular social and economic grievances as with religious issues. But after the Pilgrims had re-installed dissolved communities in their houses, the King had an excuse for further acts of forfeiture. Then, one by one, the remaining houses were dissolved, pressurised into 'surrendering' to the crown until, by 1540, all the monastic foundations in England and Wales were dissolved.

The Abbey at Fountains was far from being moribund at the time of the Dissolution; indeed, work on the great tower was scarcely finished when the Abbey met its fate. The last true Abbot, William Thirsk, was accused by the King's commissioners of embezzlement, depravity and sacrilege. If these charges served as a stick, he was also offered a carrot in the shape of a pension of 100 marks following his resignation. In the event, he became tainted by his association with the Pilgrimage of Grace and so was hanged for treason in 1537— and the pension was saved.

He was replaced in suspicious circumstances by Marmaduke Bradley, who duly surrendered the Abbey to the crown in 1539, receiving a pension of £100 while the remainder of his community received single figure sums. Since the annual revenue of the Abbey

Fountains Abbey seen from the landscaped parks of Studley Royal

was alone worth ten times Bradley's pension, the dissolution of Fountains was financially an attractive proposition and the Abbey assets included some 1,146 sheep and items of plate, metalwork and vestments worth £700.

Sir Richard Gresham had coveted the Abbey property for some time and, having bought it, he wasted no time in ransacking the monastic buildings for their carpets of roofing lead, vast painted glass windows and wooden furnishings.

Like many of the laymen who profited from the Dissolution, Gresham was a wealthy London merchant and the outlying estates, farms and manors soon became part of his merchandise, although he retained the abbey grounds for a while. Along with the remaining estates, these were sold to Sir Stephen Proctor in 1597.

At the start of the seventeenth century, Proctor built his Elizabethan-style mansion, Fountains Hall, beside the Abbey ruins. It has lasted as a well-preserved relic of the stately home of the immediate post-medieval period, with a great banqueting hall and minstrel gallery testifying to the survival of medieval influences. The Abbey grounds became

a park, and the hall and park complex passed through the hands of the Evans and Messenger families before being sold to William Aislabie of Studley in 1767. The Aislabie family had lived at the adjacent manor of Studley Royal for almost a century where they had been responsible for landscaping fashionable gardens within its 650 acres.

Following the acquisition of the Fountains park, William Aislabie and his son John began to integrate the two parks, producing a great sweep of ornamental ponds, flanked by lawns, bounded by woodlands and punctuated by temples, grottoes, pavilions and cascades. While the well-preserved 18th-century park landscape is regarded as one of the finest of its kind in England, the interest in landscaping and the picturesque possibilities of the Abbey ruins allowed for the survival of the Abbey buildings in a form more complete than is commonly the case. Therefore, visitors to Fountains Abbey may well mourn the destruction of the splendour of the monastic buildings but, as a consequence of the Dissolution and its aftermath, they are able to see not only the beautiful and still intelligible Abbey ruins, but also visit a fine mansion of the seventeenth century and enjoy a magnificent panorama of eighteenth-century landscaped park and gardens.

The Abbey has recently been acquired by the National Trust.

Phototips The landscaping of the park, the use of the Abbey ruins as a key point in the various vistas and the provision of 'surprise views' ensure that splendid photographs can be taken from almost any quarter. One of the finest can be taken from across the River Skell, now a sort of formal waterway, looking back towards the Abbey ruins, using a standard lens or a short telephoto lens. The Abbey apart, the park contains many other fine views: it was designed so that it should. Where the exterior of Fountains Hall is concerned, the wide-angle lens is essential as the tall building stands on raised ground and presents the familiar 'parallax' problem since the confines of the drive prevent the photographer from stepping back to gain a more distant vantage point.

Location About 4 miles SW of Ripon and signposted from the B6265.

ROUND AND ABOUT

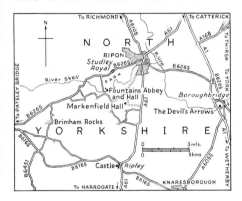

BRIMHAM ROCKS

This pocket of surrealistic scenery with its weirdly sculptured millstone grit tors is exceptional for its geological rather than its historical interest. A monastic grange did exist, however, at Brimham and carved medieval stones have been incorporated into the walls of Brimham Hall. The rocks are owned by the National Trust.

Location From Fountains Abbey, continue towards Pateley Bridge on the B6265 for about 4 miles, then take a minor road to the left, as signposted.

THE DEVIL'S ARROWS

Three of the original four great prehistoric monoliths survive. Their function is quite unknown but was presumably associated with Bronze Age religion and ritual. The fluting of the tips of the great stones is the result of natural weathering processes. The surrounding area is rich in subtle but important prehistoric rituals, including a number of earthen henges.

Location (391666) On the outskirts of Boroughbridge, between Boroughbridge and the A1.

Note Markenfield Hall is nearby and, to the SW, is the industrial complex of the Aire valley; *see* the index for page references.

Brimham Rocks silhouetted against the wintry Yorkshire landscape

Natural weathering has produced the fluting on the Devil's Arrows

Lichfield Cathedral – A Church Besieged

(Staffordshire)

There are many good reasons for visiting Lichfield Cathedral, but I include it here in the context of the religious conflicts which accompanied the Reformation and Civil War. Arbiters of architectural taste tend to place this cathedral rather low on their lists; this is because much of the work on view is the result of Victorian embellishment and extensive restoration work of the seventeenth, eighteenth and nineteenth centuries. Although the cathedral may lack the 'purity' of the architecture at, say, Durham or Wells*, we should not be deterred for this is a lovely building with a fascinating past.

The church's foundation dates back to the year 700, when a wooden church was erected to enshrine the remains of the Bishop of Mercia, St Chad, who died in 672. (The St Chad Gospels are the cathedral's greatest treasure.) It seems that the site already had long religious associations for a great stone, which may have been used in pagan rituals, lay buried beneath the high altar of the present building. Other connections with antiquity are shadowy; the name 'Lichfield' could mean 'the place of the corpses' but more probably derives from the name of the nearby Roman settlement of Letocetum, and there is a legend that British Christians were massacred here during the persecutions of the Emperor Dioc-

letian, around 300, while the Mercian cathedral seems to have been preceded by a 7th-century Celtic church.

It appears, therefore, that the original cathedral was attracted to a site of great religious importance and was not associated with a settlement of any size. Norman policy favoured urban cathedrals and so, in 1075, the see was moved to Chester and then to Coventry and it was only in 1836 that the full dignity of the foundation was regained.

Despite its demotion, the church was rebuilt after 1135, when the Saxon foundation was replaced by an apsed Norman church. By this time, the attraction of the shrine of St Chad as a focus for pilgrimage was considerable and, by the end of the century, the Norman church was inadequate.

After 1195, it was reduced by stages and then a new church began to emerge. The work accomplished in the years around 1200 included a central tower in the new Early English style. The rebuilding and enlargement bridged the periods of the Early English and Decorated styles and was only completed in 1340, by which time the Decorated era had almost run its course. The stone chosen for the work was the mellow but soft red sandstone of the Midlands, and the russet building was unique in England for its magnificent display of three great spires which became known as 'the Ladies of the Vale'. Throughout the medieval period, the relics of St Chad assured endowments and the attentions of a constant

stream of pilgrims and in the fourteenth century the Shrine of St Chad's Head was moved to a special position in the new Lady Chapel.

A recent expert study of Lichfield and its area by S. R. Bassett has underlined two very important themes in the history of our landscape: first, that the Iron Age and Roman landscapes were much more thoroughly and productively organised than was thought and, second, the importance of planning in medieval times. It was shown that some of the fields around Lichfield, which survived until the middle of the nineteenth century, were older than the Roman roads which had been superimposed upon them.

The cathedral and its close were inserted into an ancient field system and in the mid-twelfth century a planned town was laid out beside the cathedral. Although some of its features became blurred by later growth and rebuilding, particularly after a severe fire in the west of the town in 1291, sufficient evidence remains today to show that the town was originally planned in great detail on the basis of a 40-ft module. When a 40-ft grid is superimposed on the map of modern Lichfield, many of the enduring streets, like Market Street, Bore Street, Wade Street, Frog Lane, Baker's Lane and Bird Street, fit it very well.

This magnificence, however, died with the Middle Ages. Protestant opinion in the Reformation was violently opposed to the veneration of crosses, images, relics and other 'popish' symbols. In the reign of

Henry VIII, Lichfield's great asset, the Shrine of St Chad, was demolished while in the reign of his son, Edward VI, church treasures were removed, books destroyed and the valuable chantry endowments were nullified. The fabric of the great church survived—but worse was to follow.

In the course of the Civil War, relations between the church authorities and the people of the town, which had grown in the shadow of the great institution, were fractured. The town sided with the Parliamentary cause, while the churchmen of Lichfield remained loyal to the King. In 1643, Royalists fortified the cathedral close and, ironically, the Parliamentarian forces began their siege on St Chad's Day, March 2. A cannonade felled the great central tower and spire which, as they dropped, ripped a path through the roof of the church. After the Royalist surrender, their adversaries launched a frenzy of destruction, tearing down monuments, smashing the painted glass, ripping out the finely-carved woodwork, burning books and, later, stealing the communion plate and linen. The desecration culminated in a profane celebration in which cats were pursued around the building by hounds.

Prince Rupert drove out the Parliamentary forces a few weeks later, but war returned to Lichfield in 1646 when there was another successful Parliamentary siege of the Royal garrison. Another orgy of destruction followed; statues were again defaced, the bells were smashed and almost all the lead was stripped from the roof of the church. For fourteen years afterwards, the battered building was left open to the elements and became a virtual ruin.

On the Restoration of the monarchy in 1660, however, the precentor Canon Higgins, who had survived the events of 1643, assembled as many remaining members of the church community as could be found and a service was held at

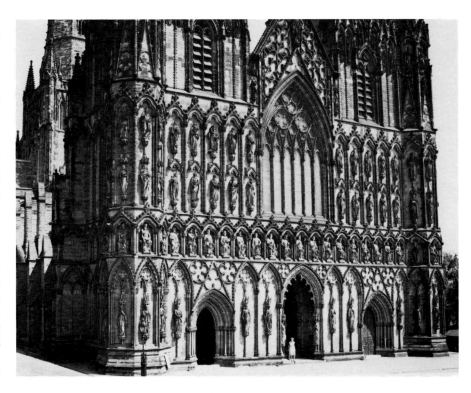

Lichfield Cathedral showing the finely detailed carvings on the restored façade

Lichfield. New canons were appointed and work began on patching up what remained of the formerly magnificent church. Within five years, funds for the restoration had been collected.

The typical Protestant church of the eighteenth century was a grimly functional building, often stripped of carving and statuary, its windows repaired with plain glass and its paintings masked by coats of whitewash. In the course of this century, many of the churches which had been erected in the Middle Ages were beginning to show signs of severe decay, although most of them had to wait until the great restoration boom of the nineteenth century for the necessary repairs. At Lichfield, much needed repair work began in 1788; the improvements

were of a modest nature, but in 1802 the cathedral received a collection of fine sixteenth-century painted glass, bought from Herkenrode, a Cistercian Abbey in Belgium which was pillaged during the French occupation of the previous year. The seven windows can be seen in the Lady Chapel.

Further restoration work began in 1842 and continued until 1908, with Sydney Smirke, Sir George Gilbert Scott and John Oldrid Scott being involved at various stages. More work has been carried out in the course of this century and the need for regular attention is exacerbated by the susceptibility of the New Red Sandstone to erosion. The magnificent tiers of statuary on the west front of the cathedral are largely attributable to the restoration of 1885, but they provide more than just a glimpse of the grandeur of the original façade which was completed in 1293.

Almost all great churches represent

the accumulation of the works of several medieval centuries. The cathedral at Lichfield is more deeply rooted in antiquity than most cathedrals and it also suffered more than any other (with the modern exception of Coventry) at the hands of zealots and vandals. Like its original construction, its resurrection is the product of centuries of devoted endeavour. The Ladies of the Vale are still arguably the most evocative landmark of the English Midlands even though, outside the Midlands, the cathedral may not have received the recognition that it deserves.

Phototips If only other authorities could adopt the same reasonable and practical policy towards photography as that which is followed by those at Lichfield! Rather than banning cameras or leaving the conscientious photographer to wonder whether he may or may not proceed, at Lichfield one pays a small fee for the right to take photographs of the interior of the cathedral.

Nothing worthwhile will be achieved with flash alone: the spaces are too vast to be lit with flash while the beautiful subtleties of the natural illumination should be captured. In short, a tripod is needed. The magnificent exterior and west front pose problems. The great height of the three spires is such that a wide-angle lens is essential. Even then, one is obliged to retreat to the furthest corners of the precinct, although one can obtain a more distant vantage point from the lane which approaches the close from the west. Even so, parked cars and fellow visitors are likely to intrude: there are no easy answers and one needs a measure of both patience and good luck. Don't overlook the finely detailed carvings on the west front and the three great doorways are pictures in themselves. An attractive view of the more distant cathedral can be obtained from the road bridge which crosses the nearby river.

Location In the centre of Lichfield, which lies a few miles to the N of the Birmingham conurbation.

ROUND AND ABOUT

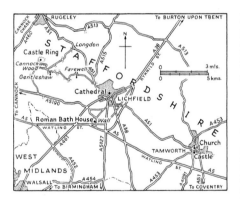

WALL

Here, on the crossing of Watling Street and Ryknild Street, a Roman bath house has been preserved, a relic from the settlement called Letocetum, where a traveller was able to obtain accommodation and stabling facilities. One can see the *pillae* of the hypocaust and, in a different chamber, the niches or lockers where bathers left their clothes.

Wall is now in the care of the Department of the Environment.

Location Proceed S from Lichfield along the A5127 and after about 2 miles follow signs on the minor road which runs to the W; Wall is about 2½ miles SW of Lichfield.

TAMWORTH

The former capital of Saxon Mercia contains several interesting monuments including a Norman keep with Tudor and 18th-century additions which contains a museum; also see the fine 18th-century town hall in red brick, and the 14th-century church of St Editha.

Location SE of Lichfield, on the A51.

CASTLE RING HILLFORT

Staffordshire lies to the N and E of the areas where the enthusiasm for hillfort building ran strongest in the Iron Age. A well-preserved ditch and rampart ring surround an island of heathland, while the panorama of Cannock Chase which is gained from Castle Ring reveals the sad destruction of other areas of old heathland by large coniferous plantations.

The hillfort is maintained by Cannock Chase District Council.

Location (045128) From Lichfield, follow signs for Rugeley and then take attractive minor roads to the W via Farewell and Gentleshaw; the fort lies just to the N of Cannock Wood and is signposted.

The ramparts of Castle Ring hillfort

Meeting the Great House in Northamptonshire

William Camden, the late 16th-century antiquary, noted that Northamptonshire was 'passing well furnish'd with noblemen's and gentlemen's houses'. Four centuries later his remarks are still true, and what are probably the two most interesting and informative of the great houses of the county appeared during Camden's lifetime. They are Kirby Hall and Lyveden New Bield—although, as we shall see, the New Bield is not quite what at first it appears to be.

Kirby Hall marks a fascinating meeting between the old and the new traditions in house building and design. It was begun in 1570, at a time when the custom of house design by craftsmen was gradually about to yield to the new practice of planning by architects. The Hall was built of excellent freestone from the famous Northamptonshire limestone quarries at Weldon and it seems to have been the creation of the mason Thomas Thorpe. Professor Pevsner believes that, like other great Elizabethan mansions such as Burghley and Longleat, Kirby Hall was influenced by Somerset House of 1548–52, but it also embodied local building styles and other features like its ornate giant pilasters and decorated motifs which were then fashionable on the continent.

Lyveden New Bield is not a large country house as it appears; it is an oppulent 'conceit' built especially for banquets

Although the Hall was progressive and fashionable in many respects, its lay-out was governed by traditions which reached back into the Middle Ages, for the ranges of buildings were still set around a courtyard which was in complete contrast to the later, compact 'double-pile' houses which were built several rooms in depth. Also, the principal range still contained the archaic design of the great hall with the kitchen to one side and the parlour to the other, so that any Norman lord would have been able to find his way around Kirby Hall with ease.

While the Hall itself is an interesting, important and appealing building, the main fascination is the accompanying gardens. Many country mansions boast of 'medieval' or 'Elizabethan' gardens, but all are in fact much later reconstructions, mostly dating from the late-Victorian and modern periods. Old houses have had many generations of owners, and sooner or later an owner will have appeared who wished to express his or her tastes in a re-organisation of the gardens; then, for reasons of poverty or a lack of interest, allowed the old arrangements to become overgrown, or else responded to the 18th-century fashion for allowing a landscape park to sweep up to the walls of the great house, causing the intervening gardens to be destroyed.

Kirby Hall is unique in that it displays a garden lay-out which dates from the 1680s. In the passage of time, the Hall became partly ruinous, and so did its gardens. However, in the course of restoration work, it was realised that the stone edgings of the garden beds remained in place, although buried and overgrown, and so it was recently possible for the gardens to be revived according to this lay-out.

Here then is an intricate geometrical pattern of flower beds which are linked by pathways and defined by low hedges in the typical formal designs of the late 17th century. Roses will have been the principal shrub planted, and lavender may have featured in the planting plans. Given the importance of the gardens, it is a little disappointing that the beds are now planted with modern hybrid tea and floribunda roses rather than with old-fashioned varieties. There are excellent elevated views of the gardens from the house itself, from the lofty bank marking the opposite sides of the gardens, or from the summit of the old 'prospect mound' which can be seen to one side of the formal beds.

The Hall—now in the care of the Department of the Environment—was commissioned by Sir Humphrey Stafford, who died in 1575. The estate was then bought by Sir Christopher Hatton, Lord High Chancellor and a favourite of the Queen, whose principal house was at Holdenby in the same county. By a strange coincidence, another set of the Hatton family's gardens survive at Holdenby, but as an overgrown archaeological monument. They were created

253

The limestone façade and geometrically laid out garden of Kirby Hall

by the same Sir Christopher Hatton in 1579–87—at the expense of two villages which were removed, while a village church was incorporated into the garden. Earthworks show how masses of earth were shifted to create terraced flower beds, a rectangular pond, a bowling green, lawn and lake.

The masters of the seventeenth century countryside took their pleasures seriously, a point which is perfectly made by the building which survives, unroofed, at Lyveden. This is the New Bield, a name which means 'new building'. The old building was the family home of the Tresham family, and the new one, now owned and typically well presented by the National Trust is, at first sight, a substantial country house. In fact, it is an opulent 'conceit' or summer house which was built as a focus for banquets and elaborately-staged entertainments.

It was begun in the 1590s and demonstrates the strong fashionable influence of the quest for symmetry, for not only is each elevation balanced and symmetrical, but each is also virtually identical. At Kirby Hall, the desire for symmetry was married to an essentially traditional lay-out, but at Lyveden New Bield, the symmetry extends all around the house and the compact shape foreshadows the more severe, 'blocky' Classical buildings of the 18th century.

Even so, some conservative influences prevailed, for the hall and parlour were large chambers on the raised ground floor, although the kitchen and buttery were placed in a basement, while a great chamber and bedroom were on the upper floor. Religion too exerted an effect, for the Treshams were devout Catholics, and the cross-shaped house plan is thought to represent Christ's Passion. Plans to crown the building with a two-storey lantern and dome, and later, to 'Palladianise' it with a cupola, were never completed.

Phototips Neither Kirby Hall nor Lyveden New Bield present any great technical challenges, although at Kirby, the height of the façade and the broad sweep of the gardens favour the use of the wide-angle lens. Sunlight is a great advantage, for the fine Northamptonshire limestone used in both buildings glows like molten gold when sunlit.

Locations Kirby Hall, lying at the end of a long drive, is reached via the A43 and the minor road from Deene to Gretton and is 11 miles NE of Kettering. Lyveden New Bield is 4 miles SW of Oundle and is reached via a field path which is signposted from the minor road having previously left the A6116 in a NE direction at Brigstock.

ROUND AND ABOUT

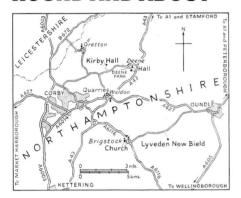

DEENE PARK

In contrast to the situation at Kirby Hall, here are seen the results of the gradual remodelling of a medieval house. Fragments of 13th- or 14th-century masonry are still displayed, while much of the fabric and lay-out of a Tudor house with a great hall and ranges of building arranged around a courtyard is well preserved. As successive owners adapted and enlarged the house, a very complicated building developed and the S. front which overlooks the terrace, waterway and park, includes 16th-century work with early 18th-century windows, early 19th-century Gothic Revival architecture and the ballroom of 1865.

The house was bought by the Brudenell family in 1514 and the 7th Earl of Cardigan (James Thomas Brudenell) who led the ill-fated Charge of the Light

The south front of Deene Park: a mélange of architectural styles

Brigade in 1854 lived here. It remains in private hands. Fine gardens and a park which contains a collection of rare trees are on view.

Location Reached by a minor road which leaves the nearby A43 for the W about 6 miles NE of Corby.

BRIGSTOCK

The stone-built village is attractive in its own right, but is celebrated for the Church of St Andrew which retains a Saxon tower and nave. There is an imposing Saxon tower arch and the exact function of the rounded W extension to the tower has not been explained.

Location On the A6116 about 5 miles SE of Corby.

The church of St Andrew in Brigstock with its lovely Saxon tower

Sedgemoor Battlefield

(Somerset)

Old battlefields are seldom the evocative places which visitors might expect. Often farming and development have so transformed the scene that a great deal of imagination and local knowledge are needed before the setting of the great events can be reconstructed. The Sedgemoor environment has been considerably affected by the reclamation of the nearby marshes and water meadows, but many of the old landmarks remain. It is, therefore, possible to retrace the advances of the armies, visit the site of their clash without being pursued by hostile farmers and see the places where the cruel events of the aftermath of battle were enacted. The battlefield site is now owned by the National Trust.

The Battle of Sedgemoor of 6 July 1685 is an important historical milestone for a number of reasons. It is often called the last or most recent battle in England. As a nobly-led provincial uprising, it had some of the features of a medieval civil war, and certainly the conflict was medieval rather than modern in terms of the callousness and brutality displayed in the course of the battle and afterwards. Unfortunately, such cruelty did not entirely disappear from these islands after Sedgemoor but surfaced at Glencoe and Culloden in

Scotland and at the scenes of many skirmishes in Ireland. Sedgemoor was also the scene of the last great religious battle in England.

The battle was a sorry affair in which an army of less than 5,000 Puritan yeomen and peasants and unemployed wool workers, who had joined a Whig and Protestant rebellion led by the Duke of Monmouth, were crushed by regular forces which were three times as numerous. The cause was already doomed for Monmouth's poorly-armed forces had failed to enter Bristol and had fallen back on Bridgwater while the army of the Catholic James II advanced into the West Country. From the tower of St Mary's Church in Bridgwater, Monmouth was able to witness the approach of the royal army; he did not wish to withdraw from the defensible line of the River Parrett and chose to attempt a daring night attack on the enemy encampment near Westonzoyland village.

It was a disaster. The royal forces were alerted by the sound of a stray shot, the armies met at around 1.30 a.m. and the battle continued until about 3 a.m. Only sixteen members of the King's forces were killed directly (though many died later of their wounds) but around 300 rebels were slaughtered on the battlefield. Some 500 rebel prisoners were then herded into the church at Westonzoyland; seventy-nine of them were wounded, and five died of their wounds inside the church. The parish records which contain a contemporary account

of the battle tell that after the prisoners were moved, frankincense and resin were burned to sweeten the air. The villagers, who are unlikely to have welcomed the royal victory, were obliged to ring the church bells in 'gratitude'.

Twenty-two rebels were hanged near the battlefield, four of them in chains; Monmouth himself was captured and put to death. The reprisals however continued. In the course of the Bloody Assizes which followed, the evil Judge Jeffreys presided as cowed juries brought the verdicts which caused 300 of Monmouth's impoverished supporters to be hanged, while a further 800 were transported to the West Indies. James II's Queen requested the gift of 100 rebels and sold them for transportation at a profit of 1,000 guineas.

Perhaps the most pitiful aspect of the whole affair was that the battle did not greatly affect the course of English history and within a few years its result was overturned. The fear of suppression by a reactionary Catholic aristocracy provided a common cause for Whig and Tory politicians, common folk, Nonconformists and the church establishment. A petition was sent to the staunch, capable and Protestant ruler William Prince of Orange who duly 'invaded' with his Dutch army on 5 November 1688 at Torbay and made a slow and stately progress towards London. Parliament chose to pretend that James had abdicated and William and his wife Mary, who was second in line to the

---

The site of the Battle of Sedgemoor (6 July 1685) lies in an area of improved pastures which stand a little above the peaty moors

English throne, became joint sovereigns.

James sought support on the continent and although his eviction brought a measure of peace to most of England, the Jacobite cause continued to threaten the stability of the northern counties where there was a substantial Catholic minority, to underlie uprisings in Scotland, culminating in the Jacobite defeat at Culloden in 1746 and to

The fine Perpendicular church at Westonzoyland where unfortunate captives were held after the Battle of Sedgemoor

encourage the cruel suppression of Catholic peasants in Ireland.

The transportation of Monmouth's rebels was remembered with bitterness in Somerset for a good two centuries after the events, but in England time has healed the old religious sores. To the credit of the landowner, the Sedgemoor battlefield site is accessible to the public and there is a small monument. It lies in an area of improved pastures which stand a little above the moist black peat of the nearby reed- and birch-sprinkled moors.

The church at Westonzoyland would be well deserving of a visit even had it

not borne such close witness to the brutal conflict of 1685. Somerset churches are renowned for the exceptional quality of their Perpendicular towers and Westonzoyland boasts a fine and early example, provided by the Abbot of Glastonbury in 1384. Inside, the standard of the carpentry in the roof rivals that of even the East Anglian churches. As has been described, the interior was the scene of cruel and squalid events but one can seek the 'little north door' through which a man called Scott, who had visited Monmouth in an attempt to trade some horses, managed to escape from the guards. He hid in cornfields until the Bloody Assizes had run their course and he survived.

Phototips The battlefield site itself is only likely to yield dramatic studies if the patterns of light and cloud are suitably ominous and lowering. If they are, then the effect can be enhanced by using an orange filter for black-and-white work or a graduated violet, tobacco or grey filter for colour.

The church at Westonzoyland is a wonderful subject; it can be photographed from the roadside if one has a wide-angle lens which is sufficiently wide to capture the full height of the tower without tipping the camera. There is also a fine view of the distant church as it soars above the moorland setting from a minor road which runs on the non-battlefield side of the village, towards Thorngrove hamlet.

Location About 3 miles ESE of Bridgwater; from Bridgwater take the A372 to Westonzoyland, or turn off the A361 Wells–Taunton road at Greylake or just N of Othery and follow signs for Westonzoyland. The battlefield lies on the outskirts of the village and is signposted from the village centre. The farmtrack leading to the memorial is marginally drivable while donations towards the preservation of the site can be given as indicated by a small sign.

ROUND AND ABOUT

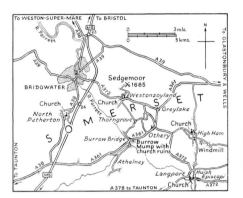

The Perpendicular church of North Petherton

BURROW MUMP

The bowl-shaped hill which juts from the flat landscape of pasture and marsh in such a surprising manner is an unforgettable landmark in the magical landscape of the Somerset Levels. It is hard to believe that the summit is scarcely more than 95 ft above sea level. Although the pimple on the crown which carries the ruins of an unfinished 18th-century church has been artificially scarped, despite its man-made appearance the hillock is a natural outcrop of Triassic sandstone and Keuper Marl. A church of one type or another has stood on the hill since at least the 15th century, but in 1836 a less lofty

The unfinished church on Burrow Mump

and inconvenient church was provided for the villagers of Burrow Bridge and the present hilltop church, begun in 1793, was never completed.

The hill has traditionally been regarded as an outer fortress guarding the approaches to King Alfred's 9th-century stronghold at Athelney, but archaeology is unable to support the claim. It is possible that a small Norman castle may have stood on Burrow Mump and there may have been a castle here in the 14th century. There are certainly more recent military associations, for in 1645, 120 soldiers from the Royalist army of General Goring—which had been defeated by Parliamentary forces under General Fairfax at Langport—took shelter in a ruined church on Burrow Mump until they surrendered to a Parliamentary detachment.

The remains of the church were given to the National Trust in 1946 by Major A. G. Barrett as a memorial to the men of Somerset who died in the Second World War.

Location Visible for miles around; overlooking Burrow Bridge village where the A361 crosses the River Parret and just 3 miles S of Westonzoyland.

NORTH PETHERTON CHURCH

Visitors to Westonzoyland or Burrow Mump and bound for Bridgwater should find time if possible to make a small detour via the A38 to see the fine Perpendicular church at North Petherton, 3 miles S of the town.

Other exceptional towers in the (old) county of Somerset are in the villages of Batcombe, Huish Episcopi, Kingsbury Episcopi, Chew Magna, Dundry, Evercreech and Chewton Mendip.

HIGH HAM MILL

This tower-mill, unusually built of stone in about 1820, is the only one surviving from a number which were once standing in the neighbourhood. It has a thatched cap made from reeds which are said to have come from Abbotsbury in Dorset. It stands in an attractive garden and is owned by the National Trust.

Location The mill, something of a landmark in this flat area, is ½ mile E of High Ham which is 2 miles N of Langport, via the A372.

Note Wells cathedral and Glastonbury are in the neighbourhood; *see* the index for page references.

The tower-mill at High Ham, dated 1820

The Avoncroft Museum of Buildings

(Hereford & Worcester)

Since the middle of the eighteenth century, there have been many crucial changes in the countryside. In the course of that century, agricultural experiment and reform were the subjects of widespread interest. The selective breeding of livestock produced new and improved strains of cattle, sheep and pigs; areas of marshland were reclaimed for agriculture; new crop rotations were developed to maintain production while preserving fertility, and the cultivation of root crops to provide winter fodder was more widely adopted. Although Jethro Tull had advocated the use of the seed drill in the 1730s, the main developments in mechanised farming took place in the nineteenth century while efficient tractors and the combine harvester were introduced during the twentieth century.

The period between 1750 and 1850 witnessed most of the Parliamentary Enclosures of common lands and the reorganisation of open-field strip farming—where it still survived—to create networks of rectangular hedged and privately-owned fields. By the same token, this was the period in which the England of the resourceful peasant finally perished.

For most of the nineteenth century,

the countryside was peopled by land-owning farmers and the hordes of their over-worked and badly-paid farm-workers until the progressive improvements in the development and efficiency of farm machinery eroded the need for so many farmhands. Although the days of the crowded fields are less than a century behind us, it is hard for us to imagine the swarms of carters, plough-men and part-time harvest workers which even a moderately-sized farm would have employed before mechanisation took its toll.

The modern countryside can be a depressing place with its lifeless, de-hedged and featureless factory fields, relentlessly rumbling machines and ugly farm buildings of concrete and corrugated iron. In the course of this century, fine old farm buildings, made of local materials, redolent of village crafts-manship and brimming with character, have toppled like ninepins. Thus it is a very small but very valuable consolation that a number of the finest examples can be seen, lovingly preserved, at the Avoncroft Museum of Buildings near Bromsgrove.

The most lovely and evocative to my eyes is the threshing barn brought here from Cholstrey in Herefordshire. It is a fine example of the cruck method of timber-framing with the main support for the walls and roof being provided by pairs of great curving cruck blades which are joined at their upper tips to provide a series of 'A'-shaped frames.

Almost invariably, the cruck-framed buildings which survive employ oak timbers, but here the black poplar—now a very rare tree in England—was used as an unusual alternative. The spaces between the framing timbers are filled with split oak pales woven between staves and the roof is neatly thatched. After the harvest wagons brought the unthreshed grain for storage in the barn and during the autumn, the great double doors will have been opened to allow the wind to blow out the chaff when the grain was threshed on the hard barn floor by farmhands wielding hinged staffs or 'flails'.

Doubtless the grain would then have been taken to a nearby wind-or water-mill for grinding. Avoncroft has a beautifully restored and working wind-mill of the post-mill type which repre-sents the painstaking reconstruction of a very dilapidated early nineteenth-century mill from Danzey Green in Warwickshire. If you are lucky, the custodian will be on hand to provide an absolutely enthralling account of the old milling process. In former times, it was often the custom for windmills to be decked out in bunting at times of national celebration; I was fortunate to see the mill at the time of the wedding of the Prince and Princess of Wales in 1981 when it was garlanded in flags and streamers—just the sort of sight that our great-grandparents may have enjoyed.

Amongst the other old agricultural buildings on display are a granary from

The windmill at the Avoncroft Museum of Buildings is shown here decked with bunting in the old manner as a celebration of the Royal Wedding in July 1981

Medieval timber-framing in the cruck-framing style seen in the interior of this fine barn at the Avoncroft Museum

original while the arched doorways in the wall date from the period when the building served as a coach-house.

Domestic buildings and an inn have also been reconstructed at the museum including 'The String of Horses' inn from Shrewsbury, built in 1576 and originally a pair of large private houses, while the Area Museum Service occupies the eighteenth-century timber-framed forge cottage brought from Wellington in Herefordshire.

However, the house which is most likely to fire the imagination is a late fifteenth-century merchant's house

The interior of a restored medieval house at Avoncroft. Note the feeling of spaciousness in such dwellings with few interior walls

from Bromsgrove itself. It was demolished in 1962 despite the efforts of a local conservational group, but fortunately the timbers were rescued. It has been reconstructed in its original form, with the hall, which is open to the rafters, being separated from a service bay where food and ale were kept (and which has not survived) by a 'cross passage' which runs through the house between the front and back doors. Two smaller rooms in the cross wing will have been used by the merchant occupier as a shop and an office while the chamber above, a 'solar', may have doubled as a private sitting-room and family bed-room. Hall-and-cross-wing houses of this type were common in the Middle Ages, not as the dwellings of humble peasants or great lords but of craftsmen, traders and lesser land-

Temple Broughton in Worcestershire in which the grain was stored in an elm-framed loft standing high above the reach of vermin on a series of brick piers, an eighteenth-century stable from Wychbold in Worcestershire in brick and timber framing upon a sandstone plinth, and the counting house from Bromsgrove cattle market, where cash changed hands and farmers and dealers haggled over discount.

There are also several craft and industrial buildings: a nineteenth-century nail-making workshop from nearby Sidemoor, and a chainshop from Cradley in the Black Country which also dates from the nineteenth century. More unusual is the cockpit from Bridgnorth in Shropshire, the scene of cockfights in the late-eighteenth century, a theatre from the early nineteenth century, which was later used as a coach-house and then as a garage. The pyramidical timber roof is

owners. Although the floor was of beaten earth, and the open hearth originally had no chimney and draughts will have rippled around the open interior, houses such as this exude a feeling of homeliness which few later dwellings can equal.

At the Avoncroft Museum of Buildings one can, in some ways, revisit the world of the crowded fields and the village craftsman. Any changes which have spared us from the bondage and drudgery of medieval peasant life or the unremitting toil, exploitation and near starvation of the nineteenth-century farmworker can surely be classed as

progress. Even so, one need only explore the wonderful buildings which were once part of an unspoilt countryside of healthy woodlands and weaving hedge-rows and compare them with the modern generation of farm buildings and practices to realise that 'progress' is a word that we use too loosely.

Phototips The challenges are similar to those described at Singleton*. The windmill, however, is a perfect subject for the less specialised photographer. With windmills in mind, it may be worth mentioning the problems of 'parallax'—the 'falling-over-backwards' effect (see

page 170). However, the technique of deliberately exploiting the parallax effect tends to work very well in the case of windmills and, by standing near the base or close to the end of a downward-pointing sail, tip the camera quite steeply upwards: the result is a picture of a building which seems to be soaring up into the sky and it works very well when white sails are outlined against a deep blue sky.

Location About 3 miles S of Bromsgrove and reached via the A38 and A4024; there is an ample car park, a shop and a tea room.

ROUND AND ABOUT

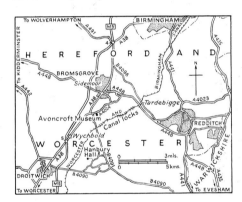

TARDEBIGGE CANAL LOCKS

The Worcester and Birmingham canal is only around thirty miles in length but some 58 locks are needed to carry barges from the Severn to the Midland plateau. The canal includes the longest flight of locks in Britain at Tardebigge where 30 locks punctuate a 2-mile stretch of canal and date from 1815. A canal-side engine house originally held a James Watt beam engine which was needed to pump water into the reservoir which maintained the canal level. The engine was

A barge approaching one of the 30 locks on the Worcester and Birmingham canal at Tardebigge

exported to the USA and the engine house was derelict until 1975 when it was restored and renovated as a beautifully-situated country club.

Location Close to the A448, about 3 miles NW of Redditch.

HANBURY HALL

The architect is unknown, but the house may have been influenced by the styles of Wren. It is of red brick, with a cupola, and built to an H-plan design. It carries the date 1701 and the interior was decorated about a decade later by Sir James Thornhill, who was simultaneously engaged in his celebrated decoration of the ceiling of Greenwich Hospital. It is owned by the National Trust.

Location About 2½ miles E of Droitwich, 1 mile N of the B4090, about 5 miles SSW of Bromsgrove.

Note The Lunt Roman fort at Baginton is close by; *see* the index for the page reference.

Bunratty Folk Park

(Co Clare)

The traditional houses in Ireland shared many features with those of Britain, although others were borrowed from south-western Europe and there were several home-grown responses to Irish conditions. The removal of Irish forests during the sixteenth and seventeenth centuries later created a shortage of mature constructional timber and this often tended to restrict the size of rooms which could be built. Stone, however, was usually abundant and most but the meanest dwellings were built of stones bedded in mortar. Clay-walled houses were common in the south-east, the damp climate of the west being generally inhospitable to building in this manner. The damp climate also encouraged the use of steep-pitched roofs. These were generally thatched but, in contrast to English thatched houses which almost without exception employ either wheat straw or reed, in Ireland one can still see many thick and shaggy roofs of oat straw, and rye straw was also used.

Although there were many regional variations reflecting the contrasts in local geology, climate and building materials, the older houses in Ireland tend to share a number of features in common: thick walls of stone; a single storey construction with an open hearth

from which the smoke found its escape through a chimney set in the ridge of a steeply-pitched roof; a rectangular plan with rooms running the full width of the house and additional rooms being added to the long axis rather than broadening the dwelling, and the absence of the hallway or 'cross-passage' so common in English vernacular building, so that

each room opened into the next.

Within the framework of these general rules, there were many differences reflecting the social status and wealth of the occupants and their occupations. The thousands of squalid sod-walled hovels or poky shanties known as 'cabins' in which masses of poverty-stricken folk lived in the nineteenth

OPPOSITE *The Bothan Scoir and* (right) *the mountain farmhouse from Kerry*

265

The Shannon salmon fisherman's house and (opposite) *the reconstructed village street*

century have disappeared along with most of their traces, but a broad spectrum of other old house types have been reconstructed in replica at the remarkable Bunratty Folk Park in the west of Ireland. They have been arranged in a village-like group, although of course the village was far less common in Ireland than it was in England and most of the forms represented would have stood alone or in small hamlet clusters. Another contrast with the traditional English village is the few outbuildings to be seen which reflects the fact that the milder climate of Ireland allowed animals to overwinter outside.

The building programme at Bunratty is continuing and a short walk away from the replica farmsteads, a much more 'Irish' settlement is taking shape in the form of a 'village' which resembles a street from a small country town dating from the years before Independence. Good old-fashioned sweets are sold in the picturesque corner shop while the pillar box is back in its bright red British livery rather than the green of the Republic.

Amongst the replica dwellings on display, one of the most basic is the salmon fisherman's house from the Shannon estuary, a two-roomed cottage of a fast-vanishing type with a thatched roof fitting low and snug, a floor of packed clay and a peat fire smouldering beneath a wooden chimney hood. There are a trio of three-roomed farmhouses

from different parts of Co Clare and the north of Co Kerry which display local variations on the theme of the single-storeyed small farmhouse. The mountain farmhouse from Kerry is particularly interesting for the paving stones of the floor were part of the dowry of a nineteenth-century bride, a customary gift when a house was being renovated for a young couple. At a lower level in the social scale, the Bothan Scoir is one small step removed from the squalor of the cabin and represents the accommodation which many farmers offered to landless labourers.

In complete contrast, the Golden Vale house is typical of the home of a prosperous farmer. It is completely furnished in a late nineteenth-century manner redolent of a smug respectability, while the back of the original building which faced the farmyard has been prettified to form a new frontage looking out over a well-planted flower garden. Overlooking the Folk Park is a far more imposing and substantial house and farm-building complex of 1804, not a replica but an important courtyard farm built by Thomas Studdert of nearby Bunratty Castle and made of stones taken from a redundant annexe of the castle. Studdert originally intended to transfer to the castle on his inheritance, but when the time came he preferred to remain at Bunratty House. The outbuildings and workshops around the courtyard now accommodate the large collection of old agricultural machines assembled by the Rev M. J. Talbot.

Although the emphasis at the Bunratty Folk Park is on replica rather than reconstructed buildings, the visitor to this remarkable site may find the trip no less rewarding than visits to Singleton* or Avoncroft* in England: it would be hard to find a stronger recommendation than this. The project—which is managed by Shannon Free Airport Development Co. Ltd. on behalf of trustees—has

266

clearly been sited in such a way as to attract the overseas visitor arriving at Shannon airport; Ireland has great depths of fascination and beauty to offer and the Folk Park provides a marvellous opportunity for understanding the real Ireland and its essentially rural roots. One can only hope that visitors will soon return in their former numbers and that the wonderful qualities of Irish country life will endure long after the tiny minority of violent fanatics have been forgotten.

Even with all its current troubles, Ireland offers an escape from the featureless arenas of modern farming and from the dismal 'No Trespassing' signs which cut short so many rambles in the British countryside.

Phototips Each building has its own particular charm and each is an easy and attractive subject. Some form of tripod or support will be needed for interior work but in most of the rooms, being quite small, flash can be used— but preferably to complement rather than to substitute for the natural light.

Location About 6 miles to the E of Shannon Airport and well signposted. There is an extensive car park, and a tea room

is housed in one of the replica buildings; there is also a craft shop and woven goods are made for sale at a weaving shed.

ROUND AND ABOUT

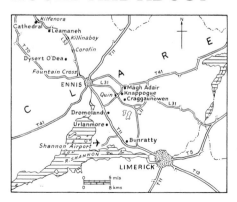

BUNRATTY CASTLE

The castle is open to the public and stands right beside the Folk Park. Although the site does not appear to have great defensive merits, the castle was originally surrounded by marsh and water and it commanded shipping moving upstream from the Shannon estuary. It was built in the 15th century and around 1500 it came into the possession of the O'Briens, Kings of Thomond. The interior furnishings have been reconstructed in a 15th-century manner.

Note Both the Burren and Craggaunowen are in the neighbourhood, and not far away is Clonmacnois monastic town in Co Offaly; *see* the index for page references.

All profits received in excess of the expenses are devoted to further improvements and restoration work by the Shannon Free Airport Development Co.

Coalbrookdale: The Cradle of Industry

(Shropshire)

Britain was the first country in the world to undergo an Industrial Revolution and Coalbrookdale has a better claim than any other place to be regarded as the birthplace of the industrial world. While modern industry is orientated towards the mass production of consumer goods, the use of electric power and exploitation of a wide variety of raw materials, in the earlier phases of industrialisation, the accent was on heavy industry with branches such as shipbuilding and heavy engineering being completely dependent upon the iron and steel industry. The Industrial Revolution embodied many strands of development, new inventions and new technologies but its explosive potential was contained until an efficient process for the mass production of iron could be established.

The old iron industry had previously employed charcoal as the smelting fuel, but the high costs and limited supplies of charcoal restricted expansion. As far back as 1619, the iron-master Dud Dudley had experimented with cheaper fuels but his results are uncertain and his iron works were wrecked by apprehensive charcoal burners. Iron had been worked at Coalbrookdale since at least the start of the sixteenth century and in 1708 a brass-caster from Bristol, Abraham Darby, bought the iron works

which had been derelict since an explosion in 1700. Darby discovered that coal could substitute for charcoal in the smelting process if its impurities were first removed by converting it to coke. The discovery did not immediately release the pent-up forces for an Industrial Revolution and the process was contained as a family secret for several decades.

The year 1760 is generally regarded as the dawn of the industrial age and it was about this time that the iron industry at large became aware of the coke process, while during the intervening years steam-powered engines had been developed to produce the powerful blasts of air which were used to raise the temperature of the blast furnace. The Darby works at Coalbrookdale prospered both before and after the secret of coke-based smelting was released and by the 1830s the iron works was considered to be the world's largest foundry.

There can be no more appropriate place in the world for a Museum of Iron than around the site of Darby's Coalbrookdale furnace. A small museum was established here in 1959 when the Old Blast Furnace was uncovered to mark the 250th anniversary of Darby's first successful experiment. However, the display which I first saw as a student in 1965 bears no comparison with the remarkable presentation which awaits the modern visitor. The Great Warehouse of 1838 was conserved by the Telford Development Corporation in

1976 while three years later the original museum was demolished and a new Iron Museum was installed in the Warehouse. It is packed with examples of the iron-master's craft, castings of many different kinds, boilers, wrought iron work, stoves and many reminders that iron was widely used for decorative as well as functional purposes. Crowning the workshop is a brightly-painted cast-iron clock tower of 1843 while in the adjacent yard you can see the old furnace which Darby inherited when he took control of the works, a railway wagon on a set of rails dating from about 1790 and a saddle tank locomotive of about 1863 which was returned to Coalbrookdale in 1959.

This section of the Ironbridge Gorge contains not only Coalbrookdale, but a unique complex of industrial monuments of different types. The best known is undoubtedly the Iron Bridge itself. This was the world's first iron bridge and as there were no earlier examples for study, it is not surprising that the constructional techniques used in stone and wooden bridges were adapted for casting in iron. This is particularly apparent in the dovetail joints which secure the base plates and the shouldered joints binding the main ribs and radials.

The River Severn was a valuable artery bearing a procession of barges carrying cargoes of coal, limestone, firebricks and pig iron to their des-

The Coalport China Works Museum where the old workshops can be seen

269

tinations along this corridor of industry. It was also a barrier to cross-valley movement and the various ferries had difficulty in operating during the recurrent Severn floods. The design of the bridge as a single-span structure was determined by the need to avoid the disruption of the barge traffic, while the steep confines of the valley posed other challenges. Parliamentary approval for this bridge across the Severn was obtained in 1776, but some of the original subscribers then began to lose confidence in the revolutionary scheme for a bridge of iron and seventeen months passed before plans for a 100 ft span structure were approved. The design was partly conceived by the Shrewsbury architect T. F. Pritchard and partly based on the ironworking experience of Abraham Darby III and his foundry workers.

Owing to the great transport problems involved, it has been suggested that the ribs of the Iron Bridge may not have been cast at Coalbrookdale, but either by the riverside or at the nearby Madeley

The cast-iron clock tower of 1843 which crowns the iron workshop at Coalbrookdale

Wood works which Abraham Darby III had bought in 1776.

By the spring of 1779, the ironwork was ready for erection and the bridge was completed by the October of the year without any disruption to the barge

traffic. Work on laying a roadway across the structure with connections to the existing road network filled 1780 and the bridge was opened on the first day of 1781. The Iron Bridge was closed to vehicular traffic in 1931 and essential reconstruction work involving the reinforcement of the north abutment and insertion of an inverted concrete arch across the river bed to hold the abutments apart was carried out between 1972 and 1974. Only one other eighteenth century iron bridge survives; it is at Cound in the same county and is also a product of Coalbrookdale.

About two miles down the valley is the Coalport China Works Museum. Several potteries were established along the Severn in the course of the eighteenth century; the Coalport works seems to date from about 1794 and expanded in 1814 when its owner, John Rose, transferred the operations of the pottery at Caughley near Broseley to Coalport. The works specialised in the manufacture of high grade utility and decorative products and in 1820 it pioneered the introduction of a new feldspar-based glaze to supersede the lead glaze which had proved damaging to the health of pottery workers.

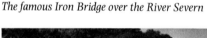

The famous Iron Bridge over the River Severn

The Bedlam blast furnace near Coalbrookdale

During the middle of the nineteenth century, Coalport porcelain enjoyed a fine reputation but the disruption of trade during the 1914–18 war proved a severe blow; in 1926 the ailing company transferred to Shelton in the Potteries and, following other realignments, the name of 'Coalport' has been part of the prestigious Wedgwood group since 1967.

Much of the canalside industrial landscape at Coalport has been conserved and you can visit the old workshops, the porcelain display which is housed in a complete bottle kiln, and the half kiln which dates right back to 1840.

Between Coalport and Iron Bridge is the 42 acre Blists Hill Open Air Museum site where a brick and tile works, a canal-inclined plane and a trio of nineteenth century blast furnaces are preserved *in situ* while pit headgear, steam engines, a saw mill, a printing shop, ironworking machinery and industrial workers' dwellings have been introduced and reconstructed from other locations. The Blists Hill mine is a typically thoughtful reconstruction, with an original late eighteenth-century shaft, a reconstructed engine house and replica headgear with the winding engine imported from Broseley.

Visitors to all the sites so far described will not yet have seen everything of interest in the Ironbridge Gorge for there is also the riverside Severn Warehouse and wharf, built by the Coalbrookdale Company in the 1840s, the Bedlam Furnaces of 1757 and the Coalbrookdale Institute which the local iron-masters provided in 1859 as a venue for classes in arts and science.

Coalbrookdale is run by the Iron Gorge Museum Trust.

Phototips The various sites provide an almost inexhaustible supply of subjects and, given a measure of sunlight, none of them is very difficult. Some will appeal mainly to industrial archaeology enthusiasts, but the Iron Bridge will prove irresistible and some of the best views are to be had from the river bank just to the E of the N abutment.

Location About 8 miles N of Bridgnorth and reached from the N and S via the A442, from the E and M6 via the A4169, and from Shrewsbury and the W via the B4380.

ROUND AND ABOUT

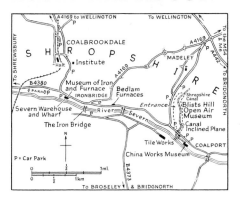

A whole day should be allowed to visit this exceptional complex of industrial sites and the authorities estimate that between $5\frac{1}{2}$ and $7\frac{1}{2}$ hours can be spent in visiting just the main attractions. There are ample car parks provided.

Note The Iron Age hillforts of Caer Caradoc and Old Oswestry, the planned town of Clun and Stokesay Castle are in the neighbourhood. *See* the index for page references.

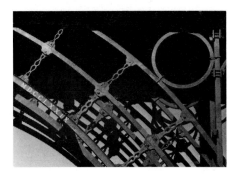

Detail of the ribs of the Iron Bridge

Wimpole Hall

(Cambridgeshire)

The countryside of eighteenth-century England was a landscape in transition. On the broad scale, the changes were enacted by gradual processes, but at the more local level of the farm or the parish, the changes could be quite revolutionary, for instance when important landowners adopted progressive farming practices or where parishes experienced the dramatic changes effected by Parliamentary Enclosure. Many traditional aspects of peasant farming still existed cheek by jowl with the newer methods, while most lowland landscapes were punctuated by the great mansions of the lords of the countryside. Many of these mansions displayed variations on the theme of neo-Classical architecture, while most were set in vast and carefully kept landscaped parks.

Wimpole Hall is one of the grandest of the East Anglian examples, massive, symmetrical and, in its way, quite striking—but restrained rather than flamboyant in style. Like Somerleyton Hall*, which became home to a different breed of magnates, Wimpole had a much older Dutch-gabled mansion as its nucleus. The first house was built for Sir Thomas Chichele around 1640 but its only obvious surviving parts can be seen

in the basement levels of the present Hall. The first extensive rebuilding was undertaken by the Earl of Radnor between 1689 and 1710. Then the house was sold and passed by marriage to the Earl of Oxford. From 1740, Wimpole was owned by the powerful Yorke family and Charles Yorke, 1st Earl of Hard-

OPPOSITE *The elegant and dignified central façade at Wimpole Hall.* (Right) *One of the mock Tudor houses in the replacement village of New Wimpole*

273

wicke and Lord Chancellor, commenced the refacing of the mansion, and the balanced and dignified central façade dates from 1742.

As was so often the case, the spectacular changes were not confined to the house, but had a dramatic impact upon the local community and landscape. The surrounding park, which is flanked to west and south by Roman roads, acquired a magnificent elm-lined double avenue, 100 yards in width and some two miles in length. The famous landscape creator, Capability Brown, worked at Wimpole between 1767 and 1773 while his lay-outs were altered by Repton around 1798.

As at Somerleyton*, the old village of Wimpole nestled beside its church, close to the walls of the splendid Hall. This intimate proximity to tenants and working folk was quite unacceptable to the noble inmates of the mansion and the village was moved twice, ending up as a row of wierd, symmetrical but Gothicised cottages alongside the present A603. Though built of a rather drab and pallid brick, these cottages dating from about 1845 were clearly intended as a Picturesque embellishment to the landscape although their thickets of aerials and the pounding modern traffic now rather undermine the effect.

The old church was not moved, but it emerged from the changes in a very different form, being rebuilt by Flitcroft in 1749 in a Classical manner to harmonise with the house, but then suffering alterations in the neo-Gothic Decorated style in 1887. The 14th-century north chapel survived as a 'storehouse of monuments' to the masters of Wimpole. The Norman font, however, may be a legacy from the first church to stand

upon the site. The latest of the large additions to the setting is the red brick stable block, designed by Kendall in 1851 and described by Professor Pevsner as 'horrible'.

Wimpole Hall survives intact as an heirloom of the age of the lords of the countryside, a symbol of the wealth and power of a now fast-vanishing class of imperious landlords. It is now an important if not particularly well-known National Trust property. In 1983, Wimpole Home Farm was opened as a modern grassland farm with a collection of rare breeds of farm animals including longhorn, British white and white park cattle, with a museum devoted to agricultural history. Sadly recent ploughing and re-seeding of part of Wimpole Park resulted in the destruction of important deserted village and ridge-and-furrow earthworks.

The church at Wimpole was rebuilt in a Classical style although fragments of the medieval church can still be seen at the rear

Phototips Free-standing and south-facing mansions like Wimpole are amongst the easiest of subjects. Although the impact of the great avenue is less striking today, an interesting photograph of the distant but commanding Hall can be taken from the side of the A603 between New Wimpole village and the junction with the A14, using a very long 300 or 400 mm telephoto lens. The National Trust has a project under hand to replant a stretch of the decimated avenue. Other attractive views are found within the grounds and at all angles to the dignified façade. Seen in winter, the glowing red brick façade, sky and snow combine to produce a striking composition in red, white and blue.

Location About 9 miles SW of Cambridge and reached from the A14 or A603 via a minor road which is very well signposted by the National Trust.

ROUND AND ABOUT

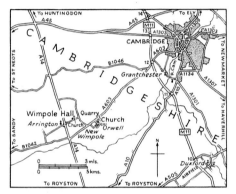

Cambridge lies within easy reach and the college grounds are accessible at most times of the year, though some restrictions may be in force during the early summer examination period. Visitors *en route* for Cambridge could pause at the villages of Orwell and Grantchester.

ORWELL

The church at Orwell, built of chalk or 'clunch' and pebble rubble, is quite typical of medieval churches in this stone-poor region, but its fine Perpendicular chancel is rather special. It is mainly of the 12th, 13th and 14th centuries while particularly good examples of morbidly-decorated tomb slabs of the 17th century are preserved inside. At the top of the field behind the church is a spectacular old clunch quarry, with caves cut in the top of its back wall.

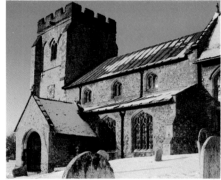

Orwell church, built of chalk or 'clunch'

Location Orwell lies immediately to the S of the A603, less than a mile to the E of New Wimpole.

GRANTCHESTER

Grantchester will interest village history sleuths because its bendy shape seems to have been acquired as the village grew towards a river crossing provided by the mill dam and the houses have been set out along tracks which wended their way through the furlong blocks in the open fields of the old village. The church is also interesting because the relics of an older Late Saxon or Norman predecessor are built into the walls at the back of the church.

Grantchester is, of course, known through the works of Rupert Brooke:

> But Grantchester! ah, Grantchester!
> There's peace and holy quiet there.

Brooke made his home at the Old Vicarage in Grantchester after leaving King's College. Byron's Pool and the walks through the celebrated Grantchester Meadows are amongst the other attractions enjoyed by visitors to this pretty but unspectacular village.

Location Grantchester is within walking distance of Cambridge and is reached by turning SE as signposted near the A603-M11 junction.

Note Very close to these sites is the Duxford Air Museum; *see* the index for the page reference.

Cottages in Rupert Brooke's Grantchester

The Industrial Revolution in the Aire Valley

(West Yorkshire)

In the old West Riding of Yorkshire, many facets of the landscape of the Industrial Revolution are preserved, and there can be few better places to explore these relics than in the Aire Valley. In the course of the Revolution, peasants became industrial workers, exchanging the near starvation, overwork and deprivation which were the lot of millions of rural workers, for the long hours of drudgery of the factory worker's life. Within the industrial community, standards of living varied considerably according to the benevolence or ruthlessness of the employers concerned, while the mill owners often lived in luxuriously appointed mansions overlooking the scenes of toil. Our exploration begins at the home of one of these employers.

Cliffe Hall in Keighley was designed by Webster in an Elizabethan style around 1830; the exact date is not known, but in 1835 it was described as 'newly built'. The original owner was one Christopher Netherwood, but in 1832 he sold the house to the Butterfield brothers, local cotton mill owners. Between 1875 and 1880, the original Cliffe Hall underwent additional building and emerged as Cliffe Castle and the owner, Henry Isaac Butterfield, filled his house with works of art. The Butterfields retained the Castle

OPPOSITE *Cliffe Castle, Keighley.* (Right) *An idea of how the wealthy industrialist lived*

until 1949, when it was sold to a former MP and Lord Mayor of London, the City of London businessman Sir Bracewell Smith. In the course of the following decade, the building was generously donated to the borough of Keighley and converted into an exceptionally fine museum and art gallery: visitors from the south seeking to understand the essence of northern civic pride can do no better than to visit the Cliffe Castle collections and see what is possible for even a small and relatively youthful town to support.

Although I have focused attention on field monuments rather than museums in this book, this is a special case since the main rooms of the Castle have been furnished to resemble their appearance when the house was home to rich nineteenth-century mill-owners. The rooms themselves are unaltered, the original chandeliers are still in place and the genteel opulence belongs to quite another world than that of the terraced housing below. The numerous display rooms in the remainder of the museum accommodate a wide variety of collections but the emphasis is on the industrial history of the locality and one of the outstanding exhibits is the reconstruction of a clog-making shop from nearby Silsden.

Bingley, a short distance downstream, is our next destination, the Bingley Five Rise flight of canal locks, our venue. The Industrial Revolution allowed the more efficient manufacture of products in far greater quantities than hitherto. However, these advances would have been nullified if raw materials could not have reached the factories, or if the manufactures could not be distributed to the market outlets. Until the railways robbed them of most of their traffic in the course of the nineteenth century, the canals provided much of the essential transport. A large portion of the network dates from the second half of the eighteenth century; the Leeds and Liverpool

ABOVE *Saltaire and* (opposite) *the Bingley Five Rise flight of canal locks*

canal at Bingley played an important role in the industrialisation of the Aire valley and encouraged the development of industries around Leeds.

Although a number of challenging engineering problems were posed, the notion of a trans-Pennine canal which would secure a link between the east and west coasts of industrial northern England was very appealing. Such a canal was authorised by an Act of 1769 and it was specified that boats 60 ft long and 14 ft wide should be able to travel from Liverpool to Hull without their cargoes having to be transferred. The first section, from Wigan to Liverpool was opened in 1774; two years later, Burnley was reached, but it was not until 1816 that the final section to Gargrave in Yorkshire was completed. At Bingley, the gradient became a problem and the spectacular answer is seen in the five inter-connected broad locks which lower the canal a distance of some 60 ft within the space of about 300 ft. This,

the most remarkable staircase of locks in England, was opened to traffic in 1774 and was a considerable success.

Each notable canal tended to create a new canalside landscape, with tow paths and lock-keepers' houses in the immediate vicinity and then the great mills, strung out beside its banks. All these features are evident around the Five Rise, while nearby is the 'Seven Arches' aqueduct, carrying the canal across the River Aire.

Proceeding along the valley, the visitor soon comes to Saltaire. Each history enthusiast has his or her own favourite periods in the past, and mine are the prehistoric era, the Dark Ages and early medieval period. Even so, of all the places that were visited in the course of field-work for this book, none impressed or excited me more than this mid nineteenth-century industrial settlement. It is a living and working monument to its founder, the industrialist Sir Titus Salt. Unlike many but not all of his wealthy contemporaries, Salt was deeply concerned for the well-being of his employees and he sought to provide hygienic accommodation for his workers to

The appealing Italianate almshouses with their bright gardens are arranged around a carpet of lawn at the approaches to old Saltaire

The Italianate style can also be seen in the tower of the Salt factory, viewed beyond the Dutch Reform church

provide schools and libraries to assist their education and prospects, and to create an industrial landscape which would be uplifting rather than oppressive and polluted like those of nearby Bradford.

He favoured an Italianate form of architecture and the capable local architects Lockwood and Mawson were employed to design the village and factory complex which was planned to look across a riverside park to unspoilt countryside beyond. Salt's textile mill is still in operation although, on first appearances, it might be mistaken for an Italian Renaissance palace or the city hall of an illustrious metropolis. Facing the mill across a carefully tended flower-bed is a remarkable Classical temple — which proves to be the Dutch Reform Church — while monumental public buildings, including the library and the Institute, punctuate the streets of Saltaire.

The little town took shape in the course of the 1850s when more than 500 dwellings were built. Although they are arranged in terraces, there is none of the gloom and deprivation which one associates with the poorer qualities of mass-produced Victorian industrial housing. The townscape is diversified by the creation of three-storeyed sections in the centres and at the ends of the terrace rows, and since the sandstone architecture of Saltaire has recently been cleaned of its acumulations of soot, the urban scenery can be enjoyed in its pristine form.

Well-scrubbed buildings now feature quite commonly in the West Yorkshire conurbation; local government in England and Wales was reconstructed in 1974 and it is said that a number of small and superseded local authorities chose to spend their remaining capital on facelifts for their boroughs. When pursued on a piecemeal basis, the cleaning of individual buildings may not always harmonise with the blackened and gritty character of the surroundings, but when accomplished on a grand scale, as at Saltaire, the effect can be both striking and attractive.

Sir Titus Salt was plainly possessed of a vision and at least at Saltaire his dream of an attractive and envigorating working environment endures. He became hugely successful by introducing alpaca wool to the worsted manufacturing process and Gillian Darley the architectural historian suggests that his investment in Saltaire may have resulted from the influence of Disraeli's novel *Sybil* which was published in 1847 and described a progressive model mill village. Although the Saltaire concept stimulated the construction of a few other model villages or suburbs, its message tended to be lost on the hard-headed majority of industrialists. Therefore, for every single local exercise in enlightened paternalism, the second half of the nineteenth century witnessed the construction of hundreds of acres of monotonous and minimally-provided terraced housing.

Phototips The three main sites described are all easy and photogenic subjects, with the exception of interior work at the Cliffe Castle museum—where you should ask permission to use a tripod. Cliffe Castle lies amongst colourful public gardens and you should always try to include a splash of colour in a photograph providing that it harmonises with the main subject: in this context, I believe that cars are always 'out', but telephone and pillar boxes merit consideration.

The locks at Bingley can be photographed from various vantage points: from the footbridges which cross the locks, looking down the flight towards the mills which line the banks; from the foot of the locks looking upwards, and from well down the canal using a telephoto lens which will reduce the perspective effect of the rising flight. Fishermen are likely to be found at the foot of the locks and figures with rods can be incorporated as interesting foreground silhouettes.

At Saltaire, only the Salt factory poses any problem because it is partly masked by shrubs. The Dutch Reform Church is a wonderful subject, but as well as the 'full frontal' viewpoint, explore the view as seen from a position a little behind and to the side of the church, where the height of the building demands a wide-angle lens. Good views of the town are gained from the various street intersections. Do not overlook the appealing Italianate almshouses with their bright gardens which are arranged around a carpet of lawn at the approaches to old Saltaire. Finally, for a particularly attractive but different study of an old, industrialised but still colourful landscape, leave the main through road near Bingley All Saints church and enjoy the scenery viewed from the bridge on the B6429.

Location The sites lie a few miles to the NW of Bradford and are linked by the A650. Saltaire is absorbed by Shipley and lies just to the N of the A650; almost all Bingley residents will be able to provide directions to the Five Rise canal locks which are within the town with street parking very close by, while the Cliffe Castle museum is on high ground on the NW margins of the town centre in Spring Gardens Lane.

ROUND AND ABOUT

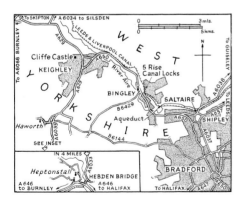

The best part of a day can be spent in exploring the three sites, but energetic visitors could proceed via Keighley and the A6033 to the old industrial centres of Heptonstall and Hebden Bridge which lie about 5 miles to the NW of Halifax. They present a striking contrast, with the beautifully conserved 18th-century textile-working village of Heptonstall dating from the industrial age of innocence; its gritstone cottages were mainly the homes of sturdy families of weavers. Hebden Bridge in the valley below belongs to a later stage in industrialisation when the factory and water and then steam-powered spinning supplanted the cottage-based industries. Its blackened terraces can be compared to the homely dwellings of the hand-loom weavers of Heptonstall or the attractive terrace architecture and civic amenities which Salt created at Saltaire.

Note NE of the Aire Valley complex lie Markenfield Hall and Fountains Abbey: *see* the index for page references.

Workers' cottages at Heptonstall

Somerleyton Hall

(Suffolk)

Somerleyton Hall and its surroundings are expressive epitaphs to the wealth and power of the early Victorian industralist and speculator and display some of the fancies of the catholic architectural taste of its period. The Hall has enveloped and largely replaced a much older mansion. In 1610, a great house in the Jacobean style was built here, inheriting its site from a succession of timber-framed houses, for a manor house had probably stood hereabouts throughout the Middle Ages. From at least the seventeenth century, the house had been surrounded by a landscaped parkland of gardens and we know that the evergreen-lined walks were praised by the historian William Fuller in 1651. Between 1672 and 1843, the house and estate were owned by members of the Allin family, although the name was changed to Anguish following a link by marriage with this more aristocratic family.

On the death of the last male Anguish descendant, Somerleyton was bought by Sir Morton Peto—a man of a very different background and much more a figure of his times. Peto was a highly successful entrepreneur, a builder of railways and the contractor involved in the construction of various important projects including the Reform Club and Nelson's Column. He had been one of the guarantors of the Great Exhibition of 1851 and, as the architectural historian Gillian Darley has recorded, he was also attracted to a variety of less spectacular causes including the Association for the Suppression of the Dog Show Nuisance in Populous Neighbourhoods!

In 1866, Peto's involvement with the Overend and Gurney Bank proved fatal to his further involvements with Somerleyton. He became bankrupt and the Hall and its estates were bought by

OPPOSITE *The clock above the stable block at Somerleyton Hall and* (right) *rebuilt cottages outside the park gates*

283

The Hall was rebuilt between 1844 and 1851

another archetypal Victorian dynasty, the Crossley family of Halifax who had made their fortune by acquiring the patent of the first mechanical carpet loom. In the meantime, Peto had transformed Somerleyton Hall and its surroundings.

The Hall was rebuilt between 1844 and 1851 to the designs of John Thomas, an obscure architect but a noted ornamental mason whose work embellishes the House of Commons. Although good stone can only be obtained at great expense throughout most of East Anglia and the body of the Hall is in russet brickwork, full use of stone can be seen in the quoins surrounds and detailed embellishments at Somerleyton as a tribute to Thomas's skills and enthusiasms. While Peto sought to perpetuate the Jacobean manner of building of the old Hall, the Victorians often found difficulty in resisting the temptation to borrow from a variety of different styles and so considerable Italianate influences found their way into Somerleyton, notably in the campanile tower.

Within and without, the Hall was packed with costly materials and *objets d'art*. The best stone from Caen and Aubigny was used; the clock above the stable block was made by the Vulliamy family and is said to have been a prototype for Big Ben, while Landseer was among the various celebrated artists who had commissions for the new mansion and items of sculpture from France and Germany were imported for the Winter Garden.

This Winter Garden, lying to the north of the Hall, was also designed by Thomas; the glass palace has gone, but the loggia remains. The landscape gardener Nesfield was involved in designing the maze for Peto; a pagoda forms the centrepiece but there is a walk of at least 400 yards between the yew hedges before one reaches it. In all, more than twelve acres of lawns, shrubberies and flowerbeds surround the mansion.

Peto's creative enthusiasms were not, however, confined to the Hall and its precincts. The destruction of an intruding village often provided an unsavoury accompaniment to the creation of an English mansion and park. As was the case at Wimpole*, Peto chose to rebuild the village and the new Somerleyton which appeared outside the park gates mirrors the eccentricity of the man and his age. Twenty-eight cottages were built, each individually designed and each loosely parodying the characteristics of traditional Gothic vernacular styles. They are redolent of Victorian patronage and were built to improve the comfort and the morality of their humble inmates: in terms of comfort, they were probably far superior to their predecessors, while the concern for morality was served by the provision of several private bedrooms, a facility not always available in truly traditional cottages.

Although I am not convinced that the effect is successful, Peto attempted Picturesque vistas by placing the cottages around a green. The Picturesque influences are strongly represented in the thatched and timber-framed schoolhouse. The creation of an idyllic and idealised 'olde worlde' village might have been more successful had more thought been given to the integration of the components, but as it is the individual dwellings seem to have been gleaned from the various architectural pattern books which were then in circulation and set down like the beads in a gaudy necklace around a pattern book green.

As was so often the case, the old village church escaped the changes and it can still be seen stranded in the park. Peto had plans to create a purpose-built church for his new village; perhaps he realised that this would result in a longer journey to services for himself and his guests so he contented himself by reroofing the original building.

Most architectural arbiters do not like things that are sham anything—and since most Victorian architecture is sham something, it tends to have had a bad press. Contemporary critics were sometimes less objective: in 1857, George Borrow described Somerleyton as 'pandemonium in red brick'—but then Peto had built one of his railways across Borrow's land, upsetting the

The isolated church at Somerleyton

writer considerably! Of the really Jacobean architecture in Somerleyton Hall, only portions of the Dutch gables are

obvious. The remainder is sham Jacobean, Italianate or sham French Renaissance—but one strongly suspects that whatever the connoisseurs or taste merchants say, the average visitor will find both the Hall and its gardens to be lovely and entrancing. They also survive as relics from the confident and ebullient world of the Victorian business magnate. The Hall remains in private hands.

Phototips Successful photography always tends to be easily accomplished where great mansions are set in landscaped surroundings and where the making of lovely vistas was ardently attempted. The creation of fine pictures was intentional and the modern photographer can exploit this. The only tip at an 'easy' location such as Somerleyton is to remember that there is not one good view to be captured, but scores—some of them panoramas, but others details of a particular architectural feature or horticultural nook.

Location About 5 miles NW of Lowestoft and signposted from the B1074.

ROUND AND ABOUT

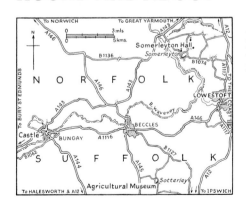

BUNGAY CASTLE

The great castle of Bungay was built in

1165 by Roger Bigod, the 2nd Earl of Norfolk, but was unlicensed. The new king, Henry II, ordered that it should be mined but the Earl of Norfolk was able to save his castle by paying a large ransom. In the SW corner of the 70 ft square keep, of which little now remains, one is still able to see the initial stages of the sapping mine which would have caused the downfall of the castle had the timbers been removed.

Location The Castle lies about 14 miles W of Lowestoft; Bungay is at the junction of the A143, A144 and A1116 roads.

Note In the neighbourhood are Burgh

and Caister castles; *see* the index for page references.

SOTTERLEY AGRICULTURAL MUSEUM

An interesting and varied collection of vintage tractors and items of old agricultural machinery is housed and well displayed at Alexander Wood Farm in Sotterley.

Location The museum lies about 5 miles SE of Beccles near Sotterley village which is situated in the angle between the A145 and A12.

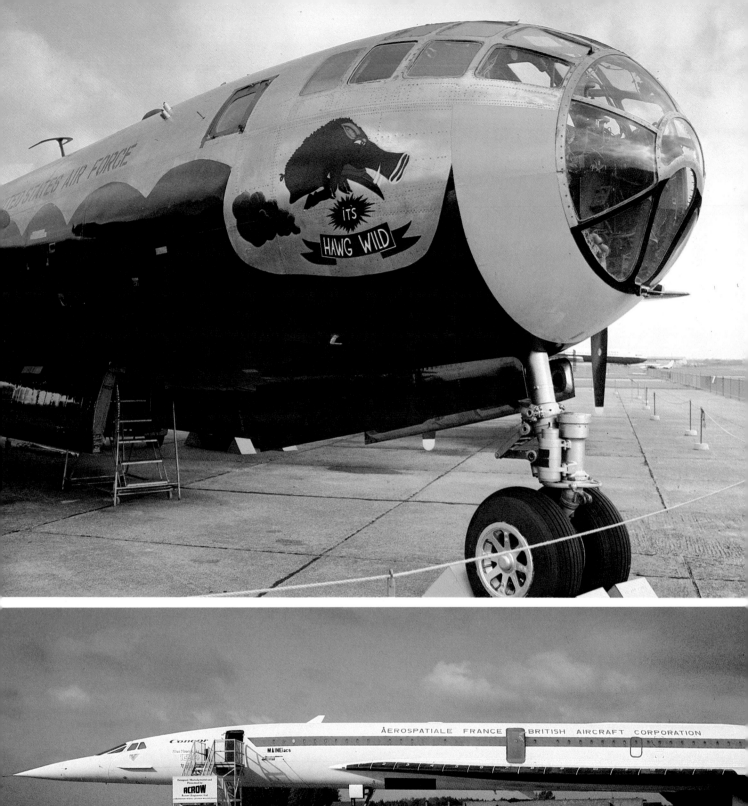

The Battle of Britain Airfield at Duxford

(Cambridgeshire)

The Battle of Britain, fought in the skies of southern England in the blazing summer of 1940, was arguably the most crucial battle in the whole of British history. If that war in the air had been lost, then British cities would have been completely exposed to Luftwaffe bombers. Even more seriously, once stripped of its air power, it is doubtful whether Britain could have prevented the landing of a German invasion force since, without air cover, the Royal Navy would have been unable to guard the British coast. The battle also had crucial psychological and political overtones. At the time, British and Commonwealth forces faced the Nazi threat alone and covert supporters and potential allies abroad gravely doubted our abilities to survive; a British defeat could have driven the USA into a policy of isolationism, while the German invasion of the USSR might have been successful had it been mounted without the rearguard threat from an unconquered Britain.

The Battle of Britain has been interpreted as a German attempt to draw the RAF, which was critically short of both aircraft and pilots, into conflict against superior odds and so annihilate the air force and pave the way for a seaborne invasion. If this strategy had been successful, the consequences would have been too awful to contemplate. By the middle of September 1940, however, the RAF had emerged victorious and grave material losses and, more importantly, severe psychological damage had been inflicted upon the hitherto victorious Luftwaffe.

Of the small and large fighter stations which were the Battle of Britain bases, some are still active and modernised out of all recognition, while others have been dismantled. One, however, has been preserved with many of its wartime apurtenances as a laudable exercise in official and voluntary conservational co-operation. Duxford airfield near Cambridge was constructed in 1917 at a time when German bombers had begun to mount daylight raids on London. Early in 1918, it became the base for three DH9 bomber squadrons and at the end of the 1914–18 war the airfield operated as a flying school. It became a fighter base in 1924 and many of the surviving buildings date from the 1914–18 and inter-war periods. One hangar was bombed during the making of *The Battle of Britain* movie in 1968, but three of the original First World War timber-trussed hangars survive and are now listed buildings. The operations room dates from 1928, and the headquarters building from 1933. For most of the 1939–45 war, the fighters operated from grass airstrips but a steel plate runway was laid in 1944; the concrete runway and taxiways date from the postwar period.

Duxford had the special distinction of

OPPOSITE *The legendary B-29 Second World War bomber, and a Concorde prototype of 1971.* (Right) *The old control building and a hangar at Duxford*

being the first RAF station to operate the immortal Spitfire, two squadrons being re-equipped with the aircraft in 1938. The brunt of the fighting during the Battle of Britain was borne by 11 Group in the zone of southern England to the south of Duxford but, during the course of the Battle, 12 Group aircraft, and the Duxford squadrons particularly, were frequently called upon for support.

Duxford became the centre of the controversy concerning Air Vice-Marshal Leigh-Mallory's 'big-wing' strategy. Proponents of the strategy believed that greater material and psychological damage could be inflicted on the Luftwaffe if they were attacked by large formations of three or even five squadrons. Opponents pointed to the time taken to assemble such large formations which then might arrive on the scene too late to intercept the enemy aircraft. There were good arguments in favour of each viewpoint and the issue is still debated.

Battle of Britain Day is celebrated on 15 September, the day on which the Duxford wing inflicted severe losses upon a German formation raiding London. The wing could not have had a more illustrious leader than the legless pilot, the late Douglas Bader. Bader was at Duxford in 1933 when he was informed that the loss of his legs in a previous flying accident would exclude him from flying duties. He rejoined the RAF at the start of the 1939–45 war and was posted to 222 squadron at Duxford; he was shortly given command of 242 Hurricane squadron which he brought from Coltishall to Duxford at the end of 1940.

In 1943 Duxford became a USAAF base with the Thunderbolts and Mustangs giving fighter cover to the day bomber squadrons of the US Eighth Air Force. The airfield returned to RAF use in 1945 and remained a fighter station until 1961. For a decade, various authorities were unable to agree upon what

Servicing an Me 109 at Duxford

should be done with the illustrious old airfield but in 1971 the Imperial War Museum began to use a hangar for the restoration of historic aircraft. A partnership was established with the volunteers of the East Anglian Aviation Society, and in 1976 the airfield and its various exhibits of historic aircraft were opened to the public. The co-operative endeavours of the Imperial War Museum, the Cambridgeshire County Council and the volunteers of the Duxford Aviation Society have allowed the venture to blossom as a successful historical attraction with more than seventy aircraft on display and periodical flying exhibitions.

The aircraft concerned are, of course, too numerous to mention, but they range in age from a British BE2C of 1916 to a Concorde prototype of 1971. Aircraft of types which once operated from Duxford include an American P-51D Mustang which has been repainted in the gaudy livery of the Mustang 'Big Beautiful Doll' which operated from Duxford under Col. J. D. Landers, commander of 78th Fighter Group, and a variant of the Gloster Meteor, Britain's first jet fighter.

Amongst the larger aircraft, the most legendary must be the Boeing B-17 and B-29 Second World War bombers. Al-

though the B-17 on display did not see war service and the B-29 flew its thirty-odd combat missions in the Korean war, both aircraft are of types operated extensively by the USA during the Second World War. Although the collection includes a Junkers Ju 52 transport aircraft, the main antagonists in the Battle of Britain are not represented, though a Hurricane fighter can be seen roaring through the Cambridgeshire skies on display days. There is now a Hurricane, loaned by the Shuttleworth Collection, that is under restoration to flying condition, and is on public view. However, a Spanish variant of the famous German Me 109 is included and there is a Spitfire, though of a later variant than was operational during the Battle.

Phototips The techniques used will depend upon whether you are seeking an objective record of the aircraft or exploring special and dramatic effects. If the latter is the case, you might experiment by shooting into the sun and capturing the effects of light mirrored from polished wing and tail surfaces, or using a wide-angle lens to exaggerate perspective, choosing a vantage point close to the propellers, rear turrets or tail fins of the aircraft. When the aircraft are treated like items of sculpture, the potential for dramatic effects is immense, though purists may prefer a more conservative approach.

There is just sufficient light in the hangars to allow photography without the use of flash or the encumbrance of a tripod, but one of the faster films should be used to ensure success for with a medium speed film of around 125 ASA you will be operating at settings of around 1/60th at f3·5 and depth of field may be a problem unless a wide-angle lens is used.

Location The Imperial War Museum, Duxford, lies close to the M11 and beside the A505 about 6 miles S of Cambridge and about 1 mile SW of Duxford village.

ROUND AND ABOUT

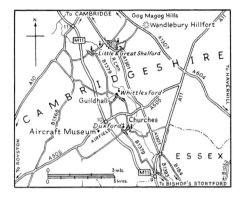

DUXFORD AND WHITTLESFORD VILLAGES

Modern farming methods have removed whatever charm this countryside may once have had, but there are a number of attractive villages. Duxford is more interesting than pretty; it is unusual in having two churches which reflect the fact that the present village results from the merging of several separate settlements including two villages, each with a church, which were aligned upon branches of the ancient Icknield Way. One church is all that Duxford really needs, but the long-redundant chapel of St John, a plain but appealing building, is currently undergoing restoration after a long period of abandonment.

Whittlesford is both pretty and interesting with several fine old timber-framed buildings and a well-preserved timber-framed guildhall which originally appears to have served a guild associated with the church. The flint-walled church embodies many periods of medieval building while the timber-framed porch is particularly appealing and its builder's name can still be seen carved on one of the timbers. Much more unusual is the pagan fertility carving of a 'sheila-na-gig' which has been re-used in the window head of the tower, just below the clock. It may have been carved in the Saxon or British periods and is of a nature that commentators usually describe as 'explicit'.

The proximity to Duxford airfield is indicated by the rows of graves of airmen in the churchyard.

Location From Duxford air museum, follow the A505 E for about 1 mile. At the crossroads, turn left for Whittlesford and right for Duxford.

Whittlesford's flint-walled church

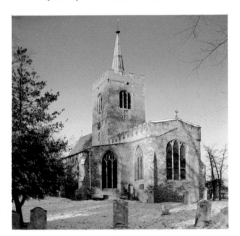

WANDLEBURY HILLFORT

Hillforts are remarkably uncommon in the E of England, but the example at Wandlebury was quite large, enclosing 15 acres. The inner bank and ditch ring was destroyed in the 18th century when the Earl of Godolphin built a mansion inside the ramparts and landscaped its surroundings, but the outer bank and ditch is fairly unchanged. A local preservation society now cares for the beautiful 18th-century beech-woods which surround the area and provide an island of loveliness in the devastated countryside of prairie farming. Wandlebury is best known for the nonsensical claim that the hill was once covered by a pageant of pagan chalk-cut hill figures; it is quite likely that the single figure of a giant was formerly visible on the hill-slope, but there is no reason to believe that he bore any resemblance to those described in the book *Gogmagog: The Buried Gods*.

It is managed by a local Naturalists' Trust.

Location If coming from Duxford or Whittlesford, proceed N through Little and Great Shelford villages; at Great Shelford, continue N along either Granhams Road or Hinton Way and join the A1307; follow this road SE for a short distance and Wandlebury is signposted to the left just beyond the brow of the hill. From Cambridge, take the A1307 SE; the hillfort is about 3 miles from the city centre.

Note Wimpole Hall is close by, while a quick trip down the M11 gives easy access to Greensted church and Hedingham Castle in Essex. *See* the index for page references.

Snow in the beech woods at Wandlebury

The Humber Road Bridge

(Humberside)

In choosing the entries to represent the different periods preceding the twentieth century, the problems of 'what to leave out?' have been quite agonising. For the modern period, the problem is of a different kind: what is worthy of inclusion? The sites that have been explored so far have been very characteristic of their ages and very worth visiting. Historians of future years will find it much easier to decide which monuments are symbolic of the second half of the twentieth century: they are likely to choose a motorway—but then, who would want to visit a motorway except for reasons of practical convenience? Coventry Cathedral has often been heralded as one of the finest contemporary architectural creations, but this is an age of dwindling church attendance and so it is not truly a symbol of its time; and can one be sure that in the year 2500 it will be as revered as our wonderful medieval cathedral creations? It would be quite wrong to suggest that modern man is incapable of creating compelling passages of man-made landscape, and the surrealistic scenery of Goonhilly Earth Station in Cornwall has been praised by more than one noted landscape historian. In the event, one modern monument proved irresistible: the Humber Bridge.

The longest single-span suspension bridge in the world, the Humber Road Bridge

With a hinterland covering the great county of Yorkshire, Kingston upon Hull grew rapidly along with the industrial cities to the west during the Industrial Revolution. The broad Humber estuary that had carried trade to Hull since the medieval period also constituted a great barrier to the assembly and dispersal of goods and greatly reduced the influence of Hull, which received its charter in 1299, on areas lying to the south, beyond the mile-wide estuary. In the course of the twentieth century, the absence of a wide and fast north–south routeway to serve areas lying to the east of the A1 caused concern and it was clear that a Humber Bridge would be an indispensable asset.

The plans for a Humber link to supersede the inconveniences of the ferry service (which was formally established in the reign of Edward II in 1315) have a long pedigree. Technological inadequacies had ruled out previous discussions of a Humber Bridge, but in 1865–67 it was possible at least to consider such a project. The idea of a tunnel was mooted in 1872 and it was felt that a railway using such a tunnel could compete successfully with established north–south railways. In the event, the navigational interests mounted a successful campaign against the rail link and many uncertainties associated with tunnelling beneath the waters of the Humber were discussed. A decade later, a proposal for a railway bridge was rejected on the grounds that

some thirty-six piers would be needed and that the forest of structures would prevent larger vessels from reaching river ports upstream.

Another bridge proposal perished in the years of stringency which accompanied the Great Depression and yet another was overtaken by the events of the 1939–45 war. Parliamentary authorisation for a Humber Bridge was won in 1959, but Hull had to wait until 1971 for government agreement for work to begin.

The Humber Bridge took almost ten years to be built. There were severe delays in construction, some of them caused by the discovery of an unsuspected artesian well beneath the south bank tower. The building costs spiralled, making the Bridge even more a symbol of its age, and the original estimate of £26 million is thought to be about a quarter of the final cost. The back-up motorways also gave rise to problems, while new estimates of population trends suggest that the level of traffic will be lower than envisaged. In the long term, however, these controversies are likely to be forgotten while the magnificent bridge endures.

It is the longest single-span suspension bridge in the world, carrying two dual-lane carriageways, a footpath and a cycle lane across the estuary, for a distance of 4626 ft between the piers, and for further distances of 1739 ft to the south and 919 ft to the north. The towers, which are unique in a suspension bridge in that they are made of reinforced concrete rather than steel, stand 510 ft above the piers, the bridge itself having a clearance above high water of 98 ft. The Bridge incorporates some 44,000 miles of wire, 480,000 tons of concrete, 27,500 tons of steel and its great structural cables are some 27 inches in diameter.

These figures, however, tell us nothing about the sheer beauty of the construction, engineered by Freeman Fox & Partners. Seen from a distance, the slender lines of the bridge are graceful, but seen from the waterside near the bases of the great towers, the effect is astonishing, with the roadway apparently disappearing into eternity in the river mists of the far shore. Modern architecture tends to be functional but little more—while, as many tower-block dwellers will confirm, it does not always even manage to be functional. The nation has every right to take pride in the Humber Bridge which not only

serves important purposes but provides a glorious focus in the bleak and level landscapes of Humberside.

It is sometimes said that the public at large is not prepared to give modern architecture the chance that it deserves. The Bridge, however, demonstrates that when the concept and design are sufficiently attractive, the public will respond. As a toll bridge, it was officially open by H.M. the Queen on 17 July 1981, and during the following weeks scores of Humbersiders gathered at the riverside to admire their splendid Bridge. With laudable foresight, the Humber Bridge Board has provided viewing areas beside the Humber, with stalls dispensing information to a highly interested and responsive public. Its working life over, the superseded ferry is moored nearby.

Phototips To capture the full drama of the Bridge, a wide-angle lens is essential. Adopting a position close to the base of a

tower, the wide-angle lens will seem to exaggerate the perspective of the receding overhead roadway and in colour photography additional effects can be contrived by the use of tinted graduated filters. If working from the viewing area on the Hull side of the river, one tends to be shooting into the sun during the middle hours of the day. This may present other dramatic effects, but it may be wise to take up a position where the disc of the sun itself is masked by one of the structures of the bridge or pictures may be flawed by internal reflections from the camera lens.

The decaying remains of wooden breakwaters lying a little to the E of the Bridge can be included in a shot in which their jagged outlines provide a counterpoint to the graceful symmetry of the Bridge.

Location The A15 crosses the Bridge to link with the A1105 and A63 on the outskirts of Hull.

ROUND AND ABOUT

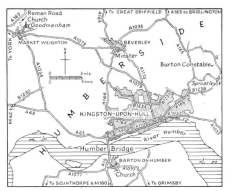

GOODMANHAM

The attractive Church of All Saints is an accumulation of many different ages of church building and will span an even longer period of religious use if the local tradition that the 7th-century 'priest' of

a pagan temple situated here was converted to Christianity is correct. Work of various later medieval periods has been added to the nucleus of the Norman chancel.

The Percy Shrine is particularly notable. The canopy is the finest 14th-century work in the country.

Location N of Market Weighton, and close to the A1079; about 8 miles W of Beverley.

BURTON CONSTABLE

Burton Constable is the home of the Chichester-Constables whose family landholdings go back to the 11th century. The Elizabethan mansion, which was built in 1570, has undergone

interior remodellings on several occasions, notably by Robert Adam in the 1750s. It stands in a 200-acre park which was landscaped by 'Capability' Brown from 1772–74. A dolls' museum is housed in what was, in the 19th century, a small theatre.

Location About 7 miles NE of Hull, and signposted via minor roads from the A165.

Note The Bridge now allows one to visit with ease two of the great English churches described in this book—Barton on Humber church which lies scarcely more than a stone's throw from the southern end of the Bridge, and Patrington near the extremities of Holderness. *See* the index for page references.

APPENDIX I and II
and INDEX

CAMBRIDGESHIRE
Duxford Battle of Britain Airfield
Duxford village
Grantchester village
Orwell village
Wandlebury hillfort
Whittlesford village
Wimpole Hall

CO. CLARE
Aillwee Cave
Bunratty Castle
Bunratty Folk Park
Chathair Chonaill stone fort
Craggaunowen
Dysert O'Dea
Kilfenora cathedral
Leamaneh Castle
Poulaphuca tomb
Poulnabrone tomb

CLWYD
Chirk acqueduct & railway viaduct
Chirk Castle
Offa's Dyke
Valle Crucis Abbey

CORNWALL
Chysauster village
Lanyon Quoit
Merry Maidens stone circle

CUMBRIA
Castlerigg stone circle
Great Langdale axe factory
King Arthur's Round Table
Long Meg and Her Daughters

DERBYSHIRE
Creswell Crags

DEVON
Buckfast Abbey
Grimspound
Houndstor

DUMFRIES & GALLOWAY
The Cairnholy Tombs
Cardoness Castle
Torhousekie stone circle

Photograph on p. 293: Caister Castle, Norfolk

DYFED
Llanddewi Brefi
Soar chapel

ESSEX
Blackmore, St Laurence's church
Finchingfield village
Great Yeldham village
Greensted Saxon church
Hedingham Castle
Ongar Castle
Thaxted village

CO. GALWAY
Kilmacduagh churches and round tower

GLOUCESTERSHIRE
Deerhurst church

GRAMPIAN
Easter Aquorthies recumbent stone circle
Loanhead of Daviot recumbent stone circle
Maiden Stone
Picardy Stone
St Fergus church

GWENT
Grosmont Castle
Skenfrith Castle
White Castle

GWYNEDD
Beaumaris Castle
Criccieth Castle
Din Lligwy
Dinas Dinlle
Llanfair slate caverns
Porth-y-Nant
Tre'r Ceiri
Ty-mawr hut group

HAMPSHIRE
Pimperne House, Butser Hill
Queen Elizabeth Country Park

HEREFORD & WORCESTER
Avoncroft Museum
Ewyas Harold
Garway
Hanbury Hall
Hereford
Kilpeck
Tardebigge canal locks

HERTFORDSHIRE
Waltham Cross

HUMBERSIDE
Barton on Humber Saxon church
Beverley
Burton Constable
Goodmanham
Horkstow, St Maurice's church
Humber Road Bridge
Normanby Hall
Patrington church
Sledmere House

ISLE OF LEWIS, WESTERN ISLES
Arnol Blackhouse
Breasclete chambered tomb
Callanish stone circle

Dun Carloway Broch
Garrabost chambered tomb
Steinacleit chambered tomb

KENT
Bayham Abbey (East Sussex border)
Knole House
Lullingstone Villa

NORFOLK
Barton Turf
Burgh Castle
Burgh Castle church
Caister Castle
Martham, Church Farm
Ranworth church

NORTHAMPTONSHIRE
Brigstock
Deen Park
Kirby Hall
Lyveden New Bield

NORTHUMBERLAND
Corbridge
Hadrian's Wall, Housesteads

NOTTINGHAMSHIRE
Laxton motte
Newark on Trent
Thoresby Hall & Sherwood Forest
Wellow

CO. OFFALY
Clonmacnois Monastic Town

ORKNEY
Broch of Gurness
Brough of Birsay
Dounby Click Mill
Kirkwall, The Earl's Palace
Maes Howe
Rennibister Souterrain
Ring of Brodgar
Skara Brae
Stones of Stenness
Unstan chambered tomb

SHROPSHIRE
Abdon lost village
Bishop's Castle
Caer Caradoc hillfort
Clun
Coalbrookdale
Heath lost village
Hopton Castle
Ludlow
Mitchell's Fold stone circle
Nordybank hillfort
Offa's Dyke
Old Oswestry hillfort
Stokesay Castle
Upper Millichope
Wilderhope Manor

SOMERSET
Burrow Mump
Glastonbury
High Ham Mill
Meare Fish House

North Petherton church
Sedgemoor Battlefield
Wells cathedral

STAFFORDSHIRE
Castle Ring hillfort
Lichfield cathedral
Tamworth
Wall

SUFFOLK
Bungay Castle
Bury St Edmunds
Clare village
Grime's Graves
Kersey village
Lavenham, church of St Peter & St Paul
Long Melford village
Somerleyton Hall
Sotterley Agricultural Museum
West Stow

SUSSEX, EAST
Battle
Bayham Abbey (on border of Kent)
Bodiam Castle
Great Dixter
New Winchelsea

SUSSEX, WEST
Singleton
Up Marden church

WARWICKSHIRE
Baginton, Lunt Roman Fort
Baginton, Midland Air Museum
Kenilworth Castle
Warwick, Lord Leycester Hospital

WILTSHIRE
The Avebury Complex

YORKSHIRE, NORTH
Brimham Rocks
Byland Abbey
Cawthorn Roman camps
The Devil's Arrows
Fountains Abbey
Helmsley Castle
Markenfield Hall
Mauley Cross
Old Byland
Pickering Castle
Rievaulx Abbey
Ripley
Ripon
Wharram le Street
Wharram Percy
Wheeldale Moor Roman road

YORKSHIRE, SOUTH
Conisbrough Castle

YORKSHIRE, WEST
Aire Valley
Hebden Bridge
Heptonstall

MAIN SITES
included
IN THE BOOK

SHETLAND

ORKNEY

Skara Brae
Stones of Stenness
Ring of Brodgar
Maes Howe

Dun Carloway Broch
Callanish
Stone Circle
Isle of Lewis

WESTERN ISLES

H I G H L A N D

INVERNESS

S C O T L A N D

GRAMPIAN

Picardy Stone ● Maiden Stone

● ABERDEEN

TAYSIDE

PERTH

DUNDEE

FIFE

DUNFERMLINE

CENTRAL

STIRLING

● GLASGOW

EDINBURGH

LOTHIAN

GALASHIELS

BORDERS

STRATHCLYDE

AYR ●

DUMFRIES & GALLOWAY

DUMFRIES

Cairnholy
Tombs

CARLISLE

NORTHUMBERLAND

Housesteads

Hadrian's Wall

NEWCASTLE UPON TYNE

TYNE
& WEAR SUNDERLAND

NORTHERN

ANTRIM

LONDONDERRY

DONEGAL

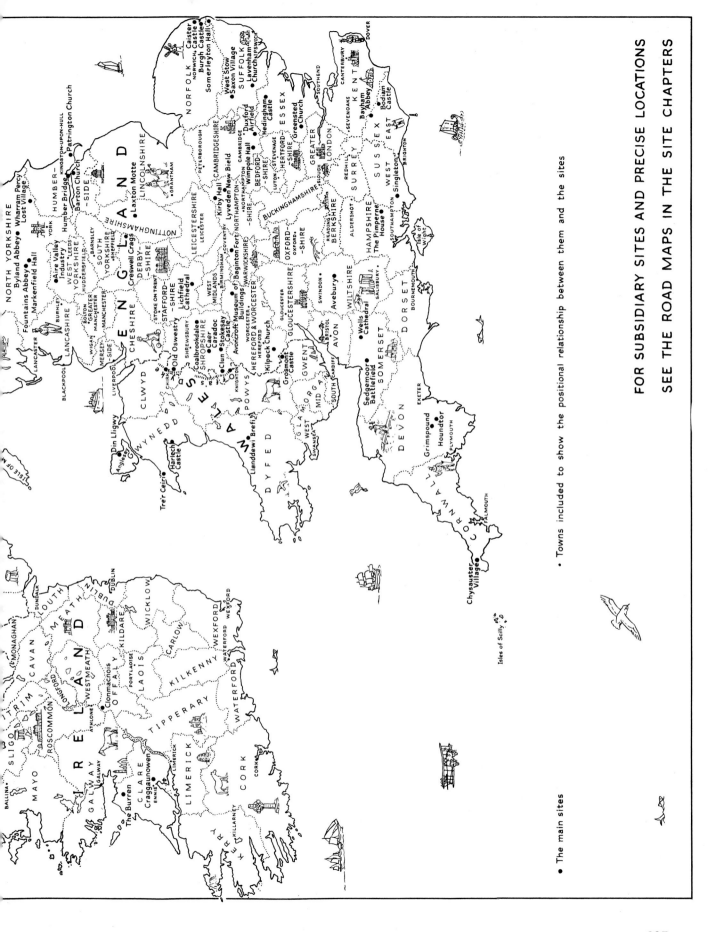

FOR SUBSIDIARY SITES AND PRECISE LOCATIONS

SEE THE ROAD MAPS IN THE SITE CHAPTERS

• The main sites

• Towns included to show the positional relationship between them and the sites

Apart from the main sites in each chapter, subsidiary sites from the same period appear in other chapters. This Appendix will give the reader both historical and geographical cross-references. See the **bold** entries in the index for the page references.

The Stone and Bronze Ages
CORNWALL:
Boscawen-un stone circle; Chun Quoit portal dolmen; Lanyon Quoit chambered tomb; Men-an-tol; Merry Maidens stone circle; Nine Maidens stone row; The Pipers; Zennor Quoit portal dolmen
GRAMPIAN:
Easter Aquhorthies stone circle; Loanhead of Daviot stone circle
GWYNEDD:
Din Lligwy burial chamber; Ty-mawr hut group
NORFOLK:
Grime's Graves
SHROPSHIRE:
Mitchell's Fold stone circle
NORTH YORKSHIRE:
Devil's Arrows

The Age of Iron
CAMBRIDGESHIRE:
Wandlebury hillfort
CO CLARE:
Cathair Chonaill stone fort
GRAMPIAN:
Mither Tap hillfort
GWYNEDD:
Dinas Dinlle hillfort
CO OFFALY:
Turoe stone
ORKNEY:
Rennibister souterrain
STAFFORDSHIRE:
Castle Ring hillfort

Roman Britain and Ireland
CORNWALL:
Carn Euny village and fogou
KENT:
Lullingstone villa
ORKNEY:
Broch of Gurness

The Dark Ages
CO CLARE:
Dysert O'Dea (rebuilt 17th century)
NORFOLK:
Burgh Castle church
NORTHAMPTONSHIRE:
Brigstock church
ORKNEY:
Broch of Gurness; Brough of Birsay
NORTH YORKSHIRE:
Mauley Cross (considered to be from this period); Wharram le Street church

The Norman Period
CAMBRIDGESHIRE:
Grantchester church (traces)
CO CLARE:
Kilmacduagh churches and round tower (probable)
ESSEX:
Ongar Castle; Priory Church of St Laurence, Blackmore (and up until 15th century)
GWENT:
Skenfrith Castle (begun as a Norman earthwork); White Castle
HEREFORD & WORCESTER:
Ewyas Harold church

NOTTINGHAMSHIRE:
Sherwood Forest
SHROPSHIRE:
Abdon and Heath lost villages; Hopton Castle; Ludlow planned town; Upper Millichope
SOMERSET:
Glastonbury Abbey
SUFFOLK:
Bungay Castle
EAST SUSSEX:
Battle Abbey
WARWICKSHIRE:
Kenilworth Castle (and up until the 13th century)
NORTH YORKSHIRE:
Pickering Castle (and up until the 14th century)
SOUTH YORKSHIRE:
Conisbrough Castle

The High Middle Ages
CAMBRIDGESHIRE:
Orwell church; Whittlesford church
CO CLARE:
Bunratty Castle; Kilfenora cathedral (probable); Leamaneh Castle (with additions up to the 17th century)
CLWYD:
Chirk Castle; Valle Crucis
DUMFRIES & GALLOWAY:
Cardoness Castle
ESSEX:
Clare church; Finchingfield and Thaxted villages; Great Yeldham church

HERTFORDSHIRE:
    Waltham Cross
HUMBERSIDE:
    Beverley church
SOMERSET:
    North Petherton church
STAFFORDSHIRE:
    Lichfield cathedral
EAST SUSSEX:
    New Winchelsea
WEST SUSSEX:
    Up Marden church
WARWICKSHIRE:
    Lord Leycester Hospital, Warwick
NORTH YORKSHIRE:
    Fountains Abbey; Old Byland village;
    Wharram Percy lost village

Period prior to the Industrial Revolution
HUMBERSIDE:
    Burton Constable
ORKNEY:
    Earl's Palace, Kirkwall
SHROPSHIRE:
    Wilderhope Manor
SOMERSET:
    Sedgemoor battlefield

After the Industrial Revolution
CLWYD:
    Chirk aqueduct and railway viaduct
DYFED:
    Bethesda Chapel and Bethlethem
    Welsh Congregationalist Chapel,
    Llanddewi Brefi

GWYNEDD:
    Llanfair slate caverns; Porth-y-Nant
    village
HUMBERSIDE:
    Normanby Hall
NOTTINGHAMSHIRE:
    Thoresby Hall
ORKNEY:
    Dounby click mill
WARWICKSHIRE:
    Midland Air Museum, Baginton
WESTERN ISLES:
    Arnol Blackhouse